Shadow Song

Shadow Song

Dorothy Keddington

Other novels by Dorothy Keddington:

Jayhawk

Return to Red Castle

NOTE: All characters in this book are fictional, and any resemblance to persons living or dead is purely coincidental.

ISBN: 0-934126-88-7

First Printing November 1985

Randall Book Co.
Salt Lake City, Utah

Lithographed in the United States of America
Executype
Salt Lake City, Utah

Author's Note & Acknowledgments

I am indebted to many for their generous and kind assistance in the research of this book and wish to acknowledge the following for their contributions:

> my husband and children, Dad and Gloria, Burt and Pat Keddington, for their love, encouragement and unfailing support
>
> My sister, Jeanine, for being a beautiful inspiration for Megan
>
> Bethany Chaffin, for providing hours of friendship, retreat and writing at "the cabin"
>
> Robert R. McKay and his magnificent "McKay Arabians"
>
> Clive Romney and 'Sound Column' Studios
>
> Detectives Kenneth Halderman, William Brusik and Ronald Parr
>
> Sandy Burnside, president, Eddie Rabbitt Fan Club
>
> Carol Warburton, for her insightful suggestions and unwavering support

Special thanks to Lt. Col. Edmund E. Hansen, friend and fellow writer, for his invaluable research assistance, expert editing, and for his wise counsel of the past three years to "Hurry up and finish that book!" I finally did it, Ed!

For Neil Diamond

from one "dreamer" to another,
thank you for the music.

Prelude

THE OBOLUS CONCERT was thirty minutes late in starting. Inside the giant coliseum, thousands of feet thundered a frustrated rhythm on the concrete floors, while laughter, giddy and gutteral, competed with whistles and shouted obscenities in an ever-rising tide. The air was saturated with odor as much as sound—cloying perfumes, rank perspiration and the pungent sweetness of marijuana smoke. Another five minutes crawled by, with security personnel nervously checking their watches. The restless crowd was agitated beyond anticipation, hovering on the brink of hysteria. The emotional frenzy focused on a small stage bathed in eerie blue light. Here, a silent silver army of sound equipment awaited the performers who would send life and energy surging through their sterile circuits.

Suddenly, the coliseum was plunged into blackness, and twenty thousand voices congealed into one deafening scream. Then flares ignited from all four corners of the stage, illuminating thick clouds of red vapor. The red mist snaked through the blackness, transforming the stage into a seething cauldron. Soft and muttered, a primal chant drifted up with the smoke, the words barely audible above the screaming crowd. As the chant grew in volume and intensity, the audience eagerly joined in. Soon the pounding words were rolling across the fetid air in waves, saturating tissue and bone, mesmerizing minds and emotions.

"Break the chains! Set love free!
Break the chains! The law is ME!"

At the height of the frenzy, four robed figures emerged from the fiery vapor like specters from hell. The hooded figures moved through the red mist, oblivious to the tumult erupting all around them. Then, deliberately turning their backs on the crowd, they closed into a circle. Suddenly, the chanting was cauterized by a savage scalpel of blinding light which sliced through the center of the stage. The figures stripped off their robes and whirled about to face the crowd's screaming approval.

Obolus' lead singer was tall and cocaine-thin; his dark hair cut short and greased back at the sides, while the top boasted stiff spikes of red and orange, like a cock's comb. Derek Durant enjoyed mocking his masculinity even as he flaunted it. Tight pants of black leather were belted low around his bony haunches and blood-red boots added another four inches to his height. Full lips were painted a glossy pink, dark brows plucked to a narrow arch, and deep-set eyes were made to appear almost cavernous by yellow and gray eyeshadow. To complete the nightmare, black spider earrings pierced both earlobes.

Bizarre combinations of leather and rhinestones, chains and animal hides swathed the half-naked bodies of the other three men; the only common element being identical bronze medallions which bounced on their bare chests.

The members of Obolus strutted about the stage, taunting the already stimulated audience with suggestive movements and obscene gestures. Then they seized their instruments and began a full-scale attack. Rage shrieked white-hot from electric guitars, drums pounded a relentless, soul-shattering rhythm, while venomous lyrics were injected into the hypnotized listeners. As the concert progressed, the stage became a battle-ground. The band made war with their instruments. Guitars were smashed, bodies contorted and exposed, and still the crowd screamed for more.

Against the shadowed wall of an exit ramp, four men and a slender, black-haired woman stood watching the frenzy. Their calm, clinical eyes were not on the performers, but the audience itself, as if the screaming teenagers were a fascinating species of laboratory animal in a scientific experiment.

One of the men, a tall blond with Nordic-blue eyes, touched

the woman's arm, then motioned for the others to follow him a short distance down the ramp where the sounds of battle weren't so deafening.

"The reservations for Lodestone were confirmed this morning," he announced. "We're booked for the first three weeks in August."

"Excellent! But it took you long enough," was the woman's clipped response.

"McLean wasn't too happy about the idea of Obolus recording an album at his studio," the tall blond informed her. "Kurt and I had a helluva time convincing him the band's reputation is just media hype."

Beside him, a stocky, dark-haired man nervously fingered his beard. "Do you think McLean will be a problem?"

"We won't allow him to be," the woman answered with icy contempt.

A policeman suddenly pushed his way past the five, dragging a thirteen-year-old girl with glazed eyes and sweat-plastered hair. Both wrists were spurting blood from self-inflicted razor cuts.

The bearded man stared at the young girl and murmured, "My God, they're destroying themselves! Maybe we've gone too far."

The black-haired woman turned to him, her eyes burning with a fierce kind of passion. "Not far enough or fast enough! If we're to succeed, we need total control—not mass hysteria!"

The bearded man said nothing, and the music raged on.

*   *   *   *   *   *   *   *

THE SINGER AND the song died in full crescendo as I switched the car radio off with a frustrated sigh. Pavarotti would have to forgive me if simple silence was more soothing to my mood than his glorious tenor. A mountain breeze, heavy with the warm scent of pines, sang through the open windows of my rented Audi 5000, and I smiled. That was all the music I needed for now. I stretched my shoulders, trying to relax cramped muscles which were the result of driving several hundred miles of Colorado's mountain roads during the past week. I was finally able to negotiate the twisting turns and steep grades without strangling the steering wheel, but I knew I would never whiz along these mountain highways like so many Colorado natives. In fact, I had grown quite accustomed to being passed by vehicles with the familiar green and white license plate.

A highway sign informed me that Estes Park was still some fifty miles away, and glancing down at my watch, I sighed again. Depending upon the road and the traffic, I had another full hour of driving ahead of me. Perhaps more. I tried to ignore my fatigue and a nagging headache by appreciating the rich gold light warming the peaks and pine-covered ridges. It was a glorious August afternoon in the Rockies, and I had nothing at all to do but drive this lovely mountain road and enjoy the scenery. I should be feeling extremely Robert Browningish: "God's in his heaven, all's right with the world." Or at least mildly content. But I wasn't. In addition to the headache, there was a vague, gnawing restlessness inside me that refused to be ignored or reasoned away. I reached for a chocolate chip cookie from the sack on the front seat and gave myself a firm order:

Megan Collier, forget about "vague gnawings" and eat a cookie instead. You have no reason to be feeling anything but happy and grateful. Especially after the week just past.

I was fortunate enough to have been given the assignment of writing and photographing a feature article on the arts in Colorado for *American Performing Arts*, a national magazine fondly devoted to "promoting public awareness and enjoyment of the arts." This particular article was the brainchild of Norm Jesperson, one of APA's associate editors. It's common knowledge to everyone on the staff that Norm's principal passion in life is to convince Easterners that there really is more between Denver and Los Angeles than stagecoaches and sagebrush. By all rights, he should have been given the assignment, but Norm's high blood pressure and Colorado's high altitudes are definitely incompatible, so the magazine's managing editor selected me to do the job instead. It was more like a paid vacation than an assignment and I knew it. So did the rest of the staff. A few offered their hearty, if slightly green-tinged congratulations, but many of the editors were miffed that a junior member of the staff should be given such a plum assignment. Most of the grumbling I cheerfully ignored, except for one particularly catty conversation. I was passing by Moira Phillips' office one afternoon when the sound of my name made me pause. Moira, a stuffy senior editor unofficially known as "Black Mariah" because of her ferocious eyebrows and penchant for wearing ghastly black knit dresses, has never been one of my favorite people. And the dialogue I overheard did nothing to alter that opinion.

"Have you heard about Megan Collier's new assignment?" she asked a secretary. "That's what comes from lots of hard work and dedication." A significant pause. "Of course, it doesn't hurt to have red hair and long legs."

The secretary laughed and added in her syrupy voice, "Maybe you should ask Megan what brand of hair coloring she uses, then the boss'll do something nice for you."

Most of the time, my sense of humor sees me through such situations, but there are a few things I will not tolerate. I was lucky enough to inherit my red hair from an Irish grandmother, *not* a bottle, and any insinuations to the contrary always stir up my equally Irish temper. The next morning I left packages of the most nightmarish shade of red hair coloring I could find on each of their desks, along with the note: "I hope this helps you with your next assignment. Love, Megan."

No matter what certain staff members might say, I knew I was up to the assignment—but I also knew that Bill Winegar, APA's managing editor, had singled me out for reasons which had nothing to do with my writing ability. My boss is an intelligent, forty-year old man who can be incredibly stupid at times. Only a fool would throw away a charming wife and three children who show every indication of growing up to be decent human beings, for a few disgusting hours of hanky-panky. I made a point of telling Mr. Winegar exactly that when he suggested we continue our business relationship "after hours." At first, I wasn't sure whether his ego could handle my blunt brand of honesty. In fact, I fully expected to be fired on the spot. Instead, we became good friends—from a distance. The "friend" idea was his, the "distance" was mine.

For that reason alone, I was grateful for the Colorado assignment. Of course, there were others. My handling of the job could open doors to a promotion as well as a raise in pay. And I suppose, deep down, I wanted to prove to the staff that my contributions to APA were worthwhile on their own merit.

My schedule for the trip was full and my calendar absolutely reeked with culture. From Los Angeles, I had flown directly to Denver where I began my assignment by enjoying an exquisite performance of the Denver Symphony in Boettcher Concert Hall. The next morning, I drove south to Larkspur for the town's annual Renaissance Festival. To see some of "merry old England" transplanted right in the middle of the Old West was a delightful bit of midsummer magic. Some of the costumes were more schmaltzy than medieval, but I was feeling too wonderful to be overly critical. Where else can one find wizards and cowboys hobnobbing over hot cross buns and barbequed beef? The entire festival was spiced with memorable anachronisms.

The following day found me driving the winding mountain road to Aspen. I had allowed myself three full days to enjoy and absorb all the artistry available there. My first afternoon and evening were spent attending workshops in connection with the

Festival of the American Theater. The next day being Sunday, I decided to relax and take in a concert at Aspen's large tent amphitheater. The afternoon was sunny and warm, the acoustics in the amphitheater were outstanding, and the program included compositions by my favorite composers. What more could one ask for?

I settled back in my seat as the orchestra tuned up and happened to notice a middle-aged couple on the bench in front of me. They were obviously in love. Every dripping look and fawning gesture attested to the fact. I groaned inwardly and glanced away, hoping they would restrain themselves during the concert. I managed to ignore the couple's besotted behavior through most of Beethoven's 2nd Symphony and a charming set of Brahm's waltzes, but when Rachmaninoff's "Rhapsody on a Theme by Paganini" began, I knew I was in trouble. I made the mistake of glancing at the couple in front of me just as the music soared to ethereal heights.

The woman was pathetically overweight and not a bit pretty. Her hair was on the greasy side and her clothes were beyond tacky. The man squashed so close to her side wasn't any more appealing. In addition to dandruff, he had a large bald spot at the back of his head and pimples on his neck.

At the precise moment the melody reached its soul-stirring climax, the man and woman turned and gazed into each other's eyes. What a ludicrous combination! The passion of Rachmaninoff and that pitiful couple! And yet, there was something in the look which passed between them that sliced through the walls of my confidence and independence, suddenly exposing the naked loneliness I thought I had learned to live with.

I built the walls back up again by working myself merci-lessly all the next day. In between performances, words flowed from my pen, rolls of film clicked through my camera, and I fiercely assured myself I was completely happy. That evening, as I watched Ballet West perform at Snowmass, I was calm and poised as usual—until the *pas de deux* from Prokofief's "Romeo and Juliet" began. Watching love's choreography intimately expressed in dance, I felt the nameless sadness sweeping over me again and found my cheeks were wet with tears.

Even now, remembering that moment was almost as painful as the experience itself. But why? My life was busy and my work rewarding. Why should I feel so unsatisfied—so empty?

My throat tightened as I stared at the road ahead. If the questions were this painful, I wasn't sure I wanted to probe deeply enough to find the answers. I brushed a few cookie crumbs off my lap and decided it was much easier to blame my mood on fatigue. I had already put in close to six hours of driving today, with only a short lunch break in Central City. If that weren't enough, the past hour had been like a roller coaster ride through the Rockies—nothing but climbing steep ridges, plunging down canyons, then climbing all over again.

My grip tightened on the steering wheel as I rounded another downhill curve and saw a camper-truck pulling a large, brown and white horse trailer just ahead. I braked slightly to allow more distance between us and counted two—no, three horses in what had to be a very expensive rig. The trailer's brakelights blinked back at me as the driver tried to maintain a safe speed on the hill. Even so, I thought he was taking the downgrade a bit fast. Then I noticed the Colorado plate on the back of the trailer. Of course. I should have known.

The road continued to follow the curve of the mountainside, with steep, forested slopes on the left and deep canyons falling away to the right. There were no lanes for passing and only a narrow strip of gravel separated the asphalt on my side of the highway from a wooded ravine far below. Looking down instead of up at the tops of fifty-foot pine trees was definitely unnerving, and after a steadying breath, I kept my eyes on the road. Thankfully, it ran fairly straight for a mile or so before making a sharp left turn around the mountain. Here, a good-sized chunk of the mountainside had been blasted away, and the rock cutting climbed some forty feet before easing back where tall pines rose even higher. On the right side of the road, a wide gravel turn-out promised a panoramic view of vistas beyond.

The mountains, the sky, the distant hills and valleys were spectacular enough, but when a large hawk swooped down from the jagged crest of the rock cutting, the beauty of the scene went beyond perfection. The bird flew directly in front of the camper-truck, then sailed out past the precipice into the endless blue. Watching the brown curve of its wings slicing silently through the air, I wondered—are hawks ever lonely?

I sighed and shifted to a lower gear. My glance in the rearview mirror was almost careless, an automatic rather than a thinking response. It came as a complete surprise to see a sleek red sports car bearing down behind me. My eyes darted ahead where the truck was approaching the blind curve, then returned to the rearview mirror. There were two men in the car. I could see them plainly now, and—yes!—the idiot-driver was actually going to pass!

I immediately braked and moved as close to the edge of the road as I dared, but the sports car was already swinging wide across the center line. As it drew alongside, I shot an angry glance to the men inside. Neither one took any notice of me. The driver was blond and good-looking. Put him in a dragon-ship instead of a sports car and he would make a great Viking. The dark-haired man slouched down on the passenger side was bearded and frowning. Suddenly, the bearded man turned his head and our eyes met. The moment couldn't have lasted more than a second or two, but it was long enough to communicate the man's fear to me. Why fear? The next instant, he averted his head and the car zoomed past.

I slowed even more, assuming the red sports car would now dart between me and the horse trailer. Instead, the blond driver maintained his reckless speed and streaked down the highway toward the blind curve as if he were racing the devil himself.

I was already holding my breath. When a motorcycle appeared around the other side of the curve, my heart gave a painful jerk, and I sank the brake pedal to the floor.

Almost as if they had rehearsed it, the sports car, the cyclist and the driver of the camper-truck each made convulsive swerves to their right. Tires shrieked and brakes screamed as the vehicles struggled for control. The sports car and the cycle missed each other by inches. I choked down a scream as the truck and horse trailer were forced off the road and onto the gravel turn-out. Stung by the violent backlash of motion, the trailer jack-knifed, tore loose from the camper and flipped over on its side. The air was raw with the abrasive scream of metal scraping against gravel and rock as the horse trailer skidded perilously close to the edge of the cliff. In that same moment, the red sports car whipped around the blind curve, and the cyclist lost control. There was nowhere for him to go—nowhere on earth but the solid rock of the mountainside. With a choked cry, I watched as the impact of the crash sent the rider catapulting through the air. I covered my face with my hands and slumped against the steering wheel.

For a long moment I was too weak to move, while reaction flooded my body in sick, shuddering waves. Then I heard a child crying. The sound sent a burst of adrenalin through my system. I didn't know whether those cries were from pain or fear or both, but at least they meant someone was alive! I shoved the car door open, stumbled out of the Audi and ran down the road.

2

A DARK-HAIRED man was running toward me with a child in his arms. The man was tall and rough looking, with frowning black brows, a mustache and the tough denim clothes of a rancher. I glanced from him to the child as we met in the road and started to ask if they were all right. I got no farther than, "Are you ---?" before he dumped the little boy into my arms with a brusque, "Here! Take him!" then ran over to the horse trailer.

Something in the man's gruff command, plus the sudden weight and warmth of the child against me, lifted the shocky veils of confusion from my mind and reality rushed in. So did the sound of crashing hooves and frightened whinnies coming from the overturned trailer. The horses' pathetic cries wrenched my insides as the dark-haired man bent down beside the trailer.

"Cinnabar, don't move! Mica, Topaz—just lie still! That's the way. I'm here, and I'll get you out. Don't move now, and I'll be right back!"

There were still a few nervous whickers and snorts coming from inside the trailer, but almost the very moment the animals heard his calm, confident voice, they stopped thrashing about. While I stood there, amazed and staring, the man left the trailer to run past my car and across the highway.

"Daddy! I want my daddy!"

A sharp kick to my hip bone made me say more sharply than I intended, "Hold still and be quiet!" but the child only squirmed and cried all the harder.

Nearby, the horses' nervous whinnies echoed from inside the trailer. Then a rush of wind swept across the lonely mountain road. And yet, when the dark-haired man knelt down and put his head on the cyclist's chest, it seemed to me as if silence were the loudest sound of all. Watching him lift a limp wrist, I felt my own heart beat more urgently, willing him to find a pulse. After a long moment, the man let go of the wrist, then glanced toward me with a slight, almost imperceptible shake of his head.

Hot, angry tears sprang to my eyes, and I fought to blink them back. This wasn't happening. It couldn't be. Disbelief suddenly blurred my emotions in a desperate attempt to push reality away. I didn't want to see more, yet my eyes remained riveted on the dark-haired man as he gently straightened the twisted legs, then dragged the cyclist's body out of the road. When I saw the bright trail of blood following behind, my knees buckled and a hot dizziness pounded through my head.

In the midst of the dizziness, I felt a small hand softly tracing the path of my tears, and glanced down to discover the child's clear blue eyes gazing into mine.

"Don't cry," he said.

I took a deep breath, not understanding why the simple words of a child should give such comfort, but as we looked at one another, the dizziness receded.

The boy was probably no more than three years old, with dark curly hair, tear-stained cheeks and a runny nose all the way down to his chin.

"I want my daddy," he said again, only this time it was a statement rather than a demand.

"I know. Your daddy will be right back," I told him, awkwardly shifting his position in an attempt to avoid that runny nose. "See, here he comes. You've got to be a brave boy now, so he can help the horses."

The child sniffed and gave me a measuring look. Suddenly, I found myself smiling into that miserable little face and saying as if nothing at all had happened, "That's better. Now let's go wipe your nose, and I'll get you a cookie."

My voice sounded almost normal, but my knees were still so shaky I could hardly walk to the car. I stumbled once in the loose gravel and quickly tightened my hold on the boy. He reached up and put both arms around my neck in a spontaneous gesture which sent the tears I had been struggling to control, coursing freely down my face.

I glanced away as the boy's father approached, hoping to hide my tears from a stranger's eyes.

"I've got a CB in my truck," he said, placing a hand on my shoulder. "I'll go radio for help."

I nodded and tried to speak, but he was already walking away.

The child didn't enjoy getting his nose wiped any more than I enjoyed doing it for him, but he recovered soon enough when I handed him a cookie. I leaned back against the seat with a long sigh and watched as the cookie disappeared in a few quick bites.

Actually, he wasn't a bad-looking little kid now that his nose was clean. His dark curls were soft and shiny, and those eyelashes had to be an inch and a half long. Dressed in Levis, a blue and white western shirt and boots of finely-tooled leather, he reminded me of a pint-sized cowboy.

"What's your name?" I asked.

"Cody," he answered, as clearly as one can with a mouthful of cookie.

The name suited him. "Well, Cody, why don't you sit here and have another cookie, while I see if there's anything I can do to help your father."

Glancing out the windshield, I saw the dark-haired man exit the truck carrying some kind of tool, a tire iron perhaps. Before I could reach for the door handle, the child was across the seat and grabbing my blouse with his grubby fingers.

"I want to come!"

I pried his fingers loose with a grimace. "Okay. You don't need to get so upset about it."

When I tried to pick him up, Cody immediately stiffened both legs and pulled away from me.

"I can walk by myself!"

"Fine! But you better hold my hand."

The child accepted the compromise without further argument and willingly slipped his hand in mine. My grip tightened as we approached the trailer and steep drop-off. Looking down, I had to fight back mental images of the brown and white trailer plummeting over the edge. It was so close! Far too close.

Cody's father lay on his back in the gravel, working with the tire iron in an effort to pry open the tailgate. Watching him groan and strain over the twisted metal, my feelings of frustration and helplessness returned.

"Isn't there some other way you could get them out?"

The man lifted his head, and I felt my I.Q. rapidly slipping away under his deprecating glance. "Horses generally run a bit large to squeeze through windows."

I backed away from his sarcasm and asked with stiff politeness, "Is there anything I can do to help?"

"Keep the boy away from the trailer and the edge," came the curt reply, then he went back to working with the jammed tailgate.

A nervous whinny sounded inside the trailer, and the man's caustic tones instantly melted into gentleness and concern.

"It's all right, boy. I'm here. Hold on a little longer, and I'll have you out."

His soft words stung as sharply as a slap, and I turned away with an angry jerk, pulling Cody after me. Obviously, the man's kindness was reserved for children and horses, and I didn't fit into either category.

Just then, a large station wagon drove around the blind curve. As the driver slowed the car, I glimpsed an assortment of small noses pressed against the windows and curious eyes straining to see. The middle-aged man behind the wheel pushed his glasses up on his nose, frowned at the overturned trailer, then drove on.

Helpless rage throbbed inside me as I stared after the station wagon.

"Forget about them and get Cody away from the edge!" came a rough shout from behind.

I swung around to see the little boy playing in the loose gravel, precariously near the drop-off and made a frightened dash for him.

Cody was completely unconcerned about the possible danger. "I'm thirsty," he said as I scooped him up in my arms. "I want a drink."

"I've got some soda pop in my car," I told him in an unsteady voice. "Let's go get you some."

As we turned toward the Audi, the child's father tossed an absent reminder over his shoulder. "Remember to say 'please' when you ask for something, Cody."

My control snapped along with my ragged nerves. "What kind of lousy father are you?" I flung back. "I don't see how you can expect your son to be polite when you obviously don't know the meaning of the word!"

I felt like an emotional idiot the moment the words were out. Gathering the tattered shreds of my dignity around me, I stalked back to the car, plopped Cody on the front seat, and reached over to grab a can of Pepsi from my styrofoam cooler. Tears were stinging my eyelids as I pulled up the metal ring with a savage twist that broke my best nail. Cody just sat there, watching me with those big blue eyes, and I didn't even have the satisfaction of saying a few appropriate words.

"Here. Be careful not to spill it on your shirt," I grumbled, handing him the drink.

Cody shrank away from me, and his chin started to quiver. Fear was in his eyes now, as well as tears. "You're mad at my daddy!" he accused.

I stared at him, and my anger crumbled in a sodden heap.

"I'm not — mad at your daddy. Not really. . . ." My voice cracked, and I looked up at the roof of the car, blinking back more hated tears. I wasn't angry—just worried and frightened and sick with shock. But I couldn't admit that, not even to a three-year-old boy. Instead, I brushed a hand across my eyes and offered a silent prayer: Dear Lord, please let help come soon!

Not two minutes later, a crusty old rancher pulled up in an ancient brown pick-up truck. The man's face had the hard strength which comes to those who live with the land, but his voice was surprisingly gentle as he offered his help. Before another ten minutes had gone by, there was a regular congregation gathered around the horse trailer, and the gravel turnout had become a parking lot. At some point, two motorcyclists stopped to direct traffic, stationing themselves on either side of the blind curve. Someone else kindly wrapped the cyclist's body in a blanket. Others brought tools, rope and strong arms. No one bothered with the formality of names or introductions. Help was needed and help was given, as simply as that.

The moment the tailgate gave way, Cody's father climbed inside the trailer. A gray mare was closest to the open door, and the man had to climb over her legs in order to reach the other two. At the back of the trailer, I could see little more than the rump and hind legs of a large bay, as he was lying directly on top of the third horse.

Murmuring soft words of assurance, Cody's father slipped two ropes around the mare's middle, and once they were secure, two lines of men grabbed hold. I stood well out of the way with Cody, along with the other spectators. None of us moved or spoke; the silent blending of will and prayers was as tangible as the sun on our faces.

The mare didn't flinch or kick once during the entire process. Cody's father stayed close to her head, calmly explaining what was going on as if she were a human being and not a horse at all. Even after the mare was safely outside the trailer, she remained perfectly still until he had untied the ropes and slipped a bridle over her head.

"All right, Mica," he said. "You can get up now and say 'thank you' to all these kind folks."

With a joyful whinny the horse rolled over and got to her feet. Exultation shone on the sweat-stained faces of the men who had pulled her out, and murmurs of admiration rippled through the crowd. The mare's coat was a glossy, silver-gray; her mane and tail, midnight black. Even more beautiful than her coloring was the proud arch of her neck, the graceful head and fine, intelligent eyes.

Cody's father led the horse a few paces away from the trailer, carefully checking her legs and walk. Relief soon replaced his tight frown, and I heard him tell the old rancher, "She's got a few scratches and bruises, but other than that, I think she's all right."

My breath came out in a sigh as I leaned down to pick up the child. "Did you hear that, Cody? She's all right!"

The boy responded with a happy nod and planted a warm, wet kiss on my cheek. The gesture left me speechless and strangely shaken. I turned away from Cody's smile to see his father leading the gray mare directly to us, while the crowd gave way on either side.

Smoky blue eyes looked intently into mine as Cody reached for the horse with a delighted, "Hi, Mica!"

"Would you mind holding her for me while we get the others out?" the man asked, adding with a devastating smile, ". . . Please?"

My cheeks flamed as bright as my hair, and I gave my undivided attention to the horse when he handed me the reins. Still smiling, the man thanked me and walked away.

Cody stopped patting the mare's velvety nose to say, "Your face is all red," and I put him down in blushing confusion.

"You stay right next to me, or the horse might step on you!" I told him sternly.

Cody looked up at me with obvious disgust. "Mica won't step on me!"

"Well, stay here, anyway. I might need your help."

The truth was I had never been this close to a horse in my life, but I would have cheerfully died before admitting how nervous I felt. Just act like you know what you're doing, and no one will be the wiser, I told myself. The mare looked at me with her dark, intelligent eyes and I whispered, "Except you, of course!"

The next rescue operation was made more difficult than the first because the large bay had to be pulled off the horse trapped beneath him. From the conversations buzzing around me, I learned that the horse underneath was a stallion.

"That's no ordinary stallion," the old rancher told a young woman standing beside him. "I'll bet that Arabian's worth more than my whole damn ranch!"

The strident wail of sirens was suddenly heard above the voice of the crowd, and turning, I saw flashing red lights racing down the canyon. Moments later, three patrol cars and an ambulance converged on the scene, but when the officers rushed into the crowd, it was not to ask questions or fill out accident reports. Instead, they added their strength to the men who were lined up, ready to pull out the second horse.

With the anxious crowd pressing as close to the trailer as they dared, I couldn't see a thing, but it wasn't long before I heard a thankful, "That's it! He's off!" and relief literally poured over the people.

Then behind me, a woman's voice cried, "Cody! Cody, are you all right, honey?"

I glanced over my shoulder and that same instant, Cody darted away from me to dive into the plump arms of a woman in her late fifties.

"Aunt Twila! Aunt Twila! Daddy's horses fell over and couldn't get up!" he cried.

"I can see that, dear. But what about you and your dad? Are you all right?"

Cody smiled and nodded, and the woman hugged him close with a thankful sigh. Then she looked at me.

There was nothing remarkable about Aunt Twila's appearance. Her simple print dress was a faded blue, the same shade as her eyes. There was more gray than brown in her hair, and she wasn't wearing so much as an ounce of makeup to camouflage the wrinkles around her eyes and mouth. Still, there was a softness about the woman; a gentle caring that lent its own kind of beauty to her plain features.

"I was behind them when the accident happened," I began, when a stocky, balding man pushed his way through the crowd and hurried to the woman's side. His rough-hewn features were creased with worry as tough, wiry hands reached out for the child.

Twila gave him a reassuring smile. "Cody's fine, Wes. He's just fine. You better see what you can do to help with the horses."

Mica whinnied a fond greeting to the stocky rancher and nudged his shoulder with her head.

"Other than some bruises, she seems to be all right," I said, placing the reins into his more knowing hands.

"Excuse me, ma'am. Are you the one who witnessed the accident?"

A tall, deeply-tanned police officer was suddenly at my side, notebook in hand.

"Yes, I am."

"I'd like to ask you a few questions. If you'll come this way, please." He gestured to a patrol car parked a short distance up the road, and I followed him through the crowd.

As the officer opened the car door, I tossed a quick glance over my shoulder, but Cody and Aunt Twila had already disappeared into the anonymous mass of bodies surrounding the horse trailer. Wes was leading the gray mare away from the throng toward a large truck with wooden sides. Suddenly, everything was under control. I got into the back seat of the patrol car with a sigh that held some loneliness as well as relief.

There was pathetically little to report. A red sports car with a Colorado license plate. Two men—one blond, one dark and bearded. That was all, and yet, it was amazing how much time it took to tell so little. By the time I had answered all the officer's questions and given what information I could, the ambulance had left, and the crowd was beginning to disperse. Glancing out the window of the patrol car, I saw Cody's father leading a beautiful sorrel stallion up the ramp and into the truck with the other two horses.

"I think that should do it, Miss Collier," the officer told me. "You'll be at Estes Park tonight if we should need to get in touch with you?"

"Yes. At the Castle Mountain Lodge."

"And tomorrow, you'll be in Boulder."

The officer repeated the name and telephone number of my motel, and I nodded. After adding one final note to his report, he glanced at me with a polite smile.

"You're sure you don't remember the license number or make of that red car?"

I lifted my shoulders in a helpless shrug. "I'm sorry. I think it might have been a Camaro, but I'm not positive."

The officer's voice held a tone of professional understanding. "Well, I guess we've kept you long enough. Thanks again."

As I got out of the car, I noticed three policemen with chalk and tape, marking the highway. There was no need to define the area where the cyclist had landed. The red stains on the asphalt were clearly visible. I shivered and walked toward the Audi. It would be good to leave this place. I glanced about one last time for Cody but couldn't see him. A state trooper was talking to Cody's father, and I didn't want to interrupt them just to say good-bye. Besides, how do you say good-bye to someone you've never really met?

I got into the car and turned the key. On the seat beside me were scattered cookie crumbs and the empty Pepsi can. For a moment, I felt a strange tightness in my throat, then I angrily brushed the crumbs onto the floor and tossed the can into a garbage sack. I wanted no reminders of this afternoon. None at all! This evening, I would attend one of the "Music in the Mountains" concert series in Estes Park and put this entire experience out of my mind. With a deep sigh, I pulled carefully onto the highway. One of the state troopers signalled me to move forward, and I drove around the blind curve without a backward glance.

3

I DON'T KNOW when I have been so exquisitely aware of my own life and life around me as I was during those remaining miles to Estes Park. The warmth of the sun, the clear mountain air, the flowers along the roadside—even the simple act of breathing became painfully profound when I realized that life could be snuffed out at any given moment.

Everytime a motorcycle or red car passed by on the highway my nerves would jump, then tighten. It was foolish to think I could forget about the accident simply by increasing the physical distance between me and that fatal blind curve. Thoughts and feelings, sounds and images flooded my mind with every passing mile, and there was no holding them back. I could still hear the shriek of tires and frightened screams of the horses. Over and over again, I saw the blood-red sports car racing around the curve, the cyclist flying weightless through the air. I thought of the two men inside that sports car. Where were they now? Had they given even a moment's thought to the death and trauma left behind them on the highway, or were they still zooming along toward some unknown destination, unconcerned and unaware?

Anger churned inside me when I realized that blond driver might never have to account for his actions, and I wished for the hundredth time that I'd been able to give the police a license number.

Questions gnawed at my mind as the miles went by. What was the cyclist's name? Was he on vacation or returning home from work? Did he have a wife and children? I would probably never have the answers, but one thing I did know. Today, someone somewhere would receive a telephone call from a serious-voiced police officer, and grief would enter a home.

A harsh thought suddenly bruised my consciousness. If I had been the one killed today, would anyone mourn my death? Would it make any difference to a living soul if Megan Collier's existence came to an end?

I thought of my father, a successful attorney living in Portland, Oregon. Ever since his remarriage, some fifteen years ago, his life revolved around his second wife and their two children. My father's sense of responsibility toward me was usually fulfilled in the form of a check, or perhaps the rare invitation to spend a holiday with him. If I had died today, I'm sure he would be sad for a respectable period of time, but his life would go on with no sense of loss and possibly even a bit of relief.

I smiled grimly, realizing news of my death would probably take at least a week to reach my mother. I hadn't seen her for more than a year and had no idea if she were still living with Ricky, a hairdresser some fifteen years her junior, or if she had moved to Acapulco with one of her other "friends." When the news finally did arrive, Mother would shed buckets of tears, throw hysterics all over the place and then be relieved that she no longer had a twenty-five-year-old daughter to remind her she was over forty.

Miles passed and I mentally went down a list of names. I had no doubt that I was liked, but was I *needed*? Had I made a difference in anyone's life or was I existing solely for myself?

By the time I reached Estes Park, I was physically and emotionally drained and totally unequipped to handle the throngs of traffic which crowded the town's narrow streets. It was half past six, and the tourists were out in full force. I stopped at a service station to ask directions, and getting out of the car, my legs felt weak and uncoordinated, like they didn't belong to me at all. I tried to ignore the waves of exhaustion crashing around inside me by giving all my attention to the young attendant as he explained how to reach Castle Mountain Lodge. Five more minutes. I could last that long. Just five more minutes.

Castle Mountain Lodge was situated along the Falls River, only a mile or two outside of town, and even tired as I was, I had no trouble finding it. My "castle" for the night was a tiny, two-room cabin with the poetic and slightly pretentious name of "River Castle 6." I dragged my suitcases inside and glanced about with approval and relief. The small living room was homier than most motels I had stayed in. The adjoining kitchen nook was cozy and clean with a wooden table and chairs, neatly-ironed tablecloth and matching curtains. Above the sink-stove combination, I found a cupboard full of dishes, some pans and a variety of utensils. Wonderful. Rather than going out to dinner, I could buy a few groceries and eat here. Right now, a bowl of canned stew would be manna from heaven. But first, I had to snatch a few minutes and rest. I made my way into the bedroom, kicked off my shoes, then collapsed on the bed with a moan.

I awoke to total darkness. It took a moment for my groggy mind to grasp where I was, but once that fact was assimilated, I remembered everything else.

There in the dark, it was safe to cry. Some of the tears were for a nameless young man who had died on a mountain road, but the rest were purely selfish. Nothing mattered as long as I carried this terrible emptiness inside! There had to be some purpose—some reason for being, other than going to work every day and coming back to an apartment or motel room alone each night.

Long after the tears had ceased, the emptiness remained. Staring into the blackness, I found myself remembering the dark-haired man at the accident—the touch of his hand on my shoulder, his voice, his smile . . . I sighed and shoved the memory away. He was only a nameless stranger. Nothing more.

I got off the bed and felt my way into the bathroom to wash my face. Now that my Irish side had spent itself in passionate tears and anguish, my English-American side asserted its common sense. I splashed cold water on my problems as well as my face and stared into the mirror. The visage peering back at me looked something like Dracula's daughter—red eyes and swollen lids, with black streaks of mascara running down a pale face.

"You may feel rotten, but you look even worse!" I told the

creature in the mirror and reached for a towel.

After undressing and putting on a loose, comfortable robe, I went into the kitchen-living room to eat dinner. This was not a hot bowl of stew, but a small carton of strawberry yogurt, which was all that remained in my styrofoam cooler. No matter how hungry I was, I refused to wander the streets of Estes Park this late at night looking for a grocery store. Yogurt would have to do.

In my present state of mind, the heavy silence of the night was far too oppressive, so I turned on the TV set for a little company. After fiddling with knobs for a futile five minutes, I was forced to accept the crackling sound and snowy picture as the best I could get. The visual offerings for the night were less than thrilling: a dreary panel discussion on the current crisis in the Middle East (when wasn't there a crisis in the Middle East?), the remaining half of an Agatha Christie movie which I had already seen twice, and a local news program. I opted for the station with the clearest reception which happened to be the news, and settled back in my chair.

The lead story was almost as tasteless as my yogurt. An impeccably dressed newsman informed me in his impeccably bored voice that several owners of bars in the Denver area were up in arms because the present law didn't permit nude dancing and the consumption of alcohol to occur in the same place. Several nightclub dancers were also upset because they didn't earn as much money in tips when they were clothed as when they "danced without a bottom." My mind immediately produced a grotesque creature whose legs were somehow connected to its waist, and I almost smiled.

One old derelict with sunken eyes and stubble on his chin insisted in coarse, almost unintelligible gibberish that this law was unconstitutional because it interfered with his freedom of speech. I did smile at that, wondering if the founding fathers would be swayed by such drunken logic. Poor old man. The only thing interfering with his freedom of speech was the percentage of alcohol in his bloodstream.

The scene cut back to the news commentator who continued with the next story. I ate another spoonful of yogurt and listened dully.

"Police are still searching for clues to the whereabouts of Denver radio station manager and concert promotor, Ross Tedesco, whose car was found at the Stapleton Airport this afternoon."

Behind the newsman, a picture of a smiling, bearded face flashed on the screen, and I nearly dropped my yogurt.

It was him! Recognition seered through me, and I leaned forward to study the man's face. The smile lightened his heavy features, but the dark hair and beard, the prominent nose and close-set eyes were exactly the same as those of the man I had seen in the red sports car. It *was* him!

The announcer went on, totally unaffected by my startling discovery. "Mr. Tedesco, a prominent member of the Denver business community and manager of radio station KVHK, is wanted by police in connection with a multi-million dollar drug bust made last night by undercover agents. Earlier this evening, one of our newsmen, Rod Malloy, interviewed Mrs. Tedesco."

The scene cut quickly to the wide porch of a fashionable brick home where a thin young man with bushy eyebrows stood talking to a lovely, dark-haired woman.

"Mrs. Tedesco, you claim to have had no previous knowledge of your husband's alleged involvement with drugs, isn't that correct?"

As the camera angled in closer on the woman's face, I saw the quick, proud lift of her chin.

"This whole thing is a terrible mistake! Anyone who knows Ross would never believe that he's anything but hard-working and honest!"

The reporter's bushy brows went up a notch. "It's been suggested by some that your husband was warned in advance about last night's raid, or he would have been among those arrested. Do you have any comment concerning those allegations?"

Stark worry, bordering on fear, tightened the woman's features, but her voice was as controlled as before. "I don't know anything about it, but I'm sure that Ross will be able to clear everything up as soon as he returns. I told you before, this is all a mistake, and I think the news media would do us all a favor if they'd concern themselves with the facts instead of rumors."

The reporter's expression bordered on smugness. "Isn't it a fact that your husband left home quite unexpectedly, and that you have no idea of his whereabouts?"

"Ross told me he had an urgent business trip," she replied coldly. "There's nothing unusual about that."

"Are you aware that your husband's car was found in the airport parking lot," the newsman persisted, "but that no flight ticket had been issued in his name?"

Mrs. Tedesco paled visibly, and her chin started to tremble. "I . . . I have no further comments," she faltered, and turning away from the camera, went into the house.

I felt an ache of pity for the woman as the camera cut back to the television studio where the news commentator summed up the story with the bland statement, "At this hour, police have issued an all-points bulletin for Tedesco. Next, on the weather, Dave Simmons reports on flash flooding in the southeastern part of the state. . . ."

I switched off the television and sat staring at the empty gray space where Ross Tedesco's picture had shocked my senses only moments before. My initial certainty began to ebb into worrisome doubt. Beards were more common than flies these days, and I'd had only a few seconds' look at the man's face. Was that really enough to make a positive identification?

My mind labored through the scant facts of the incident, trying to sort out the plausible from the implausible, the maybes from the absolutes. Ross Tedesco strongly resembled the passenger in the red sports car. That was a fact. But what should I do about it? I had already given the police detailed descriptions of both men. If I called the highway patrol now, what more could I tell them, except to say that maybe—possibly—one of those men might be Ross Tedesco.

But what if I were mistaken? After the trauma of the accident, every bearded man I saw from now on would probably look exactly like the passenger in the red sports car. I shoved back my chair and paced about the small room. If the man I had seen today was Tedesco, it would certainly account for the look of fear I had seen on his face. But so would a dozen other things.

For all I knew, Ross Tedesco might be hundreds of miles from here by now. And that would make a lot more sense than the idea of him traveling along a mountain road less than an hour's drive from Denver.

I stopped pacing and put both hands on my aching head. In my excitement, I had forgotten a simple but important detail. My cabin was not equipped with a telephone. The only way I could call the police tonight would be to traipse down to the motel office and get the owners out of bed. Put in that light, my information seemed far too uncertain to justify doing that. Maybe the best thing for me to do was forget about bearded fugitives and get a good night's sleep. I would be able to think through the whole situation a lot more rationally in the morning. Besides, if I were going to drive to Boulder and attend a concert tomorrow night, I had to get some rest.

Good heavens, the concert! I had slept right through tonight's concert! I stomped into the bedroom, slammed the door and sank down on the edge of the bed. So much for my wonderful schedule. The write-up for the "Music in the Mountains" concert would now be totally blank. I couldn't fake it. There was no point in trying, and I couldn't remember whether the series was held nightly or weekly. What a mess! Tomorrow night I was scheduled to attend a benefit concert by Cole McLean and the following evening was reserved for Colorado University's production of Shakespeare's "A Midsummer Night's Dream." I wouldn't mind substituting the "Music in the Mountains" series in place of the McLean concert, but I flatly refused to miss the Shakespearean Festival at Colorado U. I had saved that particular event until last, like frosting on the cake.

I might as well face facts. Tomorrow, or rather later today, I would have to call Mr. Winegar and ask him what I should do. After all, it might be my feature article, but it was his magazine.

I got into bed, punched my pillow into a semblance of softness and tried to relax. Simple words for the mind to say, but my body refused to obey them. Minutes and hours dragged by. I took a warm bath, then read through my notes of last night's Ballet West performance. My eyes were dry and burning from their recent flood of tears and my brain was so frazzled I knew I'd make a mess of my notes if I tried to revise anything now. Finally, at the end of the late, late show, I resigned myself to the simple fact that I was not going to get any sleep. I lay down on the bed once more and watched the feathery shadows of pine branches on the wall. Outside my window, the rushing voice of the river came to me along with the wind's soft whisper. The last thing I remember was noticing how the room's inky darkness was fading into gray. And then, at last, I slept.

I dreamed of Cody. We were walking along the edge of a narrow road, and I was holding his hand. Even in the dream I could feel the warmth of that small hand. The sun was shining, and I felt wonderfully content. Then Cody pulled his hand away and ran down the road like a frightened squirrel.

I tried to call to him, to tell him to come back, but I didn't have a voice. I could think the words, even shout them in my mind, but there was no sound. When I tried to follow after the child, my legs felt weak and boneless. Then, up ahead, I saw the blind curve. It was huge and menacing and *something* was coming. I couldn't see or hear anything, but I *felt* it. My mind called out to Cody once more: "Come back! Cody, stop!" but the words refused to leave my mouth.

Then I heard him yelling back to me, only it wasn't Cody's voice. "No! No! You can't make me! Leave me alone!"

It was coming nearer. I pushed my boneless limbs forward and reached out for the boy with a frantic cry. "Cody! Cody, come back!"

The sound of my own voice startled me into wakefulness. As I struggled out of the dream, I realized there were other voices. Outside my bedroom window, some children were arguing.

"No! You can't have it!"

"Mom said! You better give it to me!"

"No! You can't make me!"

My tense body relaxed as reality shoved the dream away, and I opened my eyes to warm, golden sunlight.

Somewhere outside, a woman's voice called, "Kevin! Amy! You come back here right now!"

The woman's tone put a stop to the childish argument and two pairs of feet raced past my window.

I sighed and reached for my wristwatch on the small night

table, then stared, unbelieving, at the watch face. Eleven-fifty!

I threw some clothes on, ran a comb across my hair and slapped on some lip gloss. There wasn't time for more. It was already two hours past check-out, and I hadn't called Mr. Winegar!

I left the little cabin and sprinted down the asphalt path to the motel office, mentally composing my upcoming conversation with the boss. If I had my way, I'd forget about the benefit concert in Boulder and finish my trip with the Shakespeare play. With a little luck o' the Irish, I hoped to be able to convince Bill Winegar of the same thing.

No such luck. Mr. Winegar was very understanding and very concerned about the accident, but I had no choice where the McLean concert was concerned. Not only did the boss insist I attend, he had even arranged for me to meet the man afterwards in a brief interview.

"Interview!" I exploded. "You never mentioned anything about an interview before I left!"

"I wasn't sure I could pull it off," he explained. "In fact, I only got the confirmation from McLean's manager late yesterday. I'd planned on calling you this afternoon with the good news."

"Good news! Mr. Winegar, I can't just walk in cold to an interview with Cole McLean! Besides, I thought the whole idea of this article was to approach it from the audience's point of view. Not too many people get the chance to talk with performers after a show."

"Look, I had to pull a lot of fancy strings to get you five lousy minutes with McLean! He hasn't granted any personal interviews for over a year, so you be there, and you be there early! I don't care if you're involved in ten head-on collisions! Got it?"

I moved the phone slightly away from my ear. Whenever Mr. Winegar gets angry or excited, his voice tends to raise in pitch and volume to a nerve-jangling intensity.

"Shall I send you the hospital bills?" I asked dryly.

There was a moment's silence on the other end of the line. "What hospital bills?" he asked. "I thought you said you weren't hurt yesterday."

"I'm talking about the head-on collisions you have planned for me."

Mr. Winegar's voice lowered to its normal pitch, and he even managed a chuckle. "I'll send a dozen roses to your hospital room every day—but you be there tonight! And enjoy yourself!" he ordered firmly.

"Yes, sir!"

"Megan. . . ." He paused, and I knew from the sudden huskiness in his voice what was coming next. "I've missed you!"

I ignored the words and the tone. "If I'm going to get to Boulder on time, I'd better be going. Good-bye, Mr. Winegar."

"Megan . . . ."

"Say hello to the wife and kiddies," I said lightly and hung up the receiver.

If Mr. Winegar hadn't insisted that I attend the McLean concert, I would have been more than happy to do so. But having been ordered to attend and enjoy myself made me want to do just the opposite. My sense of responsibility outweighed my rebelliousness as far as attending the concert was concerned, but I flatly refused to have a good time unless I wanted to!

By the time I arrived in Boulder, I was in a "fine fit o' temper," as my grandmother used to say. The fact that it was an absolutely gorgeous day with soft blue skies and heaps of woolly clouds over the mountains only made me more determined to stay angry.

Before going to my motel, I stopped at the Information Bureau on the university campus and received directions indicating Chatauqua Park and the Flat Irons Amphitheater were only a few miles from the campus. The concert was scheduled to begin at 8:30 p.m., and as there were no reserved seats, the man in the Information Booth strongly advised me to arrive at least an hour early. I gave him a frosty thank you, then headed back to my car. The poor man had no way of knowing how tired I was of "strong advice."

The remainder of the afternoon was mine just to relax and get ready, but by the time 6:00 rolled around, I was too bored and restless to stay in my motel room a minute longer. I

gathered my pens and notebook, grabbed a warm jacket and
mentally prepared myself for a miserable evening.

Chatauqua Park took me completely by surprise. One
simply doesn't expect to find nearly unspoiled mountain wilder-
ness a few blocks away from a large residential area and busy
college campus. But there it was, acres of green, sloping
meadow leading up to ridges of dark pines and the magnificent
Flat Iron Mountain range. My rebellious mood melted away into
sheer wonder as I parked and left the car in a gravel parking
area at the base of the fenced-off park. For just a moment, I
stood clutching my notebook and stared up at the mountains
where giant slabs of reddish-gray rock rose starkly from a dense
border of pines. The significance of the name Flat Irons was
immediately apparent. The shape and position of each mountain peak was identical to three household irons standing on
end. But there, all similarities ended. It seemed sadly pathetic
to me that man should be limited to crude things of his own
making when naming such staggering creations of nature. But
then, perhaps mortal words can never adequately describe the
beauty created by divine hands.

The amphitheater itself was nestled in a natural bowl at the
base of the mountains. From where I stood, it appeared very
small and far away. Two asphalt walkways bordered with log-rail
fencing seemed to provide the only access to the theater, one
on either side of the broad meadow. I'm a poor judge of
distance, but it looked as if there were at least a mile of sloping
meadow between the parking area and the amphitheater. I was
glad now that I had chosen to wear flat shoes. A walk would be
pleasant after so many hours of driving. The evening air was
mellow, and I had plenty of time. I headed for the closest of the
two paths and handed my ticket, along with my I.D. from the
magazine, to the young man stationed at the entrance.

"There's a service road down at the end of the parking lot,"
he informed me. "I'm sure it would be all right for you to use it.
Just show the guy there your I.D. and tell him Dave told you it
was okay."

Dave was blond and slender, with clear hazel eyes and a
healthy tan. Probably a student from the college. I smiled at
him and said, "Thanks, but I think I'll walk. It's a beautiful

evening."

He nodded in agreement, adding as I walked past, "Enjoy the concert!"

I choked back a retort and started up the path. Whether or not I enjoyed the concert still remained to be seen, but I thoroughly enjoyed my walk to the amphitheater. The slope was just steep enough to be invigorating, and the view was more than worth the effort. The misty gold light on the mountains changed subtly from one minute to the next, throwing the green of the meadows into sharp relief. I would have enjoyed the walk even more had I been alone, but several concertgoers were ahead of me, and others were coming up the walkways from behind. When I reached the top, I turned around for one more look at the hillside. Both paths were now crowded with a steady stream of people and far below, the parking lot was rapidly filling with cars. I quickened my pace toward the theater.

Made of huge logs and natural stone, the Flat Irons Amphitheater was breathtakingly simple in design and blended in with its spectacular mountain setting. I estimated some four to five thousand people could be seated on the wooden benches which filled the deep, grassy bowl, and there would easily be room for hundreds more on the surrounding hillside. The concert wasn't due to begin for over an hour, but already, the seats closest to the stage were packed with bodies. The excited babble of voices was all around me as I made my way down one of the grassy aisles, and in spite of my determination to feel otherwise, a tiny current of anticipation sent a quick chill up my spine.

Nine rows back from the stage, I spotted an empty space on the end of a bench and made a beeline for it. A middle-aged couple obligingly scooted over to make room for me, and I smiled my thanks. The woman was at that mysterious age— somewhere between 35 and 45—but her expression was as young and eager as the faces of three teenage girls on the row in front of us.

"I brought an extra blanket if you'd like something soft to sit on," the woman offered with a smile.

"Thanks, but I can always sit on my jacket," I told her.

The woman wouldn't hear of it. Nor was she satisfied until she had folded the blanket, placed it on the bench and made absolutely certain I was comfortable. I was a little embarrassed by all the fuss, but still pleasantly warmed by the instinct for caring in some people which makes the word "stranger" totally meaningless. After assuring her for the third time that I couldn't be more comfortable, I opened my notebook and began scribbling little characterizations and impressions of the audience around me.

I have learned that every audience has its own distinct personality, and as the minutes to concert time ticked away, I became more and more amazed by the variety of people who filled the wooden benches. Naturally, I expected the throngs of giggling, gum-chewing teeny-boppers, as well as the cooler, more sophisticated college preppies. But what surprised me was the healthy percentage of people who were (for want of a better expression) definitely "middle-age establishment." I saw every station and status—young married, swingers and singles, rich, poor and middle-class. The types and faces ran the gamut of American culture. As I wrote and observed, I found myself wondering what it was Cole McLean had which could attract such a diversified conglomeration of bodies.

My personal interests, as well as most of my previous magazine assignments, had largely been of a classical nature. Other than hearing an occasional song of his on the radio, I wasn't familiar with the man or his music. I did know Cole McLean was loosely classified as a pop-rock star and that he had a huge string of hit records and albums, but the fact he was successful didn't impress me. Success and talent aren't always synonymous in today's music business.

When the lights went on stage, the audience's excitement began to build until the sense of expectancy fairly crackled in the air around me. I turned my head to glance back at the thousands who were now seated in the amphitheater. On either side, the grassy hillside was dotted with hundreds more. It was a marvelous sight, especially with the backdrop of silent pines and softly-glowing sky. Suddenly, spontaneous applause and an eager roar of approval burst forth from the crowd. I looked quickly toward the stage where musicians were entering from the wings. Besides the usual band members, a large string section took their places, followed by some brass and wood-winds. I stopped writing and sat up a little straighter. A rock band and an orchestra? What kind of concert was this going to be?

A few minutes later, the raucous tuning of instruments ceased. The lights dimmed and softened until the stage was a glowing, luminescent jewel against the dark hillside. The woman who had given me the blanket suddenly leaned forward with a rapt expression and clutched her husband's hand. In front of me, the teenage girls tensed and huddled together with one simultaneous squeek.

I casually crossed my legs and folded my arms, thinking all this reaction was just a bit much. Then, very quietly, the music began. Laughter and conversation faded as the cellos and violas played a haunting lament in a minor key. The melody changed and grew, becoming rich and meditative, exploring solemn pathways of sound. Then violins added their high sweet-ness, like a sudden rush of wind, and the music began to build in intensity as well as volume. I felt oddly breathless as the strings soared along airy harmonies that were utterly timeless. I forgot I had made a firm resolve not to enjoy the concert. I forgot about the notebook on my lap and the audience around me. Nothing existed except the music and my response to it.

Suddenly, the violas began to tremble as the violins climbed a stairway of melody that stretched higher and higher until the evening air was taut and strained with their shrillness. A synthesizer met the strings at the apex and together they resolved the chord into one throbbing pitch. Into this brilliant fermata, the rhythmic strumming of a guitar entered unexpectedly, then there was the sudden, heart-jerking thump of a drum. More guitars and more percussion joined the strings and synthesizers in a pulsing, tribal rhythm, like the heartbeat of the earth.

At the precise moment the music reached its climax, a single spotlight captured a tall figure standing on the ramp to my left, and the audience exploded. My own gasp was completely swallowed up by the tumultuous shouts and applause as Cody's father walked confidently up the ramp and onto the stage.

4

I SAT THERE on the bench with mouth open, eyes wide and staring while the music throbbed and the audience went wild all around me. Cody's father couldn't be Cole McLean! It was crazy and impossible! But there he was—the man who talked to horses—calmly striding toward the microphone and smiling at the audience as if he were merely saying hello to a few friends instead of thousands of wildly cheering people.

I stared openly at the man, taking in every feature and detail of his appearance as if I were seeing him for the first time. The stormy blue eyes, the black hair and mustache were devastatingly the same, but apart from that, Cole McLean bore little resemblance to the gruff rancher I had encountered yesterday. Instead, he reminded me of some dashing 19th century rogue. His shirt was white, full-sleeved and gathered tightly at the wrists. The front had no buttons at all and was open nearly to the waist in a broad "v." His tanned chest with its dark, curling hair made a disturbing contrast against the whiteness of the shirt. Lean hips and long legs were molded by black trousers, while boots of supple black leather came to just below his knees.

I snatched a shaky breath as he bent down for his guitar, suddenly realizing my observations weren't exactly those of an objective reporter. I also realized I must have been totally blind as well as in shock yesterday afternoon. The man had more presence and electricity than a month of thunderstorms. One moment, he was standing there with that incredibly confident smile, while the band played and the roar of the audience subsided from avalanche volume to that of a mild-mannered landslide. The next, I saw him make a quick half-turn toward the band and close his eyes. His body tensed like a tightly-drawn bow, then he was into the music. It was just that simple, like the clicking of a switch. He began to sing, urgently, yet easily, his lean body responding to the insistent beat of the drums. Cole McLean's voice was surprisingly deep compared to the "hairy sopranos" which comprised most of today's male pop singers. There was a kind of masculine roughness to the quality which could almost be described as grating, and yet I found it compellingly attractive.

It is never an easy thing to be objective where music is concerned, simply because one's response to it is so intensely personal. Even though writing about music and the arts is my profession, I constantly have to guard against the tendency to classify music that I like as "good" or music I don't like as "bad." My objectivity toward Cole McLean lasted all of ten minutes. What can I say? The man was a poet, musician and dynamic entertainer. Not to mention the fact that if sex appeal were measured on the Richter Scale, he could have destroyed San Francisco twice over. I couldn't have taken notes if I'd wanted to, because suddenly I was part of it all—this incredible love affair between a man, his music, and the people who loved them both.

One of the first things to impress me was his stage presence. Probably, because if there's anything I detest in a performer, it's arrogance and a patronizing sense of duty. While Cole McLean demonstrated the poise and confidence which come with being a professional, he also revealed a warm appreciation and affection for his audience which had to be genuine. Throughout the concert, I was conscious of an intimate exchange of emotion flowing between the stage and the massive crowd. He belonged to us and we to him.

Like many other contemporary singers, Cole McLean composed his own material, but try as I would, I couldn't confine his songs to any one category or style. Rock, country, folk, blues—even classical—his music encompassed them all, exploring every color and nuance of human emotion. He sang of life and love, people and places in a way that was uniquely his own, and yet so relevant that each one listening could say within himself, "I know what you mean. I've felt that way, too."

The lyrics told me of his past, growing up in a small Colorado mining town. They revealed his philosophies, his loves and his sorrows. In between songs, he sometimes sat on a long-legged stool, casually picking out chords on his guitar and sharing intimate pieces of his life. He would explain what prompted him to write a particular song, or give the reason why a song had special significance to him. I marveled that he could reveal himself so easily and couldn't help comparing that to my own life with its self-imposed barriers and fences. I had always taken great care not to let anyone get too close and here was this man, opening the doors to his heart and soul and inviting the whole world to come in.

The man's versatility and musicianship constantly surprised me. After driving home a series of exhausting, hard-hitting rock numbers, he altered the mood completely by performing an instrumental suite with strings, flute and guitar which he entitled, simply, "Mountain Dawn." The audience which had been out of their seats clapping and cheering only moments before, was now silent and spellbound by a musical portrait of the coming of morning. Through the miracle of one man's musical gift, I saw birds in flight against a pale sky, heard the sounds of forest life awakening to a new day, and felt the warmth of the rising sun. The entire suite was a joyous celebration of life.

Then there was the time he had glanced up from strumming his guitar, smiled that devastating smile and said, "This next song is about a very special person in my life. He's taught me more about love than just about anyone I know. It's called, 'Cody's Smile.'"

The melody was almost childlike in its simplicity, and the man's love for his son shone like a light through the lyrics. As I listened, my angry words of yesterday returned to prick my conscience: "What kind of lousy father are you. . . ?" I cringed inwardly and stared at my tightly clasped hands during the remainder of the song.

Still another disturbing discovery came during one of his love songs. I was lost in the music, listening to his voice caress the intimate words and watching the emotion on his face when I suddenly found myself wondering about his wife. What was she like? Had this song been written with her in mind? What would it be like to be the woman Cole McLean loved? My response was so achingly physical, it jerked me upright on the bench. I blew out a shaky sigh. It was one thing to become lost in the man's music—quite another to be swept away by the man himself!

I quickly fortified the walls of my emotional defenses and just as quickly, his smile, his voice and the way he moved would send them tumbling down again. If he had abused his masculinity with crude gestures or suggestive movements, I would have had no trouble resisting him. But he didn't. Cole McLean's body had a natural language all its own that found expression the moment his music began. To state it bluntly, the man's virility wreaked total havoc on the female members of the audience. I took great pride, however, in the fact that I did not scream or jump up and down like so many of the women and teenage girls. Even so, at various times during the concert, I caught myself watching for certain mannerisms. Little things, like the way he tossed back his head, or the sensuous curve to his mouth. Even the way he pronounced certain words was enough to melt my bones. It wasn't fair! But I was totally helpless to do anything about it.

Cole McLean's music demanded a response. It was impossible to listen and not be moved. Several times during the course of the evening, I saw men and women standing on their feet, silently weeping. Other times, they laughed, sighed, cheered or sang along. And so did I. My one comfort lay in the fact that Cole McLean would never know how deeply his music had touched the secret places of my soul.

Then, suddenly, he was gone. The encores and ovations were over, and the stage was empty of his vital, living presence. Slowly, reluctantly, people began to file out of the rows, as unwilling to part with the place as they had been to part with the man. I could see it in their faces—rapture at what had been given and shared, and the emptiness, now that it was over.

The flesh on the inside of my palms was hot and stinging from the endless clapping. The night breeze was suddenly cool on my flushed cheeks. I felt drained, yet filled to overflowing.

With a sigh, I picked up the blanket I had been sitting on and held it out to the woman next to me. She thanked me absently, then moved past with a sigh more wistful than my own—leaving me standing there with the blanket still in my hands.

Her husband smiled and shook his head. "She'll be like this for a month," he said, taking the blanket. "It happens every time."

I stood aside to let him pass, then bent down for my notebook, glancing ruefully at the blank pages. How was I ever going to write an objective, concise review of Cole McLean's concert? Right now it was impossible, but maybe in a few days, or a few weeks, after some of the euphoria began to fade. I took two steps up the grassy aisle, then stopped with a jerk. I didn't have a few days, or even a few hours! My boss had arranged for me to interview Cole McLean right now!

My knees went weak, and I sat back down on the bench in a heap of nerves. I couldn't do it. But what excuse could I give Mr. Winegar? Especially after he had gone to some trouble to arrange the interview in the first place.

I'm sorry, Mr. Winegar, but I wasn't able to interview Cole McLean after the concert. Why? Well, it's not easy to explain but—his music touched places inside of me that no one has ever touched before, and I don't think I could survive meeting him face to face. Besides, he was the man at the accident yesterday. The one I yelled at. That's right, Mr. Winegar. I yelled at Cole McLean and told him he was a lousy father. Now do you understand?

Mr. Winegar would never understand. The truth sounded ridiculous, even to me. And if I were serious about keeping my job, I had better hustle my body backstage before Cole McLean left the amphitheater. A faint hope dawned. Maybe he had already gone. The thought gave me enough courage to walk up the same ramp where he had made his entrance some two hours before.

Backstage, I was met by an unsmiling security guard with a chest like a brick wall. After I gave him my I.D. and explained about the interview, he ushered me through a side door and into the sound booth where I was told bluntly to wait while he found Myron Sharp, the stage manager.

Two men, both young and bearded, looked up from an

expansive console of buttons and dials to give me polite, if curious smiles. I smiled in return and tried to impart the impression that I was definitely a personage of authority. During the next five minutes, I clung to my notebook as if it were my sanity and fed myself tiny morsels of courage. This was by no means my first interview. Since my employment with APA, I had met and interviewed dozens of musicians and entertainers. I had never had any difficulty being gracious and charming—even when the person interviewed turned out to be stone drunk and revolting. There was no reason for me to have a heart attack over Cole McLean. After all, he was only a man. And there was always the off chance he might not remember me from yesterday. It shouldn't be too difficult to paste a cool little smile on my face and pretend I had never met him either.

Suddenly, a red-faced man, whom I assumed must be the stage manager, burst into the sound room, followed by the same security officer I had met backstage. Myron Sharp was short, fat, forty and sweating. And he didn't like the idea of me interviewing Cole McLean.

"I don't know anything about an interview," he told me in tones that strongly suggested I had concocted the whole thing. "No one cleared it with *me!*"

I took a breath and smiled into his fat little face. "Bill Winegar, the managing editor of *American Performing Arts*, arranged the interview with Mr. McLean's personal manager—a Mr. Reynolds, I believe. Perhaps if I could speak to him. . . ?"

Myron Sharp fixed me with another pointed look. "I don't know any Bob Winegar."

"*Bill* Winegar," I corrected sweetly, giving him one of my dazzling smiles that I reserve especially for rude, ignorant people. "Well, Mr. Sharp, I'm sure you must be very busy, so I won't take any more of your time. Since I won't be meeting Mr. McLean, let me thank you for the concert tonight. It was marvelous! And I was so impressed with the sound system. Usually in outdoor concerts like this, the quality is completely lost."

The man's face changed from flustery red to a rosy pink. "It isn't easy to get good sound," he told me. "I've worked hard to get the bugs out."

"That's obvious, and I'm sure Mr. McLean must be very pleased with your efforts." I made a few impressive scribbles in my notebook just for effect.

Myron Sharp cleared his throat, then tilted back his head and several chins to give me the semblance of a smile. Since he was at least five inches shorter than my 5'10", he had to tilt his head back a good deal.

"Why don't you come with me and I'll see if I can find Joe Reynolds. If your interview's okay with him, it's okay with me," he said magnanimously.

"Thank you."

I followed the stage manager's bobbing bald pate down a wide hallway crowded with musicians, stage crew and other personnel, silently asking myself—why on earth am I doing this? No job is worth a nervous breakdown.

Halfway down the hall, Myron Sharp stopped one of the musicians to ask if he had seen Cole's manager.

"The last I saw, Joe was out back with some of the band," the man replied and continued on his way.

The stage manager pursed his lips, and I could read the indecision on his pudgy face. Should he make the effort to find Joe Reynolds or get rid of this red-headed reporter?

I was silently praying for the latter when he grunted and said, "You wait here. I'll go find Joe." Myron Sharp opened a door to his left and was gone.

I stood there in the hall, notebook in hand, feeling like some teenage groupie. My hair was probably a mess, and I knew my lip gloss was long gone. This was worse than horrible. But it still wasn't too late to leave. The impulse to turn and run grew stronger as two men carrying some heavy wooden risers came puffing toward me. I stepped aside to let them pass and directly across the hall, a brown metal door opened.

My heart lurched, and my mouth went dry. It was him. Not the agent, or the stage manager, but _him_, leaning wearily against the door frame. Our eyes met as another load of wooden risers went by, and his widened with immediate recognition.

It was too late to run. Besides, it's a simple fact that cement blocks shaped like feet do not move quickly. I stood motionless against the wall, as some musicians stopped to offer their congratulations on the concert. He thanked them in turn, then crossed to where I was standing.

I moistened my lips and said with a casual smile, "Hi! How's Cody?"

"Cody's fine."

We stared at each other for a moment, then he said, "You left yesterday before I had a chance to thank you."

I shrugged and smiled again. "Oh, well. There's really no reason why you should thank me."

"I think there is." Cole McLean stepped closer and took one of my hands in both of his. "I appreciate the way you took care of Cody."

I tried to pull my hand away without being obvious about it, but his grip was amazingly strong—and warm.

"I . . . I'm glad I was there to help. How are the horses?"

He ignored the question and looked down into my face. "I don't even know your name. I asked Cody later, but to him you were just the 'cookie lady' with the pretty hair."

The "cookie lady" promptly turned as red as her hair and stammered, "Well, there . . . there wasn't much time for introductions. You were busy talking to one of the police officers when I left and. . . ."

We were interrupted by a laughing group of young men who looked as if they might be members of the stage crew. One of them asked Cole for his autograph, and he let go of my hand to sign the wrinkled piece of paper.

"Look, we don't need to stand out here in the hall," Cole said after the young men had gone. "Why don't you come inside, and we can talk for a few minutes." He gestured to the open dressing room door with a nod and smile that were dangerously intimate.

"Well, I . . . no, I don't think so. You're probably exhausted and have a hundred things to do. I'll just go now and. . . ."

"Damn! I completely forgot!" he said with a tired shake of his head. "I'm supposed to talk to a reporter from some crazy magazine. But look, why don't you come sit down while I find the guy and get rid of him. It won't take long."

Before I could think of a fitting reply to this, the stage manager came rolling down the hall, followed by a tall, slender

man with dusty brown hair and thick glasses. When Myron
Sharp saw me with Cole, a broad smile split his face.

"Ah, Miss Collier, I see you've already met Mr. McLean! I'm
sorry I took so long, but Joe and I had a few other things to
discuss." He turned to the man beside him and said, "I'll meet
you in the sound room to check those tapes," gave Cole a
beaming smile, then walked swiftly away.

Joe Reynolds was dressed in a tweed sport jacket and tie,
but his manner was as casual as the smile he gave me. "I'm
amazed you got past Myron-the-Merciless. But I guess that's all
part of a good reporter's job, right?"

"I'm not a reporter, Mr. Reynolds. Just one of the
magazine's contributing editors."

Cole McLean took this in with an amused lift of his black
brows, then put in smoothly, "Miss Collier, I don't believe you've
met my manager. Joe, I'd like you to meet . . . ." He paused
significantly and gave me an inquiring look.

"Megan," I said quietly and shook the manager's hand.

"Nice to meet you, Megan," Joe Reynolds replied with
another easy grin, then turned to Cole. "Do you need me for
anything before I go see Myron?"

"No, you go ahead," Cole told him and took me by the arm.
"Megan and I have a lot to talk about."

And with that, he ushered me firmly into his dressing room.

5

COLE McLEAN'S DRESSING room was spartan and small. The cinderblock walls were painted an obnoxious off-white—definitely more "off" than white. A large, lighted mirror filled half of one wall with a formica counter below. A functional metal rack for clothes and two lounge chairs made up the remainder of the small room's furnishings.

Cole offered one chair to me and sank wearily into the other, his shirt front falling open as he did so. It took a considerable amount of self-control to keep my mouth from doing the same.

"Did you enjoy the concert?" he asked.

I smiled politely and uncapped my pen, trying desperately not to stare. "Yes. You were . . . it was wonderful!"

"Where were you sitting?"

"A few rows back—on the left side."

Cole nodded and for a moment I felt the melting inner warmth of his smoky blue eyes on my face. I glanced quickly at the notebook in my lap and turned to a fresh page.

"I hope I sang a few of your favorites tonight," he said after another silence.

"Well, actually—until tonight I wasn't very familiar with your music."

The dark brows lifted. "Oh?"

"That doesn't mean some of your songs couldn't become favorites," I went on hastily. " . . . after I hear them a few more times, of course."

"Of course."

Amusement lurked in the corners of his mouth, and I made some serious scribbles on the blank page.

"How long have you been working for this magazine—what's it called again?"

American Performing Arts," I answered without looking up. "I've been on the staff for a year and a half now."

"Do you enjoy your work?"

"Most of the time, yes."

I glanced up to see him rubbing the back of his neck and felt an unsettling physical response.

"Well, I . . . I'd better not take up any more of your time. Thank you for an enjoyable evening . . . I mean, concert."

He laughed and leaned forward. "Tell me something, Megan. Are you always this aggressive during an interview?"

There was no way I could answer him without making an even bigger fool of myself. I shut my notebook with a flourish and replaced the cap on my pen.

"It's late, Mr. McLean, and I'm sure you must be exhausted. I know I am," I added coldly and got to my feet.

Cole chuckled and stood up. "You're right. It is late. I'll pick you up about noon tomorrow, and we can have our interview along with some lunch."

I stared at him. "What?"

"It's the least I can do to thank you for all your help yesterday."

"But I didn't . . . you don't need to. . . ."

"Just give me the name of your motel, and I'll be by for you around noon."

I summoned what little composure I had left and said firmly, "Thank you for the invitation, Mr. McLean, but I wouldn't dream of putting you to that much trouble."

"It's no trouble. I'm staying in Boulder tonight, anyway." He fastened me with that intense look of his and said again, "Now where are you staying?"

I sighed and wrote the name of my motel on a sheet of notebook paper, then tore it off for him. I did not want to have lunch with Cole McLean, but right then, I think I would have signed my name in blood just to get out of there.

Cole folded the paper, casually tucked it inside his shirt front, then opened the door for me. "See you tomorrow, Megan!"

I took a gulping breath and backed away. "Goodnight, Mr. McLean."

During the drive back to my motel, I composed an absolutely brilliant dialogue with Cole McLean. Terse, provocative questions and cuttingly clever comebacks fairly gushed from my brain—now that it was too late! Whenever I thought about our actual conversation, I wanted to shrivel up and die. Cole McLean had done all the interviewing, not me! If Mr. Winegar had seen me in action tonight, my promising career with APA would have met a swift and agonizing death. One thing was certain. Tomorrow's interview had better not be a repeat performance of tonight's disaster. No more scribbles and no more blank pages!

After getting ready for bed, I tried to do a bit of advance preparation by jotting down a few questions. For nearly thirty minutes I alternately crumpled sheets of paper and stared doggedly at blank pages before realizing my emotions were too frazzled to produce a complete sentence, let alone an intelligent interview question. Finally, I switched off the lamp and climbed into bed. I lay back against the pillows and stared into the blackness, but all I could see was Cole McLean's face. Songs from the concert came drifting back to me—fragments of melody and pieces of rhyme, like a musical mosaic. There in the silence of the night, my mind listened to the memory of his voice, and I couldn't push him away.

I awoke just before nine feeling rested and relaxed—until I remembered who would be coming to pick me up in three hours' time. I ignored the sudden thump of my heart and told myself firmly this was just another interview.

The orange juice was warm and my bagel was cold, but I choked down a little breakfast in the restaurant next to the motel out of sheer necessity. There was no way I could be clever and charming if I were fainting from hunger. I took another sip of juice and reread question #3: "Has a career in music always been a motivating force in your life, or have you pursued other occupations?" Not bad. A little trite, perhaps, but it would have to do.

An hour later, I had a list of ten, semi-intelligent questions.

Most were concerned with the creative and technical aspects of his music and a few were career related. Not one was personal. Mr. Winegar might not approve, but as far as I was concerned, the less I knew about Cole McLean's private life, the better!

At 11:45, I tucked the list into my handbag along with my pocket tape recorder, then glanced in the mirror for the tenth time. A cream-colored blouse of soft crepe and smartly tailored beige slacks ought to give the right impression. Stylish, poised and professional. Cutting my hair for the trip had been a last minute decision, but I was more than satisfied with the results. The style was soft, casual, and took advantage of my hair's natural curl. I put away the tiny pearl earrings I had been debating to wear and gave myself an extra spray of Shalimar instead. Today, I needed all the confidence I could get!

A sudden knock on the door sent my heart dropping like a stone in an empty well. It couldn't be him. It was too early. Hurrying to the window, I peeked through a crack in the drapes to see Cole McLean standing outside my door dressed in tight Levis, a faded blue western shirt and cowboy boots.

I backed away from the curtains, glanced down at my dressy clothes and silently cursed Mr. Winegar, Norm Jesperson's high blood-pressure and anything else I could think of. Then I grabbed my purse, whipped on a cool, casual smile and opened the door.

"Hello, Mr. McLean."

"Hi! I'm a little early. Hope you don't mind."

"Of course not. I'm ready."

His eyes made a frank appraisal of my appearance, and I wasn't sure if I read approval or amusement in the look he gave me.

I stepped out of the room, slammed the door on my purse, and dropped my key—all in one graceful motion.

Cole bent down for the key while I quickly retrieved my purse from the door, thinking I might as well scratch "poise" off my list for today. He handed me the key with a heart-shaking smile, and the eternity it took for my clumsy fingers to lock the blasted door could have been recorded in the *Guinness Book of World Records*. When the task was finally accomplished, Cole took my arm and said, "I'm parked down by the motel office."

As we walked along the sidewalk, past the various units, a maid exited one of the rooms, pushing a cart full of cleaning supplies and soiled linen. She was young, no more than twenty, and her hair resembled a blonde atomic bomb exploding out from her head. Under an open smock, her figure was equally radioactive. There was a dangerous amount of "fall-out" spilling from her grape-colored t-shirt, and those jeans were so tight, I wouldn't be surprised if they had to be surgically removed.

The maid glanced up as we approached. When she saw Cole, her mouth dropped open, revealing a fat wad of gum the same purple shade as her shirt. The girl's pencilled brows were already painted in perpetual surprise, but her peacock-shaded eyes opened wide with recognition. It didn't take long, however, for her to recover and give Cole a seductive little smile followed by a honeyed, "Hi, there!"

Cole returned the maid's greeting with a polite nod and a smile that was faintly embarrassed, then stepped off the sidewalk to guide me across the asphalt parking area.

When we were out of earshot, I couldn't resist asking, "Do you ever get used to that?"

"Not really. I just try not to think about it."

His answer was strangely satisfying, as well as surprising. My first instincts had been to shove that seductive little smile right down her throat, but if Cole McLean could dismiss a blonde explosion in a tight purple t-shirt, so could I.

I had another surprise when Cole stopped beside a muddy brown jeep and offered me his hand. I don't know what I had been expecting. A Porsche maybe, or a Ferrari—but certainly not a jeep. As he helped me inside, I couldn't help thinking that nothing about the man fit the mold of "super star." His clothes, the jeep, even the casual way he carried himself were all so unpretentious and ordinary. And yet, after hearing him sing last night, I knew Cole McLean was no ordinary man. Besides his obvious musical talent, he had a *presence*—a kind of magnetism that all the grubby Levis and muddy jeeps in the world couldn't hide.

The streets of Boulder were congested with lunch hour traffic, and during the next five or ten minutes, our conversation was practically non-existent. Cole asked how I was feeling, and I said fine. I asked if he were still tired from last night's concert, and he said no. We both agreed the weather was wonderful. The only thing worse than our retarded conversation was the silence. When we weren't talking, I was much too aware of other things—the sun-warm tangles of his black hair, his hands on the wheel, the heavy thudding of my heart.

When Cole asked about my current assignment for the magazine, I literally pounced on the subject and gave him a non-stop travel log of my entire Colorado trip. But even that topic couldn't last forever. I ran out of things to say about the time we crossed over a steel and concrete bridge spanning Boulder Creek. Not far beyond the bridge, the road led us into a steep-walled canyon of slate gray rock. Lush willows and lofty cottonwoods lined the roadside as we followed the winding course of Boulder Creek upstream into the mountains. Perched precariously along the stream bank or pushed against the rocky gray walls, I noticed several attractive homes and cabins. The cabins were rustic enough to blend with the canyon's rough landscape, but the neat little homes with their tidy lawns and flower gardens looked flagrantly out of place. If people wanted to get away from it all and live in the mountains, why did they try to turn their yards into typical city lots? Much more pleasing to the eye were the curling trails of wild sumac which grew among the rocks, and the brilliant purple fireweed blooming along the roadside. As we drove higher up the canyon, pines and aspen replaced the willows and cottonwoods, and homes became more scarce, but I could still spot a cabin or two clinging to the rocky hillside. When we passed a road sign indicating the entrance to Roosevelt National Forest, I couldn't control my curiosity a moment longer.

"Where are we going?"

"To my ranch."

I caught my breath. "Your ranch? But . . . I thought we were going to have lunch and . . . and the interview!"

"We are," he said, flashing me a smile. "I thought you might enjoy seeing my ranch as part of your interview. Twila can serve up a better meal than anything we could get in Boulder, and I know Cody will enjoy seeing you again."

For a moment, I completely forgot the professional reasons for our luncheon plans. "That sounds wonderful! I'd love to see Cody again, too!"

The look Cole gave me was sudden and intense. "You have the most beautiful smile!"

I was unprepared for the rush of warmth that surged through me. A reply was impossible. It was much safer to pretend I hadn't heard him. After a few seconds, I asked casually, "How far away is your ranch?"

"Lodestone is a few miles outside of Nederland, about thirty minutes from here."

I nodded and gave all my attention to the passing scenery, but my heart was racing. Thirty minutes. I wouldn't last another thirty seconds if he kept looking at me that way. I glanced down at the handbag in my lap and breathed a quiet sigh of relief. The questions. A good solid interview was exactly what I needed. After fishing the list out of my purse, I gave question #1 a discreet glance, then said, "Will I be meeting Mrs. McLean today?"

I heard my voice plainly speaking the words, while inside another voice was shouting, "You idiot! That wasn't question #1!"

Cole shot me a suspicious glance, and the warmth was gone from his voice. "No. We've been divorced for a couple of years."

"Oh. I'm sorry. I was just . . . wondering. . . ."

"Are you saying you didn't know about my divorce?" he asked with edgy skepticism.

I stared at him in surprise. "Of course I didn't know. Why would I ask you something I already knew?"

"To get a reaction," he said bluntly. "People do it all the time. They poke and they prod, trying to get you to spill your insides, just so it'll look good on paper."

My face burned in spite of the cool canyon breeze blowing around us. "I'm sorry if you think I was poking and prodding. As far as I'm concerned, you can keep your insides to yourself! I wouldn't want you to spill them on my account."

"Then why did you ask about my ex-wife?"

"Because I make it a policy never to have lunch with married men—no matter how famous they are!"

His black brows lifted in surprise, then he gave me a broad grin. "Good for you, Babe," he said with a chuckle. "Good for you!"

I gave my heart a full minute to settle down to its normal rhythm, then looked at the list again. Back to question #1 and this time, no substitutions!

Before I could speak, Cole reached over and snatched the paper out of my hands. He gave the questions a quick glance, then looked at me with a curious smile.

"What's this?"

"Nothing. Just a . . . a list."

"What sort of list?"

I folded my arms and gave him what I hoped was a "poised, professional" sigh of disgust. "Mr. McLean, may I have my list back, please?"

"Certainly, Miss Collier," he replied, mimicking my stiff, formal tones and quickly transferring the sheet of paper to his left hand. ". . . after you answer my question. What kind of list is it?"

I turned away from his teasing glance and studied the gray walls of the canyon with a fierce scowl. "It's a list of questions for our interview."

"Oh, is that all?" Cole laughed and tossed the paper over his head where the wind immediately caught hold of it and sent the list pirouetting across the road.

I watched my semi-intelligent questions sail toward a rushing stream and cried, "You . . . why did you do that?"

He grinned and shrugged. "I hate lists. They're too restrictive. Too formal. I'd much rather just talk to you."

My heart took another nose-dive, but I stared straight ahead and asked tonelessly, "What would you like to talk about?"

"How about you? What do you do when you're not driving around Colorado attending concerts?"

"I .. . I live in L.A."

"Where in L.A.?"

"Near Brentwood on San Vicente," I said flatly, suddenly reminded that tomorrow afternoon would find me flying back to the coast. I glanced around at the wildflowers and pine forests with a little sigh. By tomorrow night, this moment and Cole McLean would be over a thousand miles away.

"Do you live alone?" Cole asked me then.

I knew exactly what he meant, and it angered me. Not the question so much as the shades of meaning that "modern morality" lent to it. What Cole McLean really wanted to know was whether or not I had a live-in boyfriend, and that made me furious!

"I do now," I answered coolly, "but six months ago I was living with Sam."

Cole frowned at the curving road ahead. "Sam?"

"Mmmm. We had a very 'special relationship,'" I said, trying not to gag on the words. "But things just didn't work out. Now Sam's living with a girl friend of mine in San Jose."

"Sounds like Sam really gets around," he commented, giving me a tight-lipped glance. "Doesn't that bother you?"

"Oh, it did at first. I was heartbroken when Sam left—but my landlord insisted."

Cole's frown was puzzled. "Your landlord kicked him out?"

"Oh, he didn't mind us living together," I explained, struggling to keep a straight face. "But no matter how hard I tried, I just couldn't break Sam of messing on the carpet—and you know how landlords feel about that."

Cole coughed, then cleared his throat. His expression was so taken back, I couldn't suppress my smile any longer.

Giving me a sideways glance, he asked dryly, "Sam is a dog—right?"

"No. He was my cat."

"Your cat," Cole repeated with a smile, but his voice was more thoughtful than amused.

Suddenly, my little game seemed childish and ridiculous. I glanced away, and we drove for several minutes without speaking.

Then, he looked at me and said quietly, "I'm sorry, Megan."

"Sorry? Why should you be sorry?"

"Because I think I offended you when I asked if you lived alone."

I clasped my hands together, feeling even worse. "Look, you don't need to apologize. I shouldn't be so sensitive and—

and stupid!"

"You're not stupid!" He ground out the words, and I grabbed hold of my seat as he shifted down with a hard jerk of the gears. "And thank God there's a woman left in this world who's still sensitive! If anyone's stupid, it's me for asking such a personal question."

I smiled a little. "Well, I guess that makes us even."

Cole's expression softened as we shared a look of quiet understanding. "Yes, I guess it does."

The tiny threads of tension which had been keeping such a tight hold on my emotions suddenly burst and a simple, singing kind of happiness came rushing in.

The jeep surged over a steep, pine-covered summit, then took the gentle descent toward a mountain reservoir of silver-blue water.

"Tell me something," Cole said as we drove past the reservoir. "How is poor old Sam surviving without you? Has he cleaned up his act any?"

I smiled and said, "Sam's doing just fine. My girl friend has a big white cat named Ruth, and the two of them fell madly in love—Sam and Ruth, that is," I explained with a laugh.

"Sam and Ruth," Cole repeated, his mouth curving into a smile. "That would make a great song title, don't you think?"

"Mmmm, I don't know. I think it sounds kind of biblical myself."

"I could always work that into the lyrics," he told me. "Something like . . . 'Sam the cat begat and begat' . . ."

I interrupted him with a groan. "It'll never work!"

"Why not?"

"Sam's been neutered."

Cole burst out laughing, and I made a startling discovery. The barriers were slipping away, and I didn't mind at all.

6

MILES OF MOUNTAIN scenery passed by in a lovely blur and somewhere along the way, I stopped thinking of Cole McLean as composer, recording artist and super star. Instead, I discovered a sensitive, intelligent man—one who made me feel incredibly alive. Sharing his smiles and laughter, it was impossible to remain business-like and detached. I was completely unaware we were traveling the same road I had driven only two days before until suddenly, there it was. Scarcely half a mile down the highway, the blind curve waited for us. As we approached the jagged walls of the rock cutting, it all happened again in my mind—shrieking tires, screaming horses, then silence and a bright trail of blood.

Neither Cole nor I spoke a word until the accident site was a mile or more behind us. Then he slowed the jeep, pulled off the road near a sunny aspen glen and switched off the ignition.

All around us, the light rustle of aspen leaves rose and fell in rhythm with the wind's gentle cadence, while somewhere in the forest, a mountain bird trilled his song.

"I keep seeing his face," Cole said simply, but his voice was ragged. "His eyes . . . staring up at me." He broke off and gave all his attention to scraping a microscopic piece of dirt from the steering wheel.

"I can't forget it either. I keep wondering who he was, if he had a family. . . ."

"His name was Jeff Spencer. He was twenty years old. He lived in Grand Junction, and he was going to be married next month."

I listened to him toss out the cold facts as if they were only idle statistics, while the look in his eyes tore at my heart.

"When did you—how did you find out?"

"Yesterday afternoon. I called the highway patrol."

I waited a moment to see if he were going to add anything more, then asked, "Do you know if the police have any leads on those two men in the sports car?"

Cole gave me a quick, intense look. "Two men? Did you get a good look at them?"

"Yes, but I'm not sure a description is worth much without a license number. I'm not even certain about the make of the car." I glanced at him curiously. "Didn't you see them when they passed your truck?"

Cole leaned against the seat with a frustrated sigh. "All I saw was a red blur and the back of some guy's head. I should have been paying more attention, but I . . . well, I was watching a hawk and. . . ."

"The hawk! I remember. It flew right in front of your truck."

Below his dark mustache, Cole's mouth parted in a half-smile. "Cody got all excited when he saw it. That kid loves anything that moves! Anyway, I turned my head for a second and the next thing I knew, this red car was forcing me off the road. After that, everything happened so fast. . . ."

I shivered, remembering, as a car whizzed past on the highway. In seconds, the sound of its engine was only a faint whine in the distance.

Cole straightened up and asked, "Do you think you might be able to recognize those men if you saw them again?"

I took a long breath before answering. "I think I have . . . seen one of them."

"What? Have you told the police?"

"No, because I'm not sure I can make a positive identification." I turned sideways on the seat to face him, feeling a sudden urgency to tell Cole everything that had happened. "Have you ever heard of a man named Ross Tedesco?"

Cole's face registered interested surprise. "Yes. In fact, I've met him a couple of times."

His answer left me breathless. "You've met him?"

"Yes. Why?"

"Because he — I think he was the man riding in the passenger seat of that red sports car."

"What? I'm not sure I understand." Cole's frown was perplexed. "How do you know Tedesco?"

"I don't. That is, I've never met him, but I saw his picture in a news story on TV the same night of the accident. At the time, I was positive it was him, but now . . . well, I can't help wondering if my memory's really reliable."

Cole nodded thoughtfully and leaned one arm on the steering wheel. "Tell me about Tedesco."

"What do you mean?"

"You said he was on the news. Why?"

"Oh. Well, apparently, he's wanted by the police in connection with a big drug raid made in Denver a few days ago. But now he's missing."

"Ross is missing?"

I nodded. "The news report said something about his car being found at the Denver airport, but no one knows where he is—not even his family."

Cole sighed and gave the steering wheel a thump with his fist. "I guess I shouldn't be so surprised. Still, for his wife's sake, I hope Ross isn't in too deep."

"Do you know her, too?"

"Not really. I only met her once, after a concert. Ross brought her and his two daughters backstage."

I said nothing, suddenly recalling the woman's lovely dark eyes shadowed by fear. Then my mind flashed an image of the bearded man's face. Fear had been starkly present in his eyes as well. I shivered in the warm sunshine and wrapped my arms about my sides, feeling an uncomfortable twinge of worry.

"Do you think I should have reported seeing Ross Tedesco to the police?"

"It's hard to say," he answered frankly. "Your thinking Tedesco was the man in the sports car could have been a reaction triggered by trauma and coincidence. After what happened, that's certainly understandable. And if the bearded man you saw really was Tedesco, he's probably hundreds of miles from here by now."

"I'd thought of that," I admitted.

"Well then, I can't see where telling the police about Tedesco would make much difference, one way or the other."

I sighed and shrugged. "I suppose not."

Cole's blue-gray eyes met mine with candor and tender concern. "Don't worry about it, Babe," he said softly and brushed my cheek with his fingertips. "There's nothing more you can do."

He was right, of course. After that brief touch there was nothing more I could do—speak, move, or draw my eyes away from the deepening emotion in his.

The moment ended much too soon when common sense reminded me that after today, I would never see Cole McLean again—except on an album cover.

I glanced away with considerable effort and said in a thin voice, "Shouldn't we be going?"

Cole's answer was silence and a shrug, then he leaned forward and started the motor. Without another word, he eased the jeep back onto the highway, while I tried to convince myself the sudden emptiness I felt was relief and not disappointment.

A few miles later, we left the mountain highway to take an obscure gravel side-road. At the road's entrance, a large metal sign informed me this was "Private Property" and "No Trespassing" was allowed. Near the bottom of the sign, I spotted a small but striking insignia—the letters "L" and "R" done in handsome, medieval script.

Cole slowed the jeep to a modest rate of speed as the vehicle's tires bit into the road's rough gravel surface, and I looked about with carefully controlled excitement. The ground was hilly and wooded. A dense cover of pines and aspens made a protective canopy on both sides of the road, shielding us from the afternoon sun. Everywhere I looked, wildflowers bloomed in delicate disarray and somewhere to my left, among the secretive tangle of grasses and undergrowth, I could hear the laughing voice of water.

We hadn't gone far before the land began opening up. Steep rises eased into gentle slopes where fledgling firs and slender young aspens sought the sunlight. One more curve of the hillside brought us to a small clearing. Here, the road was blocked by a heavy metal gate, and the land on either side was fenced with barbed wire and metal posts. An A-frame guard-house stood to the immediate left of the gate. Built of logs and knotty pine, it was about the size of a one-room cabin, with a door and single window in the front and a large antenna attached to its shingled roof.

Cole braked the jeep a few feet from the gate where a large sign ordered: "Stop here! Private land!" If this weren't enough to discourage casual passers-by, another sign posted on the guardhouse warned that the premises were patrolled by armed guards and trespassers would be prosecuted to the fullest extent of the law.

Even before the jeep came to a complete stop, the door to the guardhouse opened, and a beefy young man with shoulders like a linebacker came out, waving a greeting.

"Morning, Mr. McLean!"

"Morning, Ron! How're you doing?"

"Just fine, sir."

As the guard moved to unlock the gate, I took instant notice of the large revolver in a leather holster on his hip. Ron swung the gate open, gave me a wide smile, then stood aside as Cole drove the jeep on through.

I released a sigh and tried to cover a sudden attack of nerves by saying lightly, "I'm impressed, Mr. McLean. But is all this security really necessary? Your ranch has such a remote location, somehow it's hard to imagine hordes of fans milling around the gate."

Cole smiled at me, but his voice was serious. "I love the fans, but you'd be surprised how many 'crazies' there are in this old world. People who think you ought to be thrilled to death when they sneak into your bedroom at three a.m. to find out what you do or don't wear to bed. Then there are those who just want to take home a souvenir." He laughed without amusement. "That may range from a rock or bush to my clothes and stereo equipment. The funny thing is, most of them are decent people who wouldn't dream of walking into a friend's house, let alone a stranger's, and helping themselves to his belongings."

"Ah, and that's the problem," I put in. "You're not a stranger or a friend. You're a 'star,' and a lot of people think that makes you public property. Even though you give so much of yourself through your music, that isn't a tangible—a physical item someone can touch and hold in his hand. . . ." I stopped, realizing by the expression in his eyes, how personal I was sounding. Warm color flooded my cheeks, and I added lightly, "I promise not to snitch anything while your back is turned."

Cole gave me a quick glance before maneuvering the jeep around a chuckhole. "I hope I haven't given you the impression that I'm . . . well, carried away with my own importance. Security is just something I've had to accept as one of the necessary working conditions that goes along with my profession."

I met his eyes and nodded, surprised and touched that he should feel it necessary to explain this to me.

"There are times when it all seems like a giant headache," Cole went on, "but good security has been even more important since the recording studio was built."

"Recording studio? Here?"

He grinned. "Lodestone Studio has been in operation for almost a year now. We purposely keep a low profile outside the profession though, so it's no surprise you haven't heard of it. One of the main purposes of the studio is to provide a kind of getaway—a retreat where artists can come to work and record without interruptions of any kind."

"It sounds wonderful, but. . . ."

"But what?"

"Wouldn't that kind of operation be awfully expensive?"

He nodded and told me with a chuckle, "It is! But privacy is a luxury most successful recording stars are happy to pay for. In recent months, we've had some of the country's top groups and artists cut albums here at Lodestone."

"Including you?"

He laughed and gave me a smiling glance that did dangerous things to my pulse rate. "Including me."

The forest was suddenly left behind as the gravel road took us through a broad meadow where knee-high grasses rippled in the breeze. Halfway through the meadow, the road widened and split in two, with the left fork taking a westerly course toward a forested ridge, and the right fork running north, down the length of the meadow. Cole slowed the jeep near the junction and pointed to a pine-covered slope on the meadow's western side.

"The lodge and recording studio are over on that ridge," he told me. "If you'd like to see them, I can take you over after lunch. There's a rock group here now working on a new album."

Shading my eyes with my hand, I gazed at the wooded rise where a few pointed roofs caught the sun's rays. "I'd like that very much. What group is it—if you don't mind my asking?"

"Obolus."

"Obolus!" I nearly choked on the word.

"I take it you've heard of them," Cole said dryly.

"That's like asking someone from Hiroshima if they've heard of the bomb! Aren't you a little worried they might destroy the place?"

"All the more reason to have good security," he answered with a smile, and accelerating, turned the jeep down the road's right fork. "According to their manager, the group's bad-boy image is pure hype for the media. Sid's taken great pains to assure me and my staff that Obolus are really a sweet bunch of guys who need a private place to record their new album."

"Mmmm." For the sake of politeness, I made an effort to keep my voice as noncommittal as possible.

"Do I detect some skepticism in that 'mmm'?" he asked.

I shrugged and smiled. "Like you said, Mr. McLean. Obolus is all the more reason to have good security."

I glanced ahead where we were approaching a small, white-frame ranchhouse on the left side of the road. Nearby were a delapidated barn, some ancient stables and metal sheds. Cole slowed the jeep as we drew closer, and I told myself there was no reason I should be so surprised. A lot of celebrities had simple tastes. Still, even for a man with simple tastes the house was—well—I bit my lip and struggled between tact and honesty for something to say.

The house wasn't exactly run-down, but it could certainly use a fresh coat of paint. So could the tired-gray picket fence which sagged across the front yard. Both side yards were bordered by a ramshackle wire affair which probably hadn't looked any better when it was new. To be fair, I did notice the lawn had recently been mowed, and the flowers were charming. Sweet Williams, snapdragons and spiky blue delphineums were only a few of the old-fashioned flowers blooming around the house. A riot of roses trailed along the south fence and morning glory vines climbed an old wooden trellis near the front porch.

"The flowers are lovely," I said. It wasn't very brilliant, but at least I was honest.

"I'll tell Twila you said so," Cole answered. "She's always fussing over her garden."

"*Her* garden?" I asked blankly as he drove past the white-frame house and continued down the road.

Cole looked at my face and laughed. "That's Wes and Twila's place. My home is up on the ridge straight ahead."

I stared, red-faced, at the pine-covered knoll which rose up from the meadows less than a mile away.

"Did you really think. . . ?" he began, still chuckling.

"With you, I never know what to think!" I told him, then wished I hadn't given voice to my thoughts quite so hastily, as his amused expression shifted to something far deeper.

I cleared my throat and asked, "Are Wes and Twila relatives of yours?"

"No, but most of the time I forget that. The Randolphs are old friends of my folks, and I've known them ever since I can remember. Wes used to own all this land. He and Twila ran a dude ranch here for years. About the time I started looking for some ranch property of my own, Wes had to have a back operation. He and Twila decided it would be too much for them to keep the ranch going, so I made them an offer. Lucky for me, they accepted."

In the meadows to our right was a much newer barn and large, modern stables. Three-rail wooden fencing enclosed the adjoining pastures where I saw several horses grazing. As we drove by, the stocky rancher I had seen at the accident site sauntered out of the stable leading a beautiful chestnut horse with white stockings.

Cole gave the man a wave and received a brief nod in return. "You'll never find a better man with horses than Wes Randolph," he told me, pride and affection warming his voice. "I'm not here on a regular basis, so Wes takes care of my horses as well as tending to the ranch stock. When I am home, Twila keeps me from starving to death," he added with a smile.

"Who takes care of Cody when you're gone?"

Although it was a personal question, he didn't seem to mind. "I've cut back my concerts and traveling in the past couple of years, but when I am gone, Cody stays with Wes and Twila—and sometimes, with my parents."

"I only met Twila for a moment, but she seems very nice and totally devoted to Cody."

"She and Wes weren't able to have any children of their own, so Cody is like the son they never had," Cole explained, adding lightly, "I try to keep them from spoiling him, but I don't know that I've succeeded."

We reached the base of a forested knoll where the road turned right and began a gentle, curving ascent through the pines. Watching Cole's face as he took the jeep up and around a bend, I sensed a tenseness about him that hadn't been present moments ago.

"Does it bother you?" I asked.

He shot me a quick glance. "Does what bother me?"

"That the Randolphs are so attached to Cody."

"No, of course not. I wouldn't be able to manage without them." He shifted to a lower gear and released a frustrated sigh. "I guess what bothers me is Cody doesn't have a mother to love and take care of him."

"Lots of children don't," I said quietly.

Cole gave me a thoughtful glance, but said nothing.

I knew we must be getting close to the top of the hill by the widening patches of blue sky between the pines, but I wasn't able to see the house until the road made one last curve around the hillside. Then I caught my breath and stared.

Like his music, Cole McLean's home was a fascinating combination of styles, a visual extension of the man himself, colored and shaped by the rich textures of his personality. Stone steps led to an arched doorway which was part of the home's sweeping center gable. Built of rugged stone and dark-stained cedar, both the gable and the large wings extending out on either side presented a picture of solid strength. The lines of the house were dramatic and aggressively masculine, yet there was a rustic charm about the cedar shake roof, and more than a hint of romance in the old-fashioned, small-paned windows. Stately Ponderosas grew undisturbed beside the house and on both sides of a wide, circular dri··e. Other than a sloping section of lawn, Cole had let Mother Nature do his landscaping. The result was more than pleasing to th eye. I felt a sense of timeless peace and belonging about che place, as if it had grown on the hillside instead of being built by human hands.

Cole brought the jeep to a halt near the front walkway, smiled at my expression of dazed delight and said, "Welcome to Lodestone, Megan."

When he switched off the ignition, we were immediately surrounded by the quiet. No traffic, no noise, not even the sound of a bird interrupted the stillness. Then the front door burst open, and I heard a joyful, "Dad!"

Cody launched himself off the stone porch and shot down the steps like a three-stage rocket, gathering momentum with every second. I watched as his father jumped lightly down from the jeep, then ran around the front of the vehicle to swoop the little boy up into his arms. When he pressed Cody's dark, curly head close to his own, the expression in his eyes brought an uncomfortable tightness to my throat. I felt totally alone and apart from the warmth of their greeting.

Then Cody's head lifted and his blue eyes widened as he saw me. "Dad! You found the cookie-lady!"

"I sure did! And she's even going to have lunch with us!"

"All right!" Cody cried with enthusiasm and his father laughed.

Holding the little boy in one arm, Cole walked back to the jeep and offered me his other hand. Our eyes met, as well as our hands, and my loneliness melted away.

7

IF SOMEONE WERE to ask me, say twenty years from now, what it was like to spend an afternoon in Cole McLean's home, I probably wouldn't tell them much about the house itself. Not that it wasn't beautiful. The paintings intrigued me, the shelves of books, the beamed ceilings and massive, moss-rock fireplace. But twenty years from now, my choicest memories would be of simpler things—the aroma of Twila's freshly-baked bread, and the way her eyes lit up when she saw me. Cody, running to show me his favorite toys, a rock that sparkled in the sun and a horrible black spider he had trapped in a glass peanut butter jar. And Cole . . . Something told me that twenty, even thirty years from now, I would still be trying to forget, rather than remember.

We ate lunch on a large stone patio with the trees as neighbors and the Rockies for our backyard. Half a dozen stone steps led us away from the house and down a vine-covered slope where the air was sweet with the scent of honeysuckle, Shakespeare's woodbine. Rings of aspen and clusters of pine sheltered the patio on either side, while its broad, outward edge was defined by a low stone wall. The view beyond that wall thrust itself upon my soul and my senses. Below the hillside's rocky slope, meadowland stretched lazily in the sunshine, with bright ribbons of water lacing through its multi-shades of green. A dense border of pines fringed the meadows and hugged the lower flanks of a somber mountain range. Far above timberline, the mountains lifted their ancient gray heads of stone, enjoying the solitude of endless sky and drifting cloud.

The sheer expansiveness of the view made our little grouping around the redwood table even cozier. Twila apologized repeatedly as she served us, because all she had to offer for lunch was a green salad, beef stew and homemade bread.

"If you'd called to tell me you were bringing company, I could have fixed something much nicer," she told Cole with a grieved look.

"I can't imagine anything nicer than this," I said, looking down at my steaming bowl of stew with its fat chunks of beef, carrots and potatoes. "In fact, I would have given anything for a bowl of this stew two nights ago."

The woman beamed at me, placated for the moment. "Bless your heart, dear, there's plenty more keepin' hot on the stove, so don't be shy about asking for seconds."

I soon discovered that one bowl of Twila Randolph's beef stew was a meal in itself. If I hadn't been worried about hurting the woman's feelings, I never could have finished mine. Cody ate most of the meat and a few potatoes in his pint-sized bowl, but refused to touch any carrots. I watched with amusement as the child stabbed a small piece of carrot with his fork, lifted it to his mouth, and then, thinking no one was watching, dumped it under the rim of his bowl. Before long, he had a messy little ring of carrots and gravy around his plate.

Cole's eyes followed the direction of my smile and discovered his son's attempt at deception. "Eat your carrots, Cody," he instructed with gentle firmness.

"I don't like carrots!"

"Well, they like you! Carrots make you strong and healthy

Cody screwed up his face in disgust. "Carrots make me sick!"

I bit down on my lower lip, trying to keep back a smile, and buttered a second slice of Twila's heavenly bread.

Cole caught my look, gave me a wink, then turned back to his son with an exaggerated sigh. "That's too bad, son. I guess you'll be too tired to go down to the stables with us after lunch."

The boy's head lifted immediately. "I'm not tired!"

"Mmmm, I still don't think you'll be strong enough," Cole told him with mock concern. "Of course, all those carrots are just sitting there, waiting to give you lots of energy!"

Cody looked at his father, then the carrots, torn between

his desire to see the horses and his dislike for carrots.

"Do I have to eat 'em all?" he asked on a pleading note.

Cole smiled and offered a compromise. "How about three? One for every birthday."

The boy sighed and obediently stabbed a carrot. "Boy, Dad! You sure make my life miserable!"

"How old did you say your son was—three going on seventeen?" I asked, unable to suppress my laughter.

Cole leaned back in his chair and gave me one of the warm, wonderful looks my emotions had been battling with for the past hour. Those blue-gray eyes and the sensuous curve of his mouth below that dark mustache created a response in me that was disturbingly physical. Throughout lunch, I found myself making a conscious effort not to stare at him. Yet, time after time, my gaze wandered to his face, fascinated with the taut, tanned skin of his cheekbones, the rakish tilt to his brows and the laugh lines which creased the corners of his eyes. Avoiding those eyes was a bitter-sweet battle in itself, but I knew I'd be lost if I didn't.

A winged shadow suddenly flitted across the corner of my vision and turning my head, I saw a gray bird about the size of a small crow, light on the stone wall just a few yards from our table. His wings and tail were black with startling white patches; his beak, long and pointed. I smiled as the bird took note of us with an inquisitive gleam in his black eyes and jaunty cock of his head.

"There's the most striking gray bird on the wall," I said in a low tone. "I've never seen one like it before."

Cole looked over his shoulder. "It's a nutcracker. A pair of them make their nest in the pines behind the house."

Cody glanced up from his carrots as the nutcracker edged a little closer. "It's Pit!" he announced with an excited smile. "Can I give him some bread, Dad?"

"Shhh, you'll startle him if you talk so loud," Cole cautioned in a whisper, then handed the boy a bread crust. "Here. Break a few crumbs on the wall for him. Remember to go slow, son."

I smiled at Cody's exaggerated tip-toe, then asked Cole, "What did he call the bird?"

"Pit," Cole answered with a low chuckle. "His full name is

Peter Illytch Tchaikovsky, but Cody can't pronounce all that, so we just call him by his initials.''

My shoulders shook with silent laughter. "I love it! What did you name the female? No, let me guess—Clara!"

Cole grinned at me. "How did you know?"

"I figured it had to be that or the Sugar Plum Fairy."

We laughed quietly together, then Cole said, "I love it when you smile like that!"

Simple words, but the light in his eyes told me he meant them. I glanced away, giving my outward attention to Cody and the nutcracker. Inside, I was trembling. I didn't want to care about this man. I couldn't let myself!

I wasn't aware my right hand had clenched into a fist until Cole covered it with his and asked, "What's wrong, Megan?"

"Nothing. . . ."

His long fingers curved gently around mine, their touch light and undemanding. I could easily have pulled my hand away. Instead, my fingers relaxed under the warmth of his, and I raised my eyes.

"Hey, Dad! You missed it!"

Cody's voice broke through our locked glances, and we turned simultaneously to look at the child.

"Missed what?" his father asked.

"Pit ate some bread right out of my hand! How come you weren't watching?"

Cole's hand tightened around mine. "Sorry, son. I guess I had other things on my mind. What do you say we take Megan down to the stables and show her Galena's new foal?"

"You mean right now?" Cody asked, giving the carrots a covert glance.

"Right now," Cole affirmed with a grin, then turned to me. "What do you say, Megan?"

"Well, I . . . yes, that would be nice."

"You don't seem too enthused about the idea," he said as we got up from the table. "If you'd rather not. . . ."

"Oh, it's not that! It's just, I've never been around horses before—close up."

"Really?" Cole looked genuinely surprised. "You handled Mica just fine after the accident."

"I was probably still in shock."

He laughed and assured me, "If you do that well when you're in shock, you won't have any trouble now. Besides, all my horses have impeccable manners."

"Now where do you think you're off to?" Twila demanded, coming onto the patio with a tray full of brownies.

"Me an' Dad are going to show the cookie-lady to the horses!" Cody informed her, making a beeline for the brownies.

"Actually, it's the other way around," Cole amended dryly. "And her name isn't the 'cookie-lady,' son—it's Megan."

Cody bit into a fudgie brownie. "I think May-gun sounds weird."

"It's not weird—it's Irish!" his father corrected, and I laughed at the embarrassment on his handsome features.

"What about Cody's nap?" Twila wanted to know. "He should have been in bed an hour ago."

Cole helped himself to a brownie, then leaned over to kiss the woman's lined cheek. "We won't be long. Have a brownie, Megan?"

"No, thank you."

"You're sure? Twila's brownies are sinfully good," he added.

"I'm sure they are, but right now, I'm sinfully full. Thank you for the lunch, Twila. Everything was wonderful."

Cody grabbed my hand and cried, "Come on! Let's go!"

Cole took his son's other hand and together we headed for the stone steps with Twila's stern reminder ringing in our ears: "You make sure you have that child back here in thirty minutes!"

Thirty minutes later, Cody was not in his bed, but sitting in front of me on a magnificent stallion named Malachite. During the preceding half hour, I had been introduced to a dozen or more exquisite Arabians. Cole was right. His horses did have impeccable manners. In fact, the animals' intelligence impressed me almost more than their beauty. I immediately fell in love with Galena, a graceful, silver-white mare, and her foal, a spunky little gray named Gypsum. Next came Alabaster and Obsidian. The names were as lovely as the horses—Moonstone, Amber and Carnelian. When I commented on their names, Cole explained that both his father and grandfather had been miners, and he himself had long been fascinated with rocks and minerals.

"You can carry that sort of thing too far, though," he admitted with a laugh, as we approached the stalls of his newest acquisitions—two pure, Polish-bred mares named Sonata and Allegro.

I smiled as Allegro whinnied a welcome and nudged Cole's shoulder with her lovely head. "I had no idea horses were so affectionate."

"Most horses aren't," he replied, stroking the mare's satiny brown coat, "but Arabians are well-known for their communicative qualities. That's one of the reasons I love the breed."

After renewing my acquaintance with Mica, Cinnabar and Topaz, Cole suggested I take a ride on Malachite, a large sorrel stallion with black mane and tail. No one listened to my protests. It didn't seem to worry either father or son that I had never been on a horse in my life. And when I explained that I wasn't dressed to go riding, Cole just flashed me one of his grins and said the horse would never know the difference. There was no point in arguing with logic like that.

So here I was, being led across a broad, grassy meadow by Cole McLean. Mr. Winegar would never believe it. I didn't believe it!

Cody looked up and saw my smile. "It's fun, huh!"

"The most fun I've had in a long time," I told him and meant it. I never dreamed so much satisfaction could be found in simple sights and sounds—the comfortable creaking of leather, wind in the pines, the soft plodding of Malachite's hooves through meadow grass and mountain soil. And, as much as I might hate to admit it, just looking at Cole was the most satisfying experience of all. I loved the way his black hair caught bits of sun in its thick waves, and the way his broad shoulders stretched the fabric of his shirt. Watching Cole's easy, masculine stride, I was pleasurably conscious how those tight Levis emphasized his lean hips and long legs. I glanced away with a guilty smile. Very tight Levis.

We had covered little more than half the length of the

pasture when I noticed Cody's head was nodding.

"Cole," I called softly, realizing the moment his name left my lips, that it was the first time I had spoken it aloud.

He paused and turned around, awareness kindling the smoky depths of his eyes.

"I think Cody's getting tired."

"I'm not tired," the child mumbled.

"Must be all those carrots you ate for lunch," his father said with a gentle smile and turned the horse's head. "We'd better be heading back."

Cody was sound asleep by the time we returned to the stables. He didn't stir at all when I handed him down to his father's waiting arms.

As I dismounted, Cole smiled at me and asked, "How do you feel?"

"Like the horse is still under me," I answered, trying to stand without staggering. "But I loved every minute of it!"

Wes Randolph entered the stable then and took frowning note of the sleeping child. "I'll take care of the horse," he said gruffly. "You better get the boy back to the house."

Cole winked at me and handed Malachite's reins to the older man. "I know, Wes. I know. It's way past his nap time."

We walked back to the jeep in comfortable silence and after I got in, Cole lifted his son up to me. The boy's body curved naturally against mine, his small face nestled on my breast, cheeks flushed with sleep and dark hair curling damply against his forehead. It seemed right, somehow, to be holding him. Like I had been doing it all my life.

Cole and I said little on the drive back to the house, but the unspoken message in his eyes was more potent than any conversation. When he pulled onto the circular drive and turned off the motor, I sat very still, looking down at the child and praying his father didn't know how rapid my breathing had become.

Cole leaned toward me and the warm pressure of his fingers on my neck sent tingling pleasure through me. "Megan, I. . . ."

"Cole! There's a long distance phone call for you!" Twila called from the doorway, and we both jumped. The sudden movement startled Cody, who woke with a whimper.

"Hell!" Cole muttered under his breath, and swung down from the jeep. "I'll be right there, Twila! Tell 'em to hold on!"

Once inside the house, Cole left to answer the phone in his study, and Twila immediately took charge of Cody.

"Let's go up to your room, little man, and Aunt Twila will tuck you in bed," she crooned, bending down for the boy.

"No! I want the cookie-lady!"

The woman stared in surprise as Cody pulled away from her arms to grab my pantlegs. "Now Cody, you don't want to bother Miss Collier."

"It's no bother," I said. "I'll be happy to put him to bed . . . if you don't mind."

"Well, I . . . of course not. Cody's room is upstairs, the second door on your right."

Cody's dark head sagged wearily against my shoulder as I carried him up the carpeted stairs.

"I wish I didn't hate carrots," he sighed. "Then I wouldn't have to take a nap."

I smiled and opened the door to his room. If it hadn't been for a few stray toys lying about, I could almost believe we had stumbled into a miniature forest. The room was decorated in woodsy greens and browns with heavy oak furniture. Raccoons and deer, rabbits and squirrels watched us with bright, inquisitive eyes from their framed places on the walls, and there was a plentiful collection of plush animals on the bookcase and chest of drawers. Glancing about, I realized Twila must have already come up, because the shades were drawn and the bedcovers turned down.

"We better take your shoes and socks off," I said, putting the child on the double bed. "And your Levis smell like horses. You better take those off, too."

I assisted with the stockings and shoes, then Cody wriggled out of his jeans and tossed them across the end of the bed. As I pulled the covers around him, he looked up at me with a sleepy request.

"Can you tell me a story?"

I hesitated, knowing my repertoire was extremely limited, then succumbed to the appeal in those blue eyes. "What story would you like? 'Snow White' or 'The Three Bears?'"

Cody shook his dark curls. "I like made-up stories best. Daddy always makes up stories and sings songs to me."

"That must be very nice."

He yawned and said, "You can lie down if you want."

"No thanks. I'm fine."

Undaunted, the little boy smiled and patted the pillow beside him. "There's lots of room."

I laughed and said, "Has anyone ever told you you're a lot like your dad?"

"Grandma says I'm the spittin' image," he quoted cheerfully.

I laughed again and took off my shoes, then lay down on the bed beside him. Cody immediately snuggled close against my shoulder, and I felt a strange little tug at my heart.

Suddenly, I was a child again, curled up on the big iron bed in my grandmother's room. The sheets were white and smelled of lavender. At the foot of the bed lay a rose-colored afghan which Grandmother Collier would finger absently between her thin, blue-veined hands as she told me stories. Made-up stories. I could almost hear her soft, Irish voice relating nonsense tales of Gwendolyn, the beautiful purple mouse. . . .

"Once upon a time," I began softly, "there was a beautiful purple mouse named Gwendolyn."

The child's eyes widened. "Purple?"

"Purple," I repeated with a smile. "Gwendolyn was the most beautiful little mouse you ever saw. She had round pink ears and a long green tail."

Cody giggled and burrowed closer. Fingering his soft black curls, I found myself wondering if his father's hair felt the same, then decided I had better keep my mind on the story.

"One day, Gwendolyn came home from school and her father had a special surprise for her. There on the front porch was a bright red scooter."

"What's a scooter?" he asked with a yawn.

I stopped, suddenly realizing scooters had no place in the vernacular of the modern child who was raised on a diet of "Big Wheels" and ten-speeds. I spent half a minute trying to describe one, then decided it would be simpler just to change the story.

"There on the front porch was a bright red tricycle," I

amended. "Gwendolyn could hardly wait to climb on her new tricycle and go for a ride in the forest, but her father told her she must never, NEVER ride her tricycle in the forest."

"Why not?"

"Because that's where the mean old 'hunkle-dunkle' lived," I explained.

The little boy giggled again. "What's a hunk . . . a hunk. . . ?"

Cody gave up trying to pronounce the nonsense word, and I proceeded to tell him all about the magical made-up creature my grandmother had described so long ago.

Contentment. Warmth. And the touch of gentle fingers on my cheek. My eyes fluttered open to see Cole McLean's dark features bending over me. I blinked and stared at him in sleepy confusion, then wiped a hand across my eyes. He was still there and watching me with an expression that brought me fully awake.

"Oh, I . . . I'm sorry."

A hot tide of embarrassment flooded through me as I disentangled myself from the sleeping child. Avoiding Cole's eyes, I got off the bed and stepped into my shoes.

"Cody asked me to tell him a story," I explained in a whisper. "I never meant to fall asleep."

"Shhh."

Cole stepped in front of me and both hands closed firmly about my shoulders. I looked into his eyes and stiffened instinctively, afraid of what was going to happen, yet wanting it desperately. Then his mouth found mine and resistance melted into sweet release.

The kiss became a conversation in emotion. Thoughts and feelings that words would only hinder, found free expression between us. I never knew how much could be said without uttering a single word. Aching loneliness and the shadow of a deep hurt flowed from his touch, and my heart answered in silent understanding.

There in the shadowy room, with the sleeping child only a few feet away, we held each other. There was so much to know and discover. The taste and touch of him was unlike anything I had ever known.

Cole drew back slightly to look at me. "Megan . . . Megan, I can't believe this. . . ." Then he was kissing me again.

There's no telling how long our "conversation" would have lasted if a small, sleepy voice from the bed hadn't provided a startling interruption.

"Boy, Dad! You're really gettin' mushy!"

Cole and I broke away from each other with a guilty start to see Cody sitting up in bed, surveying the proceedings with mixed amounts of interest and disgust.

Cole blew out a shaky sigh. "I'm, uh . . . sorry we woke you up, son. Why don't you just lie down and go back to sleep?"

"I don't want to go to sleep. I want to go potty," Cody announced, pushing back the bedcovers.

Cole glanced at me and raised his eyes. "Well, go ahead! You don't need to tell the whole world about it!"

While Cody hopped out of bed and trotted toward the adjoining bathroom, his father grabbed my hand and pulled me out of the room.

"Come on! Let's get out of here before he starts asking questions!"

I laughed and followed him down the hall toward the stairway. "Where are we going?"

"I don't know. I don't care—just as long as we don't have an audience the next time I feel like getting 'mushy' with the cookie-lady," he told me with a look that sent liquid fire shooting through my veins.

We were making our escape down the stairs when Twila walked out of the dining room and called up to Cole, "What time would you like dinner tonight?"

He paused to glance at his watch, then turned to me. "You will stay for dinner, won't you?"

"I'd love to, but . . . I have to attend a play at Colorado U this evening. What time is it?"

"I don't think I'll tell you," he said, seizing both my hands. "Forget about the play!"

The intenseness in his eyes and voice made everything else seem unimportant. Several seconds passed before I gave him my reluctant answer.

"I wish I could but . . . the play is part of my feature article. I really have no choice in the matter.''

Cole shrugged philosophically and fixed me with another heart-shaking smile as we reached the bottom of the stairs. ''No problem. I'll drive you back to Boulder, we can have dinner there and then go to your play.'' Without waiting for my answer, he turned to Twila and said, ''Forget about fixing dinner for me tonight. Could you take Cody down to your place instead?''

Twila had been staring round-eyed during our exchange. Now she caught herself and answered with a quick nod, ''Of course. That'll be fine.''

''Great! I'll see you later.''

Cole took my arm, and I barely had time to grab my handbag off the hall table before he was rushing me out of the house.

''There's still time for a quick tour of the recording studio, if you'd like to see it,'' he told me as we walked toward the jeep.

''Yes, I would, but Cole. . . .''

He gave me a lift up to the passenger seat, kissed me hard on the lips, then ran around to the driver's side. ''But Cole, what?''

''Are you always so . . . impulsive?'' I asked, feeling the vague stirrings of an old fear. Things were moving too fast, and in a direction that could be disastrous.

''Only with you,'' he grinned and started the motor. ''Are you always so worried about the time?''

I smiled and said, ''Only with you,''—not because it was true, but just to keep things light.

On the drive over, Cole explained a little about the various set ups and capabilities of the recording studio. Somehow, I managed to keep my responses bright and interested when all the while, reality was raining cold facts on my afternoon. In the space of a few hours, I had managed to mess up much more than my emotions. I hadn't given a single thought to the interview ever since Cole had tossed away my list of questions. And the tape in my recorder was as blank as the notebook pages had been during last night's concert. I hadn't thought of anything except Cole and Cody, and how beautiful it felt to be included in their lives. Now, thoughts of our imminent good-byes weighed heavy as a stone in my breast.

I could never hope for any kind of future with Cole McLean. A freak accident and coincidence had brought us together for one afternoon, but if someone were to ask him about me one month from now, the response would probably be a puzzled, "Megan who?" And Cody. Children forget so quickly. Before too long, the "cookie-lady" would be just a blurred face in his childish memory.

We reached the base of the wooded rise where the road curved right, cutting a narrow path through the pines, and I struggled to fight the smothering fear inside me. I never should have let my defenses down. And spending this evening with Cole would only make things worse. I couldn't let that happen!

"That's the lodge straight ahead—the one with the gables," Cole said, pointing to a rustic two-story building made of whole logs and rough stone. "The lodge and a few of the cabins were originally part of the dude ranch," he told me. "The recording studio is the smaller building, there on your left."

I smiled, nodded and stared without seeing much of anything until Cole drove the jeep into a large parking area. Then my gaze sharpened and my spine went rigid. Three cars were parked in front of the recording studio, and one of them was a bright red Camaro.

8

"MEGAN, WHAT IS it?"

Cole stood beside the jeep, waiting for me to climb down.

"That red Camaro—who does it belong to?"

He glanced toward the sports car, then back at me with sudden understanding. "I know what you're thinking, but it isn't the same car. This one belongs to Kurt Gorman, Obolus' producer."

"But it has a Colorado license plate," I said, taking his hand and getting out of the jeep.

"That's because it's a rental car Kurt picked up after he flew in from the coast."

My heart stopped pounding like a jackhammer, but I still couldn't take my eyes off the Camaro. "How long have Obolus and this Kurt Gorman been here at your ranch?"

Cole grinned and shook his head as we took the wooden walkway leading to the recording studio. "Persistent, aren't you?"

"Maybe so, but I can't help being curious." I stopped and glanced back at the red sports car. "I'm almost positive the car that forced you off the road was a Camaro—exactly like that one!"

"Now wait a minute. This Camaro may look like the one you saw, but why would Kurt Gorman run me off the road, then come back here to my property and park his car in plain sight?"

"What's this about me running someone off the road?" asked a pleasant, masculine voice.

A well-dressed man in his late thirties or early forties had just exited the recording studio and was walking toward us with an interested smile. He was about my height, with sharp, well-defined features and brown hair that had been fashionably permed and frizzed. His v-neck sweater and coffee-colored slacks looked as if they had been lifted straight off the fashion pages of *GQ* and around his neck and wrists, I saw the gleam of gold.

Cole smiled and extended a hand as the man drew closer. "How's it going, Kurt?"

"Not bad. We laid down a couple more rhythm tracks today, and the boys have come up with a hot new set of lyrics. Really impressive!"

"I'm glad to hear they're getting some work done," Cole responded, then turned to me. "Megan, I'd like you to meet Kurt Gorman. He's producing Obolus' new album. Kurt, Megan Collier."

The man smiled warmly and shook my hand. At close range, he wasn't nearly as good-looking as I had first thought. The frizzy hairstyle clashed with his sharp-edged features, and there was a hardness about the mouth and eyes which made his smile seem almost artificial.

"I'm happy to meet you, Megan. Will you be recording here at Lodestone?"

"No. I'm not in the entertainment business."

"Miss Collier is my guest," Cole informed him in a tone which didn't encourage further questions.

Gorman acknowledged this with an easy nod, then asked with concern, "Did I hear you right a moment ago? I thought you said something about me running someone off the road."

"Not you, but a sports car similar to yours forced me off the road a couple of days ago," Cole explained. "Megan was in the car behind me and saw it happen. We're both still a little jumpy where red cars are concerned."

A frown tightened the man's features, and his gray eyes shifted from Cole's face to mine. "My God, that's terrible! I hope no one was hurt!"

"A young motorcyclist was killed," I told him quietly. "The driver of the sports car ran him off the road as well."

Gorman shook his head and said again, "That's terrible! Did either one of you get a look at the driver?"

"I'm sorry, Kurt," Cole interrupted, "but I promised to show

Megan through the studio, and we don't have much time."

"Of course." Kurt Gorman nodded absently and half-turned aside. Then, before we could move past, he reached out and put a restraining hand on Cole's arm. "Damn it, Cole, I know you're in a hurry, but there's something I need to ask you."

Cole glanced down at the man's hand and said coolly, "I'm sure it can wait until later."

Gorman quickly released Cole's arm and produced an apologetic smile. "I wish it could, but it concerns the concert this weekend. We all understand how you feel about having reporters here at Lodestone, but Sid and the guys in the band wanted me to ask you a little favor. There's a writer from *New Wave* magazine flying in this evening to cover the concert. You may have heard of her—Maxine Barrett?"

"I've heard of her," Cole answered shortly. "What's the favor?"

"Well, Sid and I thought it might be a good idea to invite Ms. Barrett out here for a few days. You know, have her sit in on a few recording sessions, get some interviews—if it's all right with you, of course."

Cole frowned. "How many others from the magazine will be with her?"

"There won't be any others—just Ms. Barrett," Gorman assured him. "I know I don't need to tell you how important it is to keep a good relationship with the media," he added.

Cole gave the matter a moment's consideration, then shrugged. "I guess it'll be okay since Obolus has requested it. Just make sure Ms. Barrett sticks to interviewing them and not my staff."

"I'll see to it personally. You won't need to worry about a thing," he said with effusive politeness. "I know Ms. Barrett will be most discreet."

Cole coughed to cover an amused smile. "All right, Kurt. Tell Brent to set things up for her to stay in the lodge."

Kurt Gorman was all smiles. "Thanks, Cole. I owe you one!" He glanced down at the heavy gold watch on his wrist and swore, "Lord, it's nearly six o'clock! How long do you think it'll take me to drive into Denver? Max—that is, Ms. Barrett's plane is scheduled to arrive about 7:45."

"You'd better be on your way," Cole advised. "It takes more than an hour to drive to Denver from here, and traffic will be heavy."

"Right. Thanks again." Gorman bestowed a parting smile in my direction, then started down the walkway leading to the lodge.

I looked up at Cole. "As much as I'd love to see the studio, I really need to get back to Boulder in the next hour. I had no idea it was so late."

Before Cole could answer, Obolus' producer had turned back to us and was offering, "I'll be happy to give you a lift, Miss Collier. Boulder's right on my way."

"Thanks, Kurt, but I'd planned on driving Megan back myself," Cole informed him with a firmness I was coming to know.

Gorman shrugged. "Whatever. I just thought I could save you from making the extra trip."

My pounding heart suddenly told me what I had to do.

"Cole, it might be better for both of us if I drove back to Boulder with Mr. Gorman."

For a split second, I saw the surprised hurt in his eyes, then his expression hardened into a polite granite mask.

"If that's what you want."

"I . . . I think it might be better."

Gorman's voice was overly bright. "That's great! I'll be leaving right away, but I need to run over to the lodge first and tell the guys about Ms. Barrett's arrival. If you two will excuse me. . . ." He backed away with a smile, then turned and sprinted across the lawn.

Silence lengthened between Cole and me as the first breeze of evening sighed through the pines.

"It's turning cool," I said.

Cole shoved both hands into his pockets. "It certainly is."

I tried to ignore the anger in his eyes and said quietly, "Thank you for today."

"I hope you enjoyed yourself," he responded with thin politeness.

Looking at his face, I felt a stab of loneliness go through me. Suddenly, he was the gruff rancher I had met on the road two days ago, and I was only a stranger. I turned away from him and murmured, "Please say good-bye to Cody for me."

"Megan. . . ." Behind the gruffness was a tender note that made my heart ache.

Cole stepped toward me just as Obolus' producer came out of the lodge and ran in our direction.

"Sorry to keep you waiting," he puffed, smiling at me. "Are you ready to go?"

"Yes."

Cole stood motionless on the walkway as Kurt Gorman took my elbow and led me into the parking area. Approaching the red Camaro, I felt a strange chill of uneasiness and forcibly reminded myself this wasn't the car involved in the accident. Kurt Gorman bore no resemblance to the blond-haired Viking I had seen behind the wheel of that other Camaro. Even so, I was unable to repress a shudder as I got in.

Moments later, the Camaro roared out of the parking lot, spitting gravel and stirring up clouds of dust. Something stronger than my will forced me to look back. Cole still hadn't moved.

"You look a little tired," Kurt Gorman commented as he turned the sports car onto the main highway. "Would you care for a cigarette?"

"No, thank you."

Gorman reached for a heavy gold cigarette case on the dashboard and took out a cigarette. "Do you mind if I smoke?"

"I . . . no."

"Have you known McLean very long?" he inquired politely, pushing in the metallic button on the car's lighter.

"No. Not long."

Gorman put the freshly lit cigarette between his lips and drew deeply. Puffs of smoke curled from his nostrils as he gave me a smiling glance. "I hope I didn't interfere with any plans you two may have had."

"No."

"Of course, I can understand why he'd be upset. I don't often have the company of such a beautiful redhead."

I wasn't in the mood for patronizing compliments, so I just

stared out the windshield and said nothing.

"Are you sure you're all right?" he asked again.

"It's been a long week."

"I'm sure the accident must have been very traumatic for you," he offered sympathetically.

"Even without the accident, this week has been exhausting," I said and went on to tell him a little of my assignment for the magazine. Anything to stop thinking about Cole and the look on his face when I walked away.

"It's obvious you're a very intelligent young woman—as well as beautiful," Gorman put in smoothly. "Tell me, Megan—you don't mind if I call you Megan?"

"No."

"I can't help being a little curious about this accident you were involved in," he said, stubbing his cigarette butt into the car's ash tray. "When did you say it happened?"

I hadn't said anything about when it happened, but I answered him anyway. "Tuesday afternoon."

"Strange, we didn't hear any mention of it on the news—especially since it involved someone as well-known as McLean."

"It's not uncommon to suppress some stories."

"True, but it still seems odd that McLean didn't tell us about it when he came back to the ranch."

"I . . . I'm sure he had his reasons," I faltered, not wanting to discuss Cole with Kurt Gorman or anyone else. "It wasn't exactly a pleasant thing to talk about."

Gorman quickly agreed, then fumbled in the gold case for another cigarette. "What happened, exactly?"

As I gave him the sparse details of the accident, the man's smile was replaced by frowning concentration.

"It's no wonder you were shocked when you saw my car," he commented. "Do the police have any leads on that Camaro?"

"I don't know. It had a Colorado plate, but everything happened too fast for me to get the license number."

Gorman took a long drag on the cigarette and blew out a choking cloud of smoke before asking casually, "But you did get a good look at those two men?"

A small warning switch clicked inside me. I had conducted enough interviews to become strongly aware of the emotional nuance behind questions, particularly the difference between idle curiosity and purposeful interrogation. Gorman's voice might be casual, but I wondered suddenly if his motives were.

"The sports car was traveling pretty fast when it passed me," I told him and decided to try changing the subject. "Is this the first time you've been to Colorado, Mr. Gorman?"

"Yes, it is—and please call me Kurt," he insisted with a winning smile.

I smiled in return and glanced at the passing forests. "I love the mountains, but I don't know that I'll ever get used to driving these roads."

"I rather enjoy the challenge," Gorman said, maneuvering the Camaro around a steep, twisting curve. "You know, it's a damn shame you or McLean didn't get a license number. Were you able to give the police any kind of description of the men?"

A chill of uneasiness went through me, and I thought, he really wants to know! More than that. It was almost as if he needed to know. But why? For half a second I considered lying, then rejected the idea, more curious to know Gorman's reaction to the truth.

"I have an excellent memory for faces," I told him. "I'm not sure what use it'll be, but I was able to give the police detailed descriptions of both men."

There was no change in the hard-edged features, but I thought I detected a slight tightening of his hands on the wheel.

"What about McLean? Did he get a good look at them, too?"

"No, not really."

Gorman tapped a long cylinder of glowing ash into the ashtray, and I swear his smile held a touch of relief. His voice, however, dripped with conciliatory syrup. "Well, I suppose there's nothing you can do now but try to put the whole messy business behind you."

I looked ahead, thinking, until you began your little inquisition, Mr. Gorman, that's exactly what I'd done. Now my mind was filled with disturbing questions. Was it simple curiosity which prompted the man's interrogation or something more? What if this were the car involved in the accident? Even as my emotions shuddered at the thought, common sense insisted it was only a bizarre coincidence. Just because Kurt

Gorman had a morbid curiosity about the accident didn't mean he was criminally involved. I was probably overreacting to the whole thing.

Gorman gave me a concerned glance. "I hope I haven't upset you by talking about the accident. One of my many faults is I ask too many questions. I'm sorry if I was insensitive."

I smiled and rubbed the tight muscles in my neck. "That's all right."

We drove for perhaps fifteen or twenty minutes, and there wasn't a single word in the man's conversation which might be construed as sinister. I had nearly convinced myself that my imagination had gotten the best of me when Gorman made a gushing comparison between my "titian beauty" and a clump of flaming orange wildflowers along the roadside. My suspicions were instantly aroused. Compliments are all well and good, but by now, I was aware of his pattern—make polite noises, toss in a compliment or two, then ask another question. Sure enough, only moments later he inquired, "How much longer do you plan to be in Colorado?"

"I fly back to L.A. tomorrow morning."

"That's too bad. I was going to invite you to Obolus' concert Saturday night."

I coughed to keep from smiling and thought, sure you were. Aloud, I asked, "Where are they performing?"

"At the Red Rocks Amphitheater just outside of Denver. We're expecting a crowd of close to 20,000."

"Then I doubt you'll miss me."

Gorman laughed and bestowed what I'm sure he thought was a melting look. "I still wish you were able to come. You could always include a write-up of Obolus' concert in your feature article."

"I don't think so. Somehow, I can't see a concert by Obolus having anything to do with the arts in Colorado."

Gorman stared at me, and it was supremely satisfying to see that smug look wiped off his face.

"I take it you're not overly fond of Obolus—or is it just rock music in general you dislike?"

"I never dislike any kind of music 'in general,'" I told him. "I've always been very specific about my likes and dislikes. As

far as rock music is concerned, there are several bands and
singers that I enjoy very much."

"But Obolus doesn't happen to be one of them," he
concluded in a mocking tone. "That's all right, Miss Collier. I
admire a woman who has the rare ability to be specific about
anything."

The cold light in those gray eyes made his smile seem more
artificial than ever, and I couldn't help noticing, so it's back to
Miss Collier now, is it?

"What are your 'specific' feelings about Obolus?" Gorman
pursued.

"Do you want my honest, specific feelings or my tactful,
specific feelings?"

He laughed. "By all means, be as brutally honest as you
like."

"All right, then. Musically, I have to admit that Obolus has a
fair amount of talent. But they're using that talent to produce
some of the most vile, destructive music I've ever heard!"

Kurt Gorman's expression was one of tolerant amusement.
"Who's to say that destruction is something evil? Think of the
millions of people in this country who lead meaningless lives
of conformity and control. Someone has to wake them up
before they're smothered in complacency! What better way than
music to free men's intellect and emotions? There are times,
Miss Collier, when it becomes necessary to destroy in order to
set people free."

My mouth had gone dry as I listened to him, but I wasn't
about to give Kurt Gorman the satisfaction of knowing how
much his radical speech disturbed me.

"That's a fascinating theory, Mr. Gorman," I answered
lightly. "But I'm a little confused. Are we discussing music or a
revolution?"

Gorman shrugged and his glance was cryptic. "Who knows?
Maybe a little of both."

The subject of the accident was not brought up again, nor
was Obolus and their music, but my nerves were taut and
strained from the effort of making casual conversation with the
man. By the time we reached my motel, I was totally exhausted

and had a roaring headache. Kurt Gorman insisted on seeing me to my room, voicing sympathetic concern over my pale appearance.

"I'll be fine," I assured him. "A good night's sleep is all I need. Thank you again for the ride."

"My pleasure," he said warmly. "Good luck with your article, Megan. I'll miss you at the concert," he added, offering his hand.

I refused to take it and held on to the door knob as he stepped closer. "Good-bye, Mr. Gorman. You'd better hurry or you'll be late arriving at the airport."

He got the hint, gave me a cool nod, and walked swiftly back to the Camaro.

My hands were shaking as I locked the door behind me. Now that he was gone, my nerves gave way, and felt almost too weak to stand. Was it foolish emotion or some valid presentiment that made me react so strongly to the man? I would probably never know, but Lord willing, I would never see him again!

Never see him again . . . The phrase brought disturbing thoughts of a far different man.

I walked wearily to the bed and sat down, staring at nothing. If I hadn't been so terrified of good-byes and commitments, I would still be with Cole, but there was no point in dwelling on "might-have-beens." It was better this way. Relationships might have beautiful beginnings, but the feeling couldn't last. I had seen it happen time and time again with my mother and her endless string of lovers. Love turned to hate, rapture faded into boredom and disgust, dreams dissolved into disillusionment. I made up my mind long ago that would never happen to me. Over the years, avoiding serious relationships had become a well-practiced art. I had my share of dates, and on occasion I had even permitted myself to indulge in a light romance, but I took great pride in the fact no one had ever broken down the barriers to my heart. Until now. I lay back on the bed and shut my eyes, trying to block out the memory of Cole's voice, his smile and his kiss. Tears welled up, unbidden, but I blinked them back. It was over.

Forty minutes later, I was striding across one of the beautiful, tree-lined walkways on Colorado University's campus. A hot shower and change of clothes, two aspirins and a "Big Mac" had accomplished wonders. Or so I told myself.

Dusk was falling. My favorite time of day. Cool breezes, birdsong, and the quiet gray submissiveness that comes after sunset. The outdoor setting for the Shakespearean Theater was charming and intimate. I found my seat, breathed a long sigh and got out my notebook.

This illusionary contentment lasted until Oberon made his entrance. Tonight, Shakespeare's "king of shadows" was tall, black-haired and blue-eyed. The fact he had no mustache was of little consequence. I knew I was ruined. When he looked out past the audience and said, "I know a bank where the wild thyme blows, where oxlips and the nodding violet grows; quite over-canopied with luscious woodbine. . . ." I was instantly transported to the lovely patio at Lodestone, with its woodland setting and sweet smell of honeysuckle. When Titania cuddled her changling boy, it was Cody's head I saw, dark-haired and silky.

Throughout the play, I found myself reliving precious segments of my afternoon with Cole and Cody, so that by the time Puck uttered his timeless declaration, "Lord, what fools these mortals be!" I nearly stood up and shouted, "Amen!"

Shakespeare's happy mortals all followed Oberon's advice to "think no more of this night's accidents, but as the fierce vexation of a dream." Would that I could have done the same. Instead, I returned to my motel with a notebook full of mindless scribbles and a heart full of pain. Once inside, I threw my handbag on the bed and gave the notebook a savage toss across the room. Maybe it would be better if I stopped trying to be so noble and had a good hard cry!

I was standing in the middle of the room ready to do just that when the phone rang. The sound startled me so, I nearly jumped a foot. Then I stared at the innocuous brown instrument on the bedside table, scared to death it might be Cole, and even more terrified it probably wasn't. After the third ring, I gathered enough courage to pick up the receiver.

"Hello. . . ?"

"Megan, is that you?"

"Mr. Winegar!"

"Are you all right, honey, or is it this connection that's making your voice sound so strange?"

I sat down on the bed in a trembling heap and answered, "I'm fine."

"Look, I'm sorry to be calling so late, but I knew you'd be at the Shakespearean Festival this evening. How was it?"

"All right."

"Just all right?"

I heard his chuckle on the other end of the line and tried to build a little excitement into my voice. "It was excellent. I'm just a bit tired tonight, that's all."

"I'm not surprised! You've had yourself quite a week," he said with an inflection that implied I had been indulging in other kinds of activities, all of them promiscuous.

"Why are you calling, Mr. Winegar?"

He chuckled again. "Always to the point! That's my Megan!"

I sighed and remained silent, deciding to let the "my Megan" pass this time.

"I'm calling to offer my congratulations, and to let you know there's been a slight change in your schedule," he went on. "I want you to cancel your flight for tomorrow morning and exchange your ticket for a later flight—sometime Monday should be fine."

"Monday? I don't understand. And why am I being congratulated?"

"Now, honey, there's no reason to play the innocent with me. I don't know how you pulled it off, but getting this exclusive story for the magazine could mean a nice little promotion for you."

"Exclusive story?" I repeated blankly.

"On Lodestone Studios and Cole McLean!" he exploded. "What the hell do you think I'm talking about? McLean called me a few hours ago to say you'd been out to his ranch today, but that there wasn't enough time for you to see his recording studio. Then he asked if it would be all right for you to stay the weekend as his guest and finish your article. Do you realize what this means for APA?"

For an instant, my entire body was suffused with heat and the blood was singing in my veins. I was going back . . . back to

Lodestone and to Cole!

I put a hand to my pounding heart and tried to gather my defenses as my boss raved on. "This is a first, girl! McLean has had a strict policy at Lodestone since the place opened—no press, no interviews, no pictures. And now he's asking me if you can please finish your article about the damn place!" Mr. Winegar's voice had been ringing in my ears like an electric drill. Now his volume dropped, and his tone turned confidential. "There's just one thing I'd like to know."

"What's that?"

He cleared his throat and said, "Did you sleep with McLean to get this article?"

There was a full ten seconds of blistering silence on the line before I gathered enough control to say, "Mr. Winegar, you are disgusting and filthy-minded and—and if you think I would sleep with someone just to. . . ."

"Now, Megan! Hang on a minute before you go losing your temper. . . ."

"It's too late! I've already lost it! How dare you suggest that I'd—that I'd—!"

"It's my job to suggest it," he stated flatly. "Our magazine has a reputation to protect, and as important as this story might be, I'd hate to think. . . ."

"You can stop worrying, Mr. Winegar," I said coldly. "Your magazine's reputation is perfectly intact!"

I slammed the receiver down with a crash, then got off the bed and paced around the room. Men! And that included Cole McLean! He had his nerve, calling my boss and fabricating a flimsy excuse to invite me back to his ranch! Feature article, my grandmother! Just because we had shared a . . . a pleasant afternoon together gave him no right to assume that I would jump at the chance to come running back!

I folded my arms across my chest and took a ragged breath. Since Mr. McLean had invented a convenient article for me to write, that's exactly what he was going to get—and nothing more!

9

I WAS UP and dressed, packed and on the road by nine o'clock. My preparations were accomplished with merciless efficiency and a lot of noise. Anger was my only defense against the nerve-shattering prospect of seeing Cole again, and I made good use of it.

This morning, the steep-walled canyon outside of Boulder was a grim place to be. Gray cliffs, gray sky, and a chilling breeze with the moist taste of rain on its breath. Memories of yesterday met me around every curve, but I refused to weaken. Instead, I passed the miles composing caustic little speeches for Cole McLean's benefit.

By the time I turned off the main highway and took the gravel road leading to Lodestone, my mood was as dark and threatening as the clouds smothering the mountaintops. All around me, pines and aspens shuddered in the rising wind.

Ron, big-shouldered and smiling, hurried out of the guard-house the moment I drove up to the gate. "Morning, ma'am! They're expecting you up at the lodge!" he shouted, holding onto his cowboy hat. "Do you know the way?"

I nodded and thanked him, a little surprised Cole had gone to the trouble of making my visit appear so professional.

Once more the heavy gate was unlocked and pushed open. I took a deep breath, looked straight ahead and drove on through.

Rain was spattering against the windshield as I pulled up in front of the lodge and parked the car. I took a few seconds to rehearse my welcoming remarks, then dashed up the walkway to the lodge entrance. The massive wooden door announced my arrival with a loud groan. I stepped inside, shook the raindrops from my hair, then gazed about with the wide-eyed wonder of a child.

The main room was monstrous—acres of polished hardwood floors surrounded by thick log walls and a beamed ceiling that had to be twenty feet high. The room's furnishings were no less staggering than its size. The place was a veritable treasure-trove of Native American crafts. Doeskin drapes with multi-colored beadwork hung from tall windows. Pottery and wood carvings graced the knotty pine tables. Draped over the upstairs balconies, I saw Navajo rugs with intricate patterns and bold, earthy colors. The beauty of ancient Indian culture lived in oil and canvas on the walls. Even the air held an essence of the past—pine resin, heady buckskin, and the sharp, aromatic scent of a wood fire. I looked to my right, at the far end of the room, where a great stone fireplace rose from floor to ceiling. Over its carved wooden mantle, a monstrous buffalo head benignly surveyed its domain.

"Impressive, isn't it?" said a voice.

I turned around with a start and noticed for the first time, an attractive young woman behind a carved wooden counter.

"Very impressive," I agreed.

The young woman closed a ledger she had been writing in and came forward to meet me. "You must be Megan. I'm Kathy Watkins. My husband Brent manages the lodge for Cole."

Marvelous brown eyes—large, luminous and thick-lashed—gleamed at me as I said hello. Kathy Watkins stood an inch or two above five feet and her figure was small-boned and slender. Dark brown hair hung straight down past her shoulders; her skin was flawless, and her features delicately pointed. To me, she had that rare kind of beauty which made her appear just as feminine in Levis and a western blouse as she would have in a designer evening gown.

"Cole told us you'd be arriving sometime this morning," she said, giving me a dazzling smile. "He made all the arrangements with Brent. If you'll excuse me, I'll go get him."

She left me and headed for a room near the far stairs marked "office." For a heart-stopping moment, I wasn't sure whether the "him" she referred to was Cole or her husband, and my collection of caustic speeches suddenly deserted me. Then the office door opened and Kathy Watkins came out followed by a tall man dressed in Levis, plaid shirt and a pullover sweater. Brent Watkins' dark good looks were a pleasing compliment to his wife's delicate beauty. Wavy brown hair and a well-groomed beard added to the charm of his features.

Seeing the two, I found myself giving silent approval to Cole's canny choice of employees. With their courteous warmth and attractiveness, the Watkins were bound to make a favorable impression on Cole's celebrity clientele.

"We're happy to have you here, Megan," Brent said as we exchanged smiles and handshakes. "Hope the storm didn't make your drive too unpleasant."

"No. The drive was fine."

"Cole asked me to apologize for not being here himself to meet you, but he had to fly to the coast last night on business."

My anger and suspicions collapsed under me like a broken chair. All I could do was stand there and repeat stupidly, "He flew to the coast?"

Brent Watkins nodded. "He'll be in Los Angeles for the weekend. Before he left though, Cole told Kathy and me about your feature article. We'll be more than happy to help you in any way we can."

"I . . . thank you, that's very—thank you," I said again, hoping I didn't look as foolish as I felt.

"Cole thought you might enjoy staying in one of the cabins, rather than the lodge," Kathy put in, "so he reserved the 'Mollie Kathleen' for you."

I recovered enough to attempt a smile. "The 'Mollie Kathleen'? That has to be Irish."

"That it is," Brent answered with a grin and touch of brogue. "It's also the name of an old gold mine down in Cripple Creek. Cole named each one of the cabins after mines here in the area. There's the Desperado, the White Raven, and the Baby Doe. . . ." He broke off as the ringing of a phone sounded from within the office.

"I'll get it," Kathy offered, hurrying toward the room.

"It's probably a good thing I was interrupted," Brent admitted with a chuckle. "My little footnotes about this place have a way of turning into lectures. Just ask Kathy." He pulled open a drawer behind the counter and took out a set of brass keys. Dropping them into my palm, he said, "I hope you enjoy your weekend with us."

"Thank you. I'm sure I will."

Kathy's head appeared in the office doorway. "It's for you, Brent. Long distance. Phil Collins from New York."

"Okay, honey. Tell him I'll be right there." Brent Watkins turned back to me with an apologetic smile. "This could take a while. Do you mind waiting? There's a lounge and dining room through those double doors near the fireplace."

"Thanks, but would it be all right if I just drove up to the cabin myself? My car's parked outside, and I only have a couple of suitcases."

"Sure. That's fine. Just follow the road past the recording studio. It winds up behind the lodge and through the trees. The first four cabins are being used by Obolus and their crew, the next one is empty and the last is yours. Oh, and you're welcome to have meals sent to your cabin or eat here in the dining room. Whatever suits your fancy."

"Thank you very much, Mr. Watkins."

"The name's Brent," he insisted with a grin, then headed for the office.

Outside, the rain had increased from a light sprinkle to a steady downpour. I made a mad dash to the car, fumbled for my car keys, then dived inside and shut out the storm. A tinny percussion of raindrops pelted the car roof as I leaned back against the seat with a sigh. I knew I should be feeling relieved and thankful. With Cole in Los Angeles, I could relax and write without any emotional scenes or attachments to worry about. Why, chances were probably good to excellent that I might leave Lodestone without ever seeing him at all. I sighed again and turned the key in the ignition. Somehow, the thought wasn't nearly as comforting as I would have liked.

Thunder grumbled through the forest as I drove along the narrow dirt road behind the lodge and recording studio. My windshield wipers were almost useless against the pouring rain and it was difficult to make out the various cabins. Each was set back in the trees and spaced enough distance from the others to ensure complete privacy. My heartbeat quickened when I spotted the red Camaro parked beside the third cabin, and I knew it would be a long time before I could see such a car without seeing painful images of the accident as well.

The dirt road ended in a small turn-out area. Beyond that point, the forest grew dense and undisturbed, with shadows deep under the drooping boughs of rain-soaked pines. The wind and rain all but smothered the smooth purr of the Audi's engine as I turned into the narrow driveway beside the "Mollie Kathleen." The exterior of the cabin was pleasingly rustic—log walls, a stone chimney and steep-pitched roof. I turned off the engine, debating whether to wait out the storm for a few minutes or get soaked running to the covered porch. My curiosity to see the inside of the cabin won out. With my overnight case in one hand, my handbag and keys in the other, I scrambled from the car.

The small porch provided only a minimal amount of shelter from the rain. Thrusting the brass key into the lock, I gave the door a healthy shove with my elbow, and stepped inside.

My initial reaction was—*this* is a cabin? Granted, there was a mellow, country feeling about the stone hearth and fireplace, the braided rugs and dark pine furniture. But how many mountain cabins come equipped with sophisticated stereo systems and a baby grand piano?

As I glanced about the spacious living and dining area, there was some kind of movement above me, then a masculine voice called from the stairs, "Are you ready to see the new me?"

I looked up with a startled gasp as a dark-haired man clad in brief jockey shorts came bounding down the steps, wiping his face with a towel. Then he saw me standing in the doorway and stopped as if he'd been shot. His dark eyes widened with shock, and he clutched the towel closer to his face. Something in those dark eyes struck me as familiar, but I was too embarrassed to spend time thinking what it might be.

"I'm—uh, sorry to bother you. . . . Brent must have given me the wrong cabin. I'll just go back to the lodge and get things straightened out. Sorry."

I backed out of the cabin and ran to my car, wondering what on earth was wrong with the man. I could understand his surprise, but the shock in those heavy features had bordered on fear. Even windblown and wet, I couldn't look that bad!

Brent Watkins was just leaving his office as I came trudging back into the lodge. He glanced at me with a puzzled smile and asked, "Is there a problem with your cabin?"

"Just a small one. The 'Mollie Kathleen' is already occupied."

"What? It can't be! Are you sure?"

"I just left a half-naked man standing on the stairs in a state of shock," I told him with an embarrassed laugh.

Brent stared at me in unblinking surprise. "A half-naked man...?"

"... standing on the stairs," I finished with a nod. "Perhaps there's been some mistake...?"

"There's a mistake all right! That cabin hasn't been used for over a month."

It was my turn to stare. "Then who...?"

"I don't know, but I'd better get someone from security over there right away." Brent started toward his office, then stopped, realizing he'd left me standing there. "I'm sorry, Megan. I'm sure it won't take long to straighten this out. Make yourself comfortable, and I'll be back in a few minutes."

He turned away and hurried into the office where I saw him grab a jacket, then pick up the phone on his desk. "Ed, this is Brent. We might have an unwanted guest staying in the 'Mollie Kathleen.' I don't know, but I'm leaving right now to check it out. Right. I'll meet you there."

Brent slammed the receiver down and left the office at a determined pace, scarcely pausing to take the keys from my outstretched hand.

After he had gone, I crossed the hardwood floor to stand in front of the fireplace and held my hands out to its crackling warmth. Staring into the flames, I felt a sense of uneasiness about the incident in the "Mollie Kathleen." The man hadn't acted like an intruder. In fact, his voice and manner had been quite casual until he saw me standing in the doorway. And then, that look of fear....

Footsteps and the soft murmur of voices drifted through the double doors to my right. I stiffened, suddenly recognizing Kurt Gorman's smooth, even tones, but the other voice—a woman's—was unfamiliar.

"Look, Max, I realize he's complicated matters, but I think you're overreacting to the problem. There's no way this will affect our plans for Saturday night."

"We can't let it affect our plans! I've worked too hard to get us this far!" The woman's clipped, cold words were like needles of ice dropping on frozen ground.

"He won't interfere!" Kurt assured her in a honeyed tone. "Besides, what else can we do?"

I gave a polite, but distinct cough, hating to be caught in a position of eavesdropping, and the next moment, Kurt Gorman walked through the doorway with a striking, black-haired woman. When he saw me, Gorman's expression nearly surpassed the shock of the man in my cabin, but the woman's dark eyes flickered over me without interest.

She was about thirty-five, with wraith-like slenderness and hard, pointed features. Her smooth black hair was cropped short, accentuating the sharp angles and planes of her face. Dressed in a severely-tailored pantsuit of black linen, the woman's blood-red lips and nails were the only variation in her stark, black and white appearance. Looking at her, I was reminded of a black widow spider—something dark, delicate, and deadly.

Kurt Gorman made a quick recovery, cleared his throat, then produced a winning smile. "Miss Collier—Megan! What a pleasant surprise! I thought you were flying back to Los Angeles today."

"I had a change of plans," I told him, feeling the instant scrutiny of the black-haired woman.

"Oh?" The word was definitely an inquiry, but I wasn't about to satisfy the man's curiosity and encourage further interrogation.

"Yes," I said.

"Aren't you going to introduce us, Kurt?" the woman asked, her scarlet lips parting to give me a thin smile.

Gorman laughed nervously. "Of course. Maxine Barrett, Megan Collier. I believe I mentioned yesterday that Max writes a monthly review column for *New Wave* magazine."

"Perhaps you've heard of it—'Column Five'?" Maxine

Barrett inserted in tones that strongly suggested I probably hadn't.

"Heard of it, and read it," I answered shortly.

Her black brows lifted in faint surprise.

"Megan is a contributing editor for *American Performing Arts*," Kurt went on, adding with another false laugh, "I'm sure you two writers have a lot in common."

The appraising look in Max Barrett's dark eyes said, "I doubt it," and once again, Gorman's bright tones were injected into brittle silence.

"So what brings you back to Lodestone? It certainly can't be the weather."

"Mr. McLean thought I might want to expand my article to include some information about Lodestone."

Gorman didn't bother to conceal his surprise. "That's very generous of him—especially in light of his policy barring any press or publicity."

I matched his warm tones and replied, "Yes, isn't it? I suppose Miss Barrett and I are the exceptions to the rule."

"*Ms.* Barrett," the woman corrected with an acidic smile.

"How long will you be staying?" Kurt pursued.

"Just the weekend."

This news didn't sit well with *Ms.* Barrett or Obolus' producer, but for the life of me, I couldn't understand why. Then I wondered if there might be a little professional jealousy behind their strained expressions.

"Naturally, my article will include some information about the recording studio, but I promise not to encroach upon your territory," I assured them. "Believe me, I'll be happy to leave Obolus entirely to you."

Kurt laughed and turned to Max. "I invited Megan to the boys' concert tomorrow night, but she's not a fan of theirs." Glancing at me, he joked, "Are you sure you won't reconsider my invitation now that you're staying on?"

Max Barrett gave him a venomous look and for just a moment, I wondered what they would do if I accepted.

"Thanks, but I'll probably spend most of the time writing in my cabin."

The woman gave me a strange look. "Your cabin? Aren't

you staying here in the lodge?"

"No—in the 'Mollie Kathleen'."

She and Kurt exchanged another potent look, and there was no denying the sudden tenseness between them.

Any further conversation was cut off by the abrupt entrance of Brent Watkins into the lodge. He was followed by a big man in a sheepskin jacket. Both men were rain-soaked and wore a matched set of frowns.

"Sorry to keep you waiting so long," Brent said. He gave Kurt and Maxine a brief, acknowledging nod, then answered my questioning look with, "The cabin was empty by the time we got there, but the back door was open, and there's more than enough evidence to confirm what you told me." He gestured to the man standing beside him. "Ed Garrison, here, is head of security. If you don't mind, he'd like to ask you a few questions."

One look at Ed Garrison told me the questions would be asked whether I minded or not. The man had the chest and arms of a lumberjack, the street-wise stance of a city cop, and a gritty, uncompromising stare. His brawny figure reached an easy six feet, his hair was rusty brown, and below a shaggy mustache, firm lips were clamped in a hard line.

Before the security man could speak, Kurt Gorman stepped toward Brent and demanded, "Now hold on a minute! What's going on here? Is there some problem I should know about?"

Brent exchanged glances with Ed Garrison, then said, "A few minutes ago, Megan saw a man in a cabin that was supposedly unoccupied. I don't have an explanation yet, but we're checking things out."

For once, Kurt Gorman said nothing. Beside him, Maxine Barrett was equally silent, her face a pale, tight mask.

"I don't think there's any cause for alarm," Brent assured them. "Ed and his men will conduct a thorough search of the property. Still, it wouldn't hurt to keep your eyes open."

Gorman gave Brent an approving nod, but his smile was forced. "I'll be glad to. I'm . . . uh, just heading over to the studio. The band's waiting for me. But if I can be of any help, you know where to find me." To Max Barrett, he added, "Feel free to join us any time. We'll be in the studio all morning."

The woman left without a word, her high heels tapping a rapid retreat across the hardwood floors to the stairs.

Ed Garrison watched with a frown as Gorman made a hasty exit out the front door, then turned to me. "Why don't we sit down."

His soft, husky voice suggested there might be more than an ounce of human kindness behind that rocky exterior. I followed him across the room to a grouping of leather chairs and sofas.

"That man asks too many questions," Brent grumbled, sitting down beside me on the couch.

Garrison took a chair opposite us and shrugged out of his wet jacket. "Maybe so, but what else could you tell him? He's bound to notice my men searching the grounds and want to know why. Besides, if he sees the guy, I want to know about it." He produced a notebook and pen from his jacket, then draped the wet garment on the back of his chair. Garrison's movements were spare and decisive. So was his manner.

"Now, Miss Collier. I want to know everything you saw, in as much detail as possible."

Looking into the man's dark brown eyes, I felt a strange sense of _déjà vu_. I was doing it again. Answering questions. Telling someone what I had seen. Only three days ago, I had sat in a patrol car, describing two men—one dark-haired and bearded. . .

I gave myself a hard mental shake and answered, "I had just entered the cabin when I heard a man's voice on the stairs above me."

"What did he say?"

"I've been trying to remember. It was something simple— some kind of greeting. No, I think it was a question. . . ." I paused, trying to replay the scene in my mind, but the words wouldn't come. "I'm sorry. I know this is important."

"Don't force it," Garrison advised. "It'll probably come to you later. Go on. What happened after that?"

"Well, he started to come down the stairs, then he saw me standing in the doorway and stopped. His expression was more than surprised. He seemed—shocked, almost frightened."

"Did he say anything to you?"

"No. He just stared. I assumed I'd been given the wrong cabin, so I made my apologies and left."

Ed Garrison wrote something in the notebook, then asked, "Can you give me a description of the man?"

"He was about my height, maybe shorter; rather heavy-set, with dark brown hair and eyes."

"Age?"

"Somewhere between thirty-five and forty."

"What about his face? Did you notice anything in particular about his features?"

"I couldn't see his face clearly. He was drying it with a towel as he came downstairs, and even after he saw me, he kept it close around his face."

A sandy eyebrow cocked with interest as Garrison made note of this, then he asked, "What was he wearing?"

"A pair of shorts."

"That's all?"

I met his quizzical look with a shrug and a smile. "That's all."

Garrison exchanged looks with Brent, then bent his head to scribble something else in the notebook.

I watched him write for a moment, then said, "I don't know if it's important, but—they were light brown."

Garrison's head lifted. "His eyes?"

"No. The shorts."

The hard mouth softened, and he made a sound in his throat that could have been a chuckle. Then he looked at Brent. "Interesting. The guy must have taken the time to get dressed before splitting, because I found some footprints near the back of the cabin, and they weren't made by bare feet.

Brent rubbed a hand over his beard. "This is weird, Ed. It's hard to imagine some bozo just wandering onto the property and setting up residence in the 'Mollie Kathleen,' but I don't know what else to make of it."

Garrison's only comment was a nondescript grunt as he shoved the notebook and pen back into his jacket. "I'd better get this description to Ron and the other men, then I'm heading back to the cabin area." He stood up and stuffed his big arms into the sheepskin lining of his jacket sleeves. "Thanks for your help, Miss Collier. Have Brent get in touch with me if you remember what the guy said."

"I will."

After Ed Garrison had left, Brent turned to me with frowning concern. "I'm sorry about all the trouble, Megan. I hope you don't think this is a common occurrence around here."

Suddenly, I understood part of the worry marking his face. Cole leaves for the coast, gives his manager specific instructions to take care of some reporter from a national magazine. Reporter arrives on scene to find strange man in her room. Terrific story. Great headlines. Brent Watkins probably saw them all, along with his neck in a noose as soon as Cole returned.

"I'm sure there must be a simple explanation for the whole thing," I told him. "But even if there isn't, you won't be reading about this in my article."

We stood up and Brent gave my hand a grateful squeeze. "Thanks, Megan. I appreciate you being so understanding. I know you're probably anxious to get unpacked and start working, but I'm afraid it'll be a while before I can get you into the cabin. After security finishes checking things out, I'll have to send the maids in to clean. I'd give you the cabin next door, but the plumbing's torn apart for repairs."

"That's all right. I'm in no hurry."

"If you have the time, how would like to see the lodge and recording studio? I'll be tied up, but I know Kathy would love to give you the grand tour."

"I'd enjoy that. May I take some pictures?"

Brent grinned. "Be my guest. Cole's collected some fabulous paintings and Indian artifacts. The place is a regular museum."

I smiled and agreed, "So I've noticed."

"I'll go find Kathy right now. She's always glad for an excuse to leave her paperwork." Halfway across the floor, he called back, "It's too bad Cole couldn't be here to show you around. He was madder than hell about having to leave."

After Brent had gone, I walked slowly over to the fireplace. Outside the lodge, a rolling boom of thunder added a startling note of percussion to the storm's wet symphony. Then a rush of wind sent a spiral of sparks and flame dancing up the stone chimney.

Alone once more, thoughts of mysterious intruders dwindled into insignificance. One simple irony remained. I was here at Lodestone, and Cole was in Los Angeles. I shivered and moved closer to the flames.

10

KATHY WATKINS SUGGESTED we tour the recording studio first, then finish up with the lodge and lunch. This arrangement was fine with me, but I did have some reservations about interrupting Obolus' recording session.

"They rarely get going much before noon," she told me. "Besides, they're usually so stoned, I doubt if they'll notice whether we're there or not."

I smiled at her candor as we dashed out into the rain. Holding our jackets over our heads, we sprinted the ten yards or so between the lodge and recording studio.

Once inside the building, Kathy turned to me with a guilty smile. "Maybe you'd better not tell Brent what I just said about Obolus. He'd think it was very unprofessional of me."

"Don't worry about it. I'm not a fan of theirs, anyway," I assured her.

"You're not? Wonderful! Now I won't have to think of polite things to say about them."

The caustic tone in her voice surprised me, but rather than elicit more "unprofessional" comments about the group, I remained silent.

I took a few pictures of the plush reception area, then Kathy led me down a panelled hallway where the air was harsh with the metallic screeching of electric guitars. She pointed toward the source of the noise, some double doors at the end of the hall, and shouted above the din, "The recording floor is through there! Before we go in, I'd better check with Lenny to see if they've started." She knocked on a door to our right, then pushed it open a crack. "Hi, Lenny! Are you recording yet? There's someone I'd like you to meet."

Kathy ushered me into the room, and for a moment I felt as if I had entered a miniature "Mission Control." Everywhere I looked there were dials, switches, lights and levers. Sitting behind a large console board, calmly maneuvering a course through the metallic sea of recording wizardry, was a strange, toadlike man with a cherubic face and rumpled clothes. As we came forward, he turned down the volume on the floor mikes, instantly taming Obolus' roar to a harmless whine.

"Megan, this is Leonard Gorman, Obolus' sound engineer. I believe you've already met Lenny's brother Kurt."

I smiled and nodded, trying to conceal my surprise. Lenny and Kurt? It was difficult to image the two men as distant relatives, let alone brothers. Remembering Kurt's well-built frame and fastidious appearance, I could find no similarities in the pink-faced man Kathy introduced as his brother. Lenny's thinning brown hair was unevenly cut, with one greasy strand hanging across his forehead. A frayed shirt collar and dark stains on his pullover sweater were painfully apparent. Seeing him there, swaddled in his own flesh, Lenny Gorman reminded me of an old, unloved child.

When Kathy explained to him that I was writing an article on Lodestone for a national magazine, the man's bulging blue eyes shifted to me in obvious confusion.

"Are you with Max?"

"No, I...."

"Megan is Mr. McLean's guest," Kathy told him, then gestured to the overwhelming array of tapes, speakers and sound equipment filling the room. "I really don't know the first thing about all this. If you're not too busy, would you mind telling Megan a little of what goes on?"

Lenny nodded obediently and lifted his bulk from the chair. As he began to explain the technical aspects of recording, the blankness faded from his eyes and his voice sharpened with excitement. Watching him, I saw the unloved child disappear and an intelligent, even brilliant man take his place.

I made an excellent pretext of looking fascinated and taking notes, but I didn't understand one-tenth of what he was saying. While Lenny rattled on about mid-cycles, mixes, sweetening and overdubs, my attention strayed to the glass partition overlooking the rehearsal floor.

Around six months ago, some friends had dragged me to an Obolus concert. My emotions had taken a beating that night, as well as my eardrums, and I vowed never to subject myself to that kind of torture again. But now, watching the band attack their instruments without the trappings of a screaming crowd and psychedelic lights, I felt a strange stirring of pity for those gaunt bodies and wasted faces. Without their bizarre costumes and stage makeup, the four young men looked more like malnourished members of an L.A. street gang.

Punishing the drums was Nick Bryson. Nick was your basic "biker" with greased-back hair, faded jeans and a leather vest with no shirt. Tony York on bass guitar was definitely on the "sweet" side. His dark, greasy curls bobbed up and down as he played, two diamonds sparkled in his left earlobe, and covering his scrawny chest was a pink t-shirt with the message, "Snow Queen" spelled in purple glitter.

Brawling with the lead guitars and rasping out vocals were Bruce Stoedter and Derek Durant. When I had last seen Bruce on stage, his lean, long-limbed body had been clothed in a leopard skin loin cloth and nothing else. Now, dressed in baggy, torn sweats, he seemed almost overdressed. With his virile, raw-boned face and tawny mane of hair, Bruce Stoedter was undeniably the best-looking of the four.

Secretly, I've always thought some movie producer really missed his chance by not casting Derek Durant in a horror film. With that cadaverous face and those lethal red and orange spikes sticking out of his head, Derek would have made the perfect "midnight slasher." Not to mention the fact he'd mastered the emaciated look—hollow cheeks, sunken eyes and caved-in chest.

For the past few minutes, the rock star had been casting dour looks in our general direction. Now, he stopped playing his guitar and shouted something to Lenny which, thankfully, we couldn't hear. Durant yelled once more before realizing the "mikes" were off, then flung his guitar aside and stalked off the floor.

A sick feeling in the pit of my stomach told me where he was headed. Seconds later, Derek Durant erupted into the sound booth, spewing filth and profanity in Lenny's face and demanding to know where Kurt was. The stench that came with him was almost as foul as his language.

Poor Lenny cowered in his chair, a film of perspiration covering his upper lip. "I . . . I don't know where he is," he stammered. "I . . . I haven't seen him."

Durant reached down and grabbed the man's shoulder with long, clawlike fingers. "Well, don't just sit there slobbering like an ass! Go find him!"

"There's no need for that, Mr. Durant," I said calmly. "I saw Kurt in the lodge less than twenty minutes ago. He said he was on his way over here."

Hooded eyes slithered in my direction and for five interminable seconds, I was the subject of their unblinking scrutiny. Then Durant turned to Kathy Watkins and demanded, "Who's that?" His inflection and tone were the same as if he had just noticed a piece of garbage on the floor and asked, "What's that?"

"Megan is here to write an article on Lodestone," Kathy began, her vivacious smile and manner noticeably lacking. "And since Lenny said you weren't recording yet. . . ."

"I want her out of here! Now!" he ordered flatly. "We're paying McLean a hell of a lot for our privacy in this stinking hole, and I. . . ."

"Derek, Megan is Mr. McLean's guest," Kathy inserted with controlled calmness. "She's. . . ."

"I don't give a damn who or what she is! Nobody comes in here while we're working unless I say so!" Durant jerked a scrawny thumb in the direction of the door and hissed, "Now why don't you both get the hell out!"

Kathy sent me a helpless look and turned to go. I was equally anxious to leave, but I wasn't about to let Derek Durant know that. Purposely ignoring the rock star's threatening stare, I took the time to thank Lenny for his help, then paused at the door. "There's no need to get your feathers ruffled, Mr. Durant. I never had any intention of staying during your rehearsal. I'm a writer, not a masochist!"

With that, I sailed out the door and stormed down the hall where Kathy was waiting for me. In our eagerness to leave, we nearly collided head-on with Kurt Gorman.

"Going so soon? What's the rush, ladies?" he asked, giving us both a warm smile.

"I was showing Megan through the studio when Derek Durant invited us to leave," Kathy informed him, her voice shaking with anger "—only not in those words."

"Derek can be a bit temperamental at times," Kurt agreed in the tolerant tones of a parent justifying his child's errant behavior. "I apologize if he was rude. I'll be sure and have a word with him."

"I'd advise you to choose that word carefully," I told him with a frosty look. "Mr. Durant's vocabulary seems to be limited to words describing excrement and copulation."

I didn't wait for his reaction or rebuttal, and Kathy was quick to follow suit.

Outside, the rain was still falling, but neither of us minded getting wet. Right then, I think even a deluge would have been welcome.

Kathy didn't comment on the messy little scene with Derek Durant until we were back inside the lodge. After making a miserable attempt to describe the furnishings, she turned to me with a sigh.

"Megan, what can I say? I wouldn't blame you if you wanted to walk out right now and forget the whole thing. I know it must seem like all Brent and I can do is make apologies, but . . . I want you to know how terrible I feel about what happened." She sighed again and smoothed her dark hair with worried hands. "Brent's going to be so furious when I tell him."

"Then don't tell him. He has enough on his mind right now. Please don't worry about it, Kathy. You're not responsible for the bad manners of that foul-mouthed jerk. What do you say we both just forget the whole thing?"

She stared at me in frank amazement, then smiled in spite of herself. "I don't know what to say. . . ."

"Well, you can start by telling me where on earth Cole got that preposterous buffalo head over the fireplace."

Kathy laughed with relief. "Believe it or not, old glass-eyed Bill there was a gift from a fan—a little gray-haired grandmother from North Dakota."

I have spent many a rainy morning wandering happily through museums, and my tour of the lodge was equally pleasant. While Kathy Watkins might not profess to knowing much about recording studios, she was very knowledgeable about Indian art and culture. I took scads of notes and used two rolls of film on the paintings and sculpture pieces alone.

"I keep wondering where Cole found all these things," I told her as we walked along an upstairs hallway. "It must have taken him years!"

"Not that long, really. Cole has a passion for beauty and a real knack for finding things. A lot of the paintings were purchased during his tours around the country, and most of the Indian items were bought from Charles Eagle Plume."

"Charles Eagle Plume? What a wonderful name! Who is he?"

"Charles is almost a legend around here and one of the kindest men you'll ever meet," Kathy answered warmly. "He has an Indian store a few miles south of Estes Park that's considered to be one of the finest in the country."

"I wish I'd known. I must have driven right past it the other day."

As we started down the stairs, I paused on the landing to stare at a magnificent oil painting of two rearing stallions on a rocky ledge. The artist's bold use of color and sweeping style held me spellbound.

"I love this one! Did Cole buy it from Charles Eagle Plume?"

Kathy shook her head. "That painting was a gift from the artist."

"Really?" I stepped closer and read aloud the masculine scrawl in the painting's right hand corner. "Jay Bradford. Haven't we seen some other paintings by him—the abandoned ranchhouse with that marvelous stormy sky, and the one of those Indian children playing near a stream?"

Kathy answered with a smile. "Jay's an Indian artist who lives here in Colorado, down in Manitou Springs. He's also a good friend of Cole's." Looking up at the painting, she shrugged and confided, "Jay's paintings are a bit too dramatic for my taste, but Cole loves his work."

"I can see why," I said, giving the stallions on the wall one last glance before following her down the stairs.

Back in the main room, Kathy stared at her watch in surprise. "Good heavens, it's nearly one o'clock! I know John Muir said everyone needs 'beauty as well as bread,' but I could use some lunch. How about you?"

I laughed. "As far as I know, no one ever said we couldn't have both. Let's eat!"

Beauty and bread were both plentiful items in the dining room at Lodestone. Tall windows looked out on rain-soaked forests and sloping meadows, while inside, a hearty log fire crackled in the big stone fireplace. Pictures of old mining towns and nineteenth century miners shared the log walls with brass lamps and rusty pieces of the past—a battered gold pan, an ancient pick ax and an old carbide lamp. High-backed chairs and sturdy tables of pine were grouped casually about the spacious room, each one enjoying a view of the mountains.

While the atmosphere might be rustic, the food definitely was not. Our lunch rivaled any that I had enjoyed in fine restaurants on the coast—cream of asparagus soup, warm, flaky croissants and a delectable crab salad. We were finishing up with cheesecake and coffee when Brent approached our table with the keys to the "Mollie Kathleen." He had no further information, however, concerning the mysterious intruder.

"Ed's men have made a thorough search and questioned all the staff," he told us. "But no one has seen any sign of him."

"That's hard to believe," Kathy said, frowning out at the drizzling rain. "Where could he go? Better yet, where did he come from?"

Brent pulled out a chair and joined us. "I don't know, but Ed is determined to get the answers. In the meantime, let's not worry about it. How was your morning?" he asked me, making a tactful change of subject. "I hope everything went well."

Kathy's smile suddenly drooped, and I knew she was thinking of the incident with Derek Durant.

"Your wife is an excellent tour guide," I answered. "I'm sure I have enough information and pictures for ten articles. What I need now is to get some words down on paper."

Brent shook his head. "Now that's something I can't help you with. When it comes to writing, you're on your own!"

I laughed and put my napkin beside my plate. "In that case, I'd better get to work. I've put off the inevitable long enough."

Kathy's brown eyes met mine in silent gratitude as I got up from the table. "If there's anything you need, please don't hesitate to ask."

"I won't."

"Would you like me to drive you up to the cabin?" Brent offered, getting to his feet.

"No thanks. I'll be fine."

Approaching the front door of the "Mollie Kathleen" with key in hand, I began to wish I hadn't been so quick to refuse Brent's offer. I glanced nervously around, but the forest was silent and still. The main thrust of the storm had passed by, leaving a soft rain which fell without a sound. I took a deep breath and unlocked the door.

There was no reason for me to be nervous or jumpy. I knew perfectly well Ed Garrison and security had made a thorough search of the place. In addition to that, the maids had come in to clean. Even so, before I unpacked, wrote a single sentence or did anything at all, I made my own inspection of the cabin. Every closet and every corner. It took a full five minutes before I gathered enough courage to go upstairs, and then only after I had made enough noise downstairs to frighten off a dozen intruders. Maybe it was childish and a bit paranoid, but I even got down on my knees and looked under the big Cannonball bed.

Finally, I was forced to admit what I had known all along. There was no evidence whatever of the dark-haired intruder—only a beautifully furnished cabin that was mine to enjoy for the entire weekend.

Work was a pleasure and a joy that afternoon. Directly off the upstairs bedroom, I found a small study with a gable window looking out over the forest. Besides the pristine view, the study came equipped with an old-fashioned pine desk, a modern electric typewriter and a wide assortment of stationery supplies. I spread my notes out on the desk, then glanced briefly through the drawers, taking out some correction fluid and carbon paper. Beneath the package of carbon paper, I found a letter penned in black ink.

I picked it up and read, "Darling Andrea," before my sense of decency overcame my curiosity. I was not "Darling Andrea," so I had best put the letter away and get to work. Still, what was the harm? I looked at the letter, wondering which famous recording star had written it to his lady-love, and decided to read on:

> "There are things I've never told you and hoped I would never have to tell you—parts of my life that aren't very pleasant. Try not to hate me, darling, even if you don't understand. God knows I love you and never wanted to hurt you, but. . . ."

I slipped the unfinished letter back inside the desk's bottom drawer with a sigh, wishing there weren't so many "buts" in life. "I love you, but. . . ." "I'm sorry, but. . . ." I hated them all. Poor Andrea. I wondered briefly whether she had ever received a completed version of the letter, then pushed all distracting thoughts aside and started to work.

Four-and-a-half hours later, I had typed through all my notes, made revisions and cuts and started a second draft. The article began to take on shape and substance. The concerts and events filling my week in Colorado were like multi-colored threads slowly being woven into a musical tapestry. Only one major strand was missing. Cole's concert.

After typing his name on a clean sheet of paper, I spent the next ten minutes staring out the window, engulfed by memories of the man. I pulled myself back to the present, determined to write a concise, objective review of his concert. The half hour which followed was a comic exercise in futility. The few words which finally found their way onto the page sounded more like an advertisement for Log Cabin syrup.

I ripped the paper out of the typewriter with a groan, then glanced at my watch. Six-fifteen. I decided to leave my writing block in the study and assured myself, I would be able to think much more objectively after a long hot shower and a quiet dinner.

The light sifting through the bedroom curtains was muted

and soft, dappling the carpet and nearby bed with tawny shadows. Visions of yesterday lived in those shadows. I saw Cole's dark head bending toward mine, felt the warmth and pressure of his lips and arms. . . .

I sat down on the bed and began to undress with trembling hands. Better make that a cold shower.

11

MY PLANS FOR a quiet dinner were abandoned the moment I entered the dining room and saw Kurt, Lenny and Max sipping cocktails at one of the tables. It was too late to pretend I hadn't seen them. Kurt was already on his feet and issuing a smiling invitation for me to join them. I bowed to the inevitable and walked over to their table.

Gorman was even more solicitous than usual as he pulled out the chair next to his and asked, "Can I order you a drink?"

"No, thank you."

Max Barrett gave me a cold-eyed appraisal from over the rim of her glass, and on my left, Lenny sent a vacant little smile my way before lowering his head to stare at the olive in his drink. I sighed inwardly and picked up the menu.

After taking his seat, Kurt Gorman leaned closer and put a hand on the back of my chair. "I want to apologize again for Derek's behavior this morning. He tends to guard his privacy a bit zealously at times, but that certainly doesn't excuse such rudeness."

"No, it doesn't," I agreed, turning my head away from his liquored breath.

Max Barrett tossed a few dark-eyed daggers in my direction as Kurt went on in a mollifying tone, "I'm sure this isn't the first time you've had to deal with a little bout of 'artistic temperament' in your line of work."

I glanced up from the menu. "You're right, it isn't, but I fail to see anything 'artistic' in Derek Durant's temperament."

Gorman laughed, coughed, and promptly changed the subject. "So what have you been doing all day?" he asked brightly.

"Writing. What have you been doing?" I responded, just as brightly.

The man's solicitous mask slipped just long enough for me to catch the ugly gleam of anger in his eyes, then he answered smoothly, "Naturally, we've been working on the boys' new album." Glancing toward his brother, Kurt added, "The album's coming along very well, wouldn't you agree, Lenny?"

Lenny's fascination with his olive ceased long enough for him to shrug and nod his head. Then he slumped over the drink once more.

A young waitress arrived to take our orders and after that we did an excellent job of discussing nothing in particular. Kurt and Max did most of the talking, and Max made a point of never speaking directly to me. I found the obvious snub more amusing than annoying, and it didn't prevent me from admiring the woman's graceful gestures and slender white hands. I watched as her scarlet nails creased a snowy linen napkin, then brushed away a microscopic crumb from the table-cloth. Those gorgeous fingernails were either false or the woman never did any typing, I decided.

When our dinners arrived, I happily devoted my attention to an excellent steak and baked potato topped with sour cream. Max Barrett toyed with her chef salad while she and Kurt discussed details of the upcoming Obolus concert. More than once, she made reference to some arrangements concerning a Mr. Fitzsimmons, who I assumed must be fairly important to the success of the concert. None of it concerned me, so I didn't bother trying to inject any comments.

The woman's dark eyes suddenly slid my way. "I'm sorry. I hope we're not boring you with all this talk of Obolus and the concert—especially since you don't appreciate their music."

"I may not appreciate their music, but I would never describe Obolus as boring," I said.

Kurt smiled at me, then turned to Max. "Megan and I had an interesting discussion about Obolus only yesterday. She feels their music is too—destructive—isn't that the term you used?"

I couldn't very well respond to this with a piece of steak in my mouth and Max seized the opportunity to say, "Destructive? Obolus' music is just the opposite! It's like applying therapeutic shock waves to desensitized listeners."

I smiled and went on eating my meal while Max wove her clever web of words. If I had never heard Obolus before, I probably would have been terribly impressed. According to Max Barrett, the band was living proof that it was possible to make music that really mattered. Not only that, Obolus was uncompromising, hard hitting and artistically daring. Listening to her, I was reminded of some advice given by C. S. Lewis' crafty senior devil: ". . . as I said before, it is jargon, not reason you must rely on."

Max Barrett had mastered Screwtape's counsel. Everything she said sounded wonderful, but really didn't mean much. While the woman raved on about Obolus' "palpable energy" and "densely textured songs," I sat and sipped my Pepsi, knowing full well Obolus wouldn't recognize a "densely textured song" if it walked up and bit them in the leg. When Max said something about their lyrics accomplishing, "something beyond well-intentioned rhetoric," I decided I'd had enough.

"I've been reading quite a bit about Obolus lately, and I have to agree with you. Their songs are definitely accomplishing something beyond well-intentioned rhetoric." I put down my glass and asked her, "What do you think about the recent articles suggesting that members of Obolus are practicing Satanists?"

The woman's dark eyes narrowed, and I saw a brief tightening in her face. Then she smiled and said, "Quite frankly, I think you've been reading too many scandal sheets. I'm surprised you'd bother giving credence to mere gossip and rumors."

"The lyrics of Obolus' songs aren't rumors," I said. "For that matter, neither is their name. I can't help being curious why a rock group would take their name from the bronze coin that's placed under the tongue of the dead in ancient Greek burials." There was a charged moment of silence at the table. I smiled and went on, "Names have always fascinated me, so I did a little research on the word *obolus*. According to legend, the dead souls gave the coin to Charon, the boatman of Hades, for passage over the river Styx. Very symbolic, don't you think?"

Max sipped her wine and gave me a look of utter boredom.

"Very. How long did it take you to dig all that up?"

I ignored her question and directed one of my own to Kurt Gorman. "If Obolus has no affiliation with satanic cults, perhaps you can tell me why they flaunt satanic symbols on their album covers and why their videos are full of references to occult rituals?"

Kurt smiled and answered easily, "People have always been fascinated with the occult. The subject makes for great creative lyrics. But I hardly see where that makes Obolus Satan worshippers." He chuckled as if the idea gave him great amusement.

"Rock musicians have always invited criticism, simply because they have the courage to be different," Max went on to explain. "The recent publicity about Obolus is nothing more than a vicious campaign by narrow-minded, religious fanatics. What those people refuse to accept is there are alternatives in music, as well as lifestyles."

"Are you suggesting then that Satan worship is merely a musical alternative?"

An uncomfortable silence followed my question, one in which the woman glared at me with unveiled animosity.

"I think all Max is trying to say is that every musical group deserves a measure of artistic freedom," Kurt put in mildly. "There's nothing satanic or mysterious about the fact that the occult is a great selling tool with the public. Let's face facts. Today's audiences are too sophisticated for the old 'June, moon, spoon' brand of lyrics. They demand more from performers and Obolus is inventive and courageous enough to give it to them."

I suppressed a smile and said dryly, "Somehow, I can't see where the lyrics: 'Let's yell! Hell is swell!' are all that sophisticated. And if Obolus is as courageous as you say, why do they resort to using subliminal gimmicks like 'backward masking' on their albums?"

Gorman tried to look amused, but his smile was thin, and his eyes were cold gray steel. The charged atmosphere at the table was even enough to rouse Lenny from his food fixation. He glanced from Kurt to Max to me in blinking confusion, then shrugged and reached for the wine bottle.

"You've just answered your own question," Kurt told me in

tones that suggested I was nothing more than a silly child. "Back-masking is a gimmick. And gimmicks sell records. It's only a harmless game."

"Playing with people's minds isn't a game," I said coldly. "Subliminal messages can have a powerful impact on the subconscious and. . . ."

"Really, Miss Collier," Max interrupted with a bored sigh. "All this intense emotion over dinner is awfully tiresome." She reached for a slim, silver cigarette case beside her plate, flicked it open with one of those long red nails, and took out a cigarette. "Maybe you should save some of it for your article instead."

Gorman released a brittle laugh and reached for his lighter. "I have to agree with you, Max. I think we're all getting much too serious." After lighting the woman's cigarette and one of his own, Kurt turned to me. "So how is your article coming along? You haven't told us anything about it."

I fought back a surge of rising anger and answered, "I still have a lot to do, but at least it's past the rough stage."

"Is McLean going to be the focal point of your article?" he asked, taking a long drag on his cigarette.

"Well, no . . . not really."

"I don't envy you the task of writing about McLean's music," Max said, tapping some ash into a crystal ash tray. "I reviewed his latest album a few months ago and thought I'd die of boredom before the job was finished." She glanced at her elegant hands with an abject sort of fascination, then lifted the cigarette to her mouth. "I did discover one aspect of his music though. Those insipid lyrics and soporific melodies are an amazing cure for insomnia."

I ignored the woman's smug, satisfied smile and casually placed my napkin beside my plate. "I was in an audience of close to eight thousand people the other night who would strongly disagree with you."

Max blew out a cloud of smoke and admitted, "Oh, I don't doubt he has a following of sorts—especially among middle-aged matrons."

I smiled sweetly. "Now that you mention it, I did see several women at the concert who were about your age—but there must have been twice as many teenagers and young adults."

Smoke streamed through her nostrils as she glared at me in speechless fury, while Kurt Gorman burst out with what might have been a genuine laugh. Lenny glanced up, wondering what joke he had missed, and I decided there couldn't be a better time to leave.

"If you'll excuse me, I still have a lot of work to do this evening," I said, pushed back my chair and walked away.

Outside the lodge, jeweled colors glowed softly in a sunset sky and the air was sweet with scents of the forest. I took several deep breaths, thinking it might be better for my nerves and digestion if I had meals sent to the cabin from now on. Another minute of listening to Max Barrett's biting little word games and Kurt Gorman's self-indulgent speeches, and I would have become violently ill.

Walking to the car, I heard someone call my name and glanced up to see Brent Watkins striding across the parking lot.

"Hi, Megan! You're just the person I wanted to see. I meant to drop by the cabin earlier and check on you, but it's been one of those days."

I leaned against the car door with a sigh. "I have to agree with you on that point."

Brent's welcoming smile shifted to concern as he stepped closer. "You look tired. Are you feeling all right?"

"I'll feel a lot better when the article's finished," I admitted frankly.

"Maybe you should forget about the article and take the evening off."

"That sounds nice, but I still have to write a review of Cole's concert."

Brent's smile was sympathetic. "How does anyone write about one of Cole's concerts?"

"Exactly. So far, it's not coming along very well. I wish I could hear some of the songs again, but. . . ."

"Hey, why didn't you say so? Kathy and I have all of Cole's albums over at our cabin. You're welcome to borrow any or all of them if it would help."

"Help? That would be perfect! Are you sure you don't

mind?"

"Anything to keep our guests happy," Brent grinned, and took my arm. "Come on. Our cabin's right across the way."

A few minutes later, I was back in the "Mollie Kathleen" with a stack of record albums under my arm and renewed determination to write a review so brilliant it would make Max Barrett's snide remarks nothing more than superficial slop.

I grabbed some paper and a few pencils, then kicked off my shoes and sat down on the braided rug near the fireplace. Glancing at the empty grate, I briefly considered whether I should build a fire. Evenings were cool in the mountains after sundown, and I knew I would enjoy its cheery company. But right now, I hated to spend time and energy on anything except Cole's music.

I vetoed the fire and eagerly spread the record albums on the rug in front of me. Where to begin? I stared down at nine tantalizing album covers, then picked up "Lodestone Lyric," which had an incredible photograph of Cole on horseback, looking out over rugged hills and a stormy sky. Why bother with the record inside? The cover alone was more than worth the purchase price of the album.

I set "Lodestone Lyric" down with a frustrated groan. If this wretched article were ever going to be written, I had better start concentrating on the music—not the man.

Thinking it might be helpful if I started at the beginning of Cole's career, I arranged the record albums in chronological order and put "Rough Around the Edges" on the turntable. The album was country-western in flavor and after listening to a few cuts, I had to admit the title was an apt description for most of the songs. Still, in spite of its roughness, there was something fresh and appealing in Cole's lyrics and energetic rhythms. The promise of genuine talent was definitely there.

The next album, "Cole Country," was again country-western. Most of the songs were slick, stylish and totally unimaginative—nothing but recycled versions of cheatin', drinkin', and hard times with the good ol' boys. Checking the credits on the album sleeve, I discovered Cole had written only two of the ten songs. Disappointed, I set "Cole Country" aside and went on.

"Rhythms of Life" swept me away. Emerging from the sensitive collection of songs about living and loving was a unique musical style—one that belonged to Cole McLean and no one else. I didn't need to read the credits to know Cole had composed all the songs on this album.

Listening to the title song a second time, I searched for words to describe my response. Words like fresh, innovative, and imaginative immediately came to mind and were readily rejected. I sighed and chewed the tip of my pencil. I was beginning to sound as bad as Max.

"Journey to the Heart" was romantic enough to soften the most calloused soul, and in "Lodestone Lyric," Cole gave musical expression to his feelings for the land. In it, I rediscovered "Mountain Dawn," the instrumental piece I had loved at the concert.

Hours slipped away, and the more I listened, the less I wrote. Describing Cole's music was like touching a rainbow— the colors were real and vibrant, yet always just out of reach. Finally, I gave up the attempt altogether, curled up on the couch with a blanket tucked around my legs, and let the music carry me away. In body, Cole McLean might be in Los Angeles, but in spirit he was there with me. Each song was like a key, unlocking and revealing a different part of the man. Listening to "Fool's Gold," I was sure many of the songs in that album had been written during or following Cole's divorce. The titles said it all—"Sweet, Shattered Dreams," "The Walls Inside," and "Empty Rooms." What had happened to break up his marriage? I put the record on again and found myself listening between the lines, searching for answers.

The sudden jangling of the phone made an off-key entrance into my thoughts as well as the music, and I reached for it with a sigh.

"Hello?"

"Hi! How're you doing?"

"Cole. . . ?" I dived over to the stereo to turn down the volume, then sank breathlessly on the couch. "Uh . . . hi! How are you?"

"Pretty good. I've been wondering how your day went. Brent tells me you've been working too hard."

I glanced at the sparse notes and crumpled paper on the rug in front of me. "Not hard enough. I was . . . uh, just doing a little research on the article."

Cole's voice was warm in my ear. "I wish I could be there to help."

"You are . . . I mean, you have! The cabin is lovely and Brent and Kathy have been wonderful."

"I'm glad." After a pause, he asked, "Have you forgiven me?"

"For what?"

Cole laughed. "For calling your boss and getting him to change your plans for the weekend."

I took a shaky breath. "Somehow, I didn't expect you to admit that."

"Why not? I had to think of some way to get you back, and I figured your boss had more clout than I did."

His admission left me too stunned to attempt a reply.

"You still haven't answered my question," Cole went on. "Are you angry?"

I smiled and leaned back against the cushions. "Not now."

"Megan?"

"Yes?"

"Would you mind telling me something?"

"What?"

"Why did you leave yesterday?"

Silence stretched uncomfortably on the line while I struggled to find the words.

"Look, I just want to know if it was something I said or did. If I came on too strong. . . ."

"It wasn't you. Cole, I'm sorry. . . ."

"So am I. I thought we had plans to spend the evening together. I guess I misunderstood."

The hurt in his voice cut through me, and I took a ragged breath. "You didn't misunderstand. "It's just . . . I was . . . afraid."

"Of me?"

"No—of me! Things were happening too fast and I . . . I thought it would be better to leave before. . . ." My throat tightened up, and I finished miserably, "I just thought it would be better, that's all."

Cole was silent for a moment. "I guess what I need to know now is . . . are you sorry you came back?"

I closed my eyes and answered softly, "No. No, I'm not."

"I'm glad."

Neither of us spoke for a few seconds, then he cleared his throat and said, "Well, I guess I'd better not keep you up any later. We can talk more when I get back."

"When will that be?"

"Not until Sunday. I have contract negotiations and meetings scheduled nearly all day tomorrow. But you can plan on me catching the first plane out of here Sunday morning."

"Good luck with all your meetings." It wasn't a very brilliant thing to say, but the way my heart was soaring, I was lucky to be able to talk at all.

"Thanks. You take care now."

"I will."

"And don't work too hard!"

"I won't."

"And, if you see Cody, give him a big hug for me."

I smiled and held the phone a little closer. "All right."

There was another silence, while I waited for his good-bye. Instead, he burst out with, "Damn it, Megan! I need to see you!"

"I need to see you, too. . . ." The words tumbled out before I realized what I was saying. I added a hurried, "Good night," and hung up the phone.

Some time later, the stereo turned itself off with a click, but I made no move to put on another record. Instead, I sat for a long while, just staring at Cole's picture and cradling the phone in my lap.

12

SHORTLY AFTER MIDNIGHT I got out of bed and gave up the struggle to understand my emotions. Like my response to Cole's music, I could find no simple explanation for the unfamiliar longings inside me, but hoped that a few minutes in the night air would clear my head a little. Without bothering to turn on a light, I reached for my robe, stepped into my slippers, then unlocked the sliding glass door which opened onto a small wooden balcony.

The night breeze was cool against my face as I moved to the railing and stared into the blackness. The rough shape of the hillside and feathery points of pine were outlined in ebony against the horizon, but the forest was a shapeless sea of darkness. Searching the night sky, I found only a few scattered stars peeking through the gauzy curtain of clouds. The quiet was deep and comforting. Only the breeze and the liquid movement of a stream ruffled the stillness.

"I need to see you. . . ." Cole's words played in my mind like the melody of one of his songs. The fact he had said "need" and not "want" filled me with a pleasant ache. To me, needing had always seemed more of a necessity—like sunlight and breathing air.

"I need to see you, too." I had actually said that. And what's more, it was true.

As I turned away from the railing, low, rhythmic sounds suddenly gnawed at my senses, and I tensed to listen. Somewhere in the blackness, dissonant voices pulsed through the night air like some primeval heartbeat deep within the forest. Searching the dark hillside above the cabin, my eyes fixed on a faint orange glow filtering through the heavy growth of fir and aspen. Sound and light pulsed from the spot, filling my mind with a strange sense of uneasiness. Who was out there? And why? My hands gripped the railing as the voices rose and fell in eerie cadence. Obolus.

The chanting ceased, and I shivered in the silence. Then it began again, a throbbing, primitive sound that conjured up visions of a dark time when men clawed at idols. Anger heated my blood when I remembered Kurt Gorman's glib denials about the group's involvement with the occult. And yet, if I were to go to Brent Watkins in the morning and tell him about this, I knew Obolus would flatly deny everything. Derek Durant would throw another of his ugly tantrums and Kurt Gorman would make sure in his own smiling way that I ended up looking like a fool. I could almost hear him now, calmly explaining to Brent that his boys were only roasting marshmallows and singing songs around the campfire. Without proof, it was simply my word against theirs. What I wouldn't give to expose them all as the liars they were!

I stared grimly into the darkness. The way to get that proof was right inside my purse. My pocket tape recorder probably wouldn't pick up much from this distance, but if I could get closer, I would have more than enough evidence to wipe the smile right off Gorman's face.

I hurried back inside the cabin and in my eagerness, nearly made the mistake of turning on the bedroom light. My hand froze on the switch as I realized if I could see the flames from Obolus' fire, they might also see a light in my cabin. After a steadying breath, I moved carefully to the dresser, feeling about in the darkness for my purse. The tape recorder was exactly where I had left it and for the first time, I had reason to be grateful the tape was still blank.

My hands were shaking as I slipped a warm jacket over my nylon pajamas, then exchanged my slippers for a pair of sneakers. Without another thought, I dropped the recorder into my jacket pocket, ran down the stairs and out of the cabin.

The orange glow was much less noticeable from ground level. In fact, if I hadn't known exactly where to look, I probably wouldn't have seen it. I stood at the edge of the driveway, trying to get my bearings in the darkness. Obolus must be somewhere around the reverse slope of the hillside. And with the wind coming from the east, it would carry the smoke of their fire in the opposite direction, away from the cabins and the lodge.

Walking past the gravel turn-out area, I saw something big and black looming under the trees and fear constricted my breathing. Then I realized what it was. Parked off the road, under cover of the pines, was a dark-colored van. I let the air escape from my lungs and the strong pulse beating in my throat relaxed.

When I entered the forest, my steps became stumbling and slow. There was no path and tangled undergrowth caught at my feet, frustrating any attempt to move silently. All I could do was keep my eyes on the orange glow and let it guide me through the blackness. The night wasn't cold, but the day's storms had left a moist chill in the air and the ground was still muddy underfoot. I hadn't gone far before my pajamas were clinging damply to my legs.

Over a small rise, the fire's glow was much brighter. Another ten paces brought me close enough to glimpse the undulating movement of hooded shapes. I reached into my pocket for the tape recorder and that same moment, the chanting stopped. I held my breath and froze. Had they heard me? Then, out of the silence I heard a strange, whimpering sound, like the muffled whine of a frightened animal. My eyes widened, searching the darkness for some clue to its source. Then the sound was smothered by Obolus' dissonant voices as the chanting began again.

I let out my breath, slowly pressed the "Record" button and decided to chance moving a little closer. Roughly twenty yards in front of me, the trees thinned, and I could make out the ghostly gray outline of a large rock outcropping. Obolus had built their fire in the midst of the rocks, and it was here I saw four robed figures, moving like black wraiths near the flames. Cowled hoods hid their faces and long sleeves fluttered like bat wings through the night air. Occasionally, the firelight would reveal a clawlike hand, the tip of a nose, or the bony thrust of a jaw, but that was all.

I moved cautiously behind a thick-girthed pine and held the recorder in front of me.

"Hail, Satan! He is God! Hail, Satan! He is God!"

My mind was forced to accept what I was hearing, but my spirit fought against their fervent incantations as prayers to Satan, curses, and blasphemies against Christ filled the night. Listening to their twisted souls crying out in perverted devotion, I felt the overwhelming presence of evil and knew this was no game. To the members of Obolus, Satan was not some imaginary figure with horns and cloven hoofs—he was their one true God.

I shuddered and my fingers tightened around the tape recorder as the chanting grew more intense. With their backs to me, the robed figures moved closer to the fire, forming a half circle. The tallest of the four separated himself from the others and after stepping up on a rock to face them, raised his arms high above his head. The chanting stopped.

A heavy silence penetrated the forest, one in which the sound of my own breathing seemed perilously loud. I put a hand to my throat as it came again—that strange, frightened whimpering.

The next moment, the figure on the rock threw off his robe, and Derek Durant stood naked in the firelight. In his right hand was the dull gleam of a knife.

The sight of his gaunt body filled me with revulsion and my legs went weak. I pressed against the tree for support, clutching the rough bark as Durant's voice rang through the darkness.

"We live for Satan! Our voice is his voice! We sing because we live with Satan!"

The others raised their arms and answered with a resounding, "Hail, Satan!"

Then, pointing the knife toward the flames, Durant flung back his head and prayed: "Sweet Satan, master of earth and hell, accept this blood sacrifice as a token of our love!"

He leaped from the rock and just before his naked body plunged into the blackness beyond the fire, I saw the downward thrust of his arm and the flash of the blade. A strangled scream pierced the silence, followed by Durant's triumphant, fiendish yell. Drenched in blood, he vaulted back into view, then they all went mad, stripping the robes off their bodies and swarming around Durant in a naked frenzy.

In horror, I recoiled from the scene and hurled myself into the darkness. Blind panic drove me. My only feeling was fear. My only thought to escape the suffocating presence of evil that was blacker than the night. I ran headlong through the forest until my shins smashed into a fallen log, sending me crashing to the earth. Dazed and gasping with pain, I struggled to control my breathing as well as my fear—and I listened.

Sounds of hysteria, inhuman laughter and profanity carried clearly through the night air, but there were no crashing footsteps, no sounds of pursuit. A sob of relief escaped my throat along with the whispered prayer, "Please, God, don't let them find me!"

When I tried to stand, a sharp pain shot through the fingers of my right hand, and I realized I was still clutching the tape recorder. I dropped the machine back into my pocket with a violent shudder and ran on.

Staggering, stumbling, at times half-crawling, I forced my way through the undergrowth and the darkness. I wasn't sure if I were headed in the right direction or wandering farther into the forest until I saw the black shape of Obolus' van just ahead of me. Using every ounce of strength, I ran across the road and down the driveway to the "Mollie Kathleen."

Inside at last, I leaned heavily against the door, trying to free myself of terror. Reason argued I was safe, but even a locked door couldn't block out the horror of what I had witnessed. Choking back bitter nausea, I pushed my way through the dark living room and barely made it to the kitchen sink.

The heaving sickness finally passed, leaving me weaker than before, but I forced my shaking legs to the back door to make sure it was locked. After checking the windows as well, I returned to the living room and collapsed on the couch. The blanket I had used earlier was lying across one of the cushions, and I wrapped it around me.

Sitting there in the darkness, staring at shadows in the unfamiliar room, I have never felt so alone. My taut nerves were tortured by the simplest of sounds—the refrigerator's soft whir, the creaking of a board, the night wind pressing against the windows. Knowing that the cabin had already been violated by some dark-haired stranger made it even more difficult to feel safe and secure. Going upstairs was out of the question. If Obolus came back, I would be trapped like an animal in a corner. I shivered and pulled the blanket closer.

Minutes later, the convulsive roar of an engine ruptured the night's uneasy silence, and my heart gave a painful jerk. Creeping to the front window, I parted the drapes a small sliver and stared out at the black silhouettes of bushes and trees. After a moment, I heard the van move past the cabin and down the road, but I saw nothing. The fact they had not turned on the headlights told me Obolus' desire to avoid discovery was as strong as my own. The sound of the engine faded. Then nothing. They were gone.

I moved back to the couch and reached for the comforting warmth of the blanket. I was safe. Obolus hadn't seen or heard me. There was nothing to worry about.

But would I still be safe once they discovered I had not only witnessed, but recorded the proceedings of their bloody ritual? Right now, the band's satanic involvements were a well-kept secret, but the moment I handed over the tape, all that would change. The full impact of my impulsive action washed over me in shuddering waves, and I couldn't help thinking it might be better—certainly safer, if I destroyed the tape and just forgot what I had seen tonight.

But how could I forget? Unlike a nightmare, the evil I had seen and heard and felt was real—Durant's naked body poised on the rock, the plunging knife, that fiendish yell. I buried my face in my hands, pressing the heels of my palms against my eyes, as if that would push the images away.

Dear God, what was I going to do? Taking the tape to Brent Watkins was no longer a viable solution. Not now. Obolus had to be exposed. The public might not believe it, or even care, but they had a right to know the truth. When I thought of the millions of teenagers who looked up to Obolus as rebellious young gods, I felt sick. Gorman was right. If you tell people that Satan worship is only a game, a gimmick, they'll believe it. Because they want to. To acknowledge it as anything more would be to acknowledge the existence of Satan himself, and that was something few people felt comfortable doing in this modern age. Obolus knew that. What's more, they were counting on it.

I straightened up with grim determination. Someone had to put an end to their hypocritical masquerade. If the public still wanted to idolize the rock group after learning Obolus worshipped Satan to the point of offering blood sacrifice, then it would be on their conscience, not mine.

Staring into the darkness, I suddenly realized I didn't know what that blood sacrifice was. A cold chill crept along my flesh, as I remembered that strange, muffled whimper. What was it?

Another sobering thought came on the heels of my unanswered question. The tape recording and my word alone might not be enough to verify what had taken place in the woods tonight. Before Obolus' satanic activities could be made public, I had to know what Derek Durant had killed. The thought of going back to that place, even in broad daylight, made me tremble. I couldn't do it . . . not alone.

Cole. There was no one else I could trust. He would know what to do. In fact, tonight's grisly events involved him as much as me because they had taken place on his property. The only problem was, Cole wouldn't be coming back to Lodestone until Sunday. How could I endure another day and another night in this place? Then I remembered, Obolus would be leaving on Saturday—later today, actually—to give their concert in Red Rocks. I slumped back against the cushions. It shouldn't be too difficult to stay out of their way until then, even if it meant barracading myself in the "Mollie Kathleen." Once Cole returned, everything would be all right. I didn't analyze why that should be so. I only knew that the thought of him filled me with a sweet sense of certainty and calm.

The night passed slowly. Several times, I drifted off to sleep, only to be awakened by some innocent noise. Then, long minutes would drag by with me lying rigidly on the couch, listening and wondering what it was. Finally, when pale gray light crept through the windows and the dawn chorus of birds began in the forest, I sank into an exhausted sleep.

AN INSISTENT RINGING jerked me awake, and I sat up with a gasp. Although the room was bright with sunlight, I had to fight back sick waves of fear as the ringing came again. Who would be calling this early in the morning? I glanced at my watch, startled to discover it was nearly ten-thirty. Then my eyes focused on my hands—dirty, scratched and caked with dried blood. I shuddered and reached for the telephone.

"Is this Megan—I mean, Miss Collier?" a woman's voice asked timidly.

"Yes. . ."

"I . . . I hope I'm not interrupting your writing. This is Mrs. Randolph."

My fingers tensed around the receiver, and I asked uncertainly, "Who?"

"Twila Randolph. I'm sorry to bother you. I told Cody you were probably busy, but he hasn't given me a moment's peace all morning. As soon as he found out you were back, he's been begging to see you."

At the mention of Cody's name, my suspicions melted away. "You're not bothering me," I said. "I'm sorry. I didn't recognize your voice at first."

"Are you all right, dear?" the woman asked. "You sound exhausted!"

"I'm all right. I didn't sleep very well last night."

"I'm real sorry to bother you," Twila said again, "but I promised Cody I'd give you a call. If you're not feeling up to it I'll understand, but I was wondering if you could come over for a visit and some lunch?"

"That sounds wonderful! How soon can I . . . I mean, when

would you like me to come over?"

"As far as Cody's concerned, the sooner the better," she answered with a chuckle.

The sooner the better expressed my feelings exactly. "I have a few things to do," I told her, "but I could drive down in say, half an hour?"

"That's just fine. We'll look forward to seeing you."

I hung up the phone and got stiffly off the couch, determined to put last night's disturbing events out of my mind—at least for a few hours. And yet, before going upstairs to wash and dress, my jagged nerves insisted that I check the doors once more. Both locks were solid and secure.

Glancing out the front window, I saw a tender morning sky with wispy smudges of clouds skimming the horizon. Instead of dissonant chanting, a cheerful chorus of robins echoed through the pines. I took comfort in the sound and breathed a quiet "Thank you," to the sky. Morning had never been more of a miracle.

A ten-minute soak in a hot tub did wonders for my aches and stiffness, but knowing I would be away from the cabin was the most comforting balm of all. I dressed quickly, pulling on an old pair of Levis and a soft cotton shirt. Another five minutes to blow-dry my hair and whisk on a little makeup and I was ready to go. Halfway down the stairs, I caught sight of the tape recorder resting innocently on a table. Something inside me didn't feel comfortable with just leaving it there in plain sight. I stopped and glanced around the cabin. There were dozens of places I could hide the tape, but somehow, that didn't feel right either. Finally, deciding the simplest solution was probably the best, I dropped the recorder back into my purse along with the keys to the cabin and shut the door behind me.

Driving down the dirt road, I took instant notice of the red Camaro's absence beside the third cabin. Obolus' van was gone as well. My relief was tempered by a strong sense of caution and passing by the lodge and recording studio, I glanced over the parking lot. No Camaro and no van. Perhaps Obolus and the others had already left to rehearse for tonight's concert. The thought alone was enough to make me giddy with relief. I pressed my foot on the gas pedal and urged the car out of the trees, into the sunlight.

Cody was waiting for me by the front gate. The transparent delight in his eyes promptly did away with any attempt on my part for a casual greeting. The moment I got out of the car and bent down, he ran straight into my open arms, squeezing my neck in a ferocious bear hug that nearly knocked me off balance.

"You came," was all he said.

It was more than enough.

The morning passed in simple ways. Twila had bread to bake and washing to do, so she left Cody entirely to me. First, we walked down the road to see the horses, making frequent stops along the way to examine rocks, caterpillars and whatever else caught the boy's interest. Next, he took me to see a litter of kittens in the barn. Afterwards, we explored the grassy pasture and fields behind Wes and Twila's home. To Cody, a rusty can was a treasure, a small hole in the ground an exciting discovery. If only for a morning, I delighted in seeing the world through his eyes—a world full of sunshine and surprises where darkness and chanting didn't exist.

Before going in to lunch, we sat in the back yard on the warm grass, and I showed Cody how to make necklaces and chains from dandelion stems. The child's delight soon turned to frustration when the slippery stems kept splitting up the middle, and after his third attempt ended in failure, I offered to help. Cody curled up against my side, content to watch as I carefully inserted one stem inside another.

Suddenly, he leaned forward and pointed at my hands with a frown. "Want a Band-Aide?" he asked.

I smiled at his concern and shook my head. "No. It's all right."

"Did you cry?"

"No . . . well, maybe just a little," I amended, as the memory of my dark flight through the forest shivered through me. I pushed the thought away and placed the finished dandelion chain on Cody's head with a grand gesture.

"There! Now you're 'King Cody!'"

The smile he gave me was so like his father's, I couldn't

resist the impulse to give him a kiss. Without a word, Cody climbed onto my lap, and I felt a soft yielding inside as his arms came around my neck. I leaned my cheek against his sun-warm curls, and we sat for a long moment in wordless contentment.

Cody insisted on wearing his limp little crown all through lunch, despite Twila's tactful encouragement to leave it on the back porch. Wes Randolph gave the dandelions a disgruntled glance, but refrained from making any comments. But then, as I was to discover, Wes Randolph didn't say much about anything. Most of his lunchtime conversation centered around such basic necessities as, "Pass the jam" and "I'd like some more salad." My own contributions weren't much better. After skipping breakfast and spending an active morning with Cody, I was happy to forego more scintillating discussion in favor of Twila's excellent fried chicken and potato salad. Cody filled in the gaps, giving the couple an enthusiastic, if somewhat disjointed account of our morning together.

"Know what? Me an' Megan named Tiger's kittens!" he announced proudly.

Wes grunted and Twila said, "That's nice, dear. Be careful not to gulp your milk or you'll get a stomach ache."

"Megan named two an' I named two," Cody went on. "Wanna know their names?"

Wes nodded without looking up, while Twila answered mildly, "Certainly, dear."

"Mine's 'Duke' and 'Bob Hope,'" he told them.

I smiled, thinking of the fluffy gray and white female that Cody had insisted on naming 'Bob Hope.' At least 'Duke' had been a male.

"And Megan named hers. . . ." Cody paused, his expression suddenly blank, then glanced at me for help.

"'Connie' and 'Dave,'" I said, giving the boy a little wink.

Twila stared at me and repeated slowly, "'Connie' and 'Dave'? What—unusual names."

Cody grinned. "I think they're great!"

Twila nodded vaguely. "That's nice, dear. Now stop talking and finish your lunch."

The boy's shoulders sagged as he looked down at his plate, and I felt a sudden twinge of concern about him growing up in such a silent adult world. Looking at Cody, the years fell away, and I saw myself, a pudgy nine-year-old with freckles and missing teeth, being sent to live with my father's mother. I adored Grandmother Collier, but there were times when I longed to run instead of walk down her stairs, when I ached to hear the sound of children's laughter instead of the martial ticking of the clock on the mantle. And more than once, I was sorely tempted to move those immoveable, starched doilies which covered everything from tables and the piano top to the backs of chairs.

Wes Randolph's gruff voice broke through my musings as he shoved back his chair and announced, "Cinnabar's got a touch of colic. I'm going down to the stables and check on him."

Cody was all eagerness. "Can I go, too?"

"Not this time, but I'll let you know how he's doing."

The child said nothing, but disappointment was achingly visible in his eyes. Wes didn't seem to notice this as he walked to the back door and reached for a battered brown cowboy hat hanging on a nail. "Good lunch, Twila," he grunted, pulling the hat over his balding head. Then, to me, "Come see us again, Miss Collier. It's nice to have you."

I mumbled a surprised "Thank you," to his back and after the man had gone, Twila smiled and confided, "Wes'd never admit it, but he's really quite taken with you."

I tried not to smile at the phrase. "Taken with me?"

The woman leaned across the table and said in a low tone, "I overheard him and Cole talking about you the other night, and he. . . ." She halted mid-sentence, suddenly noticing Cody's interest in the conversation. "Cody, dear, it's time for your nap. Finish your milk, then I'll tuck you in bed."

"No!" The boy scrambled off his chair, dived into my lap and promptly dissolved into tears. "When I wake up, you'll go away again," he sobbed.

"Cody, please don't cry." I picked him up, feeling the frightened desperation in the arms which clung to my neck.

"Cody's never been one to take to strangers," Twila told me quietly, "but he was broken-hearted when Cole came back without you the other day."

I stared at her, feeling a stab of conscience, and held the child closer. "It's all right, Cody. I'm not leaving. If you want me to, I'll stay right here."

The boy's head lifted and tear-filled eyes looked into mine for reassurance. "You promise?"

"I promise."

Twila's smile was tremulous, but her voice was matter-of-fact as she took a handkerchief from her apron pocket. "All right, little man, let's dry those tears. Then I'll take you to your room."

"I still don't want a nap," Cody sniffed, submitting to the handkerchief. "I'm too old for naps!"

"All right then, instead of a nap, today you can take a 'rest,'" Twila told him. "You don't need to go to sleep—just lie down for a little while, so I can do the dishes. Then, after you get up, we'll make sugar cookies. Would you like that?"

Cody nodded and offered no resistance when she lifted him off my lap. "But I'm not going to sleep!" he insisted.

"I know, dear. I know," she agreed soothingly as they left the room.

Twila returned not five minutes later, a smug little smile on her lips. "He'll be out like a light in no time," she said.

But Cody was determined to do otherwise. Twila had no sooner put the glasses into the soapy dishwater when he came bounding into the kitchen, bright-eyed and eager to bake cookies. The woman's exasperated, "Cody! You haven't been in bed for ten minutes!" had no effect on him.

"You said I didn't need to go to sleep—just rest," he reminded her with an irrepressible smile.

Twila sighed and shook her head. "I know what I said, but the cookies will have to wait until I finish washing these dishes!"

"I'll be glad to wash the rest," I offered, thinking another ten or fifteen minutes would seem like an eternity to a small boy.

"I can't let you do that...."

"Why not? I'd like to help."

"But your writing—I feel like I've kept you from your work too long as it is."

"You're not keeping me from anything," I told her. "Washing dishes is about all the mental exercise I can handle today."

The woman's expression was clearly puzzled, but she was too polite to say more. Besides, Cody was already diving into one of the cupboards for the cookie cutters.

By the time I had washed and put away the last dish, the small kitchen was filled with the warm, sweet smell of baking sugar cookies. I hung my damp towel on a rack near the sink, then sat down next to Cody, who was waiting impatiently for Twila to roll out more dough for the next batch.

"Cole didn't have the chance to tell us much about you," she remarked, deftly sprinkling flour on a wooden rolling pin. "Is your family from Los Angeles?"

"Originally, yes."

She gave me an encouraging smile. "Tell me about them."

I watched the sticky mixture become a smooth golden circle under her knowing hands, not sure what to say.

"Do you have any brothers or sisters?" she prompted.

"I have two half-brothers, but I rarely see them. My parents are divorced."

"So are mine," Cody put in.

Twila glanced down at him in surprise, as if she hadn't expected the boy to be listening, let alone understand our conversation. "Here, Cody, you can make a 'star' cookie," she said, handing him a cookie cutter. "Be sure to start on the edge of the dough."

Cody ignored the instruction as well as her attempt to change the conversation and plopped the cookie cutter down directly in the center of the dough. "My mom went away when I was a baby," he told me, adding candidly, "She didn't like me."

"Cody! Whoever told you such a thing?" Twila demanded.

"Nobody. I just know," he answered with a certainty that shocked her into silence. After pressing the cookie cutter down once more, he looked up at me. "Did your mom like you?"

"Not very much."

"Why?"

"I don't know."

"I like you," he said, the honesty in his eyes as warm and

giving as sunlight pouring through an open window.

I swallowed a little catch in my throat and told him, "That's good, because I like you, too!"

The slam of a screen door intruded upon the moment and seconds later, Wes Randolph entered the kitchen. Motioning to Twila, he said abruptly, "I need your help in the barn."

"Can't it wait? I've got a batch of cookies in the oven."

"The cookies can wait. This can't." Wes gave his wife a blunt look and stood in the doorway, waiting.

Twila's only sign of perturbance was a small sigh as she wiped her hands on her apron. "Would you mind taking over for a few minutes?" she asked me.

"Not at all."

"I won't be long. Don't let Cody eat too much cookie dough or he'll be up all night with a stomach ache," she added, hurrying after Wes' retreating figure.

As the screen door slammed behind them, Cody paused and looked at the fat glob of dough halfway to his mouth. "I never get stomach aches," he told me.

"Not ever?"

The boy solemnly shook his head, then stared at the sweet temptation between his fingers.

"I'll bet that's because you always do what your Aunt Twila tells you," I said.

I saw the flash of conscience in his eyes, and he put half the dough back into the mixing bowl. "Is this too much?" he asked, holding up the remaining piece.

I smiled at the pleading look on his face. "No, I think that's just right." Almost before the words were out, the dough disappeared into his mouth.

While I sprinkled more flour on the cutting board, Cody helped himself to another handful of dough and began rolling small pieces of it between his palms. I watched with an interested smile as he carefully placed the lumpy little balls in a line.

"What are you making?"

"A rock 'n roll band," he informed me. Pointing to the largest ball of dough, he said, "This one's the drummer. And I'm their manager."

"Oh." I kept my face as serious as his. "Does your band have a name?"

Cody considered the question for a second or two, then shrugged.

"We'll have to think of one," I said.

Cody shrugged again, more interested in sneaking another piece of dough into his mouth. He glanced up to see if I had noticed and giggled.

"Know what? You've got flour on your nose!"

I smiled and dabbed a flour-covered finger to his nose. "Know what? So do you!"

Cody rubbed his nose and laughed, then his eyes widened with surprised delight. "Hi, Dad!"

I glanced up and a sweet shaft of pain shot through me. Cole stood in the doorway between the kitchen and living room, his hair a windblown tangle of blackness, his plaid shirt wrinkled and half-open. Weariness was etched into the planes of his face, but the light in his eyes and the smile curving his mouth turned my heart inside out.

My first impulse was to run headlong into his arms, the second, to run away. Instead, I just stood there, clutching the rolling pin and staring at him with the stunned surprise of someone who has walked straight into a wall that wasn't supposed to be there.

"I'm makin' cookies with the cookie-lady," Cody announced with a grin.

"So I see."

Cole crossed the small room to give his son a welcoming hug and kiss, then made a smiling inspection of our doings. Taking a pinch of dough from the drummer's round sides, he popped it into his mouth and told Cody, "That's a great-tasting rock band you've got there."

"Dad!"

Cole laughed and his, "Sorry, son," was unrepentant.

Our eyes met over the top of Cody's head, and I tried to think of something to say. A quiet, "You look tired," was the best I could do.

"It was a long drive from the airport," he answered. "Denver was hotter than blazes."

"Oh. . . ."

The scene couldn't have been more domestic. Yet, looking at the hot beads of sweat gleaming against the tanned hollow of his throat and dark mat of hair on his chest, I have never felt less so. Wanton, yes. Domestic, no.

I took a quick breath and glanced away. "I . . . I thought you weren't coming back until tomorrow."

"So did I . . . until last night."

My hands began to tremble, and I let go of the rolling pin. Cole stepped toward me, and I said something stupid like, "I've got flour on my hands." Then he was holding me and nothing else mattered. I knew he could feel my heart's wild pounding, just as I felt his every breath as if it were my own.

"Until I saw your car parked outside, I thought you'd run away from me again," he said, the teasing softness of his mustache warm against my cheek.

"You did? Why?"

"I drove straight from the airport to the 'Mollie Kathleen,' but you weren't there. Then I stopped at the lodge, but no one knew where you were."

I drew back slightly to meet his eyes, and before I could say more than his name, Cole's mouth took mine in a brusing kiss that communicated his needs more clearly than any words.

Cody's disgusted, "Dad!" provided a potent reminder that we weren't alone, but his father's arms still held me close.

"You might as well get used to it, son," Cole told him, and to prove his point, planted another hard kiss on my lips.

I pushed him away with an embarrassed laugh, suddenly noticing the smudges of white flour smeared liberally across his shirt front. When I reached up to brush it off, Cole's fingers closed about my wrist.

"Forget about the flour—and the shirt!" he ordered in a soft growl, then raised my hand to his lips. A puzzled frown creased his brow. "I didn't realize writing was such a dangerous profession," he said, staring at the angry red scratches on my hand. "What happened?"

"I . . . that's something I need to talk to you about."

Before I could explain further, Twila Randolph bustled into the kitchen, sniffing the air and giving me a pointed look.

My gaze flew to the oven. "The cookies! I forgot all about them!"

Twila grabbed a hot pad and quickly retrieved the cookie sheet. "Well, they're a bit crisp, but they're not quite carbon," she said, setting the cookie sheet on top of the stove. "I think I'm beginning to understand why Megan forgot about the cookies." She turned to Cole with a knowing smile. "Where did you come from?"

"My sixth sense told me you were baking sugar cookies, so naturally, I grabbed the first plane out of Los Angeles."

Twila snorted. "You may have grabbed the first plane back here, but I doubt it had anything to do with my sugar cookies!"

Cole laughed and planted an affectionate kiss on her cheek. "Would you mind watching Cody for awhile? Megan and I need to talk." Turning to the boy, he said, "We'll be back in a few minutes, son. I want you to stay here and help Aunt Twila so she won't burn any more cookies. Okay?"

Cody gave his father a tentative shrug, then looked at me. "Are you coming back?"

"Of course I am! I wouldn't want to miss out on cookies and milk!"

Reassured, Cody smiled and went back to his "rock band," while Cole took my hand and gestured toward the door.

The sun was high overhead and scarcely a breeze stirred the drowsy heat of the afternoon as we stopped beside a pasture fence. Cole's look had been questioning, but he agreed without comment when I suggested we go for a walk somewhere away from the house. Now, he leaned against the gnarled fencepost and studied my face with quiet concern.

"What's wrong, Megan?"

I reached into my pocket for the tape recorder, then drew a deep breath. "Last night, I saw and heard something I think you should know about."

"I don't understand. What's that tape got to do with how you hurt your hands?"

I pressed the "Play" button and said, "Maybe you'd better listen to this first, then I'll explain."

Cole stared at the recorder, listening with frowning

concentration as Obolus' profane curses and twisted prayers filled the summer air with chilling darkness. When Derek Durant's voice cried out, "Sweet Satan! Master of earth and hell, accept this blood sacrifice. . . ." I punched the "Stop" button with a shudder.

For several seconds, Cole said nothing. Then he looked at me. "What in the hell. . . ?"

"Obolus. And hell is a pretty accurate description for what I saw last night."

"Tell me about it," he said quietly.

I tried to be matter-of-fact, but relating the incident in the woods was like living it all over again. By the time I had finished, my voice was shaking, and I was trembling from the inside out.

"Are you sure they didn't see you?" Cole demanded in a taut voice. When I nodded, he pulled me close against his chest. "Thank God for that!"

I shut my eyes and leaned against him as relief, harsh and wonderful, flooded through me. My worst fear had been that he might accept what Obolus had done and say I was merely overreacting to the whole thing.

"Do you think you could find that place again?" he asked after a moment.

"Yes, I'm sure I could."

"Good. I want you to take me there."

I stiffened in his arms. "When?"

"How about right now?"

Fear shot through me with such intensity I couldn't answer.

Cole's arms tightened around me, giving understanding as well as reassurance. "Look, I don't blame you for not wanting to go near the place, but before I can do anything about this, I have to find out what Obolus killed."

His words echoed my own thoughts from the night before, and I nodded against his chest.

"Thanks, Babe. As soon as we get back to the house, I'll give security a call and have Ed Garrison meet us at the 'Mollie Kathleen.' It won't hurt to have another witness along."

The calm certainty of his voice eased the tight cords of fear and worry inside me. "I think I'd feel a lot better if you kept this," I said, handing him the tape recorder.

Cole took the recorder from me and slipped it inside his shirt pocket.

Walking back to the house, he gave me a sideways glance and asked in the gentle voice he used for Cody, "Are you okay?"

I took a deep breath and nodded.

Cole's arm went around my waist, and there was open admiration in the look he gave me. "Do you mind telling me something?"

"What's that?"

"Why you walked into those woods last night."

I thought a moment, then said simply, "I guess because I've never cared much for liars and hypocrites."

Cole smiled. "I'll remember that."

14

ED GARRISON WAS waiting for us at the end of the gravel road near the "Mollie Kathleen." As Cole helped me down from the jeep, the security man dropped his half-smoked cigarette and ground it out with the toe of his boot.

"Look, Cole, I'm sorry about the slip-up. I didn't know you were back, or I would have filled you in on the situation myself." This, with a tight-lipped glance in my direction. Then, "I've had Ron Weaver and the rest of the men out checking the grounds since yesterday, but we haven't found any trace of the guy."

Cole stared at him. "What are you talking about? What guy?"

Garrison paused half a second, his expression matching Cole's in confusion, then gestured to me. "The guy in Miss Collier's cabin. Isn't that why you called me up here?"

Cole glanced from Garrison to me. "There was a man in the 'Mollie Kathleen'?"

I shrugged and said, "Yes, but after last night, I forgot all about him."

"Will somebody please tell me what's going on?" Garrison voiced his exasperation.

"I'll explain in a minute," Cole said. "First, I want to hear about the man in Megan's cabin."

Garrison straightened his heavy shoulders. "When Miss Collier arrived yesterday morning, she surprised some guy who was staying in the 'Mollie Kathleen.' He took off after she went back to the lodge to tell Brent about it. Like I said, we've searched the property and questioned the staff, but no one seems to know anything about him—where he came from or where he went."

Cole's expression hardened as he took this in. "You said he was staying in the cabin. How long do you think he'd been there?"

Garrison shrugged. "I'm not sure. A few days maybe, but no more than that. There was some food in the kitchen, and we found a razor and some shaving stuff upstairs."

"Sounds like he made himself right at home," Cole commented in a tight voice. "I don't like this, Ed."

"Neither do I. Brent wondered if he might be some transient who just wandered onto the property, but I don't think so."

"Why not?"

"According to Miss Collier, she heard a noise upstairs and this guy comes down in his shorts, as casual as you please. Then when he sees her, he freezes." Garrison turned probing brown eyes on me. "Have you remembered yet what he said to you?"

"No. I'm sorry. I haven't had much time to think about it. I was working most of the afternoon and then, last night. . . ."

The security man's voice was instantly alert. "What about last night?"

"We have a problem with our guests," Cole said shortly, and took the tape recorder out of his shirt pocket.

Garrison's face tightened with anger as he listened to Cole's terse account of Obolus' ritual in the woods. When Cole played a small portion of the tape, he spat out, "Those dirty bastards!" then glanced quickly at me. "Sorry, Miss Collier."

I felt a new sense of acceptance in his eyes as he asked, "What time was it when you first heard the chanting?"

"A little after midnight."

Garrison swore again and turned to Cole. "The patrols were out checking the cabin area about 11:30, then again around 1:30 in the morning. Those bas. . . . those guys either got lucky or had their escapade pretty carefully planned."

"Knowing Obolus, I doubt luck had anything to do with it," Cole said.

Garrison grunted. "So what do you want me to do?"

"Megan's agreed to take us where they held their ritual. Before we do anything, I want to know what they killed."

Garrison agreed with a grim nod and began walking toward

the forest. "Let's go find out!"

In the dappled light of afternoon, the forest was a haunt of singing birds and wild beauty. Making our way through the trees and tangled undergrowth, I found it hard to believe this was the same place I had fled in such terror. Everything looked so different, I wouldn't have been sure we were heading in the right direction if it hadn't been for the recently trampled foliage and heavy footprints in the soft earth.

We had covered perhaps thirty yards when Garrison stopped short and got down on his haunches.

"Come take a look," he said.

Cole's arm tightened around my shoulders as we stared down at a dark splatter of blood on a granite rock. There was a long moment when we all said nothing, just stared at the blood, then each other. Overhead, a squirrel scolded us for invading his privacy, breaking the uneven silence.

"How much farther is it to where they built their fire?" Garrison asked me.

I glanced ahead where sunlight spilled through narrow corridors of aspen and fir. "Not far."

The granite outcropping was an obvious landmark in the daytime and instantly identifiable. As we left the forest and entered the sunlit clearing, Ed Garrison glanced around and said, "They chose a good spot—protected from the wind, out of sight. It's no wonder we didn't see their fire last night."

A cold chill cut through me as I stared at the granite boulder where Derek Durant had stood, knife in hand.

Cole gave my hand a comforting squeeze. "Are you all right, Babe?"

Standing there in the sunlight, I didn't know how to tell him that I felt surrounded by the same smothering blackness of last night. I drew a shaky breath and answered, "I don't like this place."

The blackened remains of Obolus' fire was a stark contrast to the sun-speckled rocks. Garrison reached it first and kicked at the charred wood with his boot.

"The embers are still warm. It's a good thing there wasn't much wind last night. Looks like all they did was kick some. . . ."

Walking around to the opposite side of the fire pit he broke off and stared at the ground. "My God. . . ."

Cole let go my hand and quickly crossed the rocks to where Garrison stood, but I held back, my mind forming grisly images of some butchered animal.

"What is it?" I asked, as the two men stared in tight-lipped silence.

Cole answered with a confused shake of his head. "There's nothing here . . . except blood."

Disbelief and curiosity compelled me to see for myself. A few feet from the fire's charred remains, dark pools of coagulated blood had collected in the rocky crevices. The surface itself was spattered and stained a sticky, reddish-brown. Near my feet was a bloody, inverted cross.

"There's so much," I whispered.

Cole reached out an arm and pulled me close to his side. Looking into his eyes, I saw the same question my own were asking. What was it? Neither of us dared attempt an answer.

"I'm going to have a look around," Garrison said. "They may have dumped the carcass somewhere in the bushes."

Cole nodded, then steered me away from the blood-stained rocks. "You better sit down for a minute."

I gladly slumped down on a large boulder and took some deep breaths. "I'm sorry. The sight of blood doesn't usually make me squeamish."

"It's all right, Babe. We've both seen too much of it this past week." Bending down beside me, Cole put a hand on my knee. "Do you feel up to answering a few questions?"

"What do you want to know?"

"When you were telling me about last night, you mentioned hearing some kind of sound. Do you have any idea what it might have been?"

"Not really. It was a muffled sort of whine—like a frightened animal or. . . ." I broke off, thinking back to the hushed seconds when I had first heard that pathetic whimper. The sound had come again, moments before Derek Durant offered his black prayer to Satan, and then. . . .

"Megan, what is it?"

I released a tense breath, then looked at him. "There was a

scream—just after he—after Durant leaped off the rock. I saw the flash of his knife in the firelight, then he disappeared and I heard it. . . .'' My body turned rigid as my mind played back the grisly details. "The scream came before the yell,'' I said in a dry voice.

"What are you saying?'' Cole clutched my trembling hands in both of his. "What about the scream?''

"It wasn't Durant. His yell came after . . . after he did it. He jumped back on the rock, and I could see the blood on his body . . . and the knife. . . !''

Cole's grip tightened on my hands, and his voice was suddenly harsh. "Are you suggesting that Obolus carried out some kind of human sacrifice up here?''

"I'm not suggesting anything. I'm only telling you what I heard and what I saw!'' I pulled my hands out of his and stood up, hating the sick knot of tension inside me.

"I can't find a damn thing,'' Garrison said, coming up behind us. "Other than the blood, there's no other evidence or remains. No fur, no feathers.'' He glanced back at the blood-stained rocks and shook his head. "Whatever it was Obolus butchered last night, they must have taken it with them.''

Cole's eyes met mine for a tense moment, then he asked Garrison, "What do you think it was?''

"It doesn't matter what I think. We need answers. I'm going to take some blood samples, then go over the area again. If I get the samples into Boulder this afternoon, the police lab can check them out and tell us exactly what kind of blood it is.''

"How long before we'll know the results?'' Cole said.

"The tests take around seventy-two hours. We won't know anything much before Tuesday.''

I released a frustrated sigh. "That long?''

"The lab has to run a series of tests and that takes time,'' he explained. Garrison paused and looked at Cole. "In the meantime, what do we do about Obolus?''

Cole made a short, angry movement and shoved both hands in his pockets. "What I'd like to do is kick their butts off the ranch right now, but what I'd better do is talk to their manager.''

"Sid Rasmussen's not here,'' Garrison told him. "He left the ranch last night just after dark. Obolus have gone, too. They've got a big concert down at Red Rocks tonight."

Cole bit back his anger and asked, "When are they due back?"

"I'm not sure. Sometime Sunday, I think."

"Maybe that's just as well," Cole admitted, running a restless hand through his hair. "If I had to see any of them right now, I might do something I'd regret later. But I want to know the minute Sid gets back."

"Right. Anything else?"

"Yeah. Keep quiet about this until we get some definite answers. If somebody on the staff finds out and starts talking, we could get a lot of unwanted publicity. Tell your men what you have to and make sure they keep a close watch on Obolus after they get back. I don't want a repeat performance of last night's little show."

Ed Garrison gave Cole a grim-faced nod, then glanced over his shoulder at the blackened campfire. "I'd better get those samples."

Silence was our only companion as Cole and I walked back through the forest. I was more shaken than I cared to admit by our discovery, and Cole's tight, closed expression did nothing to encourage conversation.

When we reached the jeep, I glanced up at his tense face and said, "I'm sorry you had to come back to this."

"You're sorry! I'm the one who should apologize! When I think what you went through last night — what could have happened. . . ." He broke off and released a heavy sigh. "I'm sorry. I know you don't need to be reminded about that." The anger in his voice softened to concern as he gave my shoulder a gentle squeeze. "You look exhausted. Did you get any sleep at all?"

"Not much."

"What you need is a nice long nap."

I smiled. "That sounds tempting, but what about Cody? We promised him we'd be back for cookies and milk."

"I'll tell him the cookie-lady needed a nap. Don't worry. He'll be fine."

Cole took my hand and turned away from the jeep, but

remembering the plaintive look in the child's eyes made me pause.

"I hate to disappoint him. I can always catch up on my sleep later."

"Are you sure?"

"We did promise."

Cole smiled and something came into his eyes that started my heart pounding double-time. "That's right, *we* did," he agreed.

Color burned in my cheeks as I climbed into the jeep. It was getting far too easy to think in terms of "we" instead of "me," and I had no right to do that—just as I had no right to want his kiss the way I wanted it now.

Cole slid into the driver's side and put the key in the ignition. Then, instead of starting the engine, he reached over and pulled me into a rough embrace. His kiss completely eliminated any reticence between us, and my wholehearted response surprised him almost as much as it did me.

We broke apart to stare with shaken wonder into each other's eyes. Then Cole's mouth curved into a rakish grin. "I needed that," he said softly.

Without pausing to think, I pulled his dark head back to mine and murmured, "So did I!"

15

BY THE TIME we got back to Wes and Twila's, my appetite was definitely not the "cookies and milk" variety. My mind kept sending out faint warning signals, but I was too far gone to heed them. Cole's kisses had wrapped me in a delicious haze that no amount of common sense could penetrate.

Entering the kitchen, we were met with Twila's inquisitive stare and Cody's whining complaint that we had been gone "forever." Other than a brief, "Sorry we took so long," Cole offered no explanation. Instead, he picked Cody up in his arms and asked with pretended gruffness, "Hey, guy! Did you save any cookies for me?"

Cody grinned and pointed to the kitchen table where three plates, three glasses and a large tray of cookies had been set. "That one's yours! I made it myself," he told me with pride.

I looked at the huge, heart-shaped cookie which all but filled one of the plates. Thick pink frosting was smeared unevenly across the top and oozed down the sides onto the plate.

"It's beautiful," I said as we sat down at the table. "Almost too pretty to eat. Did you really make it all by yourself?"

Cody beamed and nodded. "An' I frosted it, too!"

"How about me?" Cole glanced at his empty plate. "Don't I rate a heart cookie?"

"I made you a star!" the boy answered, reaching for a much smaller cookie on the tray in front of us.

Cole's mouth twitched with amusement as he looked at the cookie. "A green star." He took a big bite, then gave Cody an approving nod. "Delicious!"

Father and son easily put away half a dozen cookies

between them, while I was hard-pressed to finish the giant-sized heart. As I downed the last crumb, Cody turned to his father with eager eyes. "Now can we go on a horseback ride?"

"Not today."

"Just a little one," Cody pleaded, wrinkling up his nose.

Cole shook his head and kissed the turned-up nose. "I'm sorry, son, but I have things to do, and Megan is tired. Maybe tomorrow." Glancing at his watch, he told me, "It's just past four-thirty. You still have enough time for a couple of hours' sleep."

"Enough time?"

"Before I pick you up for dinner," he said, taking my hand. "Come on. I'll walk you to your car."

There was scarcely time to hug Cody and thank Twila before Cole was steering me out of the house.

"Are you always so impulsive?" I laughed, remembering the afternoon only two days before when I had posed the same question.

Now as then, he grinned and answered, "Only with you."

We stopped beside the Audi in the tree-shaded driveway and all traces of teasing were gone as we faced each other. Two days ago, Cole had asked me to spend the evening with him, and I had snatched at any flimsy excuse to run away. The memory of that painful good-bye lived in the tortured glance he gave me now.

Touching the back of his hand to my cheek, he said softly, "Don't run away, Babe. . . ."

I gave him my lips for an answer, and it required a wonderfully long time before he was convinced I wasn't going anywhere.

Finally, Cole opened the car door for me, and I got inside. Leaning both arms on the window frame, he smiled into my eyes. "How does seven o'clock sound?"

"Just fine."

"I thought we could barbeque some steaks outside on the patio, if that's all right with you."

"It's just fine."

He laughed and bent his head to kiss me. "You're repeating yourself, Miss Collier."

"There's nothing wrong with a little repetition, Mr. McLean."

"You're absolutely right," he agreed and kissed me again. "I'll see you at seven!"

Taking a nap, or even one of Twila's so-called "rests" was a joke, but since Cole had asked me to, I felt obligated to at least try. I undressed, slipped on a silky, wrap-around robe, then lay down on the bed. After ten minutes of staring at the ceiling, grinning like an idiot, I gave up the whole idea. I was too excited, too happy, too alive to sleep! I ran downstairs instead, put a stack of Cole's records on the stereo and turned the volume up to a magnificent roar.

By 6:45 p.m., my emotional state had deteriorated from heady excitement to something resembling nervous paralysis. In deciding what to wear, the upstairs bedroom had been turned into a major disaster area. The contents of my suitcases were strewn haphazardly on the bed, chairs and floor, the bathroom reeked of Shalimar, and I had spilled my best bath powder all over the carpet. But at least I was ready. I paused in front of the bathroom mirror to brush a piece of lint off my slacks and gave my peach-colored sweater a critical glance. It wasn't exactly tight, but I never should have put it in the dryer. Leaning closer to the mirror, I applied a little more lip gloss and managed to color two teeth a rusty peach as well as my mouth. I sighed, swore, and wiped my teeth with a tissue. This was ridiculous! At twenty-five, I was hardly a teenager, and Cole McLean was most definitely a man.

Maybe that was the problem. The feelings Cole aroused in me went beyond anything I had experienced before, and I was at a loss to know how to handle them. When I was with him, I forgot myself completely, and yet on some inner level, he had a way of making me acutely aware of my own body and the heady delights of being a woman. Remembering how I had turned to him today, giving kiss for kiss and touch for touch, filled me with a rush of guilty pleasure. I took a shaky breath and left the room, thinking it was probably a good thing I could count on Cody being around to act as chaperone.

Walking down the stairs, the memory of Obolus briefly

flitted through my consciousness, but it was no more threatening than the moth beating its wings against the window screen.

At 6:55, the sound of an engine and the crunch of wheels on gravel brought an abrupt end to my nervous pacing. Seconds later, I heard his quick, confident knock on the door. Cole's greeting was casual, but something in his eyes told me his emotions were as high-pitched as mine. Walking to the jeep, I gave him a subtle, sideways glance, thinking something seemed different about him this evening. Then I realized I had never seen Cole this dressed up before. Not that Levis, a white shirt and dark gray pullover are all that formal, but combined with his black hair and blue-gray eyes, the total effect was more devastating than I cared to admit.

On the drive over, our conversation was fragmentary at best, punctuated with awkward glances and long moments of silence. The old urge to run, to protect my vulnerability behind walls of sarcasm and aloofness was battling with new desires and the growing need to be close to him. The conflict added a sharp edginess to my voice and falseness to my smile.

If Cole noticed this, he made no comment, but I was intensely aware of his questioning glance as he parked the jeep and led me around the side of the house by way of a narrow path under the pines.

The heat of the day had passed, and shadows were deep and cool as we came down the stone steps of the secluded patio. A spicy-sweet blend of pines and honeysuckle drifted on the evening breeze.

"The view is even lovelier than I remembered," I said, taking in the sweeping panorama of meadow, mountains and sky.

Behind me, Cole's voice was softly amused. "You were here only two days ago."

"I know, but. . . ."

"But what?"

"Two days ago I thought I'd never see this again."

"Megan. . . ."

I ignored the husky tone of his voice and turned away to inspect the appetizing array of food spread out on the table—hard rolls, a pot of barbequed beans, green salad and thick, t-bone steaks, all set to toss on the nearby grill.

"Everything looks wonderful," I said, then took a sharp second glance at the table-setting for two. "Won't Cody be eating with us?"

"Since he missed his nap today, Twila thought it would be better if he had an early dinner and spent the night with them."

With effort, I kept my voice as casual as his, even though warning bells were clanging inside me. "Oh, I see."

Cole stepped behind me and put his hands on my shoulders. "I thought it might be a nice change not to have a built-in chaperone around. Do you mind?"

Hearing him speak the exact opposite of my own thoughts nearly threw me into a panic, but firm hands prevented my escape.

"Megan, what's wrong?"

"Nothing. . . ."

Cole turned me around to face him. "Something's bothering you. You've been nervous as a cat ever since I picked you up, and now you've got that scared look in your eyes. What have I done?"

"Nothing. It's just. . . ." I drew a shaky breath and admitted quietly, "I'm not sure where all this is leading, and I . . . I don't know what you want."

Cole blinked and stared at me. Then, as he searched my eyes, his tense expression softened into tenderness. "I want to be with you," he answered softly. "I want to talk to you, look at you, hold you. . . ." His hands released my shoulders to cup my face instead. "What I don't want is some cheap, one-night stand. Does that answer your question?"

There was no rebuke in his voice, only honesty and a gentleness that suddenly had me blinking back the tears. Cole wiped one away with his fingertips, then smiled. "Now that we've got that settled, how do you like your steaks, my love— rare, medium or well-done?"

I smiled back, feeling the warmth of his endearment wrap itself around my heart. "Rare."

"Good! So do I."

The time passed too quickly. We talked, ate, laughed and

teased like old friends, yet there was an undeniable spark of awareness behind every smile, every touch. After sunset, a rising wind and sudden chill in the air forced us inside. I helped him put the food away, then Cole led me into a rustic family room directly off the kitchen.

I glanced about the softly-lit room with its beamed ceilings and panelled walls, amazed that Indian rugs and Navajo sand paintings could share living space so compatibly with a Colonial rocker and Chippendale armchair.

Cole motioned to a russet-toned sofa which faced the big stone fireplace. "Why don't you kick your shoes off and relax, while I get a fire going?"

Increasing awareness of our intimate surroundings suddenly made it difficult to relax, let alone kick off my shoes. As he bent down beside the raised hearth, I noticed that pine logs, kindling and rumpled newspaper were already neatly stacked in the cast-iron grate. There was little more for him to do than strike a match on the rough stone and touch the flame to the wood. I took a deep breath, trying to ease the nervous flutter inside my chest, and decided to avoid the couch for the time being. Next to the fireplace, a massive pine bookcase filled one entire wall. I gave a passing glance to the showy collection of rocks and minerals on one of its shelves, then moved closer to examine the framed photograph of an older couple, perhaps in their late sixties.

The woman was spare and straight as a rod, but her nearly gaunt figure was softened by still-beautiful features and the kindest smile I've ever seen. The man at her side was big-shouldered and heavy set. I would have found his stern mouth and stubborn jaw quite intimidating, but for the glint of humor in his blue-gray eyes.

"Those are my parents," Cole said, glancing up from the fire.

"You have your father's eyes."

"And his stubbornness," he added with a grin. "Or so I'm told." Taking an iron poker, he shifted a slow-burning log closer to the flames.

My gaze shifted from the fire to Cole's face. Seeing his rugged profile etched by flame and shadow, I was struck with a sense of awe that I should be here, in this room, with this man, sharing warm firelight and conversation.

Cole replaced the screen and got to his feet. When he turned to me, it was almost as though he knew my thoughts. "Strange, isn't it, how things happen?"

I nodded wordlessly, feeling the intensity of his gaze as keenly as the heat from the fire.

The sudden ringing of a phone made us both jump.

"That's probably my manager," Cole said, sounding a little breathless. "I'd forgotten Joe might be calling tonight. Will you excuse me?"

"Of course."

Cupping my chin with one hand, he kissed me and added softly, "Don't go away. . . ."

I waited until he had left the room, then sank down on the sofa in a boneless heap. I didn't want to think about anything beyond tonight, and yet Cole's own words were a bittersweet reminder that very soon I would have to go away—back to L.A. and my old routine, my job and my apartment. Glancing about, I found it strangely difficult to remember how my own living room looked. I sighed and leaned back against the cushions. Perhaps not so strange. Compared to the present, everything else was vague and insubstantial, like shadow patterns dancing on the ceiling.

When Cole returned a few minutes later, the tension in his voice belied the warm smile he gave me.

"Sorry to take so long, but I left some unfinished business on the coast this morning. I thought it could wait until next week, but Joe needs my decision by tomorrow."

"I hope everything's all right."

Cole shrugged, slouched down on the cushions beside me and stretched his long legs in front of him. "I don't like the pressure of having to make a big decision so fast, but I can't do much about it. Garth Bennett isn't the kind of man who likes to be kept waiting."

I shifted sideways to face him. "Garth Bennett—the producer?"

He nodded and said as if it were the most commonplace thing in the world, "Garth wants me to compose the musical score for a movie he's filming over in Ireland."

For a moment, I could only stare in open-mouthed amazement. Then I managed a stunned, "Cole, that's marvelous!"

"It is, and it isn't. When Garth first contacted me a couple of months ago, he only wanted me to write the title song. There's a big difference between that and the entire score. If I say yes, I'll have to fly to Dublin to screen the rushes and work with the crew."

"Dublin?" I swallowed and kept my voice light. "When would you have to go?"

"Ideally, a week from Monday. Two weeks from now at the latest."

"Oh."

"The crew will be through filming soon," he went on, "and Garth wants me to get a feel for the location. Apparently, the musical score is an integral part of the story, with a special love theme as a recurring motif."

I smiled and tried to shove aside the dismal prospect of Cole being thousands of miles away. "It sounds wonderful. And the chance to work with a producer like Garth Bennett is a once in a lifetime opportunity."

Cole ran a hand through his dark hair. "Don't remind me. Joe was ready to skin me alive when I walked out of the meeting this morning without giving Garth a definite answer."

I felt a guilty twinge, realizing for the first time how much he had risked to fly back to me today. "Cole, I'm sorry. . . ."

"Don't be!" He reached for my hand and gave it a squeeze. "Even if I hadn't wanted to get back to you, I couldn't have given Garth my decision. I'm still not sure."

"Why? Don't you want to do it?"

"Want to? I'm dying to do it! Composing film scores has been a dream of mine for years, but there are other things to consider. Especially the timing."

"I suppose changing your concerts and schedule would be rather complicated."

Cole shrugged this aside. "I'm not worried about the schedule. Joe can handle all that." He leaned forward, his eyes intent on my face. "The problem is, I don't know if I can handle being thousands of miles away from you."

My heart jumped a beat, and I glanced down in confusion. "But how can you say no to something this big? Especially when it's something you've always wanted to do?"

"There are lots of things I want to do," he answered softly, turning my face up to meet his. "It's all a matter of priorities."

Several kisses later, wrapped close within his arms, I could afford to be noble and unselfish. "Cole, I don't want you to give up a chance like this because of . . . well, because of. . . ."

"Us?" he filled in huskily.

I closed my eyes and nodded, loving the feel of his hand in my hair, his lips against my forehead.

"What do you think I should tell him?"

I lifted my head in surprise. "I can't make that decision for you."

"I know, but I'd still like your feelings on the matter."

I met his eyes without hesitation. "I think you should say yes."

Cole smiled a little. "Just like that?"

"You're perfect for the job!"

"I wish I shared your confidence. It's one thing to dream about composing film scores, but whether or not I can break out of the pop-rock mold is. . . ."

"Mold! No one could ever put your music in a mold, pop-rock or any other. I knew that when I heard you at the concert the other night. There's nothing wrong with the pop market, but your talent goes so far beyond it. Why limit yourself?"

Cole cleared his throat, then asked with a wry grin, "Excuse me, but is this really the same Megan Collier who told me just three days ago she wasn't very familiar with my music?"

I tried to cover my embarrassment with a laugh. "That was three days ago."

He leaned back to look at me, the warmth in his eyes like a blue flame burning in the heart of the fire. "You know, you're very beautiful—especially when you blush."

"I'm not blushing. It's . . . the firelight."

"Liar," he chuckled softly and pulled me close again. "You've got me curious," he confided after another lingering kiss. "When have you had a chance to listen to my music since the concert?"

"Last night. I was working on the review and thought it'd be helpful to hear some of your songs again. Kathy and Brent loaned me your record albums."

Cole drew back a little, his amused expression shifting to wariness. "Which ones?"

"All of them."

"All of them? Even. . . ."

"'Rough Around the Edges' and 'Cole Country,'" I finished with a teasing smile. "They're not that bad!" I said as he groaned and put a hand to his head. "Besides, you weren't responsible for 'Cole Country.' Most of the songs were written by someone else."

"How'd you know that?"

"I read the credits on the album sleeve."

Cole's glance held warm approval. "I have to hand it to you. You do your homework." Then he shook his head and stared at the fire. "I still hate thinking about that time in my life. My agent was determined to make me the latest country-western sex symbol and had total control over my career. Hank planned my schedule, chose all my songs, my clothes—he even wanted me to change my name."

"Good heavens, why?"

"He thought Cole McLean sounded too ordinary. He wanted something with more flash, more style."

"Such as. . . ?"

"Are you ready for this?" Cole's voice was as dry as his smile. "Cole Black," he pronounced with a grimace.

I couldn't keep from laughing and even he had to chuckle.

"I'm serious! He loved it. Good old Hank had everything planned right down to the last detail—skin-tight black pants and a slinky black shirt, topped off by a black cowboy hat and a whip."

"The whip was a nice touch," I said, still laughing.

Cole laughed, too, then his gaze became thoughtful. "It sounds funny now, but it's frightening how an 'image' can change your life if you let it—how you can start living and believing the words to songs. I told myself I was happy, but I'd never been more miserable in my life. Most of my songs were worthless junk, and I was constantly under pressure to make the lyrics more suggestive and sexually-oriented. When I objected, Hank reminded me I didn't have to like the rules, but I'd better play the game if I wanted to get to the top. I was young and green, and I wanted to get to the top, so I kept on playing the game, according to Hank's rules."

"Did you ever consider. . .well, getting a different agent?"

Cole nodded heavily. "Several times. If he hadn't been Shirleen's brother, I. . . ." He caught himself mid-sentence and stood up abruptly to get more wood for the fire. "Sorry. I didn't mean to bore you with my whole life story."

"You're not boring me." I watched his short, tense movements as he tossed a log on the fire, then asked what I felt must be true. "Was Shirleen your wife?"

Cole poked at the log a moment longer than necessary before giving me an assenting nod. His exasperated. "This is a hell of a time to bring up my ex-wife," was directed more to himself than me.

"Was that really her name—Shirleen?"

The tightness around his mouth relaxed at my exaggerated "country" pronunciation. "Yes. Why?"

I shrugged. "I don't know. Somehow, it's hard to imagine you falling in love with a person named Shirleen."

In spite of his laugh, the cattiness of my remark seemed to hang in the air between us.

"I'm sorry. That was a stupid thing to say."

"It's okay. There've been plenty of times when I wondered the same thing." His voice was light, but there was a bitter twist to his smile as he shoved the screen back in place and left the fire. Sitting down, Cole pulled his sweater over his head, then laid it across the arm of the couch. "I suppose we could always change the subject."

It should have been a simple thing to agree with him and dismiss the prickly subject of Cole's ex-wife along with the rest of his past. Somehow, I couldn't do it. Not when there was something I desperately needed to know. Glancing down, I ran my fingers along the ribbed edge of a cushion and said as if it didn't matter at all, "Do you still love her?"

"No. That died a long time ago." The flat finality in his voice lifted an oppressive weight from my heart, and I suddenly felt pounds lighter. "If I'd met Shirleen now, instead of five years ago, I probably wouldn't give her a second glance, but that's beside the point." Cole lifted an ankle across his knee and absently brushed the toe of his boot. "In some ways, what happened was as much my fault as hers. Shirleen was in love with an image—the image of me that her brother created. If I hadn't been so caught up in my own success, I might have realized it sooner, but. . . ."

"Caught up in your own success? Somehow, that's hard for me to believe."

"You didn't know me five years ago," he answered bluntly. "It wasn't that I had a big ego problem, but success came so fast and my life changed so suddenly that I . . .well, I sort of lost track of the things that really matter. Friends. My family." Cole leaned his dark head against the russet cushions and stared into the crackling flames. "Up until the night Hank Folsom heard me singing in a two-bit country-western joint outside of Denver, music was just a pleasant hobby, something I did for myself. I only took the job at the club because I needed some extra cash to finish my graduate studies at CSU."

My chin nearly dropped in my lap. "Graduate studies?"

Cole grinned and explained, "I was two quarters away from a masters' degree in mining engineering when Hank told me he thought 'Rough Around the Edges' could be a hit. He talked me into cutting a promo tape for him and took it back to Nashville. Three months later, Hank was my manager, and I was on the road singing 'Rough Around the Edges' at county fairs and rodeos all over the country."

I took this in with an amazed sigh. "What about your degree? Did you ever regret quitting school?"

"Not really. I went into mining engineering mostly to please my dad, and it only took a few weeks on the road to realize music was my real love." He smiled, remembering. "That first year was incredible—getting a band together, cutting my first album, seeing the country."

"When did you meet Shirleen?"

"She was a back-up singer for the band. Nothing much

happened between us for a few months. I asked her out a couple of times, and she made a point of letting me know she wasn't interested. Then, when my career started warming up, so did she." He made a derisive sound and added, "We were married almost a year before I woke up to the fact that it was the idea of being Mrs. Cole McLean she was in love with—not to mention the money. The signs were there all along, but I was too crazy about her to pay any attention to them."

"What kind of signs?" I asked, watching the bitter memories play across his face.

"Her attitude toward my music, for one. I had nothing against country-western, but there were other songs inside me—other kinds of music I wanted to write. . . ." His voice trailed off and for a moment, his eyes had the far-off look of a dreamer. "Those feelings, when the music comes . . . it's hard to put into words."

"You don't have to," I said quietly, realizing all over again that Cole McLean was no ordinary man. "I think I know what you mean."

"Shirleen never did. Neither did Hank. Whenever I wrote something that didn't fit his prescribed formula for a hit country-western tune, he'd give it a flat thumb's down, and Shirleen always sided with him. Why argue with success? she'd tell me. My first two albums went gold, and the concerts were sell-outs. Why jeopardize all that over a bout of artistic temperament? If that argument didn't work, she had other tactics and ways of getting me to give in. . . ." Cole left the sentence hanging and rubbed the back of his neck.

My imagination filled in the rest. "She must have been very beautiful," I said coldly.

He nodded and cleared his throat.

"Long blonde hair?"

"How did you know?"

"I didn't. It just goes with the name."

Cole's mouth parted in a slow smile, and the pleased lift in his voice sent hot color spreading up my neck. "Megan, are you jealous?"

"Of course not!"

His warm glance held mine until I relented with a careless

shrug, "Well, not really." When the corners of his mouth lifted in that sensuous curve, I gave up the struggle and said crossly, "I don't know whether you'd call it jealousy or not, but I can think of a few tactics I'd like to use on that selfish, manipulative little. . . ."

There wasn't the slightest taint of the past in the bruising kiss he gave me. My mouth yielded to the hard possessiveness of his, my arms went around his neck, and soon there was no past—only the present and the warm satisfaction of knowing I was the one he wanted, not Shirleen.

"Mmmm, this is much better," Cole said, slipping an arm under my legs and lifting me easily across his lap. "Talking about my ex-wife is bad enough, but having you halfway across the room is pure torture."

I smiled and kissed the corners of his mouth, my interest in Shirleen fading into the shadows. "You don't have to tell me about her. . . ."

Cole pressed my head against his shoulder and held me close, not saying anything for a few moments. Then he drew in a long breath and released it with a kind of finality, as if some decision had been made. "I want you to know," he said quietly. "It's better that you do. Ever since the divorce there've been all kinds of wild rumors about what supposedly happened—everything from me abandoning her to having affairs with women I've never met."

He was silent for so long that I felt I had to ask, "What did happen?"

"Something very natural. And wonderful. At least, I thought so," he amended with a bitter sigh. "Shirleen got pregnant. It was a surprise to both of us, but I was thrilled to death. Shirleen wanted an abortion. She thought a baby would interfere with our lifestyle, and she didn't want to miss any of the concert tours. According to her, the timing was all wrong. Maybe in a few years, we could think about having a child, but she wasn't ready yet for that kind of responsibility. I tried to reason with her, let her know how I felt, but nothing I said changed her mind." He took a short breath, and I could feel the tenseness in the muscles of his chest. "It was strange, listening to her talk about it. She looked the same, her voice was the same, but in her eyes I saw a total stranger—someone I didn't know at all."

I put my hand over his and held it tightly. "What finally changed her mind?"

"Money." He spat out the word in disgust, then told me, "The night before she was scheduled to have the abortion, we got into another argument. I finally blew up and told her if she didn't want our child, our marriage was over. She didn't believe me. When I started packing, she got a scared look in her eyes, but even then, I think she expected me to turn around and come back."

"Did you?"

He shook his head. "I spent the night in a hotel and got totally smashed. She found me the next day and said she'd changed her mind—that if the baby meant that much to me, she'd go through with the pregnancy. Then she went into this bleeding-heart routine about how much she loved me and couldn't stand to lose me. When I looked in her eyes, I knew the only thing she was worried about losing was her meal ticket.

"Everything went from bad to worse after that—my drinking, our fights, the problems with Hank. I didn't realize how much my drinking had gotten out of hand until the night I decided to play chicken with a freight train."

"Cole. . . ." I shuddered involuntarily, and his arms tightened around me.

"I was lucky," he admitted frankly. "It could have been all over. Instead, I hit a chuckhole, lost control of the car and ended up in a ditch a few yards from the tracks. I was pinned in the wreck for over an hour before anyone found me. That, plus two weeks in the hospital, gave me a lot of time to think about what I'd been doing to my life. I quit drinking and told Shirleen I wanted to make our marriage work. Then I fired Hank and told him I was going to write my songs my way or not at all."

I lifted my head to look at him, amazed at his frankness and honesty—even more amazed that he wanted me to know about this part of his life. "How did Shirleen react?" I asked quietly. "Especially when you fired her brother."

"Well, my accident shook her up pretty bad and for awhile things were a lot better between us—until she found out I'd fired Hank. Among other things, she gave me several first-class lectures about how I was nothing before I met Hank and that I'd be nothing without him. To top things off, the record company I was with tore up my contract. That didn't worry me too much until I started talking to some other companies and found out good old Hank had been passing the word around that I was unreliable and demanding too much money."

"Cole, that's so unfair! What did you do?"

"There wasn't a thing I could do, except look for a new manager and wait it out. I'd bought this property the year before, so I talked Shirleen into coming to Colorado with me. I thought it would help our marriage if we got away from Hank and all the pressures and had some time alone."

I could understand his reasoning. I could also imagine Shirleen's reaction. A spoiled young woman, used to luxuries and nightlife, suddenly moving to the mountains of Colorado.

Cole's words confirmed my thoughts. "Shirleen felt as trapped living my kind of life as I had been trying to live hers. We didn't want the same things. I don't think we ever did. And after Cody was born, she was more restless than ever. She hated the baby's demands on her time, and she resented my love for him. In March, when Cody was almost two months old, I flew to L.A. to meet with Joe Reynolds. When I got back, she was gone."

What he said neither shocked nor surprised me. Especially when I remembered Cody's painfully matter-of-fact statement this afternoon: "My mom went away when I was a baby. She didn't like me."

"Shirleen left Cody with Wes and Twila," Cole went on, "along with a letter for me. In it, she said she'd given me more than enough time to come to my senses—that it wasn't fair she should be chained to a loser the rest of her life. Hank had lined up some work for her back in Nashville, and she wanted the chance to make something of her life, no matter what I did with mine. She knew I'd understand it was all for the best and told me her lawyer would be in touch with me about the divorce."

I struggled to keep the rising anger out of my voice. "What about Cody? Didn't she say anything about him?"

"Only that he was my mistake, and she wanted a fresh start on her own. Believe me, I was more than happy to make sure she got one! Other than the Colorado property and custody rights, I gave her everything else. I wasn't about to take the chance of Shirleen changing her mind where Cody was concerned."

I frowned at the thought, my anger suddenly replaced by gnawing worry. "Has she ever tried to see him?"

Cole nodded. "About a month after our divorce was final, my album 'Rhythms of Life' was released, and my career took a big upswing. It wasn't long before I got a phone call from Shirleen telling me how glad she was about my so-called come-back. She asked if we couldn't get together sometime. Then she started to cry and said how much she regretted leaving and knew we could make it this time."

"Cole, you didn't see her. . . ?"

"I wasn't about to make the same mistake twice," he said emphatically. "She tried a few more times, even initiated a lawsuit against me. . . ."

"Shirleen sued you! What on earth for?"

Cole smiled at my indignation and pressed a kiss into my palm. "Because I refused to grant her any visitation rights."

"What happened?"

"Before the case got to court, Shirleen latched onto a new 'wonder boy' Hank was grooming and got married again. The case was quietly dropped, and I haven't heard from her since."

He fell silent, and we both stared at the fire's orange glow.

"What an empty, wasted life she must have," I said. "In a lot of ways, Shirleen reminds me of my. . . ." I caught myself in time and inserted quickly, "I'm glad she can't hurt you and Cody any more."

Cole's eyes were intent on my face. "What were you going to say? Who does Shirleen remind you of?"

"It doesn't matter."

"I think it does."

I shrugged out of his arms and sat up, feeling a familiar tightness in my throat. "Look, I . . . I'd rather not talk about it."

"Are you sure?"

Cole's face became a blur in the firelight as hot tears stung my eyelids, then slipped down my cheeks before I could blink them back.

"Megan . . . I'm sorry. I didn't mean to upset you."

"I know. It's not your fault. "It's just. . . ." My voice broke on the words.

"Hey, it's okay. You don't have to tell me." Cole's arms came around me in a gentle embrace. "Just remember, whenever you're ready to talk about it, I'll be there to listen."

I nodded against his shoulder, silently accepting the assurance of his words and arms. Past hurts faded away as I breathed in the warmth of his nearness. Beneath my palm, the beat of his heart was relaxed and steady. Very slowly, I reached up to kiss the curve of his jawline.

"Thank you."

His arms tightened around me. "Any time."

"I guess I ought to be going. . . ."

Cole's lips moved softly against my forehead. "Not yet. . . ."

Sometime later, a log broke in two and a hissing shower of sparks stirred the drowsy silence. Cole breathed a contented sigh and beneath the black curve of his lashes, one eye opened a small slit. "I guess I ought to put another log on the fire."

I sighed and snuggled closer in his arms. "Not yet. . . ."

DRIFTING BETWEEN DREAMS and wakefulness, I had the unshakeable impression I was being watched. The feeling grew stronger, driving sleep away. My heavy eyelids opened. At first, all I saw were a pair of blue eyes, wide and curious, staring into mine. Then a childish face, framed with black curls, came into focus.

"Daddy said not to wake you up," Cody whispered.

I blinked and stared at him in bleary-eyed confusion, then lifted my head, amazed to see a ray of sunlight spilling its gold across the gray stones of the fireplace. The last thing I remembered was lying in Cole's arms in the dying firelight. Raising myself on one elbow, I discovered a soft woolly blanket had been tucked around me. I smiled, stretched, then sniffed the air.

"What is that . . . odd smell?"

"Daddy's cookin' breakfast," Cody informed me, wrinkling up his nose. "But he's not very good at it."

I laughed and sat up. "Will you show me where the bathroom is? Then I think we'd better go help your dad."

Cody grinned and hopped up on the couch beside me. "First I need my 'huggers.'"

"Your what?"

Fastening both arms around my neck, he gave me a fierce little squeeze, then kissed my cheek. "Daddy says we got to have 'huggers' every morning."

I kissed his black curls and held him close. "Your daddy's right."

We entered the kitchen a few minutes later, to find Cole

standing barefoot beside the stove, staring at the contents of a frying pan with abject concentration. A blue-gray shirt hung unbuttoned outside his Levis, and his black hair was still damp from showering. I made a useless gesture to smooth my sleep-wrinkled clothes and decided it wasn't fair. No one had the right to look that good in the morning.

Cole glanced up and skipping the preliminary good-mornings, turned to me with the desperation of a drowning man. "Don't even pretend to be polite. Just tell me you know how to cook!"

I laughed, my self-consciousness forgotten. The burnt offerings on the stove demanded immediate attention, but the sight of him dictated a different course of action. Slipping my arms through his unbuttoned shirt, I wrapped them around his warm, bare back and said, "Help is on the way—but first, I need my 'huggers'!"

Even without the interruption, breakfast was beyond saving. We ended up having cold cereal and juice, which suited me perfectly. I was more than content just sharing smiles across the table.

Cody had already eaten breakfast with the Randolphs, but he downed a glass of juice and sat on a high-legged stool, nibbling a piece of toast. From the looks he gave us, I'm sure Cody thought grown-ups were a strange breed, especially when they laughed over nothing and let their bowls of "Captain Crunch" get all soggy.

For no particular reason, the lovesick couple at the Sunday concert in Aspen suddenly came to mind. Just one week ago, I had sat behind them, scarcely hiding my contempt at their simple displays of affection and secretly envying the love which had shone in their eyes. Now, I was ten times worse. I smiled into my glass of orange juice and offered the two a belated, but heartfelt apology.

"Do you have any plans for today?" Cole asked me.

"No. Nothing special."

"How would you like to take a ride this morning? On Sundays, Cody and I usually drive down to Georgetown and spend the day with my folks."

"That sounds wonderful. I'd love to go!"

His hand covered mine. "Good. I know they'll enjoy meeting you."

"I want to go for a horseback ride!" Cody interjected.

"Well, son, that might have to wait. . . ."

"But Dad! You said today was my turn!"

"Your turn?" I questioned, smiling at Cody's indignant little scowl.

"Never mind. It doesn't matter," Cole put in, motioning for the boy to be quiet.

Cody ignored his father and proceeded to explain, "Last night was Dad's turn, so I had to stay with Aunt Twila. Now it's my turn."

"Your turn for what?"

Cody grinned and pointed a finger at me. "To be with you! Dad said we were puh-sosed to share."

Cole groaned and put a hand to his head. "Look, it . . . uh, loses something in the translation."

"It sounds like a perfectly reasonable arrangement," I said, thoroughly enjoying the ruddy color tinging his tanned cheeks. "Only when is it going to be my turn?"

Cody looked stricken. "Dad! We forgot Megan's turn!"

"I'll take care of that right now," his father answered with a look that made my pulses leap. "Close your eyes, Cody."

"Why?"

"Because I feel like getting mushy with the cookie-lady."

"Yuck," said Cody and covered his eyes.

Cody was still grumbling about his horseback ride as we got in the truck and headed for the "Mollie Kathleen" so I could change for the trip to Georgetown. Cole must have used every persuasive art known to parents trying to mollify the boy, but all his reasoning and pleadings had no effect.

"If you're a good boy, we can stop in Central City for an ice cream cone," Cole said, using bribery as a last resort. "Would you like that?"

Cody scowled and slouched farther down in his car seat.

"I'll bet they have your favorite kind," Cole added in a tempting tone. "Chunky fish with peanut-butter topping!"

The boy's mouth twitched a little, but he remained stubbornly silent.

"Cody just loves 'chunky fish' ice cream," Cole told me with a wink. "It's his favorite."

"It is not!" Cody said, starting to giggle. "I like banilla."

Cole turned the truck up the gravel road leading to the cabins, and gave the boy an incredulous look. "Plain old ba-nilla?"

Cody grinned and nodded, his good humor restored. "Can I have a sugar cone?"

"Sure, kid."

"Then can we go for a horseback ride?"

I laughed and said, "That'll teach you to bribe your son."

Cole didn't answer. He had slowed the truck to a crawl and was staring at something in the trees to our left. "That's strange."

"What?"

"That dark blue Lincoln parked next to the 'Baby Doe.'" He braked to a complete stop, and I looked past him to see a late-model sedan parked beside the third cabin.

"I saw the red Camaro parked there last Friday," I commented. "Didn't Kurt and Lenny go to the Red Rocks concert?"

Cole's only answer was a tight frown as he turned the truck up the narrow driveway. "I'd better find out what's going on." He switched off the engine and opened the door. "Want to come?" As I slid out after him, he told Cody, "You stay put, son. This won't take long."

Ignoring the boy's protests, Cole took my hand and headed up the gravel pathway leading to the cabin's covered porch. Our footsteps sounded unnaturally loud in the morning stillness, and for some unexplainable reason, I found myself wanting to tiptoe. A small movement caught my eye and I glanced up to see the curtains in an upstairs window pulled shut by an unseen hand.

Cole saw it, too. "Somebody's home," he said and stepped onto the porch.

It must have been nearly a full minute before his firm knock was answered. When the door opened, it was Kurt Gorman's hearty voice and smile which greeted us.

"Cole! Megan! Sorry to keep you waiting, but I wasn't

dressed," he explained, fumbling with the buttons on his shirt.

Cole's answering smile was cordial but lacked Gorman's effusive warmth. "And I'm sorry to disturb you on a Sunday morning, but we were driving by and noticed a strange car in the driveway. I thought I'd better stop and make sure everything was all right."

Gorman paled a little, and his smile tightened to a forced grin. "Everything's fine . . . fine. Sid took the Camaro into Denver Friday night on some business, and it developed engine trouble, so we had to replace it with something more reliable."

"Is Sid back?" Cole asked.

"Uh . . . no, he stayed over in Denver with the band. The boys are always a little high after a concert," Kurt added with a false laugh. "Is there anything I can do for you?"

"There's a matter concerning Obolus that I need to discuss with Sid. When do you expect him back?"

"Sometime today. I really can't say when, but I'll have him call you as soon as he returns."

"Megan and I will be gone most of the day," Cole told him, pausing to consider the matter. "Since Sid's not here, I guess I'd better make you aware of the problem."

Gorman straightened up with sudden alertness. "Problem?"

"Yes. May we come in?"

For a moment, I thought he was going to refuse, then he opened the door and stood aside.

Coming from the bright sunlit morning, the cabin's plush living room was nearly dark. All the drapes were tightly closed and a pall of tobacco smoke hung heavy in the air.

"I apologize for the mess," Gorman said, quickly gathering up some papers scattered on a low coffee table, along with a wine bottle and two glasses. "I left the concert early with a migraine and thought I'd catch up on some work."

I swallowed a cough as Cole and I sat down on the couch, noticing that the ashtray on the lamp table beside me, was filled to overflowing.

Kurt Gorman removed a magazine from the cushion of a plaid loveseat, casually tossed it onto the coffee table, then sat down. "Now then, what seems to be the problem?"

"When we first discussed Obolus coming to Lodestone, you and Sid went to some trouble to assure me that certain aspects of the band's reputation were founded on rumor and media hype," Cole began.

Gorman nodded. "That's right. We did."

Without noticeably turning my head, I let my glance slide down to the coffee table where a gleam of silver shone from beneath a corner of the magazine. In my mind, I saw scarlet nails flicking open a silver cigarette case, and Max Barrett's elegant white hands. Shifting position on the couch, I took a casual second glance at the ashtray. Now that my eyes had adjusted to the room's dim light, the lipstick stains on many of the stubbed-out butts were clearly visible.

I looked back at Gorman's face, suddenly understanding why he had been so reluctant to invite us in.

"What're you getting at?" he was saying to Cole, his practiced smile not quite reaching those cool gray eyes.

"I want to know if you're aware of the band's involvement with the occult—Satan worship, to be exact."

Gorman's smile stiffened, and his eyes shifted to my face. The next moment he was in control again, casually crossing his legs and saying with an amused chuckle, "Obviously, you've been talking with Miss Collier. I tried to explain to her that this whole bloody business is nothing more than a gimmick, an advertising ploy. Frankly, I'm a little surprised—and disappointed—that she'd waste your time with it."

I kept silent and stared straight at Gorman, feeling the hot lick of anger inside me.

"The business is a lot bloodier than you might think," Cole told him, with a hard edge to his voice. "Friday night, Obolus held some kind of satanic ritual on my property. I don't consider that a gimmick, and I don't like it."

"Satanic ritual?" Gorman's face was as amazed as his voice. "I don't know what you're talking about."

"If you'd been with me, you could have seen your boys in action," I put in. "I was on my balcony a little after midnight when I heard some chanting in the woods and. . . ."

"Chanting in the woods?" Gorman repeated, his voice heavy with sarcasm. "If I'd thought our little discussion at dinner was going to have such a dramatic effect on you. . . ." He broke off to shake his head, then turned to Cole. "Forgive me, if this sounds rude, but I'd advise you to think very carefully before giving credence to Miss Collier's imaginings about some—some mythical ritual."

Cole got to his feet and said very quietly, "And I'd advise you and Sid to drop by my office in the lodge tomorrow morning. I have a tape recording of that 'mythical ritual' which you should find very informative."

Gorman's jaw went slack, and it took him a moment to find his voice. "A . . . a tape? What tape?" He tried to sound indignant, but it didn't work. The panic in his eyes was clearly visible.

"Let's go, Megan." Cole took my hand and ushered me to the door. "Tomorrow morning — 10:00," he said over his shoulder, then shut the door behind us.

Walking down the path to the truck, Cole swore under his breath. "Gorman's known about Obolus and this Satan business all along. I wonder how many other things he's been lying about."

"The migraine for one."

"What?" Cole stopped beside the truck to stare at me.

"Gorman may have left the concert early, but I doubt a headache had anything to do with it. I don't know if you noticed that silver cigarette case he conveniently covered with a magazine, but it belongs to Max Barrett. And there were lipstick stains on a lot of the cigarette butts in the ashtray."

Cole frowned and leaned against the truck's front fender. "I don't get it. So what if he and the Barrett woman have a thing going? Why lie about it? What the hell do I care who he sees and why?"

"I don't know. Maybe he thought it wouldn't look good, especially since Max supposedly flew in from the coast to cover Obolus' concert, not their record producer."

Cole absently rubbed his mustache and agreed. "I can see what you're saying, but it still seems. . . ."

"Hey, Dad! Let's go! I want my ice cream cone!" Cody yelled from the front seat.

"At least he's forgotten about the horseback ride," Cole

said under his breath and opened the truck door. "One 'chunky fish' ice cream cone coming up!"

I must have set some kind of record getting ready—at least for me. In a scant twelve minutes, I did my make-up and hair, slipped on a light summer skirt and blouse, then blissfully turned my back on the disaster area upstairs. By ten-forty-five, we were on our way.

The morning was ripe with August sunshine and brilliant blue skies. It didn't matter that a warm wind out of the south and puffy cumulus clouds mushrooming over the mountains promised rain. Let the rain come, I thought, as Cole's hand closed firmly over my knee. Today was a gift, and I wasn't going to spoil it by thinking of anything beyond this moment.

We had been on the road a little over an hour when the gentle motion of the ride combined with soft music on the radio, took its toll on Cody. I watched out of the corner of my eye as his head nodded, then his eyelids drooped. Soon he was sound asleep, chin on his chest, his small body completely relaxed.

"Poor little guy," Cole said softly, observing his son with a tender smile. "Twila told me he was up at the crack of dawn, raring to go for his big day with the cookie-lady."

I touched the boy's soft cheek, my thoughts wandering back to Cole's disturbing revelations of last night. How could Shirleen leave him? Just walk away and casually abandon a two-month-old infant to pursue her own selfish interests? I had been part of Cody's smiling existence for only a short time, but already he had added a rich store of love to my life. Simple joys that his own mother would never know or experience—making dandelion chains, rolling out dough for sugar cookies, sharing 'huggers' in the morning.

"He's so perfect," I said. "Does it ever amaze you that he's yours?"

Cole's eyes left the road to briefly touch mine, then glance at his son once more. "It scares me sometimes, how much I love him. Especially when I think how close I came to not having him at all. When Cody was a baby, I used to go into his room at night just to make sure he was still breathing."

I leaned my shoulder against his in silent understanding. He smiled at me and began humming along with a song on the radio. Almost as if it had a will of its own, my left hand moved to rest on his firmly-muscled thigh.

Moments later, the barking voice of a disc jockey intruded on our quiet intimacy. Cole reached across me to switch off the interruption, when the sound of Obolus' name stopped him short.

"A dream come true has turned into a nightmare for a Denver teenager. Police suspect foul play, but as of this hour, there are no leads in the bizarre disappearance of a teenage girl from a rock concert. Fifteen-year-old Julie Bellis was one of six local teenagers to win free tickets to the Obolus concert held last night. As one of the winners in the contest sponsored by radio station KVHK, Miss Bellis and her date were driven to the concert by chauffered limousine and promised a personal interview with band members after the show.

According to witnesses, Miss Bellis was last seen leaving the amphitheater early in the concert with a middle-aged white male allegedly posing as a security guard. Members of Obolus were unavailable for comment concerning the. . . ."

Cole gave the radio dial a quick, hard twist, cutting off the announcer's strident voice. "Those guys attract trouble the way rotten meat attracts flies," he muttered. "I don't know if I can wait until Tuesday to get rid of them."

I nodded and stared at the sunlit road ahead of us, not sure if I should give voice to the nagging thought on my mind.

"What is it, Babe?"

I released a tight breath and met his concerned look. "You don't suppose there's any connection, do you?"

"Connection?"

"Between Obolus and the kidnapping."

Cole's dark brows narrowed in a frown. "What makes you think there might be?"

"I don't know. Maybe I'm just being overly suspicious, but the whole thing sounds like a set-up, with the radio contest and everything."

"It could have been, but Obolus wouldn't have anything to do with the contest. The radio station and contest promoters would be the ones to organize and sponsor that."

"Oh."

Cole put an arm around my shoulders and pulled me close against his side. "Hey, after what you saw on Friday night, you have every right to be suspicious. To tell you the truth, I've had it up to here with Obolus and this whole mess, but there isn't a thing I can do about it until we get the results of those blood tests."

"I know."

"What do you say we tune out the world for a while?" he suggested, turning his head to give me a quick kiss. "Right now, the only thing that matters to me is being with you."

I relaxed against him with a sigh, daring to kiss the tanned smoothness of his neck, his jaw, then the corner of his mouth. "It frightens me. . . ."

Cole's arm tightened around me. "There's no need to be. I won't let them hurt you."

"Not Obolus."

"What then?"

I leaned my head on his shoulder and whispered, "Being so happy."

17

CLOISTERED IN A high mountain valley, Georgetown was a haven of Victorian homes and lusty relics of the old mining days when the little town had reigned as one of Colorado's "silver queens." Because of its sheltered location, a hundred feet or more below the freeway, I had driven right past the town earlier in the week, completely unaware of its nineteenth century charms.

Light and shadow chased each other across the pine-covered slopes above the town and gray clouds were boiling through the mountain passes as Cole turned the truck onto Georgetown's historic Main Street. Driving past the white columns of the post office and antique store fronts, spatters of rain were already pelting the dusty ground, causing tourists to cover their heads and scramble for shelter inside one of the shops.

Cole left Main Street to take a steep side-road and in scarcely more than a block's distance, we were out of the business section and into a residential area of well-kept homes.

"I can't believe this! I feel like we've lost an entire century somewhere between here and the freeway," I told him, glancing about with delighted eyes at steep Mansard roofs, quaint carpenter's lace and widow's walks with wrought-iron fencing.

"After dinner, I'll give you a proper tour of the place," Cole promised. "This storm shouldn't last long."

As if to dispute his statement, the rain began in earnest with a violent rush of wind and sudden clap of thunder. Cody awoke with a startled cry, and I quickly unsnapped his seat belt, lifted him out of his car-seat and onto my lap.

"It's all right. It's only thunder."

Another deafening boom rumbled above us, and Cody covered his ears. "I don't like thunder!"

Cole turned left, off a hilly side-street and parked the truck in front of a small, two-story house set back from the road in a secluded cover of trees and bushes. "Tell Megan whose house this is," he said, ruffling the boy's curls.

Cody lifted his head off my shoulder long enough to peer through the rain and mumble, "Grandma's house," then burrowed against my shoulder once more.

"It's like a storybook house," I said, taking in the old-fashioned porch, long windows and intricate woodwork. The narrow lap-siding was painted a light green and the steep-sided roof was brick-red. "Did you really grow up here?"

Cole touched my cheek, his glance teasing. "Red Ridinghood lived right down the street, and the three little pigs are over on the next block."

Cody's head lifted, and his blue eyes were half-believing. "They did?"

Cole laughed and took the boy off my lap. "Come on. We're going to have to make a run for it, or we'll get soaked."

The rain came down in a pounding fury that afternoon, but my senses were tuned to gentler things—the gravelly sound of Alex McLean's voice muttering an unintelligible blessing on the food, the warm pressure of Cole's hand finding mine under the table, the heavenly smell of roast lamb. I found myself storing up all the sounds, smells and images of that Sunday dinner, much the way a squirrel hoards nuts and seeds for the coming winter.

The dinner itself was a feast for the eye as well as the palate. In addition to the lamb, there were new potatoes with thin red skins, buttered asparagus, hot rolls with homemade raspberry jam and a dish of tangy mustard pickles. My compliments on the meal drew a smile and modest "thank you" from Cole's mother, and Alex McLean was quick to tell me, "Good cooking is a tradition in Mary's family. Her grandmother used to run a boarding house over in Black Hawk, and its reputation for hospitality was known for miles around. Folks used to say you could always count on getting a good hot meal at Mrs. Clark's place, whether you had money or not." Alex McLean's blue-gray eyes were a mirror of Cole's as he winked at me and added, "And if you were Irish, you could sit at the table!"

I suspect my Irish ancestry may have had something to do with Cole's father's inimitable brand of hospitality, because he teased and flattered me quite shamelessly throughout the meal. Whenever she thought her husband had gone too far, Mary McLean would insert a cautioning, "Now, Alex. . . ," which he cheerfully ignored.

Once he told her with a grin that made his craggy face appear almost boyish, "Don't be worryin' yourself, Mary-darlin'. You should know by now that the more I like someone, the more I enjoy teasin' 'em a bit."

At the end of the meal, Cole's father rose from his place at the head of the table and moved to his wife's chair. Bending down in a gesture that struck me as almost courtly, he kissed her on the mouth and said, "That was a fine meal, Mrs. McLean."

The woman's brown eyes glowed at his praise. The look of open affection between them made me glance down at my plate, touched and a little embarrassed with the realization that this man and woman loved each other. More than that, they were still in love with each other.

Cole put an arm about my shoulders and glanced out the dining room window at the drizzling rain. "I guess my guided tour of Georgetown will have to wait awhile."

"That's all right. It'll give me time to help your mother with the dishes."

Cole got up and pulled back my chair for me. "In that case, if you don't mind, I think I'll lie down for a few minutes."

I touched a hand to his face. "Of course I don't mind. You look tired."

Cole leaned his cheek into my palm and for a moment, I forgot we weren't alone in the room. Then Cody tugged at his father's hand and asked, "Can I go outside? I want to catch worms on the sidewalk."

"Not now," his grandmother instructed with quiet firmness. "Your father's tired. You go read the 'funny papers' with your grandpa."

Five minutes later, Cole was sound asleep on the floral

couch in the living room, one arm across his face, the other hanging down over the side. Cody was on his grandfather's lap in a big armchair, listening to Alex McLean's lilting rendition of the Sunday comics.

I stood for a few seconds, a glass of mustard pickles in one hand and the butter plate in the other, memorizing the scene in my mind and wishing this moment, no—this feeling of quiet belonging—could last forever.

Cole's mother accepted my help in the kitchen with a smile and the simple instructions, "The butter goes in that cupboard there on your left, and you can put the rest of those pickles back in the jar."

I did as she asked, thinking Mary McLean's kitchen was a cheerful place to be on a rainy afternoon. Painted yellow cupboards stretched as high as the ceiling and the counter-tops beneath were inlaid octagons of green, white and yellow tile. The single enamel sink had no garbage disposal, and the metal faucets above it came directly out of the wall. I smiled as Cole's mother reached down to get two dishpans from under the sink, thinking I hadn't seen one like it since I left my grandmother's house. Glancing around, the refrigerator and an old gas stove appeared to be the only modern appliances in the room. I knew very well that Cole's income could have purchased a dozen dish-washers and microwave ovens if his mother had wanted them. And somehow, I doubted whether it was pride which prompted the refusal of such modern conveniences. The more we talked, the more I came to realize that Mary McLean was perfectly content with her home the way it was. She needed nothing more.

Once the dishes were washed, dried and put away, Cole's mother satisfied my interest and curiosity by taking me on a quick tour of her home. My pleasure in the polished, hardwood floors and Victorian fixtures brought a smile of pride to her lovely face.

"This home used to belong to my parents. When my father died, Alex and I moved in to help take care of Mother. Cole was born here, and except for a few years during the war, I've never lived anywhere else." She paused in the doorway of a small bedroom so I could enter. "This is Cole's room," she said.

The furnishings were attractive, but simple—a dresser and chest made of dark pine, a large oval rug in forest green, and an old iron bed covered with a spotless white chenille bedspread. Hanging above the bed was a painting of two white stallions, their manes flying against a stormy sky.

Cole's mother followed my gaze. "Ever since I can remember, he's been crazy about horses. Seems like that's all he wanted and dreamed about when he was a boy. Of course, living here, there was no way we could get him one," she added wistfully.

I touched her shoulder as we left the room. "Sometimes, dreams have to wait."

She smiled at me. "Sometimes they do."

The master bedroom had wonderful carved woodwork around the door and windows and an antique bedroom set of rich, dark walnut. But what intrigued me most was a framed black and white photograph sitting atop a high bureau. The radiant faces of a handsome young man in uniform and a slim young woman in a flowered blouse smiled back at me. The man's resemblance to Cole was striking—wavy black hair, strong jaw and broad shoulders.

"That picture was taken the day Alex and I got married," Mary McLean told me, a soft smile on her lips. "That was forty-three years ago next month."

I looked into her still beautiful face, amazed at the love I saw shining in her eyes. "Forty-three years. . . ."

She nodded and took the photograph from its place on the dresser top to dust the glass with her apron. "My parents weren't too pleased when I told them Alex McLean wanted to marry me. Now, I can understand why. It was wartime and my dad was ill and out of work. They barely had enough to live on and couldn't afford to give me a nice wedding. Mother begged me to wait awhile, but Alex and I couldn't stand the thought of being apart. He only had a few days leave, you see, before he was transferred." She sighed, then smiled. "I didn't care about having a fancy wedding, or even a wedding dress. So I bought myself a new blouse and a purse and thought I was the luckiest girl in the world. Mother and Dad invited a few friends over and had a nice little wedding breakfast for us here at the house. I remember telling them not to worry because it wasn't fancier. I was Mrs. Alex McLean—and that's all I needed to be happy." She rubbed an imaginary speck of dust from the corner of the frame before placing it back on the bureau. "It still is," she told the young Alex softly.

A lump came into my throat which refused to be swallowed. Mary McLean turned to see the liquid brightness shimmering in my eyes and put both arms around me.

"I'm so glad Cole brought you to meet us," she said. "I can't remember when I've seen him so happy."

Later that afternoon, the rain stopped, and Cole and I walked down into the town with Cody riding atop his father's shoulders. Occasionally, I caught someone doing a well-timed double-take as we wandered through the stores, but for the most part, Cole enjoyed the same anonymity of any other tourist.

Cole insisted on buying me a glittering speciman of iron pyrite with a miniature pewter miner on top, and Cody proudly presented me with a plush mouse dressed in a gingham apron and cap. "She's not purple, but you can still call her Gwendolyn," he said.

The hours passed too quickly. Shadows were long across the lawn as we walked back to Cole's parents' home in the green-gold light of late afternoon. Cole waved to a few residents who were sitting on their porches, enjoying the rain-fresh air, but the little town seemed half-asleep, dreaming in the mellow light. Into the stillness came the sweet, sad whistle of a train, and I stopped to listen.

"There's a song in that sound—music from the past," Cole said, "but I've never been able to capture it. I can't count the times I used to sit down by Clear Creek and listen to that train. The wind would carry its whistle for miles along the canyon."

"It's a lonely sound," I said as the whistle came again, sounding farther away.

The spell of the past was broken when Cody started to squirm from his perch atop Cole's broad shoulders. "Dad, I need to go potty!"

Cole laughed and swung the little boy down to the ground.

"We're almost to Grandma's house. You better run on ahead."

Cody needed no further urging to take off down the street at a dead run.

"Watchin' that boy of yours is like seein' you a few years back, young Alex," came a thin, raspy voice.

Cole and I turned together to see an elderly man easing his bony frame onto the porch steps of a white-frame house to our right.

"I'd say more than a few years," Cole replied with a smile. "How're you doing, Eskel?"

"Well, considering my age and my habits, not too bad," the old man answered, striking a match on the stone steps and putting it to the pipe clamped firmly between his lips. After drawing deeply, Eskel gave Cole a sly wink and nodded in my direction. "I can see I don't need to ask how you're doin'. It's real nice to see you and your missus."

Cole grinned and put an arm around my waist, not bothering to correct the man's mistaken assumption. "It's nice to see you, too, Eskel. Take care now."

We continued down the street, and I was sure my face must be as red as the petunias growing in Eskel's flower garden. "Why did he call you 'young Alex'?" I asked, hoping to divert Cole's attention from my embarrassment. "I didn't realize Cole was a 'professional' name."

"My full name is Alex Coletti McLean," he told me. "Alex after my father and Coletti. . . ." He paused to open the wrought-iron gate to his parents' yard, then said, "There's an interesting story behind that name. If you ask Dad, I know he'd love to tell you about it."

I did just that as Cole and I were sitting around the kitchen table with his parents, enjoying fresh-baked apple pie and ice cream. Cody had made short work of his dessert and was outside in the cool twilight, happily hunting bugs.

"Now that's a story worth retelling," Alex McLean pronounced, setting his fork beside his plate.

"I think it's dreadful," Mary put in with a shudder.

"That it is, Mary-darlin', but it's a story to be remembered all the same." Alex stared out the kitchen window, lost in memories for a long moment, then glanced at me. "I was a lad of nine or ten when my dad was shift boss at a mine near Silver Plume. One of the men under him was a young Italian named Alphonso Guisseppe Coletti. Dad never could pronounce his name right," he added with a chuckle, "so he just called him Al. Most everybody did. Dad cared a lot about his men, and even though Al Coletti was only a 'mucker,' they got to be real good friends."

Cole saw my puzzled look and put a hand on his father's shoulder. "Before you go on, maybe you'd better explain to Megan what a 'mucker' is."

His father nodded and told me, "Muckers were the men who did all the shoveling—usually around ten cars per day. Mining was a 24-hour operation, you see, and it was back-breaking work. The only thing lower than a mucker was a 'carman'—they were the ones who pushed the cars full of ore. Anyhow, Coletti was a hard worker, and it wasn't long before the big boss moved him up to bein' a miner. A miner's job was to drill holes, then set the charges," he explained. "And at the end of the shift, he'd do the blasting."

"That sounds awfully dangerous."

"Everything about mining was dangerous," Cole's father told me with a grim nod. "Besides the blasting, there was always the risk of cave-ins and bad air. And the sulfide ores formed sulfuric acid that'd eat the clothes right off the men's backs. Al never worried about all that. He was a devil-may-care sort of fellow. Danger or no, he always had a smile on his face and a joke to tell." Alex smiled to himself, remembering. "Al used to come by our house real regular after his shift, and I never got tired of listening to his stories. In my eyes, Al Coletti was the nearest thing to a hero that I ever expected to meet. He used to win drilling contests with his double-jack. Nobody else could match him. One time, he came over to show us the double eagle $20 gold piece he'd won. I remember him tellin' my dad that someday, when he had a son, it'd give the boy something to brag about. A boy needs to be able to brag about his dad, he used to say. Not too long after that, Al dropped by to tell us he was getting married. Bein' the young scamp that I was, I couldn't understand what he was so happy about, and I was real embarrassed when he kissed me and my dad on both cheeks and said, if he was ever lucky enough to have a fine son like me, would Dad mind if he named him Alex." Cole's father drew a long breath and stared into his coffee cup. "Two weeks later, Al drilled into a missed hole—one with the dynamite stick still in it. The explosion blew his hands off and both his eyes out. I'll never forget the night Dad came home from the mine and told Mother what had happened. He said there was blood all over the walls where poor Al was feelin' around with those bloody stumps, tryin' to find his way out." Alex McLean shook his head, as if to rid his mind of the gruesome image, then straightened his big shoulders.

"The whole town went to Al's funeral, and the foreman shut the mines down that day. That was when I found out he had no family to speak of, only an aunt on on his mother's side. His father's line of the family died with him. That didn't seem right to me, especially when I remembered how much Al had wanted a son of his own. Walkin' home from the funeral, I told my folks that Al Coletti's name wasn't going to die out—that someday, when I had a son, I'd give him that name." Alex McLean gave Cole a fond glance, then quickly gulped down the rest of his coffee.

"That's enough of sad stories," Mary put in briskly. "Cole, you haven't sung a song for me yet."

Cole frowned at his watch. "I'm sorry, Mom, but it's getting late. We won't be back to Lodestone until after nine, if we leave right now."

"You're not going anywhere until I hear a song. Five minutes won't make that much difference, one way or the other."

Nearly an hour later, Mary McLean reluctantly agreed we ought to be on our way. My throat was aching as I hugged Cole's parents good-bye, and it took concentrated effort to keep smiling, especially when Cole embraced his mother and said, "I'll see you next week, before I leave for Ireland."

Earlier in the day, when Cole had told his parents about Garth Bishop's proposal, I had shared in their pride and excitement. Now, the mere mention of it was a painful reminder that my meager part in Cole's life was rapidly nearing an end.

The drive back to Lodestone was a silent one. Making light conversation was a chore my emotions couldn't handle, yet anything more serious was totally out of the question. It was past ten and fully dark by the time Cole took the forested road leading to his hilltop home. Cody had slept most of the way, but the cold air roused him as Cole carried him from the truck to the house.

"Where are we?" he mumbled, lifting his head off his father's shoulder.

"We're home, Tiger."

"Where's Megan?"

"I'm right here."

Inside the house, Cole switched on the hall light, then turned to me. "I won't be long. Just make yourself comfortable."

"Do you mind if I put Cody to bed? I . . . I'll probably be gone before he wakes up in the morning and. . . ."

There was no need to say more. In fact, it was the first time either of us had made actual reference to my leaving.

Cole handed me his son without a word, and the little boy's arms immediately tightened around my neck.

"I don't want you to go!"

"I told you Megan had to leave, son. You know that," Cole said brusquely and walked away.

There was a bittersweet feeling of déjà vu as I carried the child upstairs and helped him undress for bed. The ache in my throat grew worse when I tucked the bedcovers around him and looked into his sleepy blue eyes.

"Can you tell me a story?" he asked with a yawn.

"A made-up story," I said softly.

Cody nodded. "'Bout the purple mouse."

I gathered him in my arms with a stifled sob, needing to hold his warm little body against me one last time.

Cody drifted off to sleep long before Gwendolyn encountered any danger from the "hunkle-dunkle," but I lingered by his bedside for several minutes, watching his peaceful sleep with silent tears running down my face. Finally, I turned off the beside lamp and softly shut the door behind me.

Before going downstairs, I slipped into the bathroom to

bathe my eyes with a cold washcloth. I sniffed and stared at my red-eyed reflection, berating myself for ever letting down the barriers. Why did caring have to hurt so much? It would have been better if I'd never met Cole McLean. I threw the washcloth down in angry frustration and left the room.

The soft strains of a guitar led me through the dark house to the family room. My anger melted away as I paused outside the open doorway to listen. I'll never understand why certain harmonies evoke such a deep emotional response in me. I only know that although I was hearing the haunting strains for the first time, it was as if my heart had always known and loved the melody.

Edging forward, I saw Cole sitting on the stone hearth, his dark head bent in rapt concentration, with the tawny blend of flame and shadow playing across his face. I'd made no sound, but he must have sensed my presence, because his fingers suddenly paused on the strings, then he glanced up.

"Please, don't stop. That's beautiful."

Cole's eyes followed me across the room. "You've been gone so long—is everything all right?"

"Cody wanted a story," I answered, trying to keep my voice light. I was about to sit down on the couch when Cole gestured to a large pillow near his feet.

"Come sit by me."

I did as he asked, feeling a hard, fast pulse begin to beat in my throat. "I love that melody you were playing. Is it the love theme for the movie?"

He smiled a little and strummed a few chords. "No. I guess I should have been working on that, but . . . last night, I was watching you sleep and the words just started coming. . . ."

The pulse in my throat beat faster as Cole's eyes touched mine in the firelight. Then he began to sing. . . .

"My love is like a shadow song
　　half-remembered in the dusk
But there's no one here to listen
　　Arms to hold me, eyes that trust.

Will you ever hear the music,
    see the pain behind the smile?
Will you ever let me touch you,
    taste the kiss and stay awhile.

Must our love remain a shadow song,
    chasing dreams that die at dawn
Never knowing, or becoming,
    while the heartache lingers on. . . ."

The night kept its silence for a long moment. Then, Cole lifted the guitar strap over his head and laid the instrument down beside the hearth. "It needs another verse, but I'm not sure how to end it."

"I love it—I love you!"

Saying the words aloud was terrifying and wonderful. So wonderful I had to tell him again. Then his arms reached out, and our faces touched and words were no longer necessary.

The release of love inside me was like a floodgate yielding to the rushing torrents of spring after a long, frozen winter. Holding him, kissing him, I felt as if I were drowning in a warm, dark well of happiness.

Rational thought didn't exist until Cole raised his head and asked, "How does Ireland sound for a honeymoon?"

I stared at him in total amazement. "Honeymoon?"

He pressed a gentle kiss on my lips. "I love you, Megan. I need you with me."

"But Cole. . . ."

"Look, I know things have happened pretty fast."

I nodded breathlessly and sat up. "So fast, I can't believe this is real. I . . . I've tried so hard not to let it happen. . . ."

"Why?" Cole raised himself on one elbow and looked at me. "Why shouldn't we fall in love?"

"Because. . . ." I shook my head helplessly and blurted out, "Because loving someone hurts too much!"

Cole was silent for a moment. "I know someone's hurt you. I've known it since we met. The day of the accident, when I saw you standing by the road with Cody in your arms and tears in your eyes—there was a sadness in you, something that reached out to me." He touched my cheek and asked softly, "Who hurt you, Megan? Who was he?"

"Not he . . . my mother."

Cole stared at me, comprehension gradually replacing the stunned expression on his face. "Your mother's the one you were talking about last night," he said finally. "The one like Shirleen."

I nodded and glanced away to watch the shuddering flames.

"Do you want to talk about it?"

"I don't know if I can. I've tried before, and all I do is cry."

Cole took a handkerchief from his pocket and placed it in my lap. "There's nothing wrong with crying," he said, giving my hand a gentle squeeze.

Strangely enough, I didn't cry. Cole's handkerchief remained wadded up in my clenched hands, as it all spilled out—the burden of hurt and resentment I'd carried over half my life. Even before their divorce, my parents had taught me that love was a selfish emotion, demanding constant gratification, always seeking to manipulate and control. Afterwards, I became a pawn each used to hurt the other. For two years, I was tossed back and forth between them, knowing all the while that neither one really wanted me. My father was caught up in his burgeoning law practice and only half-aware of my presence in his sterile apartment. Mother was always too busy trying to "find herself" to notice me. She tried a modeling career for a while, then painting, but nothing satisfied her for long. Her relationships with men were much the same. I remember coming home from school to find all the doors locked and a strange car in the driveway. Sometimes, there was a note on the screen telling me to go play with a friend for a few hours. Other times, she wasn't so discreet. Even now, the memories made me shudder.

I shrugged them away with a long sigh. "I promised myself that I'd never let anyone hurt me the way she did—that I wanted no part of marriage, or children or—or love."

Cole ran a hand along the rough stone of the hearth, then glanced up at me. "Do you still feel that way?"

When I didn't answer, he took hold of my shoulders and said, "Megan, you're not your mother!"

"I know . . . but, I'm still her daughter."

"And what's that supposed to mean? That selfishness is passed on through the genes like some damned birth defect? You can't believe that!"

"I don't know what to believe any more. Being with you and Cody, seeing your parents, it's all been so wonderful. . . ." I broke off and fought back the tears. "But I'm not sure if I can trust what I feel!"

Cole's arms pulled me close. "Megan, I love you! I don't want to be alone any more. I don't want either one of us to be alone. The thought of losing you scares the hell out of me."

My tears wet his cheeks, and our kiss was salty with the taste of them. "I don't want to lose you either."

"Then marry me!"

I pulled back to stare at him.

"Marry me," he repeated softly.

"Cole, it . . . it isn't that simple."

"Why not? We love each other. Cody adores you. Nothing would make him happier than to have you for his mother."

Cody's mother. The thought made my head spin.

"But — we need to be sure! For Cody's sake, we have to be, and that takes time."

"Time." Cole released me and shook his head. "You leave for L.A. in the morning, and I fly to Ireland next week. The idea of a long-distance romance doesn't appeal to me. What reason is there for waiting?"

"There are lots of reasons!" I felt more tears coming and angrily brushed them away with the back of my hand. "I don't know what to do about my job and . . . and my apartment. I just need some time to think. . . ."

Cole got to his feet and faced the dying flames. "How much time do you need?"

It seemed an eternity before I was able to tell him, "I don't know."

Another eternity passed away before he answered in a stranger's voice, "It's late. I'd better get you back to your cabin."

DARK GLASSES HID my swollen, red-rimmed eyes from the young man behind the counter of the car rental agency in Stapleton Airport. He gave me a pleasantly generic smile, along with several papers to sign, then made polite noises while I scribbled my signature on the various forms. Handing over the keys to the Audi, I felt hot tears suddenly fill my eyes. I dropped the keys on the counter, grabbed a tissue out of my purse and hurried down the concourse. This was ridiculous! It was only a stupid car. After last night and this morning, I was amazed I had any tears left.

Someone was calling my name. I swallowed a sob and turned around.

"Miss Collier! You forgot your luggage!" The young man had left his desk to come after me, his pleasant expression sharpening to concern when he saw my face. "Would you like me to get someone to help you with your bags?"

"No, thank you. I'll be fine." I hated polite lies, but sometimes they were easier than the truth.

After my baggage was checked in and my reservations taken care of, there was nothing else to do until departure time. I took a deep breath, trying to rid myself of the constant need to hurry which seemed to permeate the very walls of Stapleton Airport. Coming back to crowds and noise and confusion after the simple peace and beauty of the mountains was a definite culture shock.

I glanced at my watch with a sigh. Only 9:40. Since my plane wasn't scheduled to leave until 10:15, I had plenty of time to buy something to read.

It took nearly ten minutes to find a magazine shop in the

airport's huge mall, and I didn't dare allow myself more than half that time to browse. I bought a copy of the *Denver Post* and a paperback novel that looked as if it would require a minimal amount of brain cells to read, then started back down the concourse at a brisk walk.

My heart contracted in a painful jerk as a plump woman with a small, dark-haired boy in tow came hurrying toward me. The child's short-legged stride couldn't begin to match his mother's rapid pace and every time he lagged behind, the woman would yank him roughly by the arm and bark out the impatient command to, "Hurry up, or we'll be late!" The boy's mother noticed me staring at them, softened her tone to a threatening rumble, then pulled the child along even faster. In seconds, they were out of sight, melting into the autonomous mass of expensive-suited businessmen with attaches and the polyester-salesmen types who talked too loud and smiled too wide. I bit my lip and walked on.

There were only four other passengers waiting at Gate 52; two businessmen already in conference, an elderly woman engrossed in a steamy paperback, and a teenage boy plugged into his Sony Walkman. I chose a solitary seat near the window, placed my tote bag and purse on the empty chair beside mine to insure a small measure of privacy, and picked up the newspaper.

On the front page, a picture of an attractive teenage girl accompanied the headline, "Denver Teenager Feared Kidnapped." My eyes caught the name "Obolus" in the article below and I began reading with interest. The information was basically the same as that given in the radio announcement Cole and I had heard yesterday, except for some additional facts concerning the missing girl's parents, a Colonel and Mrs. Foster Bellis of Evergreen, Colorado. Colonel Bellis was presently engaged in a research project at the Fitzsimmons Army Hospital. A spokesman for the hospital declined any comment on the nature of the project, or whether there might be any connection between the kidnapping and Colonel Bellis' position at the hospital. Colonel Bellis would not say whether any ransom demands had been made.

I quickly scanned the rest of the article for further

information about Obolus, then turned to page A-7, where the story continued. Glancing over the sea of speckled newsprint, my grip tightened on the paper, and I drew a taut breath.

There he was. That bearded face. Those dark eyes. The broad nose. Above the photograph, a stark caption announced, "Station Manager Found Slain." I bent over the page, my mind reeling with the bloody facts. The nude, mutilated body of Ross Tedesco, age 38, was discovered late Sunday afternoon in a wooded ravine near Allenspark. Cause of death, pending an autopsy, multiple stab wounds. Tedesco, who had been missing since Tuesday, was being sought by police for alleged involvement in a cocaine ring operating around Denver. Denver police, in cooperation with the Boulder County Sheriff's Department, suspect the killing was drug-related.

I skimmed over the list of Ross Tedesco's business and civic accomplishments to focus on the brief information at the column's end: Survivors—wife, Mrs. Andrea M. Tedesco; daughters, Lisa, Amy. . . .

"Darling Andrea. . . ." The words penned in black ink suddenly swam before my eyes and dizzy waves of shock washed over me. "There are things I've never told you and hoped I would never have to tell you—parts of my life that aren't very pleasant. . . ."

My heart was pounding hard and fast as I stared at Ross' photograph once more. Very slowly, I covered the lower portion of his face with my hand, then slumped back against the seat. Dear God. Ross Tedesco was the man in the "Mollie Kathleen." I knew it as surely as I knew he had been the passenger in that red Camaro. In my mind, I saw him bounding carelessly down the stairs of the cabin, wiping his face with a towel. I heard his deep voice asking, "Are you ready to see the new me?"

The "new me. . . ." The beard! That's why I hadn't recognized him! My hands were clammy with perspiration as I reread parts of the article. My eyes riveted on the terse description: "cause of death, multiple stab wounds." Multiple stab wounds . . . the flash of a blade in the firelight . . . that strange, frightened whimper . . . Durant's hideous yell . . . .

I shut the newspaper with a violent shudder, trying to block out the nightmare images of four hooded shapes, moving in the firelight, offering dark prayers to Satan. I closed my eyes, but the images were still there—Derek Durant, leaping on the rock, his naked body drenched in blood, and the frenzy which followed.

Dear God, they killed him! Obolus killed Ross Tedesco!

The newspaper crumpled beneath my clenched fingers as I tried to control my racing, terrified thoughts. Cole! I had to tell him! Warn him! Fear constricted my breathing as I remembered his meeting this morning with Kurt Gorman and Obolus' manager. Obolus themselves might be there! The moment Cole played that tape, they would know. . . .

I shoved the newspaper into my tote bag, grabbed my purse and ran blindly down the concourse.

The phone rang eight times, but no one answered at Cole's home. I didn't have Wes and Twila's number, but thank God, Cole had given me the phone number of the lodge. I punched the numbers with shaking hands, and Kathy Watkins' pleasant voice answered after only the second ring.

"Kathy, this is Megan. I'm calling from the airport. Is Cole there? He's not? Do you know where you could find him? It's very important."

Her polite voice was apologetic. "I'm sorry. Cole had a meeting with Kurt Gorman and Obolus a little while ago, and I haven't seen him since then."

"Oh, Lord — no!"

"Megan? What's wrong? Can I help you with anything?"

"No! No, nothing. Kathy, could you get Brent for me?"

"Brent's not here. He . . . ."

"Then Ed Garrison! Tell him I have some important information that he. . . ."

"I'm sorry. Ed's driven into Boulder this morning, but I expect him back after. . . ."

I slammed the receiver down in frustration, whirled around and collided with the ample bosom and numerous packages of a middle-aged woman. The packages went flying, and so did a string of curses that would have curdled the blood of a sailor, but I didn't stop to help or apologize.

When I rushed back to his desk, the man at the car rental

agency was busy talking on the phone. I grabbed a few seconds to catch my breath, then demanded, "I need my car back! I . . . I've had a sudden change in plans."

Putting a hand over the mouthpiece, he smiled his generic smile and told me, "I'm sorry, Miss Collier, but the Audi you were driving has already been taken back for. . . ."

"Then get me something else! I don't care what, as long as it's fast!"

One eyebrow raised slightly. "If you'll wait just a moment, I'll be right with you."

"I don't have time to wait!" I reached into my purse and slapped two $20 bills on the desk in front of him. "Will this help cut through the red tape?"

His generic smile instantly became genuine. "Yes, ma'am!"

Five minutes later, I was zooming out of Stapleton Airport in a sleek black Porsche. The mid-morning traffic was fairly heavy, but once I hit the freeway outside of Denver, I was able to keep the speedometer up to 70 mph and over. I made Boulder in less than an hour. Soon, I was racing up the gray-walled canyon, passing cars and whipping around the winding turns as skillfully as any native.

As the miles sped by, snatches of conversation and small incidents, like puzzle pieces, began snapping into place. The red Camaro rented by Kurt Gorman was the car involved in the hit-and-run accident. I no longer had any doubts about that. Ross Tedesco and the blond-haired driver must have been on their way to Lodestone when the accident occurred. But why? I had no answers. Not even wild guesses. But in order for Ross to be hiding in the "Mollie Kathleen," he had to have known someone on the ranch. He didn't break in, which meant someone must have given him a key. And brought him food. It could have been one of the staff, a maid perhaps, but somehow, I doubted it. Especially when I remembered the tense look of worry on Kurt and Max's faces when Brent had told them about the intruder in the "Mollie Kathleen." Max had reacted strangely when I first mentioned that I was staying in one of the cabins. If she and Kurt were hiding Ross, it was little wonder. That would also explain why Ross' greeting had been so casual—until he saw me. But what connection did Ross Tedesco have with Kurt

Gorman and Obolus? Drugs? Thinking over the implications in his unfinished apology to Andrea, made that a definite possibility.

I gripped the steering wheel a little tighter, trying to remember whether I had put Ross' letter back inside the drawer, or left it on top of the desk. What if the maids came in to clean and discovered it? Or threw it away? I released a tense breath and pressed my foot down on the gas pedal.

I didn't dare let myself think about Cole or the fact Kathy Watkins hadn't seen him since the meeting with Obolus. He had to be safe. He had to be. . . .

At eleven-forty, I turned off the mountain highway to take the gravel road leading to Lodestone. Ron Weaver was surprised, but smiling when I skidded to a stop in front of the guardhouse.

I tried to fend off any questions with the hurried explanation, "I'm sorry to bother you, but I left some important papers in my cabin."

"It's no bother," Ron said, "but if you'd called, we could have. . . ."

"Have you seen Mr. McLean this morning?"

"No, ma'am, I haven't." The guard walked leisurely to the big gate and took out his keys. "Would you like me to call him for you or maybe someone at the lodge?"

I nodded quickly. "Yes, if you would. Tell Cole that I'm back and need to talk to him. It's very important."

"Will do."

I drummed my fingers on the steering wheel, mentally urging him to hurry. The moment Ron pushed the gate aside, I was through and gunning the Porsche up the gravel road.

Scant minutes later, I pulled into the parking area, squealed to a stop beside the dark blue Lincoln, then ran up the walkway to the lodge.

Inside, I found Kathy Watkins perched on a long-legged stool, engrossed in paperwork at the front desk. Her welcoming smile faded when she saw me.

"Megan, what. . . ?"

"Has Cole come back yet?"

"No, I. . . ."

"Then get someone to find him!"

Kathy's dark eyes widened with the beginnings of fear. "I will, but can't you tell me why. . . ?"

"It'll take too long to explain. Just get someone from security to find him. Please!"

She nodded and slid off the stool.

"Oh — before you go, could I have the keys to the 'Mollie Kathleen'? There's something . . . some important papers that I left in the desk."

Her troubled expression deepened as she reached into the desk drawer. "Megan, what's wrong?"

"I'll tell you later."

Snatching the keys out of her hand, I turned and ran across the expanse of hardwood floors to the front door. It opened just as I reached for the handle, and I suddenly found myself face to face with the tall Viking driver of the red Camaro. The man must have seen the shocked recognition in my eyes, because he looked me over with a curious smile.

"Hi, there. Have me met. . . ?"

From behind, I heard a clipped, cold voice. "Sid, could I talk to you for a few minutes?"

I half-turned, just enough to catch the angry glitter in Max Barrett's dark eyes as she strode toward us, then fled out of the lodge as if the devil himself were at my heels.

Backing out of the parking lot, I flung a hurried glance behind me, then sent the Porsche screaming up the gravel road to the cabins.

It couldn't have taken more than a few seconds, but it felt like an agony of hours that I stood on the porch, wrestling with the lock. I almost wept when it clicked, turned and finally gave way.

The letter was exactly where I had left it—in the bottom drawer of the desk, under the carbon paper. I quickly tucked it inside my handbag and hurried from the room.

Going down the stairs, I heard the angry roar of a car's engine and froze to listen. It was coming toward the cabin. I reached the open front door just in time to see the Lincoln pull into the driveway. One glimpse of the blond head behind the wheel was enough to send me racing for the back door.

Behind the cabin, a wooded hillside tumbled down some fifty yards or more in a steep tangle of pines, aspen and dense undergrowth. There was no path, but far below, through the sunlit flutter of leaves, I could see the safe haven of the lodge.

The going wasn't bad. Hanging onto branches and taking skittering side-steps, I was able to manage the steepness of the slope fairly well, but it would have been sheer foolishness to run. Halfway down, I heard an angry male shout from above. Sharp needles of fear shot through me, but I didn't pause or look back. In less than a minute, I was out of the trees and approaching some small service cabins. I flung a quick look over my shoulder, relieved to see no movement on the hillside. Other than the sharp chatter of a squirrel, there was no sound at all.

Once past the service cabins, my shaking legs were strengthened by a growing sense of security. I slowed my pace to a brisk walk and headed across the green expanse of lawn behind the lodge and recording studio. I had no sooner reached the wooden walkway between the two buildings when I heard a car moving down the gravel road at a high rate of speed. Fear came rushing back, and I froze on the walkway, fully expecting to see the blue Lincoln whip into the parking area. Instead it shot past, disappearing into the trees below the lodge.

As I stared at the cloud of dust slowly dissipating in the sunlight, four men exited the recording studio and headed toward the lodge. My breath caught in my throat. I wanted to turn and run, but I was suddenly too weak to move.

Intent on their own discussion, Obolus didn't notice me at first. Then Bruce Stoedter tossed a casual glance my way, tensed, and grabbed Derek Durant by the arm. Durant stopped. Conversation ceased as all four men turned to stare at me.

Standing there in the sunlight, my fears and vulnerability exposed to their gaze, I felt stripped and naked. Derek Durant's hooded eyes held mine in a malignant moment of communication that terrified me far more than his explosive temper. He knew. They all knew I had been the one to witness their secret ritual. More than just a ritual. I had witnessed and taped the murder of Ross Tedesco.

HOOFBEATS, CLATTERING OVER rough ground drew Obolus' attention away from me. Looking past them, I saw a horse and rider taking the gravel road into the parking area at full gallop. Derek Durant stared at the black-haired rider urging his sorrel stallion straight for us, then made a quick retreat toward the lodge. The others followed him without a word, and the threat of a confrontation disappeared as quickly as it had come.

I was alone on the walkway when Cole reined Malachite and leaped from the saddle to the ground. In less than a moment, his arms banished the blackness, his kiss erased the fear. Overwhelming relief and the unexpected sweetness of being in his arms again drove everything else from my mind.

"Thank God you came back," he muttered against my neck. "I drove over to the cabin this morning, but you'd already left. I've been half-crazy ever since. . . ."

I stiffened in his arms, realizing what he must be thinking, and not knowing what to say.

Cole felt my withdrawal and drew back to look at me. "Ron said you had something important to tell me," he began, a thread of uncertainty in his voice.

Seeing his rough, unshaven jaw and the bruised weariness around his eyes and mouth, made me feel even worse. I glanced down and said quietly, "I do—but it doesn't concern us."

Cole's arms dropped away from me. "Why did you come back?"

"I had to warn you. . . ."

"Warn me?"

"About Obolus!" I drew a short, tense breath. "They killed him. Obolus killed Ross Tedesco."

"What? Megan, what are you. . . ?"

"Ross was the man hiding in the 'Mollie Kathleen'! I didn't recognize him before because he'd shaved off his beard, but when I saw his picture in the paper, I knew where I'd seen him and what he'd said when I. . . ."

"Hold it, hold it! Just slow down a second. How do you know Ross was murdered?"

"The article's in this morning's paper. His body was found a few miles north of here, near Allenspark."

"My God," Cole uttered hoarsely. "Look, I can understand why you're upset, but that still doesn't mean. . . ."

"Ross died from multiple stab wounds," I said in a flat voice.

Cole's mouth tightened, and I could see a tense muscle working in his jaw. "Where's this article? Do you have it?"

"Yes, it's. . . ." I started to open my purse, then remembered. "The newspaper's in my tote bag. I must have left it in the car."

Cole glanced around the empty parking lot. "Where's your car?"

"At the cabin. I drove up to get Ross' letter and. . . ."

"What letter?"

My breath caught in my throat in a strangled gasp. "Oh, no! I nearly forgot! You've got to stop him!"

"Who?"

"Sid! He was the driver of the red Camaro!"

"Sid Rasmussen? Megan, do you realize what you're. . . ."

I nodded impatiently and went on in a rush. "Sid and Ross were on their way to Lodestone the day of the accident. I'm sure of it. And Sid knows I recognized him. That's why he came after me when I was at the cabin."

Cole frowned, struggling to take this in. "Sid came after you?"

"Yes! His car was blocking the driveway, so I had to come down the hillside instead. . . ." I stopped to draw a frustrated breath. "I know it must sound crazy, but you've got to believe me! You've got to stop him!"

"Sid passed me on the road when I was riding over here," Cole said. "The way he was burning rubber, he's probably long gone by now, but I'll check with Ron at the gate. Come on.''

He took my arm and turned toward the lodge, but I pulled back.

"I can't go in there!"

"Why not?"

"Obolus. . . ." I shuddered and shook my head. "You go ahead. I'll wait here."

Cole saw the fear in my eyes and said tersely, "I'll be right back."

After he had gone, I dropped down on the grass, not wanting to move or think and desperately wishing it was all a nightmare. Beside me, the stallion grazed contentedly, his teeth making short, cropping sounds as he pulled up the grass. The hot sun, beating down on my neck and back, affirmed what I already knew. This was no nightmare.

Cole returned moments later, a worried frown narrowing his brows. "Sid's gone. But Ron's going to try and get a license number on the Lincoln, then notify the Highway Patrol."

"I'm sorry—I should have told you about him right away."

"That's okay. He won't get far." Cole picked up Malachite's loose reins, then offered me his hand. "Come on. I'll give you a boost up."

"A . . . a boost?" I glanced uncertainly at Cole, then the massive stallion.

"You can ride with me up to the cabin," he said. "I want to see that newspaper article, then I want you to tell me everything you know—from the beginning."

Detectives Randall Goff and Don Burdick from the homicide squad of the Boulder County Sheriff's Department, arrived at Lodestone shortly before one o'clock.

Maybe it was his slick, emotionless smile or the patronizing greeting he gave Cole, but I took an instant dislike to Randall Goff. His looks were pleasing enough—light brown hair, a lean muscular build and an excellent tan. The man looked as if he would be more at home on the tennis court in white shorts and Vuarnettes than investigating a crime scene. Goff's mouth had a cocky smirk about it, even when he wasn't smiling, and his eyes were about as caring as cold, cut glass.

Don Burdick was probably around the same age as his partner, but a salt and pepper beard, plus an extra twenty or thirty pounds on his stocky frame made him appear much older. Like Goff, Detective Burdick was dressed in casual slacks, an open shirt and sportcoat. But instead of loafers, he wore a showy pair of cowboy boots. One pantleg was partially stuffed in the top of a boot, showing off the handsome leather.

As Cole ushered the two men into the lodge and made the necessary introductions, Burdick gave a simple nod, then stood, hands in his pockets, frankly admiring the buffalo head over the fireplace. Of the two, I secretly hoped Randall Goff's "take-charge" attitude was only that—an attitude. But minutes later, Goff instructed Burdick to investigate the site in the woods with Ed Garrison, then turned his patronizing smile my way.

It was nearly four o'clock by the time the two detectives completed their interrogations and investigation. At Randall Goff's request, Cole and I, along with Ed Garrison and Brent Watkins, met with them in the lodge office to discuss their findings. I knew exactly what Goff was going to say. I'd known from the moment he interviewed me with that detached, professional voice and that detached, professional stare.

After frowning at his notes for a suitable length of time, Randall Goff cleared his throat, then glanced up at Cole. "I want you to know, up front, that I appreciate your concern about the alleged events of the past few days, and I'm going to take all the legal steps available to me to follow through with this investigation. But I hope you can understand that right now, the only evidence we have of a crime taking place is purely circumstantial."

"There's nothing circumstantial about those blood stains in the woods," Garrison inserted gruffly.

"I'm aware of that, Mr. Garrison," the detective conceded with a tolerant sigh. "But until we have the results of those lab tests, the evidence is still circumstantial. For all we know, that could be chicken blood or goat blood on those rocks." Randall Goff turned his expressionless eyes on Cole once more. "As I said, I'm sorry, Mr. McLean, but with facts as they are—legally, there isn't a thing I can do for you. It might help to know that we have strong reason to believe Ross Tedesco's murder was drug-related. In fact, my men are questioning some viable suspects today."

Cole's only comment to this was a cold-eyed stare, and Randall Goff glanced down, fastidiously straightening his notes. "Naturally, I can understand why Miss Collier would be disturbed about certain similarities between Tedesco's death and the ritual she witnessed Friday night, but as yet, we have no proof that there's any connection between the two incidents. Detective Burdick and I questioned members of the band, and they admit to holding a. . . ." He paused as if searching for the proper terminology. ". . . a religious rite of some kind, but as you know, there's nothing illegal about that. And all four men deny knowing anything about Ross Tedesco, other than the fact he worked with their manager to set up the Red Rocks concert."

"What about Kurt Gorman and Max Barrett?" I broke in, trying to control my frustration. "Did they admit to knowing anything about Ross?"

The detective sighed again and thumbed through his notes. "According to Mr. Gorman's statement, neither he nor his brother have ever met Ross Tedesco. Ms. Barrett's statement is the same." Goff glanced up from his notes, that irritating smirk playing about his mouth. "I'm sorry, Miss Collier, but other than the letter you found, there is no physical evidence to support your claim that Ross Tedesco was on this property. And since the letter has no signature or date. . . ." He held up the piece of paper with a careless shrug. "It's really of little value."

"It wouldn't hurt to have a handwriting expert check it out," Don Burdick amended, taking the letter from his partner. "I'll take care of it," he said, giving me a nod.

"Thank you."

"Let's talk about Sid Rasmussen for a minute," Cole said. "And the fact he left the property in such a hurry after seeing Megan."

"Since Mr. Rasmussen wasn't available for questioning, there's very little to talk about," Goff countered. "According to Mr. Gorman, Sid Rasmussen had some legitimate business in Denver. His leaving the ranch had nothing to do with Miss Collier."

"Then why did he follow her up to the cabin?" Cole persisted.

Goff tapped an irritating rhythm on the desk with his pencil, but his voice was as nonplussed as ever. "Again, Mr. McLean, since Mr. Rasmussen wasn't here to answer any questions, I can't give you an answer. But we have no reason to suspect that...."

"That red Camaro is a damn good reason!" Cole told him heatedly.

"The highway patrol has been alerted about Rasmussen," Don Burdick told Cole. "They have a description of him and the vehicle. I'll let you know when they pick him up."

I leaned back against the couch, not wanting to speak or look at either detective. Goff gathered up his notes, and after giving Cole a polite string of meaningless assurances, promised he'd be in touch if there were any further developments. Feelings of frustration, anger and utter helplessness raged inside me as Brent ushered the two detectives from the office. Had I overreacted? Jumped to the wrong conclusions?

Ed Garrison rose from his chair, but Cole stopped him with a quiet, "Could you wait a minute, Ed? Detective Goff may be through with his investigation, but mine is just beginning."

Garrison sat back down, a pleased glint in his brown eyes. "What've you got in mind?"

"Starting now, I want Obolus placed under surveillance. Around the clock. But make sure your men keep things under cover. I've been threatened with enough lawsuits for one day."

Garrison nodded. "I think it'd be a good idea to have a guard outside the 'Mollie Kathleen' tonight and another man on your place."

I looked from the security man to Cole, my frustration disappearing in a flood of relief. "You mean — you still believe me?"

"Don't be an idiot. Of course, I believe you. Just because Goff's and Burdick's hands are tied up in legal red tape doesn't mean I have to sit back and do nothing." Turning to Garrison once more, he added, "Don't worry about having someone guard the 'Mollie Kathleen.' Megan will be staying at my place. I don't want her anywhere near Obolus."

My pulse rate suddenly skyrocketed, as Garrison agreed to this arrangement with a satisfied nod. "Sounds good. Anything else?"

Cole's expression was grim. "Yeah. Don't take any chances with those guys."

"No problem." Garrison's voice was completely self-assured. "It'll be just like the old days in L.A.," he said and left.

The rest of the afternoon dragged by. Twila brought over a casserole and a big chocolate cake for our dinner, then discreetly left. I managed to eat a little of the casserole, but couldn't touch the cake. I knew the letdown of tension, plus the fact that I'd spent more time crying than sleeping the night before, were largely to blame for my fatigue, but the awkward restraint and distance between Cole and me made things even worse. Thank heavens for Cody. He was overjoyed by my unexpected return, and his happy chatter filled in many an uncomfortable silence between his father and me. His only complaint was that I would be sleeping in the spare bedroom used by his grandparents, and not with him.

After dinner, Cole gave in to Cody's pleadings for a horseback ride, but insisted that I lie down and rest. They hadn't been gone five minutes when the doorbell chimed through the empty house. I dragged myself off the family room couch and hurried to the front door.

Kathy Watkins stood on the stone porch, a smile on her face and a paper sack in her arms. "Hi! I passed Cole on the way over here and he said you were resting, so I won't stay. But when Brent told me your luggage was somewhere between here and L.A., I thought you might enjoy having a change of clothes." She handed me the sack and declined my invitation to come in, adding with another smile, "I know we're not the same size, but I hope these will do—at least temporarily."

"Thank you. That's very thoughtful. I. . . ." My jaw dropped as I caught a glimpse of black lace and filmy black nylon beneath a teal blue sweater.

Kathy smiled demurely at my startled look. "Brent gave me that nightgown. With your hair and skin, I know you'll look gorgeous! Well, I'd better be going. Let me know if there's anything else you need."

"I . . . I will. And thanks again."

I shut the door and leaned against it, not sure whether to laugh or cry at Kathy's presumptive assessment of Cole's and my relationship.

By the time Cole and Cody returned from their horseback ride, I had showered and changed into the teal blue sweater. The cotton sweater, which would have been comfortably loose on Kathy Watkin's petite frame, clung to me with revealing snugness, but at least it was clean and a welcome change from the wrinkled blouse I had been wearing all day.

Cole's smile was openly admiring as we took Cody upstairs for his bath. "You ought to wear Kathy's clothes more often," he said. "You do a lot more for that sweater than she ever did."

I laughed, feeling the color rise in my cheeks. "I doubt Brent would agree with you on that point."

Some of the restraint disappeared as we got Cody ready for bed and took turns telling him bedtime stories. But when the little boy knelt down and leaned his dark head against my knee, I was at a loss to know what to do.

Cody didn't need or expect my help. In his own childish fashion, he rattled off a quick round of "thank you's," then asked God to bless his dad and all the horses and Uncle Wes and Aunt Twila. He paused a second, then added, "And please bless Megan, that she won't have to go away and leave me anymore. Amen."

I couldn't speak or say good-night. The ache in my throat was too tight, and the tears were too close. Cody hugged me, then his father and hopped into bed. Tucking the blankets around him, I was intensely aware of Cole's thoughtful silence as he stood behind me. After turning out the light, we left the room and Cole headed toward the stairs.

"It's been a long day," I said, pausing at the doorway of the room next to Cody's. "If you don't mind, I think I'll go to bed early."

Cole hesitated a moment, then turned and walked down the shadowy hallway without a word.

20

MOONLIGHT SPILLED ITS pale, milky glow across the big brass bed in the spare bedroom. Outside my window, a chorus of crickets squeaked their splintery serenade, while the rustle of the breeze added its soft music to the night. I turned over with a restless sigh, my thoughts haunted by the simple plea in Cody's prayer. What was wrong with me? Part of me ached to stay, to be part of his and Cole's life forever, yet still another part was terrified of making such a commitment. And so tonight, I had run away again, retreated to this prim, Victorian bedroom when I could have spent the rest of the evening with Cole.

I sat up with a moan and gave my pillow a merciless punch. Resting on top of a dresser near the bed, I could just make out the dark outline of the sack containing Kathy Watkins' black lace nightgown and peignoir. I almost smiled, thinking it was a far cry from the one I was wearing. In one of the bureau drawers, I'd found a simple, high-necked gown which I was fairly sure must belong to Cole's mother.

I punched my pillow a few more times, then lay back down, determined to put thoughts of Cole and black lace nightgowns firmly out of my mind. Ten minutes later, I got out of bed and picked up the sack. Where was the harm in just trying it on? No one would ever know. . . .

Standing in front of the mirror, I smiled at my reflection and decided Kathy was right. I did look gorgeous. The bodice, what there was of it, was sheer black lace held up by thin, nylon straps. The filmy skirt clung to my body's curves in silky black folds. I turned around in front of the mirror, idly wondering what Cole would do if I waltzed downstairs dressed like this, then put a hand to my middle, surprised by the deep, sensual ache I felt inside. I knew exactly what he'd do. And unless I wanted to confirm Kathy Watkin's suspicions, I'd better stay right where I was.

With a shaky sigh, I moved to the window and sank down on the cushioned bench beneath it, letting the night breeze cool my heated skin. I don't know how long I sat there, wrestling with my emotions and desires, but when the breeze grew chill, I turned out the light and got back into bed. It was going to be a long night.

The sound of men's voices and a harsh, metallic squeak roused me from a restless sleep, and I immediately stiffened in alertness. Someone was in the hallway outside my room. One of the husky whispers I recognized as Cole's, but the other was unfamiliar. The name "Obolus" had me out of bed in an instant and hurriedly wrapping the peignoir around me. I switched on a small lamp, then opened the door.

The arc of light fell across a heavy metal revolver on Ron Weaver's hip, as well as the sophisticated portable radio in his hand. Cole stood beside him, wearing a pair of Levis and nothing else.

I stepped toward the two men and asked in a tense whisper, "What's wrong?"

It was several seconds before either one answered. Following the direction of Cole's stunned expression, I began to realize why and wrapped the peignoir more closely around me.

Clearing his throat, he said, "We . . . uh, didn't mean to wake you."

"That's all right. I wasn't really asleep. Has something happened?"

"Not yet." Cole hesitated slightly before adding in a low tone, "Ed just radioed Ron that Obolus have left their cabins and are headed somewhere in the van."

Dark fear pressed upon my heart, and I took a steadying breath. "Where?"

Ron answered, "We don't know. Ed's keeping a safe distance behind them." Glancing at Cole, he added, "They ought to be reaching the fork in the meadow any time now."

Seconds later, Ed Garrison's husky voice came over the

radio. "Ron, this is Ed. Do you read?"

"I read you. Go ahead."

"Obolus have just taken the left fork, and they're headed your way. Does Cole know?"

"I'm right here." Cole took the walkie-talkie from the security guard and asked, "What do you think they're up to?"

"I don't know, but they're all dolled up in some black robes, and they're driving without lights. Doesn't look good. I've alerted Tom at the gate, and he's notifying the police."

"Where are they now?"

Tense seconds of silence followed Cole's question. Then Garrison's voice came across the radio, sounding more taut than before. "They've just passed Randolph's place. How do you want me to play this, Cole? Just give the word, and Ron and I will stop them right now."

Cole frowned and drew a long breath. Right then, unarmed and half-naked, he looked even more dangerous than the brawny security guard beside him. "Before you do anything, I want to find out what their game is," he answered grimly. "Let's give them enough rope to hang themselves."

"Don't take any chances," Garrison warned. "They could be armed."

Ron took back the radio and said, "I'll cover things here, but you better alert Tom to be ready for some back-up."

"I'll call him now. Over and out."

Cole looked at Ron. "Which door do you think they'll try?"

"Depends whether they split up or not," the guard answered, drawing his .357 magnum from its leather holster. "If I cover the stairs near the dining room, I'll be able to see them if they enter from the front or back doors."

Cole agreed and told him, "I'll grab my rifle and cover the upstairs in case they try to break through the door to the balcony."

Ron Weaver turned without another word and ran down the stairs, disappearing into the well of blackness below.

"Cole — please, be careful." My trembling voice betrayed the pounding fear inside me.

"I will." His arms reached out, pulling me against his bare chest, and there was nothing gentle in the kiss he gave me. "I want you to stay in Cody's room—and don't come out until I tell you!'' His mouth took mine once more, then he was running silently down the dark hall, leaving me even weaker than before.

After switching off the lamp in my room, I turned the knob to Cody's room and slipped inside. My bare feet moved noiselessly across the thick carpet to his bedside, where I stood, staring down at his small form under the bedcovers. The sound of his breathing was relaxed and even, totally unlike my own shallow breaths. Leaning down, I touched a hand to his dark curls, then tiptoed back to the door and leaned against it, listening.

Minutes passed and the only sounds were Cody's peaceful breathing and the frightened pounding of my heart. Then a slight movement and metallic click outside the door sent panic shooting through me.

''Megan?''

I put a hand to my breast and released a pent-up breath. ''Yes?''

''Stay put, Babe. They're coming.''

I swallowed the painful dryness in my throat and flattened my back against the door. Sometime later, it couldn't have been more than a minute or two, I heard a slight pushing sound, splintering wood, then furtive whispers. The flesh prickled on my arms and I knew they were in the house. I leaned closer to the edge of the door, every muscle in my body tensed to listen.

Cole's bedroom was through the wall from Cody's. I couldn't be sure, but I thought I heard movement there. Moments later, my ears caught the soft swish of their robes moving down the hall. I held my breath and bit down so hard on my lower lip, I could taste the blood.

All in the same moment, a sliver of light appeared under the door, there was a startled intake of breath, then Cole's voice booming like a rifle shot in the deathly silence.

''Hold it! Drop those knives and put your hands behind your heads! I said drop the knives!''

The soft thuds on the carpet which followed his words sent a sick chill through me, and my knees went weak.

''Ron! We've got company!'' he called down the stairs. Then, ''All right, downstairs! Keep those hands up, Durant!''

I waited a few seconds, until the shuffling footsteps had moved past Cody's room, then opened the door a small crack. Only a few feet away, four black-robed figures moved slowly toward the stairs. Cole stood near the head of the stairs, a rifle raised to his shoulder. Nick Bryson and Tony York had taken a step or two down when Durant gave Bruce Stoedter a sudden, violent shove. Cole jumped back, but not quickly enough to prevent Stoedter from charging straight into him like a wild animal. Head down and arms outstretched, he made a desperate grab for the rifle. Derek Durant seized the moment of confusion to lunge back down the hall, his black robes passing so close by my door I could have touched them. Like a giant bird of prey, Durant swooped down and plucked up one of the knives. In frozen horror, I saw his clawlike fingers clench the handle, blood-lust burning in his eyes. All Durant saw was Cole's bare back, now exposed to him, as he and Stoedter wrestled for the rifle. Durant's hideous yell joined my terrified scream as he ran for Cole. The next second, my ears were ringing from a thunderous report as Durant's body slammed into the wall, then crumpled on the floor, spatters of scarlet oozing from the front of his robe. Stoedter jerked around to see what had happened and got the butt of Cole's rifle across the side of his head. The rock star staggered and fell just as Ron Weaver reached the top of the stairs, gun in hand.

I started forward, then stopped, hearing Cody's frightened cry behind me. I ran back to his bedside and found the child sitting up in bed, eyes wide.

"I heard a boom."

"It's all right," I said, cradling him in my arms. "Everything's all right now."

Cody clung to me, fear still edging his voice. "Will you stay with me?"

I held him closer. "Yes, I'll stay."

The trust of a child is an amazing thing. All I had to do was lie down beside Cody, murmur some soft words of comfort, and in a few minutes he was sound asleep. For me, it wasn't that simple. Lying there in the darkness, my mind couldn't rid itself of the bloody scene in the hall. Again and again I saw Derek

Durant rushing toward Cole, blade raised, his face crazed with murderous hate. If Ron Weaver's aim or timing had been the least bit different, Cole might have been the one lying in a pool of blood.

I had nearly lost him. . . .

I shuddered with the realization and stared into the darkness, seeing things clearly for the first time.

A while later, I had no idea how long, the door to Cody's room opened a small crack, and Cole's husky whisper came through the blackness.

"Megan? Are you all right?"

"I'm fine."

"How's Cody?"

"Sound asleep," I whispered back.

"Could you come out in the hall a minute?"

I slowly lifted my arm from behind Cody's head and discovered he was lying on top of the peignoir. I had to slip both arms out of the sleeves in order to sit up, then Cody rolled over with a sigh—right on it. I got off the bed with a sigh of my own, forced to leave the robe behind.

The lights from downstairs diluted the darkness in the hallway and cast a dusky glow on Cole's naked arms and shoulders as he stood outside Cody's room.

"Are you all right?" My voice was scarcely more than a whisper.

He nodded slowly, and I felt a warm flutter inside as his eyes moved over me. I could have stayed in the shadows. Instead, I stepped toward him, my own gaze lingering on his bare chest with its dark cloud of hair, before lifting to his face.

We stood for a few seconds, not speaking or touching, then I went into his arms with a little cry.

"Cole . . . thank God you're all right! I was so frightened . . . when I saw him coming after you with the knife."

"Shhh, it's all right, Babe. It's over."

"Don't let go of me. . . ."

"I won't." His hands molded themselves around my back, my waist and my hips. "I won't. . . ."

Over his shoulder, I saw the dark shadow of blood on the

wall, and I had to know. "Durant — is he?"

Cole shook his head. "He's lost a lot of blood, but I think he'll make it. Ed and Ron have him and the others tied up in the study. The police will be here soon."

I stiffened with apprehension. "Will I have to talk to them?"

"Yes, but there's nothing to worry about. We've got a lot more than circumstantial evidence this time."

I shuddered and pressed myself against him. The warmth of his skin burned into mine where our bodies touched, and I suddenly found myself responding to his nearness in a way that had nothing to do with comfort or concern.

Pulling back a little, I murmured, "I . . . uh, guess I'd better change. I'm not exactly dressed to meet the Sheriff."

"So I noticed." Cole looked down at me with a smile that turned my emotions inside out, then fingered one of the nylon straps. "Do you mind telling me where this came from?"

"Kathy brought it over . . . along with the sweater."

Cole's hands curved around my bare shoulders. "Remind me to give Kathy a nice, fat raise," he said huskily, then bent his head to kiss the curve of my neck and throat.

I leaned against him with a sigh, lost in the dark rapture of his touch and my own throbbing desire.

"I'd better go," he said, his voice low and unsteady. "You're not the only one who's not dressed to meet the Sheriff." He kissed me once more and whispered, "I'll see you downstairs."

Alone in my room, I sat on the edge of the bed, shivering with joy and the quiet realization that my decision was made. I couldn't leave. Not now. Not ever. I loved him. I loved Cody. And nothing would ever change that.

Peace welled up inside me, spilling its warmth and sweet assurance into my soul. I smiled in the darkness and wiped away happy tears, knowing I had run away for the last time.

21

FOR THE NEXT few hours, my personal feelings had to be set aside in deference to more immediate police matters. Answering questions, giving statements, signing complaints—the whole procedure was getting to be so familiar, it almost seemed routine. How could violence ever be routine? Somehow, it didn't seem right that I should be able to recount tonight's horrifying events in such a calm, coherent way. That my voice should sound so normal. Even when I overheard Detective Burdick telling Cole that investigating officers had found cans of gasoline behind the house, I couldn't seem to feel anything. Was I really that callous? That hardened? Or had shock cushioned my mind from the ugliness of reality?

The answer came as I wearily climbed the stairs to check on Cody. In the hall at the top of the stairs, a cleaning woman was on her knees, scrubbing the blood stains out of the carpet. Seeing the bright streaks of red, a sick dizziness suddenly engulfed me, and I made a clumsy grab for the railing.

"Are you all right, Miss? Maybe I'd better get Mr. McLean!"

I hung on to the railing, as she hurried to my side. "No, don't bother him. I just need to lie down."

Leaning on her supporting arm, I made it into the bedroom and sank down on the bed.

The woman stood over me with worried eyes. "Are you sure you're all right? I still think I should get Mr. McLean."

"I'll be fine. I just need to rest for a few minutes. Thank you." I took some deep breaths and shut my eyes to stop the room from spinning.

By the time I felt able to go downstairs again, the cleaning woman had gone and so had the police. Lights and the sound of voices led me from the hallway to the living room where I found Cole talking with the Watkins and Ed Garrison.

"There's no way we're going to avoid all the publicity that's going to come from this," Brent was saying. "In fact, I wouldn't be surprised to see a camera crew outside the gates a few hours from now."

"Megan. . . ." Cole stood up as I entered the room and moved quickly to my side. "I thought you'd gone back to bed. Are you feeling all right?"

"Fine. Just a little shaky."

"Come sit down."

Seated close by his side, with a strong arm firmly around my shoulders, the last of the queasy weakness began to subside.

"I don't want any reporters allowed on the property," Cole went on in answer to Brent's comment. "Ed, you'll have to instruct your men, especially whoever's assigned to the gate, not to have any dialogue with the press. 'No comment' is going to have to be the rule of thumb. And that goes for the staff as well," he told Brent and Kathy. "The last thing I want is for some careless talk to damage the case against Obolus. And Kathy, the phone calls coming in will have to be screened. Unless it's my folks or one of my managers, I'm unavailable."

Kathy nodded as her husband leaned forward to ask, "What do you want me to tell the Gormans about tonight? You can bet Kurt'll be full of questions."

"I don't care what you tell him, just as long as he and Lenny are off the property by tomorrow night," Cole answered wearily. "Since Sid's taken off, you'll have to get in touch with someone from Obolus' road crew to come haul off their instruments and equipment. Is that Barrett woman still here?"

Brent shook his head. "Kurt drove her to the airport this afternoon, not long after the police left."

"Good. That's one less problem we have to deal with."

"It's all so incredible," Kathy murmured, pushing back her dark hair. "I still don't understand why — why they did it. . . ."

"The threat of exposure," Ed Garrison answered bluntly. "In some ways, Satanists are a lot like the Mafia. Complete secrecy is a vital part of their existence. When Obolus found out that

Megan had taped their ritual, she became an immediate threat. So did Cole. In Obolus' minds, the only way to prevent that exposure was to kill them and burn the evidence."

Kathy paled and leaned closer to her husband.

"They must have been crazy to even attempt it," Brent said angrily.

"Not crazy—desperate," Garrison told him. "And so high on 'coke' they thought they could get away with anything." In the silence which followed, he got to his feet. "I'd better be going."

Cole stood up and put a hand on the big man's shoulder. "Thanks again, Ed."

"Don't thank me. You and Weaver did all the work," he grunted. On his way out, Garrison added, "Just so you know, there'll be a man outside the house for the rest of the night."

Brent and Kathy left soon after, and Cole and I were finally alone in the house.

"Four o'clock," Cole sighed, glancing down at his watch. "I ought to be exhausted, but I don't think I could sleep a wink. How about you?"

"I've been running on nerves for hours."

"Are you hungry?"

Just the thought of food was enough to make me ill. "No, but I'll be glad to fix you something. We hardly touched Twila's chocolate cake at dinner."

Cole gave me a crooked grin as we walked toward the kitchen. "I hate to admit this—it seems sacrilegious or something—but a piece of cake and a tall glass of milk sounds great."

I smiled and kissed his cheek. "I'll get you some right now."

"Thanks, Babe."

Cole stretched out on the sofa in the family room while I took the cake out of the cupboard and a carton of milk from the refrigerator. The mundane tasks brought a much needed feeling of normality to a night which had been anything but that. Moving about the kitchen, looking in drawers for plates and utensils, I found myself wondering what it would be like if this were my kitchen . . . my home.

The thought took my breath away, and I stood staring at the milk carton in a daze. This was hardly the ideal time to tell

Cole about my decision. Common sense said I ought to wait, but my pounding heart and sweaty palms insisted otherwise.

Dishing out the cake, I tried to think what to say. How should I tell him? It wasn't very original, but maybe, "I love you and want to marry you more than anything else in the world," might not be a bad place to start.

I put the glass of milk and plate of chocolate cake on a small tray and carried them resolutely into the family room.

For someone who didn't think he could sleep a wink, Cole was doing a great imitation. I looked down at his weary face and closed eyes with a tender smile, then carried the tray of food back to the kitchen. It didn't really matter when I told him. From now on, all my time was his. . . .

A soft knocking roused me from a deep, dreamless sleep. I opened one eye to find Cole standing beside my bed.

"I'm sorry to wake you, Babe, but Detective Burdick just called. They've picked up Sid Rasmussen and want to know if you'll come down to the Sheriff's office to make a positive I.D."

I sat up with a start. "Where did they find him?"

"At the airport, around six this morning. Apparently, he gave the police quite a chase." Anticipation gleamed in his eyes as he bent down to kiss me. "Maybe now, we'll get some answers."

Cole and I walked up the cement steps to the Boulder County Sheriff's Department just before nine. By nine-fifteen, I had picked out the tall blond from a string of other men in the line-up.

"You're absolutely sure," Randall Goff questioned as we left the room.

I gave him a cold glance. "Absolutely."

"Have you had a chance to question Sid about Ross Tedesco?" Cole asked as we followed the detective to his desk.

Goff nodded and gestured for us to sit down. "Rasmussen's admitted to knowing Tedesco," he said, shoving back his chair.

"And?"

"All he'll say is that he was trying to do a favor for a friend. He denies knowing anything about Tedesco's drug connections, and he's even more adamant about the murder. Rasmussen claims he was in Denver Friday night."

"Do you believe him?" I asked.

Goff glanced at me and answered flatly, "Yes, but I haven't told him that. Rasmussen knows a lot more than he's telling, and I'm hoping a murder charge might provide the necessary incentive to get him to talk."

I breathed a small sigh, thinking Detective Randall Goff might be human after all.

"What about the lab tests on those blood samples?" Cole pursued. "Have you got the results yet?"

"They came in a few minutes ago." The detective picked up a yellow sheet of paper from the sea of colored forms on his desk. His face revealed nothing of his feelings as he told us, "The blood was human. B negative."

A sudden tightness gripping my chest made it difficult to breathe. "And Tedesco's blood? I assume you've checked that out."

Goff nodded again. "B negative."

Cole took my hand in a firm grip. "What about Obolus?" he asked the detective. "Do they know about the blood test?"

"They'll know soon enough," Goff said, straightening a stack of reports. "As yet, no formal charges have been filed against them. I have a few more details to work out before extradition papers are prepared."

Cole stared at him, anger blazing in his eyes. "Extradition papers? Are you telling me you let them go?"

"After bail is posted and paid, we have no choice." Goff reshuffled the already perfect stack of papers and avoided Cole's eyes. "Their lawyer flew in from L.A. not too long after they were booked. Obolus flew back to California in a private Lear jet around five this morning." The detective glanced up, saw Cole's face and made a helpless gesture. "At the time, we had no reason to deny bail."

"If murder isn't a good enough reason, I'd like to know what is!"

"I'm sorry, Mr. McLean. . . ."

"Like hell you are!" Cole shoved back his chair and took my hand. "Come on, Megan. Let's get out of here."

Walking down the hallway toward the front entrance, he stopped short and glanced around. "We'd better find another way out."

"Why? What's wrong?"

Cole nodded toward two men carrying mini-cams who were headed our way, and a slim blonde with notebook in hand. "Let's leave the press to Detective Goff. Right now, I'm in no mood to be polite."

As we cut quickly down a side hall, a dark-haired woman dressed in black came out of the women's restroom and turned our way.

"Cole, isn't that Mrs. Tedesco?"

He nodded. "And she doesn't look up to handling a lot of questions. Andrea?"

The woman glanced up at the sound of her name, recognition bringing a momentary flicker of life to her drawn features and darkly-shadowed eyes.

"There's a group of newsmen headed down the front hall," Cole said, taking hold of both her hands. "Megan and I thought we'd avoid the crowd and find another way out. Care to join us?"

Andrea Tedesco nodded gratefully and followed his lead. A few twistings and turnings brought us to a back exit near the cafeteria.

Outside, Cole glanced around the parking lot behind the building. "Looks like the coast is clear. Where are you parked?" he asked her. "We'll walk you to your car."

"I don't want to put you to any trouble," she began, her dark eyes looking bewildered.

Cole gave the woman one of his melting smiles and took her arm. "It's no trouble." He paused and added quietly, "I'm sorry about Ross."

Andrea Tedesco's fragile composure nearly crumbled. Tears filled her eyes, and her chin began to tremble. After a deep breath, she answered thinly, "Thank you. I'm parked about a block from here."

As we walked through the parking lot toward the street, Cole gave her an encouraging smile. "There wasn't much time for introductions before, but I'd like you to meet Megan Collier. Megan, Andrea Tedesco."

The woman's lovely eyes touched mine, her expression questioning. "Did you know Ross?"

"No. I saw him briefly, a couple of times," I answered, not knowing what else to say.

Andrea Tedesco stared straight ahead. "I don't understand," she said softly. "Why was Ross at your ranch? The police told me he was hiding in one of the cabins. I . . . I don't understand. . . ."

"Neither do I," Cole said gently. "I'm sorry. I wish I had some answers."

"A Detective Burdick called me last night," she went on. He said someone had found a letter addressed to me. I came down this morning to identify the handwriting."

"The letter — have you seen it?" I asked.

She nodded and stared down at the asphalt.

"It's his, isn't it?" I said.

The woman glanced at me, her dark eyes puzzled. "How do you. . . ?"

"I found the letter."

Andrea Tedesco stopped walking, then reached for my hand. "Thank you. I — I wanted to thank whoever found it. After all the — the horror and shock of the past few days, it helped to know Ross was thinking of me. That he. . . ." Her voice broke on a strangled sob.

When Cole put a comforting arm around the woman's shoulders, she broke down completely. "I knew something was wrong," she said between sobs. "I've known it for a long time, but Ross would never talk to me. Ever since he got back together with the 'Fifth Column' things haven't been right. All those unexplained meetings . . . and the lies. . . ."

Cole stiffened slightly as he held her. "The Fifth Column?"

Mrs. Tedesco fumbled in her purse for a handkerchief and wiped her eyes. "It's a singing group. Years ago, when Ross went to the university here in Boulder, he and some friends from SDS had a group by that name."

"Who were those friends?" I asked quietly. "Did you ever meet them?"

"No. . . ." She blew her nose, then took a ragged breath. "I didn't meet Ross until a few years later. I'd never heard of the

Fifth Column until. . . ." She broke off and gave us an embarrassed glance. "I'm sorry. I don't know why I'm bothering you with all this."

"It's no bother," Cole assured her. "If we can help. . . ."

"You have helped," she told him with a sad smile. "I'd better go. My car's just across the street." She pressed Cole's arm, then paused to look at me once more. "Thank you again — for the letter."

Cole's expression was thoughtful as he watched Mrs. Tedesco walk away. "The Fifth Column. That's an unusual name for a singing group."

"Why do you say that? Considering the names of some groups, the Fifth Column sounds fairly tame."

Cole took my arm and headed for the side street where he had parked the jeep. "Do you know the meaning behind that name?"

"I guess I don't."

"The term refers to undercover agents operating within a country or organization."

"What?"

Cole gave my startled look an affirming nod. "Those agents paved the way for military or political invasion, using such methods as sabotage, propaganda, infiltration—even terrorism. I can't help being curious why a singing group would choose that particular name for themselves."

I drew a quick breath, as my memory was jolted by a disturbing coincidence. "And I can't help being curious why someone writing a music review column for *New Wave* magazine would name it. . . ."

"Column Five!" Cole stopped short and grabbed my arm. "Those college friends of Ross'—it'd be interesting to find out who they were."

"Cole, do you think. . . ?" I couldn't put words to the fear growing inside me.

"I don't know." He paused, then started down the sidewalk at a brisk walk. "But I think I know a way we can find out."

"How?"

"The campus is only a few blocks from here. The library or journalism department ought to have back copies of the university newspaper."

I smiled and quickened my pace to match his.

Fame has its advantages. As Cole and I approached the Information Desk at the library, the bored young woman sitting behind it was pointedly informing two male students that she was too busy to show them where a reference book was. As soon as they turned away, she took a paperback copy of _Tropic of Cancer_ from under the desk and began to read. When Cole asked where we might find copies of old campus newspapers, 'Carolee,' according to the name badge pinned on her blouse, glanced up with an impatient sigh, took one look at Cole and nearly fell off her swivel chair. Not only did Carolee tell us where to find the newspapers, she insisted on escorting us to the microfilm area, getting the films we were interested in, then giving Cole sugary instructions on how to load the machine.

"Is there anything else I can do for you, Mr. McLean?" she asked with an adoring smile.

"No, thanks. This is fine."

"If you need something—anything at all—just let me know."

After Carolee had floated away, I pulled out a chair for Cole and brushed off the seat with a sweeping gesture. "Is there anything I can do for you, Mr. McLean?" I asked, mimicking the girl's breathy tones. "Anything at all?"

"As a matter of fact, there is," he said, sitting down and pulling me onto his lap. "Do you realize I haven't had a kiss all morning?"

I glanced around, noticing four or five heads turned in our direction. "Cole . . . we have an audience."

"Then let's make it a good one. I like to make my audiences happy."

His kiss stifled my laughter, and I quickly scrambled off his lap to sit in the chair next to his. A few feet away from us, a serious-looking young man was staring fiercely at a book, giving every indication that he hadn't noticed a thing—except for the fact that his ears and neck were a violent crimson.

I picked up a box containing microfilm. "This could take a while. What year would you like to start with?"

"How about 1966? I don't think Ross was over forty, and if I remember right, SDS wasn't founded until the early sixties."

I peered at the black and white print moving past on the screen. "I remember hearing about the riots and protests back then, but I was too young to understand what it was all about. I'm not even sure what SDS stands for."

"Students for a Democratic Society," Cole answered, studying the screen.

"Impressive."

He nodded. "SDS was a strong political force on campuses all over the country in the middle to late sixties. By the time I entered college in the mid-seventies, the organization had split into several factions, including groups like the Weathermen." Cole stopped the microfilm to view a headline announcing, "SDS Plans Protest Rally Against War."

We quickly skimmed the accompanying article, but found no mention of the Fifth Column. Half an hour later, we had covered only the first nine months of campus newspapers for that year, with the same result. Nothing.

"Maybe we should try a later year," I suggested. "When anti-war sentiment was running higher. Say, 1968."

"Good idea." Cole handed the microfilm to me, then loaded another reel.

The campus papers in January and February of 1968 contained only brief mentions of SDS activities; then in March, we both caught the headline, "Protest Rally Results in 10 Arrests," and stopped to read. Again, no mention of a singing group called the Fifth Column. Then, in late April, we spotted a small article with the headline: "Fifth Column Rocks Campus Complacency."

Some members of the university administration have branded them "Marxist folksingers," but to the 15,000 students who turned out for Friday night's concert, the Fifth Column is a gutsy musical phenomenon that's taking this campus by storm.

Their songs, such as "Cancer of the Mind" and "Destroy to Build" may sound suspiciously like leftist propaganda, but lead singer, Maxine Berenstein had this to say about the group's philosophies: "If there's a point to our band, or an overriding theme, I think we'd have to say that there are alternatives in music, the same as alternatives in life. You don't have to be rich. You don't have to fit in. You can do whatever you want. Nobody tells you what to do.

Cole blew out a quiet breath and squeezed my hand. "That sounds like our Max. I think we're onto something."

In the following months, the Fifth Column was a frequent headline maker. Critics accused them of proselyting revolution and campus unrest, while supporters applauded their controversial blend of music and violent politics. Maxine Berenstein gained particular notoriety after her arrest for dancing topless at a rally. Her published comment following the arrest read: "I am freer behind bars than the ignorant pigs who walk the streets."

In still another issue, when campus reporters asked the group if they considered themselves to be socialists, Kurt Gorman responded: "I can't answer for the others, but I consider myself a revolutionary communist."

In September of that year, the singing group was on hand to welcome national officers and members of SDS at the convention where leaflets were passed out giving full instructions on how to make bombs and explosives. Beside the article was a picture of four men and a slender, black-haired woman.

Cole and I stared down at the young faces of Sid Rasmussen, Kurt and Leonard Gorman, Ross Tedesco and Max Barrett. Then he began rewinding the film.

"I don't know about you, but I've had enough."

"More than enough."

"Before we go, I think we ought to make copies of some of these articles—especially the picture, and drop them by the Sheriff's office."

My voice was skeptical. "Do you really think Detective Goff will do anything about it?"

"I'm not going to waste my time with Goff. But I think Burdick will be very interested to know that Kurt Gorman and the others were lying through their teeth about knowing Ross."

When we stopped by the Sheriff's office, both detectives had gone to lunch. Cole left the copies on Burdick's desk, scribbled a quick note, and we left.

"Do you want to stop and get a bite to eat before we head back?" Cole asked, as I climbed into the jeep.

"I'm not very hungry, but a cold drink sounds wonderful."

Cole stopped at a fast food drive-in and came back with two double cheeseburgers, fries, and two large lime-aids.

"You don't eat enough," he told me as I stared at all the food. "Besides, I can't think on an empty stomach."

Driving back along the winding canyon road, there was much to think about—and very few answers.

"People don't lie without a reason," Cole said, finishing the last of his drink. "In light of the drug scandal, I can understand why Kurt and the others wouldn't want to admit to knowing Ross—but it still bothers me that they were all at the ranch at the same time." He shook his head. "I don't know—it just seems like too much of a coincidence."

I nodded agreement. "Even though Kurt and Lenny and Sid had legitimate reasons to be there, I have the feeling Max's trip to cover Obolus' concert was nothing more than that—a cover."

"So what were they up to?" Cole threw out a frustrated sigh. "We know Ross must have been pretty important to the group, otherwise Sid never would have picked him up last Tuesday, much less taken the risk of hiding him in the 'Mollie Kathleen.'"

"What I don't understand is how Obolus fits into all this. What possible motive could they have for killing Ross?"

Cole frowned at the road ahead. "I don't know, but I think it's pretty safe to assume that Ross was aware of Obolus' satanic activities. Especially, since he and Sid were the ones who planned the Red Rocks concert. A lot of people in the business know about groups like Obolus and look the other way."

I glanced sharply at Cole. Suddenly, my heart was beating high and fast.

"Megan, what is it?"

"I'm not sure. Maybe nothing. But your mentioning the

plans for the concert reminded me of something." I took a quick breath, thinking back to the morning I had arrived at Lodestone. "Last Friday, I overheard a conversation between Kurt and Max as they came out of the dining room. Kurt was saying something about someone—it must have been Ross—complicating things. He tried to reassure her by saying she was overreacting to the problem, that it wouldn't affect their plans for Saturday night. Max told Kurt they couldn't let it affect their plans—that she'd worked too hard to get them that far."

Cole's expression was rigid, his features taut as tightly-strung wire. "Did Max say what kind of plans?"

"No. Right after that, she and Kurt saw me and that put a quick end to the conversation."

Cole was silent for a moment, then he looked at me. "Try to think. Was there ever another time when you were with Kurt and Max that they might have said something—anything—about plans for Saturday night?"

"The only other time was Friday evening when we had dinner together. They both talked quite a bit about the concert. I remember Max referring to a Mr. Fitzsimmons several times. I assumed he must be fairly important because she acted so smug every time she mentioned him. Poor Lenny was so out of it, he never said much of anything. . . ." I broke off with a sharp intake of breath. "Oh, dear God, it couldn't be. . . ."

Cole's hands tightened on the wheel as he maneuvered the jeep around a tight curve. "What?"

"The plans for Saturday night and—and Mr. Fitzsimmons!" I snatched a tense breath, trying to slow my racing thoughts. "Maybe it's only a crazy coincidence, but I read in the newspaper that Julie Bellis' father works for Fitzsimmons Army Hospital. He's involved in some kind of research with. . . ."

"Wait a minute. Who's Julie Bellis?"

"The girl who was kidnapped at the Obolus concert! Remember when we heard the radio announcement? The news report said she'd won tickets to the concert in a contest sponsored by some radio station—KV—something or other."

"KVHK," Cole answered slowly, looking as if he'd been struck a hard blow full in the face.

"Ross Tedesco was the manager of a Denver radio station,"

I said. "Do you know which one?"

He nodded, then shoved his foot down on the gas pedal. "KVHK. And if what you're thinking is true, Kurt and Max had a lot more going on Sunday morning than a romantic interlude."

My eyes widened. "That's right! I'd nearly forgotten about Sunday morning. Kurt even admitted he left the concert early."

"That's one thing he couldn't lie about and get away with. Whoever's at the gate keeps a log of all arrivals and departures, along with the time."

I stared down at my clenched hands. "Do you think we should tell the police?"

"We're closer to Lodestone than we are to Boulder. If we turned back now, Gorman might be long gone—and so would Julie Bellis."

"But, what if we're wrong . . . wrong about everything?"

Cole shot me a tight-lipped glance. "Let's pray to God we are," he said fervently.

WE DROVE UP to the guardhouse and main gate a scant fifteen minutes later.

"Has Kurt Gorman left the ranch yet?" Cole asked before Ron Weaver could say a word.

"We've had a few reporters trying to get in, but no one's come through the gate since I came on at seven."

Cole sprang down from the jeep and called over his shoulder, "I'd better alert Ed," then ran inside the guardhouse. In the short time it took Ron to unlock the gate and push it open, Cole was back behind the wheel.

The guard frowned as he took note of Cole's stormy-eyed expression. "More trouble?"

"Could be. No one leaves, Ron." He shifted into first gear and gunned up the road.

We had almost reached the meadow when Cole braked the jeep in the shade of some tall aspens. "Here he comes."

Through the thinning trees ahead, I could see the brown stripe of road cutting through the meadow, and a sleek gray automobile headed our way.

Cole quickly backed up the jeep and parked it sideways across the road. Only seconds later, the gray car was upon us and skidding to an angry stop.

The window on the driver's side went down with a whisper, then Kurt Gorman's frizzy brown head leaned out. Today, there was no polite mask, no smiling pretense of civility on his hard-edged features.

"What's the problem?" he called out. "I've got a plane to catch!"

Cole slid out from behind the wheel and approached the

gray Buick. "Before you catch any planes, I have a few more questions that need to be answered."

"I haven't got time. If you have more questions, talk to the police. I've already told them everything I know.'

"Not quite everything," Cole said. "I'm sure the police would be very interested in why you lied about knowing Ross Tedesco."

"Lied? What the hell are you talking about?"

Cole met Gorman's angry expression with controlled calm. "I'm talking about the Fifth Column."

The man's face went as gray as his eyes. Through the windshield, I could see Lenny on the front seat, nervously mopping his face with a handkerchief. The next moment, Kurt had recovered enough to insist, "You have no right to keep me here, McLean! In fact, you're the one who told us to leave, so get that damn jeep out of the road before I move it for you!"

"Cool down, Gorman. You're not going anywhere until I get some answers. Why don't you turn the car around and head back to the lodge."

Gorman's mouth was ugly. "I said I had a plane to catch."

"And I said, turn around."

Gorman threw the Buick into reverse, backed up a few feet, then floored the gas pedal. Cole leaped aside just in time, and the next second, I was jolted out of my seat as the Buick scraped its way through the narrow gap between Cole's jeep and the road-side trees. Cole dived back to the jeep and leaped behind the wheel as the Buick screamed down the road in a choking cloud of dust. He'd no sooner turned the jeep around when we saw a sturdy Blazer heading straight for the Buick.

Gorman gave his horn a long blast, but Ron Weaver kept the Blazer squarely in the middle of the road. I gasped and gripped the side of the jeep, afraid he and Gorman were going to crash head-on. At the last second, Ron whipped the Blazer to the left and Gorman hit the brakes. There wasn't time or room for either vehicle to pass, and the Buick caught the Blazer broadside in a crunching spasm of tearing metal and breaking glass.

In the same moment, Cole and I were out of the jeep and running down the road. Cole immediately headed for the Blazer, but Ron was already getting out of the vehicle and shrugging aside his concern.

"That was nice timing," Cole told him. "But why did you leave the gate?"

"Ed called just after you left. He saw Gorman driving away and thought you might need some back-up."

I glanced over to the Buick where Lenny was slumped over on the passenger side, holding a bloody handkerchief to his face.

When I started toward him, Cole put a restraining hand on my arm. "Stay back, Babe. Ron and I can handle this."

One look at the guard's magnum revolver told me he was right. Holding the heavy pistol with both hands extended, Ron ordered, "Out of the car, both of you! Hands behind your head!"

White-faced and shaking, Lenny staggered out of the Buick, still holding the bloody handkerchief to his temple, while his brother faced Cole with all the pious dignity of a martyr wrongfully accused.

"I can ruin you, McLean," he muttered with cold anger. "Ruin you and everything you have!"

Cole ignored him and quickly glanced in the back seat of the Buick. "Nothing here," he told me, then walked past Gorman to the driver's side.

Kurt stiffened, his gray eyes darting nervously from Cole to the security guard. "What do you think you're doing? Give me those keys!"

Kurt made a sudden move toward Cole, but Ron Weaver dodged between them and leveled his revolver at the older man's chest.

"Don't try it Gorman! On the ground! Hands behind your head!"

Gorman's mouth curled in a derisive sneer. "You go to hell!"

"I said, on the ground!" Ron grabbed him by the arm and yanked him away from the car, then physically threw Kurt to the ground, while Cole walked around to the trunk, keys in hand.

"Damn you, McLean! You have no right! You touch that car, and I'll sue!"

Ron put a foot on the man's back and said in disgust, "Shut up, Gorman. You're so full of it, your eyes are brown."

I stepped closer as Cole inserted the key, my heart hammering in my throat. The lid gave way with a small whoosh of sound, and we found ourselves staring down at the crumpled body of a young girl. Her hands and feet were tightly bound and above a thick, adhesive strip, her pale face was glazed with sweat.

Cole quickly removed the tape, then put a hand to the girl's neck. He looked at me and nodded. "She's alive. . . ."

Some five hours later, Cole and Cody and I were sitting around the big pine table at Lodestone, eating grilled cheese sandwiches and chicken noodle soup. All Cody knew of the day's affairs was that his father and I had had some business to take care of. Now that was over, he could fill us in on more important matters, such as the fact that Tiger's kittens had their eyes open and this morning Uncle Wes had caught a weasel in the barn.

Cole gave the boy a weary smile and mumbled, "He's not the only one catching weasels," then got up from the table to answer a knock on the back door. He returned moments later with Ed Garrison.

The security man gave me a polite nod. "I'm sorry to interrupt your dinner, but I just got back from Boulder and thought you might want to know about some. . . ." He glanced at Cody and finished discreetly, ". . . interesting developments."

Cole gestured to a chair, then turned to Cody. "How would you like to finish your dinner in the family room and watch a video?"

The boy gave his father a knowing glance. "More business?"

"Sorry, kid," Garrison said with a throaty laugh. "More business."

While Cole situated Cody in the family room, I passed the security man the plate of sandwiches and asked, "How's Julie Bellis?"

"She'll be in the hospital for a few days," he said, accepting a sandwich off the plate. "Kurt and Max kept her pretty doped up while she was here, but the doctor said her condition's stable." He took a bite of the sandwich. "She'll be okay, but her taste in music'll never be the same."

I smiled at Ed as Cole came back into the kitchen and pulled his chair closer to mine. "There are times when Walt Disney can be a terrific babysitter," he said, then turned his attention to the security man. "So what's up?"

"Plenty. Burdick's been interrogating Sid Rasmussen and the Gormans most of the afternoon.

I shook my head. "I can't imagine Kurt Gorman admitting to anything."

"He didn't. But a little plea bargaining worked wonders on Lenny. And ever since Sid Rasmussen decided that hit-and-run charges were a lot better than murder and kidnapping, he's become very talkative. Between the two of them, Burdick's put together a hell of a story."

Cole put an arm around my shoulders. "You've got our attention, Ed," he said dryly. "How about some details?"

"The little detail you two came up with this morning is what got things moving," Garrison answered with a satisifed smile.

"You mean the Fifth Column?"

He nodded and put down the sandwich. "According to Sid and Lenny, Max Barrett was the motivating force behind the group, with Kurt a close second. The band broke up in the early seventies, about the same time SDS started falling apart. Sid tried to make it on his own as a singer, but had more success managing other rock groups. The Gormans ended up on the West Coast, working for some recording company. Ross was the only one who stayed in Colorado. After being a D.J. for awhile, he moved up the ranks at KVHK until he became manager."

"What about Max?" I asked him, my curiosity aroused.

"Lenny and Sid were both a little vague about her activities, but in piecing things together, it seems she traveled a lot after college and did some free-lance writing. She spent a few years in Cuba and Central America researching the revolutions, then moved to the Middle East. By the time she showed up again in this country, it was under the name Max Barrett, not Maxine Berenstein. According to Lenny, she got the group together for 'old times sake' about four years ago. They started talking about SDS and the problems with the world as they saw it, and this led to other meetings. It wasn't long before Max managed to convince the rest that it was their 'calling' to be the great liberators of this generation. Even though SDS failed in its goals to change society, it still wasn't too late for them to free young people from the so-called tyranny of the 'establishment.' According to Max, the capitalist system was immoral and long overdue for destruction. The way to bring about this destruction wasn't through open rebellion like the old protest marches, but from the inside—by appealing to kids' minds and emotions.''

''Music,'' Cole said quietly.

Garrison's eyes widened. ''How did you know?''

''Music is the language of emotion,'' Cole answered. ''Words communicate ideas, but music communicates feelings. Put the two together and you have something pretty powerful. A lot of protest singers in the sixties believed their music would bring about a sort of bloodless revolution. I wonder sometimes if they weren't right.''

Garrison stared at Cole. ''That's exactly what the Fifth Column wanted—a revolution, using rock music instead of bombs to reach the youth. But I'm not so sure any revolution is bloodless. Too many people want to free the world, even if it means blowing it to pieces. Max and company aren't much different. Freedom to them means throwing out the family, religion, government, the works.''

''That's not freedom—it's anarchy,'' Cole said soberly.

I leaned against him with a sigh. ''The frightening thing about all this is the kids don't even realize what's happening. They think they're being entertained, not taught by a bunch of radicals.''

Garrison agreed, then went on, ''About three years ago, Rasmussen started managing a punk band called, 'Acid Dreams.' Max heard them and decided the band was just what the Fifth Column needed to help further their cause and philosophies. Promoting a rock band takes a lot of money, and that's where Ross Tedesco entered the picture. Tedesco made the mistake of getting involved in drugs, and Max capitalized on this—maybe blackmail might be a better word,'' Ed amended, ''because Ross was never as sold on the 'cause' as the rest of them. Anyway, Max threatened to expose Ross' drug activities unless he funneled some of the drug money into the group. The interesting thing about all this is, somewhere along the way, 'Acid Dreams' became involved with the occult and changed their name to 'Obolus.' At first, Max and the others weren't too happy about this, but when record sales started going up and the concerts became smash sell-outs, the group couldn't really complain.''

Ed leaned forward, resting both elbows on the table. "It was the ideal set-up. Ross provided the financial backing with his drug money; Kurt was there to produce the albums, with Lenny as soundman. And Max used her influence in journalism and *New Wave* magazine to sell Obolus to the public. Even the Satan-business seemed to work in their favor because it was controversial and sparked a lot of conflict between kids and their parents, which was exactly what the Fifth Column wanted. Then, about nine months ago, Lenny got wind through a friend in the business, of some plans the army had to conduct experiments with 'infra' and 'ultra' sound.''

"Infra and ultra sound?'' Cole said. "I've never heard of it.''

"I don't know much about it either,'' Garrison admitted, "except 'infra' deals with sound below the normal hearing frequencies and 'ultra' is above. Because of his work as a sound engineer, Lenny knew all about it, including the fact that experiments had been done in the past with the idea of using sound for subliminal methods of crowd control. Lenny started asking questions and found out Colonel Bellis was supervising a research project at Fitzgerald Army Hospital. When he told the others, Max and Kurt decided this infra and ultra sound business was just what they needed to speed up their little revolution. All they had to do was figure out a way to get hold of the classified information, then Lenny would use it to develop a method of feeding subliminal messages and propaganda over the sound system at concerts, as well as on record albums.''

"Kidnapping Julie Bellis was the way,'' Cole said heavily.

Garrison nodded. "And the classified information on infra and ultra sound was the ransom. The arrangements were fairly simple. Sid set up the Obolus concert at Red Rocks with Ross Tedesco, and to make sure the Bellis girl was there, they rigged the contest sponsored by Ross' radio station. Getting reservations for Obolus to record at Lodestone was the final part of the plan. What better place to hide the girl than a private, out-of-the-way resort? Everything went smoothly until an undercover police operation exposed Ross' drug connections. Max and the others were worried that Ross' arrest, and the resulting investigation might jeopardize their plans, so they agreed to hide him in the 'Mollie Kathleen' for a few days."

"How does Obolus fit into all this?" I asked him. "What motive did they have for killing Ross?"

"The same motive they had for trying to kill you and Cole," Ed answered bluntly. "The threat of exposure. Apparently, Obolus never knew they were being financed by Ross' drug money. In fact, they didn't know anything about the Fifth Column until last Friday. After you surprised Ross in the 'Mollie Kathleen,' he grabbed some clothes and headed for Sid's cabin. When Ross barged in, Sid was having a meeting with Derek Durant. Sid couldn't just hide the guy and expect Durant to keep quiet about it without giving him some kind of explanation. He told Derek that Ross was an old friend who'd done them some favors, but Durant didn't buy it. They got into an argument and Ross lost his cool. He made the mistake of telling Durant that it was his money that'd bought Obolus their success and said he could ruin their career by making public the group's satanic activities. Sid finally calmed things down and Derek left. Then Kurt and Max showed up with the news that you were back at Lodestone. Rasmussen was afraid you might recognize him as the driver of the Camaro, so he took off that evening for Denver, leaving Ross alone in the cabin."

"And that night, Obolus made sure Ross couldn't carry out his threat to expose them," Cole finished.

Garrison nodded. "Kurt and Max nearly panicked when Ross showed up missing the next morning, but decided to go ahead with their plans to kidnap the Bellis girl. They didn't find out Ross had been murdered until late Sunday. Sid suspected Obolus might be responsible, but he didn't dare do anything that might draw the police's attention to Lodestone. They had too much at stake."

"What happened to the information on infra and ultra sound?" I asked him. "Did they get it from Colonel Bellis?"

Ed Garrison shook his head and gave me a satisfied smile. "The pick-up was set for late Monday afternoon, but before Kurt and Max could leave the ranch, you showed up and all hell broke loose."

Cole glanced at me with a wry grin, "Megan does tend to have an unsettling effect on people."

Garrison chuckled. "So I've noticed. All things considered, I'd say Obolus and the Fifth Column had a pretty lousy weekend and we're damn lucky they did. The only thing that bugs me is the way the Sheriff's Department is handling Tedesco's murder."

Cole frowned. "What do you mean?"

"Goff doesn't want anything to do with the satanic angle, and he's leaving that out of all his reports," Ed answered with a frustrated sigh. "The way it stands now, the Sheriff's Department is calling Tedesco's murder a 'drug-related crime.'"

I stared at him in disbelief. "How can they do that? What about the tape and . . . and my statements? Detective Goff can't dismiss all that!"

"I know, but he can downplay it, especially with the press. This isn't the first time the police have been unwilling to admit the relationship between crime and satanic cults."

"It's got to come out sometime," Cole insisted. "There's too much evidence to ignore, especially after last night."

Garrison shrugged. "Let's hope so, but people usually end up believing pretty much what they want to believe, in spite of the facts. When all this hits the news, you can bet there'll be those who insist the whole thing's a plot cooked up by the Moral Majority or some religious group to persecute another poor, maligned rock band."

"Yes, but there'll be others who recognize Obolus for what they really are," I said. "Murder is still murder, whether the motive stems from drugs or Satan worship. I can't believe Obolus will get away with it."

Garrson leaned back in his chair, his canny eyes holding mine. "Maybe not, but what about all the other groups just like Obolus and worse? Their music's like a slow-acting poison, eating away at kids." He shook his head, then pushed back his chair. "If I hear any more, I'll be in touch. Burdick said he'd keep us up to date.''

''What about Max?'' Cole asked, getting up from the table. ''Has she been picked up yet?''

''Not yet. Gorman supposedly took her to the airport yesterday afternoon, but her name wasn't on any of the passenger lists. She could have used an alias. The FBI's in on it now, and there's an inter-state bulletin out for her arrest.'' Garrison's hard glance softened as he looked at me. ''Thanks for the sandwich, Megan. Try to get some rest.''

After Ed Garrison had gone, I gathered up the dinner dishes and carried them to the sink.

''Why do I have the feeling that it isn't over?'' I asked Cole with a worried sigh.

''What's bothering you?''

I leaned against the counter and met his eyes. ''Max. She frightens me—now more than ever. Somehow, I can't see her giving in or running away. She's worked too hard and too long to give up now.''

Cole put his arms around me. ''I know how you're feeling, Babe, but try not to think about it anymore. Burdick's a good man and like Ed said, the FBI's on the case now. Max won't get far.''

''I hope not, but I can't help worrying. We ruined everything for her, and I'm afraid she might. . . .''

Cole's lips brushed against my cheek. ''Might what?''

''I don't know—try to get back at us, somehow. Who knows what she's capable of?''

''There's no way she can hurt us now,'' Cole said, drawing me closer. ''I won't let her.''

The ringing of the wall phone brought us out of a thoroughly satisfying kiss and Cole crossed the room to answer it. I cleared away the rest of the dishes, only half-listening to his brief ''yes-no'' conversation.

''That was Kathy,'' he said, hanging up the receiver. ''Your boss just called the lodge for the third time today, demanding to know where you were and what the hell was going on.''

''Mr. Winegar! I forgot all about him!''

''So did I.'' Cole faced me with a shame-faced grin. ''He

called this morning, but I forgot to give you the message. Then he called again while the police were here."

I sighed and ran a hand through my hair. "I was supposed to be back in the office yesterday afternoon. I can imagine what he's thinking."

"Would you like me to talk to him? I'm sure once he understands the circumstances, there won't be any problem."

"Thanks, but I might as well face the music." I winced, then laughed. "I don't believe I just said that."

Mr. Winegar's reaction was true to form. Explode first and ask questions later. His anger didn't bother me nearly as much as the sticky, hurt tone of voice he always used to inspire feelings of guilt and shame in his employees.

"Megan, why didn't you call? I've been half out of my mind with worry! And today, all anybody would tell me was that you were involved with the police in some murder investigation. Why didn't you return my calls? It isn't like you to be so selfish and inconsiderate."

"I'm sorry, Mr. Winegar. I didn't receive the message until just now—but you're right, I should have called."

It was difficult to sound sufficiently contrite when Cole was leaning against the counter, arms folded across his chest, watching me with a smile that was warm enough to melt my bones.

"When can I expect you back?" Bill Winegar went on. "Can you get a flight out tomorrow morning?"

"I . . . I don't know."

"Tomorrow afternoon, then. Just let me know the flight number, and I'll meet you at the airport."

I drew a long breath. "That won't be necessary."

"Nonsense! In spite of what you've put me through, it's the least I can do. Just give me a call before you leave."

I paused a moment, then said, "I'm sorry, Mr. Winegar, but I won't be coming back to L.A.—at least, not right away."

Cole straightened up, the amusement wiped off his face while Bill Winegar's voice boomed in my ear, "Not coming back! What are you talking about?"

I smiled at Cole, then said, "Mr. Winegar, I'd like you to be the first to congratulate me. I'm getting married."

Cole was beside me, his arms around my waist, before my boss recovered enough to stammer, "Get . . . getting married? Megan, are you crazy?"

"No, just happy."

"If this is your idea of a joke, I don't think it's a damn bit funny! I suppose the next thing you're going to tell me is that you're marrying Cole McLean. . . ."

Cole took the receiver from me and said, "That's right, she is!" then hung up the phone.

We laughed and hugged each other, then Cole took my face in his hands. "Megan, are you sure? I've been doing a lot of thinking since Sunday night, and I don't want to rush you. I'll wait as long as you want. I just want you to be happy."

I smiled and kissed him. "Being Mrs. Alex Coletti McLean is all I need to be happy. How does tomorrow sound?"

Cole's jaw dropped, then his surprised look was replaced by a rakish grin. "The only thing better than tomorrow, would be tonight. But I want things to be right for you. What about your family? Wouldn't you like them to be there?"

"The only people I want to be at our wedding are your parents—and Cody, of course."

Cole kissed me and said softly, "We could drive down to Georgetown in the morning. . . ."

"That sounds like a wonderful idea."

He kissed me again, then asked, "Shall we go tell our son the good news?"

"Our son. . . ." I smiled and took his hand.

23

COLE AND I both agreed that aside from his parents, we wouldn't tell anyone about our plans to be married. There were legitimate reasons for a trip to Georgetown, and Cole left messages with Brent and Ed while I helped Cody pack some extra clothes. At 8:30 sharp, we got into the truck, then drove down the forested road away from Lodestone. Cole's expression was almost as boyish as his son's, and I was positively giddy with excitement.

Passing by the stables, Cole slowed the truck and glanced at me. "I forgot to tell Wes and Twila we were leaving. I'd better stop and let them know. It'll only take a minute."

"That's fine. I'm in no hurry," I teased.

Cole laughed and kissed me. "Well, I am!"

Twila Randolph was coming out of the chicken coop, her flowered apron full of eggs, as Cole pulled the truck into the driveway. Leaving the motor running, he ran across the side yard and planted a big kiss on her cheek.

"You're looking especially glamorous this morning, Twila."

She chuckled and shoved him away with one hand. "You watch out you don't make me drop these eggs!"

"I just thought I'd let you know you won't need to do any cooking for me today. Megan and I will be spending most of the day in Georgetown."

"Again? You just saw your folks on Sunday."

Cole smiled and ignored her question. "We'll be back sometime this evening," he said, gave her another kiss, then ran back to the truck.

As his father got behind the wheel, Cody leaned his head out the window and yelled, "Know what, Aunt Twila? Megan's going to be my new mom!"

Twila let out a whoop and dropped the eggs.

Cole sighed and looked at me. "So much for trying to keep things quiet."

I was a little afraid that the suddenness of our plans might be an imposition for Cole's parents. I needn't have worried. The fact that her son had foisted a wedding upon her with scarcely half a day's notice didn't bother Mary McLean in the least. The moment we drove up to the house, she hurried out to meet us and announced with sparkling eyes, "Now I don't want you to worry about a thing. Everything's all planned. We can have the ceremony here at the house. Alex has already made arrangements with the minister, and I've got Mrs. Neumann down the street to bake the cake. She was thrilled to have a chance to put all those cake decorating classes to use."

Cole laughed and hugged her. "It's a good thing Mrs. Neumann took those classes or the wedding would've been ruined."

We left her busily preparing chicken salad with Cody as chief taster, then drove into town to get the license and buy me some clothes.

"I hope you realize we're completely breaking with tradition," I said to Cole as he parked the truck alongside a small boutique. "It isn't every bride who has the groom along to help her pick out a wedding dress. In fact, it's supposed to be bad luck to even see the bride before the wedding."

Cole walked around the front of the truck to open my door. "I don't believe in bad luck. Let's make our own traditions!"

Getting out of the truck, I caught glances with a frizzy blonde who was parked directly across the street in a dark-colored Mustang. She abruptly looked away and slipped on a pair of sunglasses.

"What is it?" Cole asked.

I shrugged away a momentary feeling of disquiet and said, "Just another woman who can't take her eyes off you. I guess that's something I'm going to have to get used to."

Cole gave the blonde a brief, uninterested glance as she pulled away from the curb, then took my hand. "Come on. They might have something you'll like in here."

As we searched through two small racks of dresses, Cole frowned and apologized, "I'm sorry there isn't more to choose from. Georgetown is big on tourist items, but a little short on fashion."

"Don't worry. If we can't find a dress, I'd be just as happy with a new blouse and a purse."

"What?"

"Never mind." I smiled at his puzzled expression, then lifted a simple, white silk dress off the rack. "What about this one?"

Cole nodded his approval.

I took one look at the price tag and put the dress back. "On second thought, maybe we'd better look for something else."

"Why? Is it the wrong size?"

"No . . . the price tag is the wrong size," I whispered.

Cole glanced down at the tag and chuckled. "It'll be tough on the budget, but I'll manage somehow," he said dryly. "Here's the dress, my love."

Two hours later, Cole had bought me almost an entire trousseau. Walking back to the truck, arms loaded with packages, he said, "I keep thinking we've forgotten something."

"I can't imagine what. You've bought me far too much as it is."

"Not half as much as I'd like to," he grinned, stopping to dump his load in the back of the truck. "But there's something. . . ." Cole deposited my share of the packages, then gave the back bumper a smack. "The wedding license!"

"Oh, that."

"Yes, that!" He laughed and kissed me. "We'd better hurry! It's already twelve-fifteen."

Ten minutes later, we were dashing down the steps of the old courthouse, license in hand. As Cole unlocked the door on the passenger side, I looked past him to see a brown Mustang parked across the street and the same frizzy blonde behind the wheel. Something in the woman's cold-eyed stare struck me as familiar, and I shuddered.

"That blonde I pointed out to you earlier, is parked right across the street," I told Cole under my breath. "She's watching us."

Cole's smile was unconcerned. "What if she is?"

"There's something. . . ." I hesitated, hating to give voice to the unreasonable worry inside me. "Never mind. I guess I'm still a little jumpy."

"That's a bride's prerogative," he said as I climbed in the front seat. After getting in the driver's side, Cole turned and drew me into his arms. His whispered, "I love you, Megan," made me forget everything else. . . .

Alone in Cole's parents' room, I surveyed my new clothes laid out carefully on the bed and congratulated myself for feeling so calm. Stepping into the white silk dress, I decided it was just another silly tradition to assume all brides were jittery and nervous on their wedding day. I felt perfectly fine—except for the fact that my fingers were suddenly too clumsy to zip up my dress. Halfway up, the zipper caught in the fabric and refused to budge. Standing there, struggling to release it, my mind went back to the countless times my mother had called me into her bedroom to help with a zipper or buttons. I remembered the anxious note in her voice as she asked the eternal question, "Do I look all right?" Like the enchanted mirror in the fairy tale, I would give the proper assurances of her beauty and attractiveness, silently wishing that just once, she would look at me and say the same.

Where was she now? What would she think of my marriage? Part of me ached to see her, to have her with me. Yet, I knew only too well that Mother's presence would mar, rather than brighten, my wedding day.

There was a quiet knock on the door, then Mary McLean poked her head inside. "Can I help with anything, dear?"

"I'm almost ready, but could you give me a hand with the zipper? It's caught on something."

The woman deftly released the fabric, finished zipping the dress, then stepped back to look at me. "You look beautiful," she said warmly. "And your hair—it's so lovely! Alex's mother was a redhead." She paused and added, "So was my daughter."

I turned to face her. "Cole never mentioned he had a sister."

"He never knew her. Anne was born nearly five years before

I had Cole. She only lived a few hours. . . ."

The pain in her eyes made it difficult to know what to say. A quiet, "I'm sorry," seemed grossly inadequate.

"It's all right. Nothing ever takes away the ache inside, but maybe the good Lord was just trying to teach us patience." Smiling that beautiful smile, she hugged me and said, "After all these years, He's finally given Alex and me a lovely red-headed daughter. . . ."

I came down the stairs of the old house on the arm of Alex McLean. Cole was waiting for us in the living room, with Cody and the minister. A dark gray suit and white shirt made his black hair seem even blacker and brought out the deep blue-gray of his eyes. In his lapel was a single red rose.

My mouth was dry as his mother handed me a small bouquet of roses. I vaguely heard Alex McLean introducing me to the minister, heard my own voice making some reply, and promptly forgot the man's name. Cody was hiding behind his father's long legs, staring up at me in timid wonder.

Then Cole took my hand, and the enormity of what I was doing flooded over me. I was marrying Cole McLean! How had it all happened? Suddenly, it seemed impossible and unreal. Exactly one week ago, I had sat spellbound in an audience of thousands, listening to this man sing. I had even dared to wonder what it would be like to be the woman Cole McLean loved. Now, his eyes and his voice told me I was that woman.

The words of the ceremony floated through my consciousness. Like one in a dream, I heard Cole's confident, "I will," followed by my own soft answer.

Reality returned when the handsome face of the man who was now my husband, bent to give me our first kiss as man and wife. Cody, who had been wide-eyed and silent throughout the ceremony, pulled on his father's pantleg and demanded, "Hey, Dad! It's my turn! I wanna kiss my mom!"

I laughed and picked him up, smiling into the blue eyes that were so much like his father's.

Cody wrapped his arms around my neck in a fierce hug. "I love you!"

"I love you, too. . . ." My voice broke on the words.

Cole's arms came around us both. Tears were bright in his eyes. Smiling at him, I felt completely surrounded by the warmth of my family's love.

"I hope you don't plan on leaving right away," my father-in-law said as we sat around the dining room table enjoying chicken salad, hot rolls, and Mrs. Neumann's magnificent wedding cake. "Mary and I thought we might take Cody for a train ride over to Silver Plume and back."

"We did?" Mary McLean's expression was blank until she caught the look in her husband's eyes. "Oh, that's right, we did."

Cody glanced up from his wedding cake with excited eyes. "A train ride? All right!"

"Sounds fine to me," Cole answered and gave my shoulder a squeeze. "What do you say, Mrs. McLean?"

The pride in his voice sent color rising in my cheeks. "What about his nap?" I said stupidly.

"If Cody gets tired, he can sleep on the way back," my mother-in-law assured me.

"We'll be gone for close to three hours," Alex added with a sly look, "so there'll be plenty of time for you two to get some rest."

Five minutes later, they were gone, and Cole and I were standing alone by the stairs, grinning at each other like a pair of idiots.

"We've had a very unconventional wedding," he said, searching my eyes. "I hope you're not . . . disappointed with anything."

"Disappointed? I've never had such a beautiful day in my life. But, it's still a little hard to believe we're married."

Cole swooped me into his arms and started up the stairs. "I think I can take care of that."

In the warm, drowsy silence of the afternoon, I lay in my husband's arms, the sheets tangled around our feet. Through the open window, a soft breeze barely stirred the curtains.

"Do you feel married now, Mrs. McLean?" Cole asked with a sensual smile.

I breathed a long, contented sigh and kissed his hair-roughened chest. "Mmmm. I feel wonderful."

His arms tightened around me. "I know. . . ."

I laughed and looked into his eyes with happy wonder. "I never knew loving someone would be like this."

Cole took my face in his hands. "Neither did I," he said softly. After a long kiss, he lay back on the pillows and stared at the ceiling. "I think I can finish our song now."

I smiled and rose on one elbow, listening as he hummed the melody and watching the mellow shafts of sunlight play across our bodies, his firm and tan, mine pale.

"Thanks to you, there aren't any more shadows," I whispered and bent to kiss him.

In the midst of the kiss, we heard the sweet, sad whistle of the train. Cole turned over on his side and glanced at the clock on the bureau. "It can't be five o'clock already."

When the whistle came again, he lifted his head to listen. "The train's still a few miles down the canyon. They probably won't be here for another fifteen or twenty minutes."

I pulled him back to me with an eager sigh. "That's good. . . ."

24

THE SKY WAS still light, its deep blue glowing with sunset ribbons of coral and pink, as we drove up the wooded hillside to Cole's home—our home—I realized with wifely pride and new confidence.

Walking hand in hand up the stone path, Cole suddenly frowned at the dark house. "I thought I turned some lights on before we left this morning."

"I'm sure you did," I said, feeling a sudden return of tension as he unlocked the door.

Before Cole could touch the light switch, the living room and hall lights came on with blazing brightness and a chorus of voices shouted, "Surprise!"

Cody's startled squeal ended in delighted laughter, as Wes and Twila, the Watkins, Ed Garrison and half a dozen others rushed forward to congratulate us. Gaudy crepe paper streamers dangled from the hall banister and balloons were everywhere, from the lights to the potted plants.

Cole's face was blank as he stared at the laughing throng. "How did you. . . ."

"Twila let us in on the big secret," Kathy confessed, giving him a hug and kiss on the cheek. "We hope you don't mind."

Cole laughed and hugged her as Ed Garrison came forward, his shaggy brown mustache turned up by his smile. "Even if you didn't check with me first, I want you to know you have my approval," he told Cole.

"Thanks a lot, Ed."

"Mind if I kiss the bride?"

Before Cole could answer, Ed dipped me backwards and a cheer went up from the crowd as he proceeded to do just that.

Cody partied with the best of them, doggedly insisting he wasn't tired, until I found him curled up in a corner of the couch, a partially eaten cookie in one hand, and the string of his balloon firmly clutched in the other.

Twila started toward him out of habit, then caught herself and glanced at me. "Would you like me to put Cody to bed?" she asked hesitantly, not sure if I would misinterpret the offer.

I smiled, thinking how strange it was that our roles had suddenly been reversed. "Thank you. I'd appreciate that."

Her gentle eyes met mine in a moment of quiet understanding, then she leaned down and gathered the boy in her arms.

Besides Twila, I sensed a subtle change in attitude on the part of several members of Cole's staff. Suddenly, I was no longer the journalist who was treated with more reserve than respect—I was Cole McLean's wife. For some, that bridged a certain distance between us; for others, it created one which hadn't been there before. Thankfully, Kathy and Brent Watkins were as warm and friendly as they had always been and made no secret of the fact that our marriage had their wholehearted approval.

Excitement ebbed into pleasant fatigue as I sat down on the couch, sipping a cup of punch. Across the living room, Cole was chuckling over a joke Ron Weaver had told him.

Kathy sat down beside me and smiled as she followed the direction of my gaze. "Next to Brent, you married the most wonderful man I know," she said. "Besides which, he's sexy as hell."

I choked on my punch and laughed at her frank description.

Kathy laughed, too, then added, "Maybe you better not tell Brent I said that."

I smiled and teased, "I know. He'd think it was very unprofessional of you."

"By the way, you can keep the nightgown," she said, giving my elbow a nudge. "Just consider it a wedding present."

"I wouldn't dream of depriving Brent of one of his pleasures," I told her. "Besides, I bought one almost exactly like it in Georgetown today."

Kathy's smile was full of womanly wisdom. "Smart girl!"

I was taking my empty cup back to the table a few minutes

later when a nameless thread of worry suddenly tightened around me. Cody. I stiffened, then shrugged the feeling aside. Twila had come down nearly ten minutes ago to tell me he was sound asleep in his bed. I took a deep breath and walked out of the dining room. Reason insisted Cody was safe, but something else—a feeling or prompting I didn't fully understand—warned of danger.

Cole left Ed Garrison to come to my side. "Are you okay, honey? It's getting late. If you want me to, I'll get rid of everybody."

"I'm fine, but I think I'll go check on Cody."

"I thought Twila said he was asleep."

"She did, but . . . it won't hurt to check again. I'll be back in a minute." I turned and headed for the stairs, leaving Cole staring after me.

In the shadowy darkness of the hall, the feeling was stronger than ever. I ran towards Cody's room, noticing the door was ajar, then stopped dead as my eyes caught some movement at the end of the hall. Cold air from outside suddenly fanned my cheeks, and I realized the door to the outside balcony must be open.

I reached the balcony just in time to see a woman's slender shape running across the moonlit lawn, carrying something in her arms.

My heart froze with dread as she turned and glanced back toward the house, moonlight catching her dark eyes and pale face.

"Max. . . ." The name came out in a dry croak, then I flung myself across the balcony and down the stairs. "Max! Stop!"

My scream pierced the calm night as her slight figure disappeared into the blackness of the pines. I paused in a moment of terrified indecision. If I went back for help, she might be gone before anyone could find her. There was no time. No time! With a muttered prayer, I ran across the lawn.

I was moving blind, once I reached the trees. I stumbled along, a few yards at a time, pausing to listen for her running footsteps and harsh breathing. She was heading for the road below the house. I forced my legs to go faster, afraid that Max might reach her car before I could catch up to her. But when my feet stumbled onto the road's hard surface, she was nowhere to be seen. I glanced around wildly, gasping for breath, then heard her below me, running down the hillside itself. Arms outstretched, I dived down the steep slope.

The moon had not yet risen, but my eyes had adjusted enough to the darkness by now to make out the thick silhouettes of pines and black clumps of bushes. It wasn't long before I reached the next loop of the switchback. Stopping to listen, I realized Max was still keeping to the trees. The pines growing on this area of the slope were much farther apart, and some yards down, I thought I glimpsed a dark, running shape. As I paused to gauge the woman's distance from me, I realized with a sick chill that she had stopped as well. I strained to listen, eyes wide against the blackness, but there was nothing—only the barest whisper of a breeze in the tops of the pines.

Fear rose in my throat as seconds of dead silence passed. Finally, I couldn't stand it any longer and called down into the blackness, "Cody! Cody, I'm coming!"

The answer to my cry was a sharp crack, and the sudden splintering of wood some yards to my left. For a moment, I was too stunned to comprehend what the sound was. The second shot was much closer. I dropped to the ground as the bullet bit into a pithy trunk only a few feet away. Crouched in the darkness, I realized I was more angry than frightened and decided two could play this game. Feeling about, I found a heavy rock, a little larger than my fist, and flung it off to my right.

Max's third shot followed the path of the stone, and this time I saw the tiny orange flash not twenty yards below me. My anger died when I heard Cody's muffled whimper, and I had to stop myself from calling out to him. The next second, snapping wood and heavy footsteps told me Max was on the move. Crouching low, and using trees for cover, I took up the chase.

Moments later, I heard the roar of an engine somewhere above me, then another. Soon, two sets of headlights were bathing the dark forest in swerving arcs of white light. For a brief instant, one of the beams caught Max Barrett's dark form, lunging through the pines. Then she was gone. Behind me, one of the vehicles wheeled around a sharp curve, then appeared on the road below. The second followed suit with a squeal of brakes as it took the turn.

I raced on, hope surging through me, until Ed Garrison's gruff shout brought me up short. "Stop right there, Barrett! Let go of the boy!"

Max's answer rang clear and cold through the night air. "Unless you want me to blow a bullet through his brains right now, don't either one of you take a step!"

I gasped and gripped the rough bark of a pine tree as Cody's frightened whine came from below, followed by Cole's strained, "Max . . . in the name of God, don't. . . !"

Garrison's voice was tight but firm. "Drop the gun, Max. You can't get away with it now. It's all over, and you know it."

"You drop the gun!" Max cried shrilly. "Drop it, or I'll kill him!"

I bit down on my lip and slowly edged forward toward the voices.

"Ed, do as she says," Cole said in a ragged voice. "Max, don't hurt him — just tell me what you want — we can work something out."

"It's too late for that. You've ruined everything—everything I've worked for! All I want now is to see you suffer. And I can't think of a better way than to watch your son die."

"My God, Max. . .you can't. . . . Please. . . ."

She was directly below me, not more than five or six feet. The jeep's headlights outlined her form in an aura of blinding white light. Cody was pinioned against her left side, and a small revolver in her right hand was aimed directly at his head. Cole stood on the road below, flanked by Garrison, Ron Weaver and another security man. Helpless agony stared out of their eyes.

Max saw their fear and enjoyed it. "Maybe, it would be more satisfying to shoot you first and have the boy watch his father die," she taunted, moving the pistol away from Cody to wave it carelessly at Cole.

"No!" Without a second's thought, I dived toward her and grabbed for the gun.

My scream caught her off guard, and Max whirled around as swiftly as an adder. A twisted branch caught my ankle that same moment, and I went down on top of her. I heard Max's enraged cry, felt a sharp pain in the back of my head and that was all.

The nightmare was back. I could see Cody ahead of me, running toward the blind curve where something waited—something black and evil. "Cody! Come back!" I tried to run after him, but my legs wouldn't move. "Cody!"

"It's all right, love. Cody's fine. He's fine."

Cole's voice came into the dream, fading in and out, like an echo. I opened my eyes to see his face above me, one half in shadow, the other side lit by a harsh white light. My swimming thoughts cleared, then sharpened into focus, like the features of his face. I stared at the tears on his cheeks and fear, sharper than the pain in my head, shot through me.

"Cody. . . ."

Cole gathered me close. "He's all right, darling. He's fine. He was thrown clear when you jumped Max."

I closed my eyes and sagged against him. My tears joined his as we held each other.

After a moment, I tried to sit up and realized I was lying near the road with a rough jacket wrapped around me. I searched the darkness beyond the headlights' glare. "Where is he?"

"Ron's taken him back to the house." Cole smoothed the hair away from my face and helped me to a sitting position. "How do you feel?"

"All right, I think. Except for a headache." I rubbed a tender spot on the back of my head. "What happened?"

"After you jumped Max, she rolled over, and you hit your head on a rock."

I heard footsteps approaching in the darkness behind us, and seconds later, Ed Garrison materialized. In his left hand he carried something frizzy and pale.

The man's grim expression softened into relief when he saw me sitting beside Cole. "We found her car parked in the trees near the bottom of the hill," he said. "Among other things, this was in the backseat."

I stared at the blonde wig in his hand, suddenly remembering the woman I had seen in Georgetown. "What kind of car was

Max driving?"

"A brown Mustang."

Cole's voice was stunned. "That blonde you pointed out to me this morning—Max must have been following us."

"Probably waiting for a chance to snatch the kid," Garrison said bluntly. "The party at the house tonight gave her the perfect opportunity."

"How did she get through the gate?" Cole demanded.

"Max caught Mark off guard and hit him over the head with her revolver, then stole the keys."

I looked away from the blonde wig with a shudder. "Can we go now? I want to see Cody."

Garrison's big hand was surprisingly gentle as he reached out to touch my cheek. "You're some kind of lady," he said gruffly, then walked away.

I couldn't seem to stop shivering as Cole helped me into the jeep. He ran quickly around to the driver's side and asked again, "Are you sure you're okay?"

"Just cold."

"I'll have you home in a minute." Cole turned the key, then paused to look at me. "Can I ask you something?"

I nodded and drew the jacket more closely around me.

"How did you know? If you hadn't gone upstairs to check on Cody when you did. . . ." He broke off and asked again, "How did you know?"

I shook my head and leaned against him, remembering the inner prompting which had come so forcefully. "Mother's instinct, I guess. . . ."

Cole kissed me, then eased the jeep up the dark forest road to Lodestone. "Let's go home."

Postlude

ON A WINDY October afternoon, some eight weeks later, I was strolling a sandy shore near Dublin, in western Ireland. The music of the sea mingled with the mewing of the gulls and my son's delighted laughter as he played tag with the waves and searched for shells in the damp sand.

In this legendary land of folklore and wild beauty, I half-expected to see some fairy troop descending the stony path from the cliffs above me. Instead, I saw the tall form of my husband, his black hair blowing in the wind as he raced down the path to our sheltered cove.

"I thought I might find you here," he said after a welcoming kiss.

"You're through early today. How did your meeting with Garth go?"

Cole's smile broadened, and I saw the excited gleam in his blue-gray eyes. "I finished the love theme, and Garth's crazy about it."

"Cole, that's wonderful!" I threw my arms around his neck. "You've been struggling with that theme for so long. What happened?"

He laughed and hugged me close. "You're not going to believe it!"

"Tell me!"

Cole grinned at my impatience and took hold of both my hands. "Okay. I spent the entire morning working over those two melodies, but no matter what I tried, it just didn't feel right. Garth was due to come over at two and by one-thirty, I was so frustrated I was ready to tear up the piano keys. Finally, I gave up and decided to work on something else. I was playing around with a piano arrangement for 'Shadow Song,' and the next thing I know, Garth's voice is booming out, 'That's it! That's the love theme. I knew you could do it!'"

I stood there, gaping at him. "Our 'Shadow Song'?"

"I tried to explain that it was a song I'd written for you, but Garth just gave me that sober look of his and said, 'No wonder it's inspired.'" Cole's smile was teasing. "You know, I think the man's half in love with you."

I laughed. "That's too bad, because I'm in love with someone else."

Cole put an arm around my waist, and we began walking across the sand toward Cody. "Do you mind if I use our song for the movie?" he asked, his eyes serious.

"Of course I don't mind. I think it's wonderful! Now that you have the love theme, how long do you think it will take to finish the rest of the score?"

"Not too long. A couple of months. Four at the most."

"That's good."

"Why?"

I glanced up at him and said casually, "Well, I realize it'll be quite a change for you after composing a film score, but . . . I was wondering how you'd feel about writing a lullabye?"

Cole walked on a few more steps before stopping with a clumsy jerk. "Megan. . . ?"

I smiled as his expression of stunned surprise exploded into joy.

"When?"

"May. . . ."

Cole smiled and put a gentle hand on my stomach.

Mere words could never describe his smile, or my happiness at that moment. Then his lips found mine, and there was no need for words—only the timeless music of the waves and the gulls, blending with windsong and its whispered promise of forever.